PRAISE FOR *THE GREY BASTARDS*

"An action-packed, sneakily smart adventure. Half-orc and all badass, Jackal is a hero you won't soon forget"
Scott Sigler, *New York Times* bestselling author of *Alive* and *Infected*

"You find yourself truly in the world French has created, and it all becomes wonderfully familiar and convincing. The world-building creates exactly the kind of seamless transition that makes fantasy literature compelling, informative and just plain fun"
R. A. Salvatore, *New York Times* bestselling author

"It's a wild ride on the hog, filled with brutality, battle and bravery. It's coarse and crass and also loveable, and after this, I have high hopes for what French might do in the future"
Bibliotropic

"Mr French: I envy and admire you for this story you've crafted. *Bastards* is brutal. *Bastards* is brave. *Bastards* is utterly fearless and unashamed of being what it is. I greedily await more from Jackal and co., and fully intend to hound you for news about the hoof – a truer set of bastards you'll never meet . . ."
Fantasy Faction

"*The Grey Bastards* . . . is a book that I just absolutely fell in love with. It's dark and brutal, but it is also unapologetically its own animal. This is unlike any other grimdark books I've read recently, and because of that, because of this author's unique vision and his incredible talent, this one left a mark on me. I want more"
Bookworm Blues

"Kudos to Jonathan French for writing such a different story and having the guts to follow through and not take any easy routes with his characterisations, world history and even politics . . . *The Grey Bastards* has instantaneously catapulted him into my must-read list"
Fantasy Book Critic

"A thoroughly entertaining, downright excellent read. I loved it and definitely want more . . . In case I didn't make it clear I recommend *The Grey Bastards* without reservation"
Lynn's Books

"I f*cking loved this book. *The Grey Bastards* went down like a shot of good top-shelf tequila: warm and smooth, but with one hell of a spicy kick"
Bibliosanctum

"French has crafted an ambitious but intricate plot. I never knew what was going to happen next or whether Jackal would live to tell the tale. This is a sign of a good book in my view . . . potentially one of my favourite books of this year"
The Qwillery

"This is a filthy book, but it is a damn good one. For fans of: Nicholl's Orcs, Gentle's *Grunts*, Cook's Black Company, of course. But also Abercrombie's First Law"
Pornokitsch

"This epic fantasy is a boisterously good read . . . I thought the ending was spot on, and I'm excited to read book two"
Rosalyn Kelly

THE GREY BASTARDS

JONATHAN FRENCH

www.orbitbooks.net

ORBIT

First published in Great Britain in 2018 by Orbit

5 7 9 10 8 6 4

All characters and events in this publication, other than those clearly in the public domain, are fictitious and any resemblance to real persons, living or dead, is purely coincidental.

A CIP catalogue record for this book is available from the British Library.

ISBN 978-0-356-51164-1

Printed and bound by CPI Group (UK) Ltd, Croydon CR0 4YY

Papers used by Orbit are from well-managed forests and other responsible sources.

Orbit
An imprint of
Little, Brown Book Group
Carmelite House
50 Victoria Embankment
London EC4Y 0DZ

An Hachette UK Company
www.hachette.co.uk

www.orbitbooks.net

Rob, this one is for you, brother. You better fucking know why.

Chapter 1

Jackal was about to wake the girls for another tumble when he heard Oats bellow for him through the thin walls of the brothel. Ugly, early sunlight speared through the missing slats in the decrepit shutters. Jackal jumped from the bed, shaking off the entangling limbs of the whores and the last clouds of wine swimming in his head. The new girl slept right through, but Delia groaned at the disturbance, raising her tousled red locks off the cushions to squint at him with naked disapproval.

"The fuck, Jack?" she said.

Laughing quietly, Jackal hopped into his breeches. "There is a large bowl of porridge calling my name."

Delia rolled her bleary eyes. "Tell that big thrice to hush. And come back to bed."

"Would that I could, darlin'," Jackal said, sitting on the bed to pull on his boots. "Would that I could."

He stood just as Delia's fingers began to coax at his back. Not bothering to find his brigand, Jackal snatched his belt from amongst the girls' discarded garments on the floor, buckled it on, and adjusted the fall of his tulwar. He could feel Delia's eyes on him.

"Hells, you are a pretty half-breed!" she said. The sleepiness was gone from her eyes, replaced by a well-practiced look of hunger.

Jackal played along, purposefully flexing as he gathered his hair back and tied it with a leather thong. Giving Delia a parting wink, he threw open the door and hurried from the room.

The corridor was dim and abandoned, still clinging to the bleak stillness of dawn. Jackal walked through to the common room, not breaking stride as he stepped around the pitted tables and overturned chairs. The sour stink of spilled wine and sweat were all that remained of the night's revels. The door leading outside was cracked, the bright, intruding light already promising a sweltering day. Jackal stepped into the morning glare, clenching his jaw and eyelids against the assault of the sun.

Oats stood by the well in the center of the yard, the slabs of muscle on his broad back shining with water. Jackal jogged up and stood beside his friend.

"Trouble?"

Oats lifted his chin slightly, pointing with his spade-shaped beard down the dusty track leading to the grounds. Jackal followed his gaze and saw the shimmering shapes of horses approaching. Putting a hand at his brow to shield his eyes from the sun, he looked for riders and was relieved to find them.

"Not horse-cocks."

"No," Oats agreed. "Cavalry."

Jackal relaxed a little. Human soldiers they could handle. Centaurs might have meant their deaths.

"Ignacio?" he mused. "I swear that pit-faced old drunk can smell his payment from all the way at the castile."

His friend said nothing, continuing to scowl at the approaching cavalcade. Jackal counted eight men, one clutching a banner that no doubt bore the crest of the king of Hispartha. That blowing bit of silk meant little in the Lot Lands and Jackal kept his gaze fixed on the man up front.

"It's Bermudo," Oats said, a second before Jackal picked out the captain's identity through the dust.

"Shit."

Jackal found himself wishing he had not left his stockbow under Delia's bed. Glancing over, he noticed Oats was completely unarmed, the half-full bucket from the well still clutched in his meaty hands. Still, the brute's appearance was often enough to discourage a fight. As was said amongst the members of the hoof, Oats had muscles in his shit.

Jackal was no stripling, but his friend was a full head taller. With his bald head, ash-colored skin, corded frame, and protruding lower fangs, Oats could pass for a full-blood orc as long as he hid the Bastard tattoos that adorned his powerful arms and back. Only his beard marked him for a half-breed, a trait Jackal had not received from his human half.

As the riders fanned out around the well, Jackal grinned. He might not be able to pass for a thick, but he was big enough to give these human whelps pause. Their clean crimson sashes, brightly polished helmets, and petulantly brave faces marked them as fresh arrivals. Mustachios must have been in fashion in the courts of Hispartha, for drooping from every upper lip was something akin to a furry horseshoe. Every lip except Bermudo's. He looked like one of those long-dead tyrants found on the old Imperium coins, all long nose and close-cropped hair.

The captain reined up.

He took a moment to survey the yard, his attention lingering on the stables Sancho maintained for his guests.

Jackal lifted his chin in greeting. "Bermudo. Breaking in some new boys, I see. What, did they demand proof that a man can still get some quim in the badlands?"

"How many are with you, Bastards?"

It was an offhand, almost lazy question, but Jackal did not miss Bermudo's concern.

"Not here to ambush you, Captain."

"That is not an answer."

"Certain it is."

Bermudo turned to catch the eye of one of his riders and flicked a finger at the stables. The chosen cavalero hesitated.

"Go check the stables," Bermudo said, as if instructing an idiot child.

The man snapped out of his puzzlement and spurred his horse to the west side of the yard. His compatriots watched his progress. Jackal watched them. All held demi-lances and round steel shields, with scale coats for further protection. Five of them had grown tense, betrayed by the tautness in their reins. The last one looked bored and produced an overwrought yawn. The errand runner had dismounted, tied his horse to the post, and now strode into the stables. A moment later, Sancho's stableboy stumbled sleepily into the glare. The cavalero followed not long after.

"Three hogs and a mule team," he reported when he rode back.

"The team belongs to three miners," Jackal told Bermudo. "From Traedria, I think. They're not here to ambush you either."

"No," Bermudo said. "They have dispensation to prospect in the Amphora Mountains. I know because I issued them the writ. You, however, have no such dispensation."

Jackal looked at the empty surrounding sky with awe. "Oats? Did Sancho's place get spirited into the Amphoras while we slept?"

"The peaks look smaller than I remember," Oats said. "Invisible, even."

Bermudo remained humorless. "You damn well know my meaning."

"We do," Jackal said. "And you damn well know Captain Ignacio allows our presence here."

"Did he assure you of that before leaving here last night?"

Oats's face clenched. "Ignacio wasn't here last night."

It was true, but Jackal would have preferred not to give that away just yet. The captains hated each other, but that didn't explain Bermudo biting at Ignacio's name as if it were bait. It also didn't explain his presence at the brothel. The noble captain did not employ Sancho's girls and was rarely seen this far from the castile.

Jackal attempted fresh bait. "Don't let us stall you from getting inside. Sure you're all eager to relieve some spend."

Bermudo sniffed.

"Observe, men," he said, his gaze resting on Jackal and Oats while also ignoring them, a skill only noble-born humans could master. "A pair of half-breed riders. From the Grey Bastards hoof. You will learn to distinguish them by their hideous body markings. Some you will come to know by their absurd names. Despite the allotments, they all think this entire land belongs to them, so you will find them in places they do not belong, like this establishment, blatantly ignoring the fact that it rests on Crown land. It is within your power to expel them in such instances. Though it is often best to allow them to sate themselves and move on. Unlike a pair of rutting dogs, it takes more than a bucket of water to discourage half-orcs in heat. They are . . . slaves to their base natures."

Jackal ignored the insults. He looked beyond Bermudo and smiled at the cavaleros arrayed behind him. "We *do* love whores. Pardon. We enjoy seeking our ease with willing company. Reckon that's how you'd say it up north. Either way, Sancho and his girls are always hospitable."

Bermudo curled his mouth with distaste, but it was the yawning cavalero who spoke, his mouth now settled into a comfortable sneer.

"I would never pay for a woman willing to lay with half-orcs."

"Then you best start fucking your horse," Oats rumbled.

Jackal smiled as the eyes of the new cavalero grew wide. "He's right. You won't find a whore in the Lot Lands who hasn't been spoiled by us. I'm sure they would take your coin, but don't be offended, lad, if they fail to notice your pink little prick is even in."

The man visibly bristled. Looking closer, Jackal noticed his mustachio could not quite conceal a harelip. The other six were casting uncertain looks at the back of Bermudo's head, searching for guidance. The captain's helmet was hanging from his saddle, and he carried no lance, but his hand had drifted to the grip of his sword.

"Make trouble," Bermudo said, his face turning flinty, "and I will drag you behind my horse all the way back to your lot, whatever arrangements you have with Ignacio be damned."

Jackal hooked his thumbs in his belt, getting his hand closer to his own blade. He could posture as well as the captain. "There is no quarrel here."

"Not unless you make one," Oats put in.

Bermudo's eyes flicked between Jackal and Oats. Was he actually considering spilling blood? Would this arrogant ass risk a feud just to save face in front of a gaggle of outcast nobility with new saddles and wet dreams of heroism?

Bermudo's jaw bulged as he chewed on his pride, but before he came to a decision the harelip rode up to the well.

"You there," he said to Oats, gesturing with his lance. "Fill yonder trough."

Jackal let out a snort of derision and watched as a ripple of uncertainty passed through the recruits, every eye on their outspoken comrade.

Bermudo shot the man a warning look. "Cavalero Garcia—"

The youth waved him off. "It is all right, Captain. We have half-orc servants at my father's villa. They have to be kept well in hand or they turn mulish. Clearly these two have gone undisciplined for too long. A lack of humility that is quickly remedied. It is all in how you address them." He looked languidly down at Oats. "I said fill the trough. Step to it, mongrel."

Jackal heard the strained creaking of wood as Oats's knuckles paled against the bucket. This was heartbeats from coming to blood.

"You want to get your new arrival in hand, Captain," Jackal said. It was not a suggestion. "He might not know what an angry thrice-blood can do to a man."

Bermudo's haughty manner was showing cracks at the edges. He saw the situation turning ill, same as Jackal. But he set his jaw and allowed the insubordination.

Shit.

Nothing to do but control whose blood was spilled, and how much.

"So, Captain," Jackal said, "what did this fop do to be banished here? Gambling debts? Or, no, Oats had it before, didn't he? Your man got caught with his father's favorite stallion. Riding it without a saddle. Inside the stable."

The smug cavalero stamped the butt of his lance into Jackal's face. He did it so casually, so lazily, that Jackal had plenty of time to avoid the blow, but he let it land. Pain overtook his vision and he reeled back a step, snapping a hand to his throbbing nose. He heard Oats snarl, but Jackal reached out blindly and laid his free hand on his friend's trunk of an arm, stopping any retaliation. Spitting, Jackal waited for his head to clear before straightening.

"You will keep a civil tongue," Cavalero Garcia told him. "Speak with such impudence again and I shall have you horsewhipped in the name of the king."

Jackal looked directly at Bermudo and found nervousness infecting his face. But there was also a creeping look of satisfaction.

"King?" Jackal said, sucking the last film of blood from his teeth. "Oats? Do you know the name of the king?"

"Such-and-Such the First," Oats replied.

Jackal shook his head. "No, he died. It's So-and-So the Fat."

Oats gave him a dubious squint. "That don't sound right."

"Wretched soot-skins!" Garcia exclaimed.

Jackal ignored him, throwing his arms wide in a mock flummox.

"The name escapes us. Anyway, he's some inbred, overstuffed sack of shit that weds his cousins, fucks his sisters, and has small boys attach leeches to his tiny, tiny prick."

This time, Jackal caught Garcia's lance as the man thrust and used it to yank him from his mount, angling him to collide with the well's roof on the way down. The horse shied away, whinnying. Garcia floundered in the dirt, sputtering wordless rage as he tried to stand. Jackal grabbed the cavalero's cloak, pulled it over his head, and punched his face through the dusty cloth. He fell flat.

The horses were balking at the disturbance, but the men were stilled by shock. Bermudo had visibly paled.

Jackal motioned at the fallen Garcia. "I think that's a good lesson for these virgins, Captain. You agree?"

Bermudo was no fool. He saw the chance being offered. With a curt nod, he took it.

Garcia, however, was still conscious. And less wise. Sitting up, he yanked the cloak from his head, revealing a mouth dripping blood and venom.

"Captain," he seethed, an accusing finger sweeping between Jackal and Oats. "I demand these two be brought back to the castile and hanged."

Jackal laughed. "Hanged? You're not dead, frail. A trade of insults, you bust my nose, I smash your teeth. That's it. It's done. Now go inside, get your cod wet, and forget it."

Garcia was deaf to good sense. His vengeful stare shifted up to Bermudo.

"*Captain?*" He spoke the rank, but it sounded far from the respect due a superior.

Jackal and Oats shared a look. What was this? Certainly not the first time cavaleros and hoof riders had come to blows. It happened at Sancho's more often than anywhere. It was time for everyone to ride on.

A gem of sweat studded the center of Bermudo's upper lip. He looked torn, chewing on a choice that was making him angry.

"Bermudo . . ." Jackal tried to get the man's attention, but was shouted down by Garcia.

"You will languish here forever, Captain!"

It was a threat. And it made up Bermudo's mind.

"Take them!" he commanded.

Bermudo tried to draw his sword, but the bucket took him in the brow before the blade was half free. Oats had thrown with such force that not a drop of water spilled until the bucket smote the Captain's skull. He fell from the saddle, unconscious before he even struck the dust of the yard.

Jackal kicked Garcia under the chin, sending him sprawling before he could squeal further. Rather than intimidate the other riders, the violence against their comrade steeled their courage and all six lowered their lances. Jackal drew his sword and tossed it to Oats in one motion, keeping hold of Garcia's lance and leveling it against the impending charge.

Before the cavaleros could spur their horses forward, their gazes snapped up to stare wide-eyed. A voice rang out from behind Jackal's head.

"Think twice, you prickly lipped eunuchs!"

Jackal smiled. The voice was ill-humored, commanding, and familiar. The cavaleros were lowering their lances, every mouth agape.

"Perfect timing, Fetch!" Jackal called over his shoulder. He gave the men a gloating smile before turning around. A moment later, his own jaw fell open.

Fetching stood upon the roof of the brothel with a stockbow in each hand, both loaded and trained on the riders. She was stark naked.

"You're bleeding, Jack."

Jackal managed a grunt and a nod. He had known Fetching since childhood, but neither of them were children anymore.

Her pale green flesh was flawless, lacking the ashy grey tones found in most half-orcs, and smooth save where it rippled with muscle or swelled with curves. She had both to spare. Her dark brown twistlocks were unbound, falling to her shapely shoulders. She held the heavy stockbows steadily, the points of their quarrels unwavering between the prods. It was an impressive sight. And based upon the stunned silence behind him in the yard, the cavaleros thought so as well.

Clever Fetching, always using every advantage, though she needed few.

"You're bleeding," Fetch repeated, "and I am awakened very early. Someone is going to die."

Garcia had managed to stumble toward his fellows and pointed with a quivering finger.

"You filthy ash-coloreds!" he shrieked through his swollen lips. "You will all dangle from a gibbet! Take them, men! Take them!"

"That one," Oats grunted.

"That one," Fetching confirmed, and shot Garcia through the eye.

He fell backward stiffly, the fletching of the quarrel blossoming from his left socket. The cavaleros cursed and struggled to keep their shying horses under control.

"I got one bolt left," Fetching announced. "Who would like it?"

There were no volunteers.

Jackal spun on the cavaleros.

"Before any of you say anything fool-ass, like, 'My father will hear of this!' remember—no one cares a fig for you back north in whatever civilized jewel you called home. If they did, you wouldn't be here."

Jackal swept every man with a steady gaze, noting which ones looked away.

"What are you, third-, fourth-born? At least one of you is likely a bastard. You were all fobbed off here to be forgotten. To patrol the borderlands and watch for orcs. You have no station, you have no privilege." Jackal tossed Garcia's lance onto his corpse. "*He* forgot that. Don't make the same mistake. If you want to survive your first skirmish with the thicks, you best begin to look kindly on us half-breeds. We are what keep you safe. Bermudo's right. We claim this land as our own. But we aren't the only ones. The orcs call this land Ul-wundulas. They think it's theirs. You won't prove them wrong by believing you're better than they are. Your fathers can't help you here. The king, whatever his name is, can't help you here. Only we mongrels can help you here. Welcome to the Lot Lands."

Stepping back, Jackal gave Oats a nod. The brute picked the unconscious form of Captain Bermudo off the ground as if he were a child.

"Didn't take more than a bucket of water for you, 'Mudo," he said, and slung the man over the back of his horse. He handed the animal's reins to one of the cavaleros.

"Take him back to the castile," Jackal told the men. "Tell Captain

Ignacio that Cavalero Garcia defied Bermudo's orders and struck him. He fled on horseback rather than face discipline and was last seen heading into centaur territory. The Grey Bastards have volunteered to go searching for him. But we're not confident he'll ever be found. When Bermudo comes around, he will want to remember it that way. You all will. Unless you want a war with the half-orc hoofs."

No one responded. Each face had gone pale and placid.

"Now is the part where you all nod!" Fetch called down from the roof.

Every helmeted head bobbled up and down.

Jackal extended a guiding arm toward the track. Within minutes, the cavalcade was a shimmering smudge on the horizon.

Jackal found Oats staring at him and shaking his head.

"What?"

"Nice speech, Prince Jackal."

"Suck a sow's tit, Oats."

Jackal probed at his nose while Fetching jumped down from the roof, the well-developed muscles in her long legs absorbing the impact.

"Next time you go out to make pretty words with the frails, don't forget to bring a thrum," she said, tossing Jackal the spent stockbow.

"And next time you come to our rescue, you should wear that," he retorted, sweeping a hand at her nakedness.

"Lick me, Jack!"

"Didn't one of Sancho's girls already do that?"

"Yes," Fetch replied, turning her back to head for the door of the brothel. "But like all the whores, she would rather have had her head between *your* legs."

Jackal stared brazenly at the dimples above Fetch's pert backside until she disappeared into the shadows of the whorehouse.

A cuff from Oats on the back of his head brought him around.

"We need to get back."

Jackal scratched at his chin. "I know. See to the hogs."

Before Oats could head for the stables, the same door that had so recently enveloped Fetching now disgorged the brothel's proprietor. The pleasant swell in Jackal's cod immediately withered.

Maneuvering his corpulence through the jamb, Sancho came heavy-footed into the yard, his small mouth held in an oval of witless alarm.

What little hair the man had left was already soaked with sweat, a slick black stain across his head. Sancho stared at the cavalero's corpse and shook his head slowly, causing his ill-shaven jowls to jiggle.

"I'm ruined."

Jackal snorted. "Don't tell me that this is the first man to die here, Sancho."

"The first cavalero!" the fat man said, his voice sounding choked. "And not even one of Ignacio's commoners, but a fucking blue blood! What have you done?"

"Rid you of a future troublesome guest," Jackal told him. "Fair wager, that piece of hogshit would have beaten your girls."

"That I can handle! But the body of exiled gentry is not so easily managed."

"It is. Contact the Sludge Man." Jackal gestured at Garcia's sprawled carcass. "Let him dispose of our deceased friend."

The whoremaster's large, moist face went pale at the mention of the name.

"He and our chief have an understanding," Jackal said before Sancho's panic fully took root.

"You sure you want to involve him?" Oats put in, an uneasy look on his bearded face. Jackal wasn't sure who he meant, their chief or the Sludge Man, but he didn't bother to clarify. This was the way through.

He kept his attention on giving Sancho instructions. "Send a bird. When he gets here, give him the body and the horse. Tell him it's for the Grey Bastards."

"And what about me?" Sancho demanded. "What do I get for being your agent in this?"

Jackal took a deep breath. "What do you want?"

"You know," Sancho told him.

"I do," Jackal conceded. "Fine. I'll tell the chief."

The whoremaster eyeballed him for a moment, then nodded. Giving the cavalero one final, grudging glance, Sancho stomped back inside.

Oats clenched his jaw. "Claymaster won't be pleased."

"Our days of pleasing him are almost over, so he better start getting used to it," Jackal replied, breathing out hard through his sore nostrils. "Get ready to ride."

Chapter 2

The day was hot long before the sun was high. Jackal rode point, setting a quick pace to allow the air to flow across his skin. Hearth was well rested and eager to run, so Jackal gave the hog his head, gripping the bristles of his mane in one hand. Keeping his heels tucked and gripping the barrel of the animal with his thighs, Jackal kept an easy seat, settling into the rhythm of Hearth's trot.

The rugged, sun-bathed plains of Ul-wundulas spread out in every direction, each boulder and piney shrub passing by with a whispered rush of wind in Jackal's ears. He tried to imagine the time, not so long ago, when the hoofs did not exist, when half-orcs were slaves and the hogs they now rode were only beasts of burden. Those years were not so far gone, only a few decades past, a handful of years before Jackal's own birth, yet he found them difficult to picture. He lived for the ride, for the feeling of a strong beast beneath him, huffing like a bellows and chewing the leagues into a dusty cloud behind pounding hooves.

Hearth was a formidable pig and bred for speed, generations removed from the cumbersome beasts who were yoked to wagons and watermills during the Orc Incursion. The Claymaster and the other old veterans said those first hogs were tireless and keen, but their strength was meant for the pulling of great weight. The great bearded deer-hog, that is what humans called these animals, but amongst the half-orc slaves who tended them they were affectionately known as barbarians.

The name had stuck, but the barbarians now ridden by the mongrel hoofs were true mounts, no longer draft animals. Only three-quarters the height at the withers of a Hisparthan stallion and shorter of leg, they were less swift than a horse over short distances, but unequaled over longer runs in rough terrain due to their frightfully compact and effective musculature. They were all but hairless from the flank to the shoulder, possessing only a crest of coarse bristles along their spine, sprouting from the mane growing about the neck and dangling from the lower jaw. A pair of tusks emerged vertically through the skin of the long and tapering snout, eventually curving back sharply toward the beast's forehead. These tusks never stopped growing, and wild barbarians of advanced age had been found with the tusks beginning to penetrate their skull. Through careful breeding, they were made to sweep back sharply toward the rider. Dubbed swine-yankers, these tusks could be gripped and used to direct a hog's head in desperate circumstances, though even a domesticated barbarian would resist such manipulation, requiring a rider to be no weakling. Certainly, few humans were capable and stuck with their precious horses. Frails on foals, as Warbler had often said.

Another set of tusks protruded upward from a barbarian's lower jaw and were the animal's most vicious form of attack. Hearth's were particularly long, a source of pride for Jackal, along with the hog's golden-hued hair. Far comelier than Oats's lumbering, mud-colored mount, aptly named Ugfuck.

Just after midday, Jackal called a halt at a broad, glittering tributary of the River Lucia to rest and water the hogs.

"What's the matter, Jack?" Fetching said as she dismounted. "Delia and the new girl drain your balls so sore that you can't make an uninterrupted ride home?"

"We're not stopping for me," Jackal replied, smiling. "It's so Oats's fat sack of a pig doesn't expire from the heat."

"Don't you listen, Ug," Oats said, kissing his hog on the head before urging him to the water with a swat on the rump. Snorting noisily, Ugfuck joined Hearth and Fetch's unnamed hog on the bank. They were trained not to wallow while wearing a saddle, but they sucked vigorously at the flowing water.

While the barbarians drank, Jackal squatted beside them and dipped his kerchief into the river. After wringing it out, he tied it back over his head to keep his hair from his face. His brigand was still tied in a roll behind Hearth's saddle. It was against the code of the hoof to ride without armor, but Jackal hated the weight of the vest. Once, he had painstakingly removed all the iron plates riveted between the leather. When the Claymaster found out, he forbade Jackal to ride until he repaired and cleaned the brigands of every rider in the hoof. Still, when away from the Kiln and out of the chief's sight, Jackal preferred to ride bare-chested.

Oats's considerable shadow fell across the riverbank and Jackal turned without rising. The brute never rode without his brigand on. His stockbow was held low in both hands. A quiver hung from his belt at the hip, his tulwar opposite. Oats had also tied a kerchief about his bald head and stood gazing across the wash. Fetch was equally equipped, but she had stridden knee-deep toward the center of the river to fill her skin.

"She did good this morning," Oats said, careful to keep his voice low.

Jackal nodded. Amongst the hoof, deserved praise was usually voiced openly. But not to Fetching. She never responded well. No matter that she had ridden with the Grey Bastards for going on four years, she still saw everyone as pandering to her. And maybe, sometimes, they were. Amongst the eight half-orc hoofs in the Lot Lands, she was the only female rider. Her place was hard fought, and well won, but she had reasons to be dubious of kind words. That was why she never named her hog, worried it would be viewed as weakness, no matter that they all did it. Hells, Oats had named his first hog Gorgeous, and Polecat still rode a sow called Lavender.

"Fetching!" Jackal called out across the water. "You ride point when we leave."

Fetch acknowledged this by raising her stockbow.

"Nice gesture," Oats said.

"Nah," Jackal said, standing and smiling at his friend. "I just want to look at her ass some more."

Oats grinned behind his beard. "You really do want to die young." They both laughed. "What was that shit with Bermudo? Couldn't tell who was giving the orders. Don't think the captain could either."

"Sounded like that Garcia had a way out of the Lots for him."

Oats hummed an agreement. "Not anymore."

A question came to Jackal's mind, sobering him.

"What were you doing in the yard unarmed, Oats?"

The brute shrugged, not relaxing his vigil as he spoke. "Woke up hot. Went to the well for a dunk."

"Never thought to go back inside, get your thrum? You had time."

Oats shook his head, his gaze going back across the river.

"It could have been centaurs, Oats."

The thrice-blood dismissed this with a wrinkle of his lip. "We haven't gotten a warning from Zirko yet."

"They don't just ride during the Betrayer Moon, half-brain."

"It was daylight in Crown lands, Jack."

"It was sloppy!"

"Sloppy?" Oats growled, turning a glare on Jackal. "And who else came out without a thrum? Certainly wasn't Fetching."

"No, I just came out without a stitch," Fetch said, stepping out of the river. Jackal hadn't even heard her approach. "You two get any further in each other's faces, you'll be kissing."

Jackal and Oats both turned their heads to glower at her.

"Well, go on." Fetch smirked. "Always knew the pair of you were hard for each other."

Jackal laughed first and was rewarded with a companionable shove from Oats, which nearly sent him sprawling into the river.

"Can we get moving, then?" Fetching asked. Not waiting for a response, she gripped one of her hog's swine-yankers and pulled him away from the river. The barbarian loosed a few agitated squeals, but Fetch coaxed him away with one arm and swung herself into the saddle. Jackal and Oats were astride their own mounts within moments.

"Careful not to drift too far east when we reach the Lucia proper," Jackal warned Fetch. "Last thing we need is to trespass on Tine land."

Fetch flashed him a grin. "You afraid of elves, Jack?"

Before he could retort, she put heel to hog and rode swiftly away from the river.

Oats snorted a laugh.

"Come on, you ugly fuck," Jackal said.

Oats stroked between his hog's ears. "I'm the only one who gets to call him that."

"I meant you."

Despite her flippancy, Fetching did a fine job leading them, not once straying into elven territory. Still, Jackal kept an eye eastward as they rode, certain that behind him, Oats was doing the same.

The war had left much of Ul-wundulas denuded, as the armies of man and orc felled timber to fuel their fires, build their defenses, and replenish their weapons. In the thirty-odd years since the battles ceased, wildfires had prevented much from returning. What forests remained clung to the high places, nestled in mountain valleys where the fighting had been sparse. After the war, when Hispartha had awarded vast portions of its reconquered southern kingdom to its allies, the elves managed to draw much of the rare woodlands, claiming large swaths of mountain range in the doing. The lots were supposed to be random, but the elves' spellcraft had no doubt played a part in their luck.

As Fetching picked their trail south, Jackal frowned at the brooding peaks of the Umber Mountains to his left. Somewhere deep within the Umbers was Dog Fall Gorge, stronghold of the elven hoof. Miles of garigue and shrubby foothills separated Jackal and his friends from the range, but the Tines patrolled their lands jealously and were swift to descend on any who set foot on even their farthest borders. Fortunately, they encountered none of the rust-skinned savages on their eerily silent harrow stags.

"Doesn't mean they aren't there," Jackal said to himself more than once.

He breathed easier when, nearing dusk, Hearth splashed across the Winsome Ford. They were now back in Grey Bastard lands. Jackal eased his hog's trot until Oats drew alongside and together they caught up with Fetching.

"Jack," Oats said, giving Jackal a pointed look.

"What?"

Fetching shook her head. "Your brigand, fool-ass."

"Shit," Jackal hissed and reached behind his saddle for the vest.

"One of these days we're not going to remind you," Oats said.

Riding side by side across the sandy flats, the three hogs surged forward, their snouts full of the smell of home.

Every hoof in the Lot Lands had a strong place to hole up. The humans had their castile, with its high towers and resident wizard. The elves had the seclusion of Dog Fall, defended with archers and sorcery. The centaurs trusted to their crumbling shrines and the belief in their mad gods.

The Grey Bastards had the Kiln.

As the central chimney grew upon the horizon, Jackal felt a pleasant stirring in his chest. He took his greatest pleasure while ranging astride his hog, but if he had to be idle, there was no place he would rather be than here.

Dominating a flat expanse of plain dotted with stubborn shrubs and boulders, the Kiln was an unsightly, sprawling compound, its buildings surrounded by a roughly oval foundation wall of pale brick. Five times the height of a half-orc, the wall sloped inward, laden with triangular buttresses and dimpled with load-bearing arches, then topped with a palisade of stone and latticed timber covered in render. From the outside, only the great chimney could be seen, rising high and imposing from the middle of the compound.

Vineyards and olive orchards thrived within thrumshot of the walls, worked by the people living under the protection of the Grey Bastards. As Jackal, Oats, and Fetching rode through the cultivated land, they saw humans and half-orcs ending their day's labors. None of these folk lived within the Kiln, but made the short walk to Winsome, the town that had sprouted up not a mile from the stronghold.

"All right," Oats said as they neared the shadow of the wall. "Who's going to tell him?"

"He won't listen to me," Fetch said.

"Fuck you both," Jackal griped. "You know I'm going to do it. Give me the coins."

Oats produced the jingling bag that held the Grey Bastards' portion of the profits from Sancho's brothel. He tossed it to Jackal just as they entered the Kiln's only gate, housed along the south-facing short side of the oval.

Unlike other fortifications, the gateway of the Kiln did not lead directly to the interior of the compound, but was blocked with stonework halfway beneath the thickness of the wall. A single sally port was set into the left wall of the gatehouse, big enough for two hog riders to enter abreast. This tunnel ran within the entire circuit of the foundation wall, before coming to another port, which debouched into the interior yard. In times of siege, the great oven in the center of the compound that gave the Kiln its name could be kindled, the flow of hellish air directed into the passage. Any attackers not wishing to scale the scorching walls would be forced to traverse the passage and complete the circuit, then break down the gate, all before they roasted alive.

In its twenty-six-year history, none had ever attempted assault on the Kiln.

At the moment, the portcullises of the sally ports were raised and the wall passage cool. There was no need for light; the hogs knew their way blind. Jackal and his companions rode single-file, hugging the left wall of the passage in case other riders were exiting. As soon as they emerged from the darkness and entered the compound, they rode directly for the meeting hall.

Jackal reined Hearth up outside the low building and dismounted, as did Oats and Fetching. A half dozen slopheads were waiting. They practically tripped over one another hurrying to tend the hogs.

"Can I take him to the pens for you, Jackal?" one of the young half-orcs managed, fawning and eager like all hoof hopefuls.

"No," Jackal replied. "Let him cool down."

"Just water, slophead!" Fetching barked at the youth approaching her barbarian.

Oats leaned down in front of his hog, butting his forehead between the beast's eyes. "All right, Ug, if one of these little shits so much as passes wind in your presence, eat them."

Jackal pushed through the door and led his friends into the dim embrace of the meeting hall, leaving the hopefuls outside. Despite its name, the meeting hall was a low-ceilinged structure that resembled nothing more than a rude tavern. Roundth and Hobnail were already well into their cups, waiting for the rest to arrive.

"Fill a mug for you three?" a slophead behind the counter asked.

Oats and Fetching went directly for the offered drink, while Jackal crossed the common room and headed straight for the hoof's voting chamber. One of the double doors was open, so he entered without bothering to announce his presence.

The Claymaster hunched behind the head of the great table, scrutinizing a pile of maps.

The chief was ravaged by old wounds and the lingering effects of the plague he had caught during the Incursion. That pox had killed tens of thousands on both sides, human and orc. Half-breeds fared no better. Yet the Claymaster, tough old shit that he was, refused to die. The disease was no longer catching, but it continued to flare up within him nearly thirty years later, taking a torturous toll on his once powerful frame. The outbreaks caused his joints to swell and his skin to become rife with weeping pustules. Linen wrappings, stained with dirty yellow blotches, now covered practically his entire head, with gaps left across his eyes and mouth. The hunch of his twisted back was more pronounced with each passing year and the fingers of his left hand were so engorged they looked ready to burst.

Jackal swallowed a groan when he saw Polecat hovering over the chief's shoulder. They both looked up as he came into the room. The Claymaster's face was impassive beneath his bandages, but Polecat produced a leering grin.

"He's back! Sancho got any new lovelies, Jack?"

"One," Jackal replied.

Polecat's eyebrows jumped with excitement. "Where's she from?"

"Anville."

"Oh," Polecat groaned, his beady eyes narrowing. "I bet she's pale and pliable."

"Get your head out of your prick!" the Claymaster said, thumping Polecat with his elbow. "Sit down, Jackal. Stop distracting this hatchet-faced fuck."

Jackal did as he was told, taking his usual chair two seats removed from the Claymaster's left.

The Grey Bastards' council table was a coffin-shaped behemoth of darkly stained oak. The Claymaster sat at the wider end with the diagonal shoulders to his left and right always empty. The long, tapering body of the table held a score of chairs on each side, yet only nine throwing axes sat upon its surface, each representing the remaining voting members of the hoof. Jackal had never known the table to be full. The Grey Bastards had numbered sixteen when he had joined their ranks seven years ago, but orc raids, centaur attacks, and internal strife had whittled away at their numbers. Admittance to the brotherhood was strict and the amount of worthy slopheads rising to sworn members was too few to keep up with the losses.

Grocer was already present, sitting closest to the Claymaster's right. He nodded as Jackal sat down, but said nothing. The willowy old quartermaster was stingy with everything, including words.

Oats entered with a frothing flagon in each hand. He sat next to Jackal and slid one of the mugs over.

"If I'd wanted one, I would've gotten it," Jackal groused halfheartedly, taking the drink just the same. He was in the midst of his first deep pull when Oats responded.

"Seemed like a waste to pour it out after I washed my cod in it."

Jackal sputtered, more from laughter than alarm.

"You rinse your balls in it too?" he asked, wiping the foam from his mouth.

Oats grinned. "Not *mine*."

"They were mine, Jack!" Roundth proclaimed as he entered the chamber, Hobnail close behind. "I would have dipped my wick too, but you know it won't fit. The mouth of those mugs is too narrow to handle all my—"

"ROUNDTH!" Oats, Jackal, Hobnail, and Polecat joined Roundth in the old joke. The stocky mongrel loved to trumpet the origin of his hoof name and it was always worth a laugh.

The Claymaster did not so much as grin.

Roundth and Hobnail took their seats and made a few rude, good-natured gestures across the table at Jackal, which he returned. Like him and Oats, the pair was still dust-stained from riding.

A few minutes later, Hoodwink drifted in, sitting silently at the far end of the table, away from the rest of the hoof. This was something the Claymaster would not allow anyone else to do, but Hood had been a free-rider for a long time and the solitary ways clung to him. The chief would not risk losing a member for the sake of forced camaraderie.

Nearly every inch of Hoodwink's blanched skin, including his hairless scalp, was covered in ragged scars, crisscrossing over the tattoos of the hoofs he had ridden with over the years. Pale, puckered lines marred the ink of the Skull Sowers, the Tusked Tide, and the Shards, and those were just the ones that Jackal could make out. Every one of those brotherhoods had once accepted Hoodwink into their ranks, and every one had cast him out. It was a wonder he was still alive. With none willing to take further risk on him, Hood had ridden nomad for years before the Claymaster offered him a place with the Bastards. The vote had barely passed, but the hoof needed the numbers and, whatever his offenses, Hoodwink was a formidable mongrel. After two years, Jackal was still wondering how long he would last.

The Claymaster glanced around the table and grimaced.

"Am I going to have to throw a stick out there?" he asked, pointing through the doors toward the common room. His question and his gaze were directed at Jackal and Oats.

Fortunately, Fetching entered the chamber before they had to answer. She was talking with Mead, but Jackal suspected she had heard the chief's remark. Likely, she had been waiting for it, controlling the derision since she could not stop it. Quickly breaking off their conversation, Fetch and Mead went and sat at opposite sides of the table. Likely the youngblood would have sat next to her if he thought it would not make his attraction any more obvious.

Despite several standing bets between Jackal and Oats, Fetching had not yet broken any of Mead's bones. Surprisingly, she seemed to enjoy his consistent attempts to be friendly. Other than Hood, who forever felt like an outsider, Mead was the only member of the hoof newer than Fetching, rising from the ranks of the slops last winter. He was young and confident and wore his hair in the fashion of the Tines, shaving it along the sides to leave only a broad strip down the center of his head, worked into plumes. The older Bastards frowned on that, but Mead spoke the elf tongue, a rare skill amongst half-orcs, and a welcome one for the hoof.

As the room quieted, the Claymaster leaned back in his chair.

Looming behind him, a massive tree stump stood upon its side, anchored to the ceiling with heavy chains. Its old face held uncountable rings, the wood grey with age and pitted with dozens of sharp grooves. These wounds were a permanent tally of the votes cast against the Claymaster's will, the marks left behind from axe blades hurled deeply into the stump. One axe was lodged there still, stuck into the wood just over the Claymaster's left shoulder as it had been the past twenty years.

Warbler's axe.

"I know you're all tired," the Claymaster began, "so let's make this palaver quick. Grocer, how are our stores?"

The quartermaster's scowl deepened as he calculated. "We're well provisioned. Though, that next load of timber can't get here quick enough."

"How long could we keep the Kiln burning if we were attacked?"

"Two days," Grocer answered. "Might stretch to three."

The Claymaster grunted, not liking the answer, but accepting the truth. "I'll send a bird to Ignacio. Find out if he's heard when we can expect those wagons from Hispartha. Mead? Any luck with that shit from Al-Unan?"

"Only a little, chief," Mead replied. "Getting it to burn is simple, but it's damn hard to control. It doesn't need fuel, but it will consume anything it touches. Salik almost lost a hand to the stuff."

"Who?" the Claymaster asked, giving Mead a chance to correct his mistake.

"One of the slops, chief," Mead said without flinching. "Anyway, I'm still worried about what the green fire will do to the ovens."

"Keep on it," the Claymaster told him and pointed a finger, "but don't burn down my damn fortress." He turned his chin up, peering down to the end of the table. "Hood? You have any trouble with that errand?"

"No, I did not," Hoodwink answered, his unblinking eyes leaving the surface of the table long enough to address the chief.

Jackal shot Oats a questioning look, but he didn't seem to know what Hood had been sent to do either. That was nothing new, and the mysteries were getting tiresome. One of these days, Jackal was going to lead a vote and find out, but now was not the time. He doubted he would have the support needed and, besides, he was moments away from stirring up enough trouble for himself. He figured the chief would go to his favorites next, ask Roundth and Hobnail for their report on the Shards, but the Claymaster's next question was directed at Oats.

"How did we do?"

Oats motioned to Jackal, who tossed the bag of coins onto the table. The Claymaster's face remained impassive beneath his bandages as Grocer reached over and hefted the bag, weighing it in his palm.

"Feels light."

Jackal nodded, inwardly cursing the old miser. "Two of Sancho's girls took sick most of last month, and one ran off with some Guabic merchant. He's brought in a new girl, though, from Anville. She will help make up for the loss."

The Claymaster leaned forward. "Did you remind that fat frail that if he doesn't make good on his end, the Grey Bastards might find they can no longer patrol around his brothel?"

Again, Jackal nodded. He had given Sancho no such reminder. There was no need. The whoremaster had lived in the Lot Lands a long time, long enough to know the dwindling cavalero patrols from the castile could no longer ensure his safety.

"There's something else," the Claymaster said, not a hint of a question in his gravelly voice. The chief's eyes flicked to Jackal, then to Oats and Fetching, then back again. "What is it?"

Jackal took a deep breath. He had wanted to volunteer the information before the chief suspected, but the Claymaster missed nothing. Despite his increasingly crippled form, his mind remained as keen as the head of a thrumbolt. He waited on Jackal to respond, his bloodshot eyes staring fixedly from between the foul wrappings.

"Bermudo came to the brothel this morning," Jackal said, feeling every eye at the table settle on him. "He had seven new cavaleros with him. I don't think he expected us to be there. Tried to act the hard man."

Polecat sniggered. "That snobby frail fuck."

"He goad a fight?" the Claymaster asked.

"Not him," Jackal replied. "But one of his new fops tried to make Oats his damn valet. We gave him the old Grey Bastard charm and he hit me. I gifted it to him, and gave Bermudo a chance to rein his peacock in, but he didn't take it, so we did it for him."

"You killed the peacock," the Claymaster observed without feeling.

Jackal nodded. Polecat, Hobnail, and Roundth thumped the table with approval. That was good. Jackal felt his nerves begin to calm.

"And," he went on, using the growing favor, "we knocked Bermudo senseless. Made sure the other cavaleros understood the way of things in the Lots."

Jackal looked around the table, thankful to see Mead smiling and even Hoodwink nodding slowly down at the end.

"What about the body?"

Jackal turned back at the Claymaster's question.

"Figured on the Sludge Man."

The Claymaster was silent for a long while, his only motion the blink of his eyelids.

"Ignacio will back us," he said at last. "But if that prick Bermudo decides he wants some comeuppance—"

"He won't," Jackal put in. "We made ourselves plain."

The Claymaster did not look convinced.

"And Sancho?" Grocer asked. "What does that coin clipper want for going your way on this?"

Jackal met the quartermaster's stare. "Just that the Bastards start paying for quim. No more free thrusts as part of our protection bargain."

The bandages along the Claymaster's jaw bulged as he grit his teeth. Polecat and Roundth issued wordless sounds of disgust. Grocer's expression could have soured wine.

Jackal raised a placating hand. "That arrangement had to end anyway. Some of the girls were starting to resent it."

The Claymaster slammed his good hand down on the desk. "The girls?! What kind of cockless maggot is Sancho that he's worried about what a bunch of whores think? Or is that your own sympathies coming through, Jackal? I know you're all but wed to that red-haired hussy, got her gagging for your mongrel meat. You looking to her needs instead of the interests of this hoof?"

Jackal shook his head, opening his mouth to answer.

"Don't you say a fucking word!" the Claymaster warned, thrusting a distended finger outward. "You throw me a half-empty bag of coin before ensuring me it's going to go back to proper weight, *then* you say some of that weight is gonna be our own shine coming back to us because we have to start paying for cunny? *And* we might have to start watching out for reprisals from the castile all because you three"—the finger jabbed at Jackal, Oats, and Fetching—"couldn't keep from killing some arrogant frail so fresh from the north that he still smelled like incense from his father's fucking manor? Which one of you actually ended him?"

Jackal felt his teeth grinding. He heard Fetch take a breath.

"That cavalero struck a Grey Bastard!" he said, before she could speak. "And he did it in front of a half dozen other noble brats new to the Lots. Do you want tongues to wag that a rider from this hoof can be chastised by some blue blood? Do you want the Tines hearing that? What about our brother hoofs? We cannot be cowed by Hisparthan gentry, chief."

"Damn right," came Hoodwink's soft voice from the far end. Jackal did not risk a glance at the others, but the table was silent.

"No, we can't," the Claymaster agreed, his voice thick with anger. "But as leader of this hoof, I also cannot allow my riders to make choices that might bring blood we are not ready to shed or spill. Now. Which one of you killed the cavalero?"

"Who do you think?" Jackal replied. "I did."

Next to him, he felt Fetch's entire body go taut. She was angry, just as Jackal knew she would be, but she was no fool and did not question or contradict his lie in front of the hoof.

The Claymaster's head slumped slightly. "Looks like you're going to be nursemaiding the slopheads for a while, Jack."

Jackal seethed. He stared at the Claymaster, his jaw so tight it began to throb. They had done the right thing, protected the reputation of the hoof. And now he was to be punished for it? Jackal felt his hand drifting across the table to the axe in front of him. He would cast against the chief's decision. Surely the rest would back him.

Just then the doors of the chamber were thrust aside. A slack-jawed hopeful stood in the jamb, his wide eyes darting uncertainly around the room.

"Hells, say their name and one fucking appears," the Claymaster groaned. "What do you want?"

The slophead jumped at the chief's tone.

"R-riders returned, Claymaster," the slop stammered. "Scouts from . . . from Batayat Hill."

"Out with it!" the Claymaster said. "What do they report?"

The slophead's mouth went up and down ineffectually a few times before he finally got the word out.

"Thicks."

Chapter 3

Jackal sat astride Hearth, waiting with the rest of the hoof as the Hogback unfolded. The narrow passage through the foundation wall was perfect for defense, but not ideal for fast egress. The Claymaster had found a way around that back in the early days and paid some Hisparthan siege engineers to construct his solution.

A hinged wooden ramp lolled down from the palisade into the compound's yard. Three powerful barbarians were harnessed to a great vertical axle, which turned a chaos of gears that Jackal had never been able to comprehend. Once the hogs were urged to walk, the Hogback split, a second ramp rising up from the first, yawning into the sky until it overtopped the palisade and touched down on the ground beyond, all in a matter of minutes. More than enough time for the Grey Bastards to marshal in full arms.

"I hate these damn night raids," Roundth complained as he buckled a brace of heavy javelins to his saddle.

"Me too," Fetching said as she secured a second quiver of thrumbolts to her harness. "No chance to see exactly how few brains you've got when a thick knocks you from the saddle and your skull gets dashed against a rock."

Roundth snorted. "I won't expect any tears from you, Fetch, you cold lizard."

Jackal ignored the banter. His own gear was already affixed across Hearth's shoulders.

Oats bumped him on the shoulder. "Stop brooding."

"I'm fine," Jackal replied.

"You're not. Your head is still back at that table, pissed off at the chief. Let that go for now, Jackal. We got a fight coming."

"Slop duty." Jackal gnashed his teeth. "We did the Bastards proud today and slop duty is the reward."

Fetching's head snapped around, fury in her face. "We?"

Before she could say another word, Jackal jabbed a finger at her. "Don't you go saying something stupid to the Claymaster on my account! I don't need more shit work because you don't know when it's best to keep silent."

Fetching's neck went tight as further ire boiled up in her face, but her eyes darted to Roundth and Mead, who were close by and watching the little dustup with interest. Swallowing hard, Fetch jerked her mount to face away from Jackal.

All nine sworn members of the Grey Bastards were assembled, even Grocer, his sinewy old root of a body looking odd in full kit. The pair of slop scouts who had spotted the orcs were conversing with Hobnail, likely trying, and failing, to convince him to let them ride with the hoof. Slopheads made good eyes, and the older ones helped patrol the Lot, but until they were blooded into the brotherhood, they did not ride into battle. Jackal had half expected the Claymaster to order him to stay behind as well, but his punishment would have to wait. With orcs on the raid, they could not afford one fewer rider.

As the Hogback reached its vertical apex, the Claymaster rode into the yard. His twisted back no longer allowed him to sit in a saddle, but he drove a chariot with skill, pulled by a single giant of a hog named Big Pox. Stopping between the ramp and the hoof, the Claymaster faced his riders, his misshapen bulk imposing in the fresh night.

"We got orcs in our lot!" he rumbled. "If I gotta say a damn word about how we handle that, you mongrels aren't my hoof. We make for Batayat Hill. Ride out!"

The Grey Bastards put heel to hog and thundered past their chief. They hit the ramp at speed, crested it, and went charging down the opposite slope. Jackal had both hands in Hearth's mane, keeping his arms loose as the hog surged onto flat ground. Ahead, Hobnail took point, his barbarian kicking up a wake of dust. Jackal and the rest of the hoof spread out into an arrowhead formation, four to a side. Oats, the last rider in the left spur was behind Jackal. It was always comforting having the brute at his back. Looking to his right, Jackal saw Fetching directly opposite him in the other spur, between Polecat and Hoodwink. She kept her eyes fixed ahead. The Claymaster rode rearguard in his chariot, between the ends of the spurs.

Jackal settled into the ride, feeling his stockbow jostle against his back. Ahead of him, Grocer's ropey mass of hair flew in the wind. Behind, the Hogback would already have been raised and the slopheads would have manned the palisade, nearly three dozen young half-orcs with spears and shields. The fires would be quickly stoked, the flues from the great oven opened to flood the wall passage with deadly heat, securing the Kiln until the hoof returned, burning wood they could ill afford to lose. Grocer was probably sick with the thought. Jackal would no doubt be hearing him gripe about the waste for the next fortnight while he was penned up within the compound, molding the slops into future riders. But for now, he was out on the plain, borne along by pounding hooves, hunting the enemy.

An old saying still existed from the days of the Incursion: "The orcs have the power to conquer the world, but to do it, they will have to walk."

Jackal reckoned it was true, on both accounts. The thicks had no affinity with animals. Every living beast responded to them like the predators they were, and so, the orcs knew nothing of husbandry, or taming, or domestication. It was their sole disadvantage. Cunning, vicious, dreadfully strong and unnaturally tough, orcs were terrible foes. They were three times as strong as a man and twice as fast. The Hisparthans learned early in their battles with the thicks that infantry was useless. Only mounted warriors had a chance of victory against an orc force of equal numbers.

The nobility of Hispartha had brought half-orcs and hogs together as servants for the war, but it was the thicks who inadvertently formed the first hoof.

During one of countless inconsequential battles, the orcs broke the Hisparthan cavalry and the frails routed, abandoning their baggage train to be slaughtered. The half-orc slaves took up what arms they could and threw the yokes off the barbarians. The hogs became their mounts and they charged the orc horde. The barbarians endured wounds that would have felled a horse and delivered their share of injury with their sweeping tusks. Even ill equipped and untrained, the half-orc slaves were stronger than any human and every bit as ferocious as the thicks. Their natural prowess gave the Hisparthans time to rally and the orc lines were shattered.

The Claymaster had been at that battle, as had every original member of the Grey Bastards, most now dead. They proved their worth as more than slaves that day. They could do more for the war than serve as drovers and potters and gravediggers. Even the pompous human nobles could not fail to see the power of the mounted half-orc, and soon all mongrel slaves were given a chance to fight for the Crown.

The end of the Orc Incursion saw the eventual freedom of all half-orcs in Ul-wundulas, but more important to Jackal's way of thinking, it saw the establishment of the Lot Lands. After years of bitter fighting and the toll taken by the plague that effectively ended the war, the southern half of the country had been left all but abandoned. Hispartha had neither the stomach nor the numbers to resettle Ul-wundulas, so they allowed their allies to draw lots and gifted great parcels of land to those willing to defend them against further aggression from the orcs.

Bringing swift, brutal resistance to thick raids was the purpose of the Grey Bastards. And the Fangs of Our Fathers, the Cauldron Brotherhood, the Orc Stains, the Sons of Perdition, and all the rest. It was Jackal's purpose, blood to balls.

Batayat Hill stood near the southeastern border of the Bastards' lot, nearly twenty miles from the Kiln. After a full day's travel from the brothel with little rest, Hearth was far from fresh, but the hog punished the ground, keeping pace with the group without any signs of flagging. Jackal rubbed him proudly on the shoulder.

The hoof reached Batayat.

The hill was a sullen formation of exposed rock. Much of the soil around it had eroded, but stubborn shrubbery somehow thrived within the cracks of the rocks. Like all of his fellow riders, Jackal's vision was sharp at night, a gift from whatever thick had raped his human mother. As the hill came into view, he spied no movement upon the rocks and no band of orcs on the plain below. Thicks raided in small bands called *ulyud*, the orc word for hand, and each was led by a *t'huruuk*, the arm. The scouts had reported two full *ulyud* in the area, meaning twelve orcs.

From the point of the arrowhead, Hobnail slowed the formation, swinging south to circle around Batayat. The hill covered a broad expanse and Jackal did not like their reduced pace with the dark rocks so close at their left. The average orc was nearly seven feet of bulging thews, allowing them to move at daunting speed. From a dead stop they were swifter than any mount, able to sprint forward and close in before a horse or hog could gain enough distance to outpace them. The key to survival was to keep moving.

Jackal reached down behind his hip, gripped the bridle of his stockbow, and slung it around. As Hearth continued to trot, Jackal held his seat with his legs and yanked back on the bowstring until it settled into the pawl. Another advantage of orc blood: a human would have needed a windlass to pull back on the metal prods of such a heavy stockbow. Reaching into the quiver at his belt, Jackal drew a bolt and loaded the thrum. He returned his left hand to Hearth's mane while his right held the weapon at the ready. All around him the other Bastards did the same.

Rounding the southern edge of the hill, the hoof struck east and swept the rocks for a sign.

Nothing.

Jackal bit back a curse. If the thicks had seen them coming and sheltered atop Batayat, the Bastards would be facing a battle they could not win. The hogs would be of little use amongst the rocks, and fighting orcs on foot without superior numbers was a sure way to see every member of the hoof feeding the flies by morning.

As the formation came around the eastern slopes and turned north, Jackal grinned.

"There you are," he whispered.

The hoof had just crested a rise at Batayat's feet, giving them a good vantage of the orcs, not a half mile distant. The two *ulyud* were running across the rough plain below the hill, headed north, their backs turned to the Bastards, unaware of their presence. Had they known they were being pursued, they would have turned and charged or taken up a position in the rocks. Thicks did not flee.

Hobnail kicked his hog forward. The hoof followed.

Hearth plunged down the slope and Jackal clung to his bristles with one hand. His eyes darted from the orcs to Hobnail, waiting to see what he chose to do. In a fight, the hoof followed the point rider.

Jackal's mind ran faster than his hog.

There was no hope of felling twelve orcs in one charge. The *ulyud* ran beside one another, but there was a gap between them big enough for the hoof to pass through if they tightened the arrowhead. This would allow them to let loose on both bands, each spur sending their thrumbolts into the closest group. But the leftmost *ulyud* could make a dash for the rocks before the hoof could wheel for another pass. Hobnail saw the risk and aimed the formation directly at them. Jackal approved. Hob was going to lead them in a tusker, a ride-through intended to shatter the six orcs in one brutal charge. It was a bold move, and the right decision, but if the charge stalled it would expose the right spur of the arrowhead to a counterattack from the other *ulyud*. The Claymaster too, in his slower chariot, was vulnerable.

Jackal shot a quick look over at Fetching, riding in the right spur. Her teeth were bared in gleeful anticipation of bloodshed.

The orcs caught scent of them and turned just before they were within thrum range. All six were bald, pitch-skinned in the darkness. Their heavily muscled bodies were clad in kilts of animal hide and sleeveless hauberks of mail. Heavy iron plates, festooned with thick spikes, protected them at stomach, knee, and forearm. Most brandished the heavy scimitars favored by orcs, though two wielded broad-headed spears. The *t'huruuk*, the leader, was always the largest, fiercest orc. Jackal watched as he bellowed quick commands at his *ulyud*, waving his great blade. The orcs spread out quickly, forcing the Bastards to widen their arrowhead. Jackal hoped the riders on the right spur were keeping one eye on the other thicks, lest they be taken in the flank.

The hogs tore across the plain and closed the distance.

Hobnail took his shot. The string from the stockbow thrummed deeply, quickly followed by shots from Roundth and Mead. Jackal did not see if their bolts found a mark, focusing his own aim on one of the spear-wielding orcs.

The furious squeals of hogs filled the air as the tip of the formation met the orcs. Just ahead of Jackal, Grocer thundered toward the *t'huruuk*, letting a bolt fly. The shot went wide and the orc leader rolled, coming to his feet between the spurs of the formation. He issued a guttural, undulating war cry and raised his massive scimitar. Jackal quickly changed his target and swung his stockbow to the right, squeezing the tickler just before he drew even with the thick chieftain. The bolt took the orc in the belly, but snapped against his iron gut plate. Jackal pulled his hand out of Hearth's mane and gripped the hog's left swine-yanker, pulling down hard. The barbarian's head dipped and he veered just as the *t'huruuk* swung his curved blade. The stroke hissed through empty air as Jackal rode past.

Releasing his grip on his stockbow and allowing the weapon to fall to the end of its strap across his body, Jackal snatched a javelin from his saddle. Another thick was ahead of him, raising his spear to cast at Grocer's passing hog.

Jackal threw first.

The javelin sunk into the orc's exposed armpit, arresting his attack, but the brute kept his feet. Jackal guided Hearth straight toward the thick and the hog whipped his head sideways, goring the orc with a swipe of his tusk. Ripped off his feet from the force of the blow, the orc tumbled bloody to the ground.

Jackal was now past the *ulyud*, but he heard the sounds of squealing hogs and thrumming stockbows behind him as Oats, Hoodwink, and the Claymaster gave the thicks a taste of the rearguard. Hobnail steered his hog to the right, leading the hoof to wheel around for another charge. While Hearth slowed as he made the turn, Jackal retrieved his stockbow, using his legs to stay in the saddle as he reloaded. Once the weapon was ready, Jackal made a quick count.

Ten hogs. Ten riders. All had made it through.

With no more need for stealth and the thrill of battle blazing in his chest, Jackal opened his mouth and let loose the hoof's war cry.

"Live in the saddle!"

"Die on the hog!" the Grey Bastards responded as one.

The formation came around and straightened the path of their mounts for another charge.

The orcs were closing ranks, the untouched *ulyud* rushing to join up with their bloodied brethren. Only two thicks lay unmoving upon the ground. A third, the one Hearth had struck, was on his knees, but still alive and clutching his spear.

"Hells, these fucks are hard to kill," Jackal told his hog.

The *t'huruuks* were still standing and formed up next to each other, blending their war bands into a single force of ten. The numbers were now even, but the orcs were prepared and eager to spill blood.

As the hoof pounded toward the thicks, Hobnail raised an arm straight up, then quickly hooked his elbow over his head, pointing his fist to the left.

Jackal grimaced. A shank shot? Had Hob lost his mind?

The maneuver was nothing but a harrowing action, requiring the riders to turn sharply just before reaching the orcs, the spurs of the arrowhead interweaving into a single line while the riders let loose with their stockbows. It slowed the hoof considerably and would never kill all the orcs in one pass. The Bastards would be lucky if the thicks didn't break for Batayat Hill while they turned. Now that the *ulyud* were joined, they likely would and then it was a boulder hunt. Hob needed to order another tusker or send the left spur around the orcs ahead of the right, whittle at them with a scorpion's jest or a viper tongue.

While Jackal clenched his jaw in frustration, Hobnail stuck to his signal and jerked his hog left, leveling his thrum to the right and sending a bolt into the orcs. Roundth and Mead followed seamlessly, guiding their barbarians from running side by side to single file as they turned. Jackal saw at least one thick fall. Grocer and Polecat were next. As they made ready to turn, one of the *t'huruuks* roared in fury and darted forward. The thicks followed him. Desperate to get out of their path, Grocer missed his shot, and Polecat didn't even have time to loose a bolt.

Jackal was now riding directly beside Fetching, the pair of them making headlong for the charging orcs. Her voice filled his right ear, yelling over the rushing air, savagely elated.

"Fuck this shanking shit! Another tusker, Jack?!"

"Right down their throats!" he agreed, and pulled the trigger of his stockbow.

The bolt sped over Hearth's head and struck an orc in the arm. Fetch's bow thrummed and a thick fell with a shaft in his neck. Jackal had just enough time to drop his stockbow and tear his tulwar from its sheath before Hearth crashed amongst the orcs, the hog's tusks rending one thick's leg as he barreled through. Slashing left and right as he passed, Jackal felt his arm vibrate with the impact of his blade on orc armor. One of the *t'huruuks* sprang at him, its scimitar held high in both hands. A javelin screamed over Jackal's shoulder and hit the orc chieftain in the chest, tearing through his mail and striking with such force it knocked the brute backward.

Oats.

Jackal issued a silent thanks that his big friend had followed him into the press. He only hoped Hoodwink and the Claymaster had shown equal balls. To Jackal's right, Fetch laughed as her dripping tulwar took an orc's hand off.

Only one thick lay between Jackal and open plain, the injured one with the spear. In a display of unnerving vitality, the orc dragged himself to his feet, ignoring the gaping wound Hearth had left in his thigh. Jackal swung his tulwar in a sideways arc as he passed, shearing through the orc's spear shaft and slicing into his collarbone. Grunting, the orc collapsed and Hearth emerged from the battle.

As his hog continued to put distance between him and the orcs, Jackal turned in the saddle. Fetching had won through, Oats and Hoodwink not far behind. Hood looked unsteady in the saddle and as he rode closer, Jackal saw he was clutching a seeping wound on his shoulder. Farther back, Jackal saw the twice-wounded orc with the shattered spear was again regaining his feet, but Big Pox charged right over him, trampling him beneath his hooves and the wheels of the chariot as the Claymaster drove out of the melee.

Jackal and the others reined up a safe distance from the thicks and waited on the Claymaster to reach them. Four thicks were still on their feet, rallying around the single surviving *t'huruuk*. All of them appeared injured. Hobnail and the rest of the Grey Bastards had now wheeled back around, and were preparing another charge. To Jackal's surprise, the Claymaster reached for the war horn affixed to his chariot and blew three short bursts, the call to regroup.

"Chief," Jackal said, "we could hit them from two sides and finish this."

The Claymaster shook his head. "No. We're going home."

Jackal could not help but throw a gawking look at Oats.

"What are you looking at him for?" the Claymaster demanded. "Was I fucking unclear?"

"No, Claymaster," Jackal replied. "But if those thicks reach the rocks and hole up, we risk all going in after them."

"Did your skull get thumped back there, boy? I didn't say anything about going in after them. I said we are going back to the Kiln."

"And leave thicks alive in our lot?" Fetching asked, trying and failing to keep the challenge from her voice.

The Claymaster turned his large frame slowly to face Fetch. "I'm going to explain something to you. And if I am still explaining it when the rest of the boys get here, I ain't gonna be pleased." The Claymaster put a cruel emphasis on the word "boys" as he kept his hard stare on Fetching. "Not a one of those orcs ain't wounded. They came with two hands, two arms. They're leaving with an arm and four fingers. Thicks don't choose their numbers randomly. Whatever they came to do, they won't try it now. Let them limp back south and take the tale of their defeat with them. Now, do you want me to give them another tale to take back? About how the leader of the Grey Bastards cut the tongues out of the mouths of two of his own hoof for questioning his orders? Because I have had enough of Jackal's voice today, and honestly, Fetching, if your tongue isn't licking my cock, I got no damn use for it."

Beyond the Claymaster, Jackal watched as the orcs clambered in amongst the rocks of Batayat. He did not say another word and neither did Fetch. When the others rode up, they seemed equally perplexed at the chief's order, but no further challenges were voiced.

The hoof took its time getting back. There was no need to tax their hogs further. Everyone was silent, each rider keeping his eyes open for additional threat while worrying at his private thoughts. Jackal knew his brothers. It would not sit well that they allowed the orcs to escape. The Claymaster was headed quickly toward a vote to remove him from the head of the table. Hells, it was past time. Jackal just had to make sure none of the others beat him to the axe toss.

The chief again blew his horn when they were within sight of the Kiln, signaling the slops to lower the Hogback. The ramp was down by the time the hoof reached the walls and the hogs crossed over quickly, each one eager for the pens.

"Get the damn ovens doused!" the Claymaster bellowed at the slops. "I don't need all our wood burned up over a dozen thicks."

"No, you let it burn up for seven," Jackal muttered so only Oats heard. His friend gave him a cautionary frown.

After the Bastards dismounted, they began leading their hogs to the stables. As they passed the entry gate, Jackal flinched away from the heat still pouring out of the wall passage. It would be hours before it cooled enough to use.

"Forgive me, my friend?"

Jackal and the others cursed at the sound of the voice, taking a few startled steps away from the tunnel from which it emerged.

"Who the fuck said that?" Roundth demanded.

Fetching and Hoodwink already had their stockbows pressed hard into their shoulders and trained on the shadowy opening. Jackal shot a look at Oats and raised his own thrum.

A figure leaned forward out of the darkness behind the portcullis.

"A thousand and one apologies, friends. I did not intend alarm."

It was a half-orc, one Jackal did not recognize. He was fleshy, going to fat, but his face was youthful, bearing a black beard and mustachio, perfectly trimmed. A turban was wrapped about his head, his body clad in the robes of the east. There were many rings upon his pudgy fingers, which casually gripped the iron bars of the portcullis. Those bars, Jackal knew, were too hot to touch. It was difficult for him to even breathe this close to the infernal mouth of the tunnel, but the intruder standing inside it was not even sweating. He regarded the semicircle of pointed stockbows with serene indifference.

"If one would be so kind as to allow me entry," he said pleasantly. "I assure you all, I am merely a humble visitor."

"No, you're not."

It was the Claymaster who spoke, shouldering his way between Hobnail and Grocer. He took two stiff steps toward the gate and stood in the hellish waves of heat as he stared at the turbaned half-orc.

"You're a wizard," the chief said. There was a smile on his face, beneath the bandages.

Chapter 4

WHAT DID YOU DO THIS TIME, JACK?"

Beryl didn't even look up as Jackal entered the orphanage, keeping her attention focused on the squalling babe she was cleaning. He was never sure how she did that, though she always claimed to know every child she ever raised by smell. All about the long, low-ceilinged room, young half-orcs ran, toddled, crawled, or simply sat. Every one of them was making more noise than a hog in rut.

"Grab Wily before he sticks his hand in the pot," Beryl said calmly, tilting her head slightly over one shoulder.

Looking toward the familiar fireplace, Jackal saw a stout little drooling thing reaching a pudgy hand toward the bubbling porridge pot hung over the low flames. Springing over and around the other children, Jackal managed to reach the child and snatch him up before he learned a hard lesson. The small mongrel giggled as he was hoisted into the air.

"You going soft, Beryl?" Jackal teased, balancing the child on his hip. "Time was you let burning be the reason we didn't go near the hearth."

Lifting the dripping infant out of the washbasin, Beryl shrugged. "This batch is smarter than you were." She dried and swaddled the babe with practiced hands and handed it off to one of the older girls before finally turning to face Jackal, eyeing him up and down.

"Well? Claymaster didn't send you here for nothing. Out with it."

Jibes aside, Beryl had not gone soft in the least. Though well past fifty, she retained a strong, comely figure, though fuller in the hips and belly than she had been when Jackal was under her care. Her long chestnut locks, tied up in a practical pile, had lost none of their color and her arms were as sinewy as ever. Half-orc females lose their minds long before their bodies, as was often joked around the hoof when Fetching was out of earshot.

Jackal opened his mouth to answer, but before the words came out, the boy he was holding stuck an entire fist in. Careful to keep his teeth from hurting the child, Jackal went on with his explanation, allowing the child's hand to make an incomprehensible mumble out of his speech, not stopping until the little mongrel was belly-laughing and Beryl cracked a smile.

"So, you're not in trouble," she said. "You're just here to be amongst those your own age."

Lip-chewing on the boy's hand until he laughed harder, Jackal gave Beryl a wink. He turned and looked at the child's chubby face, eyes clenched tight with glee, then expelled the hand from his mouth with an overexaggerated spitting sound.

"Hells," he said, cocking his eyes to look past the boy's lips. "This little slobberer's already got his lower fangs."

Beryl gave a slow, tired nod. "Makes me glad my wet-nursing days are over. Wily there is not yet two and already bigger than most twice his age. Not much hair, but strong, hungry, and, as you said, lower fangs cutting already. I don't envy Thistle. That little beast is at her tit night and day. Reminds me of Oats at that age. Bald, fanged, and breast-crazed."

Jackal smiled. "Not much has changed there."

He lowered Wily down and set him on his unsteady feet. The boy squealed and went toddling off after one of the older children.

"How long you exiled here to Winsome?" Beryl asked, sweeping her gaze across the room in a silent warning to the children that she was still watching them.

"Until the Claymaster says I can ride again."

"Are you really going to let me hear what you did from the bed-warmers, Jackal?"

"No," he said. "No, I killed a cavalero at Sancho's, giving him the opening to ask the hoof to start paying for his girls. *That* only earned me slophead tending, but then I questioned the Claymaster's decision in the field, so . . . here I am."

Beryl cocked her head disapprovingly to one side. "Jackal!"

"He allowed five thicks to escape, Beryl! He wasn't thinking clear.

None of us could believe the order, but only Fetch and I had the guts to say something."

Beryl threw her arms up at the mention of Fetching's name. "Still risking yourself for that one. I might have known."

Jackal swallowed a snarl of frustration and kept his voice from rising. "There was no risk. I spoke up first. We—"

"Challenged the Claymaster," Beryl cut in, her mouth forming a hard line.

"No," Jackal protested. "We just wanted to know why he was letting a bunch of orcs run free in our lot."

Beryl shook her head in that disappointed way Jackal knew as a child. "He was fighting full-bloods long before you were born, Jack."

"So it's my fault he's lost his taste for it?"

Beryl's eyes flashed and she looked around before taking a step toward him.

"Enough!" she said, her tone hushed. "Cissy and Sweeps are right outside hanging linens. What happens when they hike up to the Kiln tonight and whisper what you said to Polecat while they're all squirming beneath his blankets? Or one of these little ones repeats what they heard to Thistle? She's still walking home bowlegged most nights from Roundth's bunk. Some of the village girls aren't even bedwarmers, but they're not above letting a slophead have his way every now and again in hopes he'll be a rider soon. You think they don't gossip? What are you going to do when half the hopefuls are whispering that you are making a bid for the hoof?"

Jackal held up a hand to try and stall her tirade, to no effect.

"You won't be ready for the Claymaster's response. And there will be one more empty seat at that voting table."

Beryl's voice broke a little at the last, causing Jackal to look away and pretend not to have noticed. After more than twenty years, Warbler's absence still pained her.

"Don't worry," he said, watching the children play. "The chief's more interested in filling a seat right now."

"One of the slops showing promise?" Beryl asked.

"No. We had a stranger show up at the Kiln last night, dressed and spoke like he was from Tyrkania or somewhere."

"So?" Beryl shrugged. "What makes some dune lover so special?"

"Claymaster thinks he's a wizard."

Beryl almost succeeded in hiding her surprise. "Is he?"

Jackal wrinkled his mouth. "The ovens were lit and there he was, standing in the wall. He should have been cooked, Beryl, and long before he made it all the way to the yard gate."

"Those desert-dwellers are accustomed to heat," Beryl said, but even she didn't sound convinced.

Jackal decided not to mention the stranger touching bare flesh to blazing metal. "Whatever he is, the chief was giddy as a slophead with his first whore. Never seen him like that, even Grocer looked disturbed."

Beryl folded her arms in front of her. "The Claymaster's wanted a wizard in the hoof for as long as I've known him, Jackal. The castile has one, it's said the Tines practically shit them, but none of the half-breed hoofs have ever been able to bring sorcery to their tables. If this stranger really is a wizard, it could help the Bastards." She fixed him with a long, studying look. "But you don't think so."

"I don't know what to think. The Claymaster was holed up with this creep all night. Only came out long enough this morning to order me down here."

"Well, don't look too crestfallen over it," Beryl said, snatching up one of the damp rags on the table and throwing it at him. "Neither you nor that son of mine visit anymore."

Before Jackal could say anything, one of the orphans, a thin little girl, maybe three, ran up and grabbed his fingers, trying to tow him over to where she was playing.

"Go on," Beryl waved him away. "Let them get used to you being here and then I'll put you to work."

Jackal spent the morning tussling with the boys and chasing the girls. It was strange to be back in the province of his earliest memories. The orphanage had changed little, the smell of the place an instant reminder of his years under its roof. Winsome was within sight of the Kiln's walls, yet Jackal avoided setting foot in the settlement if at all possible.

He had left at twelve, walking the mile to the Kiln to join the ranks of slopheads and begin his path to the hoof. Now, fifteen years later, he had his own hog and a back covered in Grey Bastard tattoos. Every last one of the dozen or so boys currently living under Beryl's care would try for the same, but few would succeed. Jackal knew he was a living image of who they were in their dreams. As for the little girls, they were already in love with him, their abandoned hearts knowing nothing of what a father was, but yearning for one all the same. For many, that yearning would mature as they did, turning into a desire to become a bedwarmer, a Bastard's favorite toss. But today, they were all young and blessed with ignorance, girls and boys both, not yet knowing the hard truths to come.

As the day drew on and Jackal played with the children outside, garnering approving looks from Cissy while she hung the wash, he began to understand why he avoided this place. It was not to escape haunted memories; most of his days at the orphanage had been happy. It was because he did not enjoy facing the unattainable.

Jackal would never have children.

All male half-orcs were sterile. His father, and the fathers of every child in this room, was a thick. The seed of the orc was strong, able to take root in humans with ease, and once a woman was impregnated, no amount of herbs or teas could flush it out of her. Some frails killed themselves rather than carry a half-breed. Some endured the seven-month pregnancy and, if they survived the birth, dispatched the babe in whatever way they could stomach. Fortunately for Jackal, and every half-orc breathing, some allowed their mongrels to live.

The nobility of Hispartha still prized half-breed servants, and handsome children fetched a high price up north. Within the Lot Lands, the half-orc hoofs made it known that all human women willing to rear their own half-breed children were welcome to live under the protection of the hoof. The village of Winsome had sprouted up near the Kiln because of this arrangement. And yet, many babes still turned up simply abandoned, their mothers refusing to kill them or sell them or raise them, simply wanting to be rid of them. That was how Jackal, and scores of orphans since, had come to Beryl.

She had come to Winsome from her own pillaged town, a thick's get already growing inside her, for half-orc females could sometimes conceive. Rarely, human seed would quicken in a half-orc's womb, but most often it was a thick that put a babe in their bellies. A child born from such a pairing was called a thrice-blood, or simply a thrice.

Bigger, stronger, and more orcish in appearance than a common half-breed, a thrice was a rare occurrence and it was even more rare that they were abandoned, for few half-orc women succumbed to that weakness. Beryl certainly had not. She accepted the Grey Bastards' protection, vowing her thrice-blood babe, if it were a boy, would become a formidable member of the hoof. Half a year later, Oats was born. Beryl raised him alongside the town's foundlings, including an infant who would become her son's closest friend.

Jackal looked at the child Beryl had called Wily and wondered if he was a thrice. The husky monkey was certainly fearless, mingling easily with the older children. He definitely reminded Jackal of Oats, who would have dominated the orphanage if his mother had not kept firm control of him, as she did with all her charges.

Four days passed with no word from the Kiln. Beryl kept Jackal busy replacing the broken tiles on her roof, ridding her garden of vipers, and repairing the loose bricks in her chimney. When those tasks did not occupy him, she turned him over to the foundlings and Jackal soon gave more shoulder rides than he could count. At night, he slept outside beneath the portico, his stockbow close at hand.

Winsome had only been threatened once in its history, when a band of centaurs rode through on one of their rampages. Jackal had been about nine and could still remember huddling in the root cellar with Oats, Fetch, and Beryl and the other children as the horse-cocks screamed madly nearby. They'd killed eight people that night and wounded a score before the Claymaster led the Grey Bastards down from the Kiln and chased them off. Had it been the Betrayer Moon, the hoof might not have been able to stop them.

True to its name, the Betrayer could wax on any night, enrapturing the centaurs and sending them out to murder. The dread moon would often go years without showing its face, only to appear twice in as many months. It was said that the centaurs summoned it to align with their mad whims, but who could say for certain? None had ever entered one of the horse-cocks' protected groves and returned with an answer. Whatever the cause, the Betrayer Moon was a lingering fear, a celestial axe that hung, invisible, above the Lots. Its arrival could not be accurately predicted, save by Zirko, and the little priest had not yet sent warning. Jackal kept his thrum loaded just the same.

On his fifth day in Winsome, he finally succumbed to Cissy's come-hither stares and snuck off with her, ducking down the narrow dead-end courtyard between Beryl's and the cooper's workshop. Cissy was a half-orc Jackal had known in the orphanage when they were younger. She had been about ten when he left and had grown into a sweet, plain-faced girl with a pleasingly sizable backside. Polecat had been shagging her and another of Beryl's helpers, a frail named Sweeps, but had not yet chosen a favorite.

"Cat finds out about this, he is going to want my scalp," Jackal said as Cissy gnawed eagerly at his neck. He was already shirtless from his chores and she ceased her mouth's attentions long enough to step back and gaze at his torso, her hands running over his arms.

"Hells, Jackal!" she said. "Next to you, he's damn weedy."

Jackal chuckled. "What do you see in that lazy-eyed letch, anyway?"

He said it teasingly, making it clear that he bore Polecat no ill will, nor was there any competition between them.

Cissy's wide eyes left his chest and sparkled wetly up at him. "He is just the right amount of rough."

Jackal raised his eyebrows and nodded, affecting a pondering expression, then he snatched for Cissy without warning, making her gasp and laugh as he seized her around the arms. Spinning her around, he pulled her back against him and slowly put a hand over her mouth to hush her giggling breaths. She was a good deal shorter than him, but raised up on her toes to rub her backside in just the right spot. Parting her lips, Cissy got her mouth around one of his fingers and bit down, just enough to hurt. One of the cooper's cast-off barrels was just to Jackal's left. He shoved Cissy over its slightly buckled top, keeping his finger in her mouth. With his free hand, he raised her skirts up over her hips, revealing her sage-colored rump, and hooked a hand behind her knee to raise it up onto the rim of the barrel. Cissy moaned and arched, wordlessly encouraging him as her teeth held his finger fast. Jackal was unlacing his breeches one-handed when the alley of the courtyard darkened.

Fetching stood there, little more than a silhouette against the bright sun.

"Jack. We need to talk."

Jackal took a step away from Cissy, who rose from the barrel and threw her skirt down with a frustrated expulsion of breath.

"It couldn't wait half an hour?" she demanded.

Fetching stepped to one side of the alley mouth. "Get going, Cissy."

Throwing an angry look at Jackal, Cissy hurried out of the courtyard. Fetching leaned away as she passed, as if the other girl's life would rub off on her, drag her back to the station she narrowly avoided. Jackal leaned against the barrel.

"That one gives you too much credit," Fetching said as she approached. "Half an hour?"

Jackal ignored the bait, waiting for Fetch to broach the subject she came to address. She was dust-stained, fresh off her hog. As she came close, Jackal could smell her, the earthy aroma of hard riding mixed with her familiar scent.

"Claymaster tell you how long you got to stay here?" she asked.

"I was hoping you were about to tell me."

Fetching wrinkled her nose. "No. The chief doesn't talk to me even when he isn't courting some fat conjurer."

"Anything come of that? Who is he?"

Fetching rolled her eyes. "I don't know. Claymaster's had me on patrol since Batayat."

"You came out of it unscathed," Jackal said. "Not even slop duty."

"No," Fetch agreed. "Claymaster doesn't want me around the hopefuls, even as punishment. Figures they'll be too preoccupied with visions of bending *me* over a barrel." She kicked at Cissy's former perch, unbalancing Jackal in the process. He stood to keep from falling, bringing him even closer to Fetching. She was just a hair shorter and eyed him boldly.

"Why did you do it? Why did you claim to have killed that cavalero?"

"Because we all had a hand in it. You, me, and Oats. But if the Claymaster knew it was you who pulled the tickler, the punishment would have been worse than slop duty. When it comes to you . . ."

Jackal trailed off, knowing he did not need to explain to Fetch what the Claymaster thought of her.

"No more, Jack. The hoof is never going to treat me as one of them so long as you don't."

Jackal wrinkled his face. "I would have done the same for Oats!"

"Would you?" Fetching shot back. "That's pretty big of you, considering he had not one word to say out at Batayat. He could have backed us!"

"Oats picks his fights carefully, Fetch. Which is more than either of us can boast."

Fetching held up a hand, giving him the point. "Then you got to start letting me deal with the shit that comes from the fights I pick. I don't need your swinging cod getting between me and the Claymaster or any other member of this hoof. Understand?"

Jackal nodded.

"Say it!"

"I understand."

Fetching set her jaw and nodded, her eyes softening slightly. Then she slammed a fist up into his balls.

Jackal grunted and bent over double, the sudden dull pain giving way to a foreboding numbness before the real agony shot upward and lodged in his throat, trailing nausea through his entire body.

"The fuck, Fetch?" he managed between coughs.

"That was a favor," she said, leaning down to put her face level with his.

"A . . . favor?"

"So you'll be too sore to try and spread Cissy's cheeks again. That hussy is looking to make the Kiln her permanent home. Soon as you stick that troublemaker in any of her holes she is going to see a clear path to your bunk."

Jackal tried to glare at her through teary eyes. "We were both just looking for a break in the drudgery."

"That's what *you* were doing, halfwit. But she'd throw Polecat over in a heartbeat. Cissy's not about to stay with that weasel-faced pederast if she can get you. So, unless you're ready for a bedwarmer, keep out."

Fetching straightened and began to leave the courtyard, her stockbow bouncing slightly against her lower back.

"And you're welcome."

Jackal hobbled in slow circles for a long time after she was gone.

Chapter 5

A slophead came to fetch Jackal back to the kiln after eight days. The young hopeful was out of breath, as if he had run all the way from the compound.

"What's the matter, slop?" Jackal dug. "You can't sprint a mile without getting winded?"

The slophead tried to steady his breathing, causing his lips to twitch and his face to pale.

"Hells, Biro, breathe," Beryl told him from her chair on the portico. "Don't let this one tug your ear. Jackal swooned like a virgin the first time he was made to run back to Winsome with a message. Took me forever to bring him around."

Jackal snorted. Some of his fellow Bastards would not have taken kindly to being teased in front of a slophead, but he found Beryl's story amusing, all the more so because it wasn't true. Jackal trimmed a few more artichoke stems with his knife, dropping the heads into the basket between him and Beryl, before standing. Sheathing his knife, he picked up his brigand and stockbow.

Beryl looked up at him with a tiny smile. "Good to have you around, Jackal."

He leaned down and kissed her once, then stepped off the portico and into the hot sun.

"Let's go," he told Biro.

Nodding rapidly, the slophead spun on his heel and began jogging up the dusty trail that ran through Winsome. Jackal continued at a walk, squinting at the retreating slop until the youth realized what was happening and turned around.

"The Claymaster said to bring you back quickly!" Biro called back.

"Then he should have sent my damn hog," Jackal replied, not bothering to raise his voice.

The foundlings, now aware that he was leaving, came scurrying from their play to surround him, following in a laughing, living cloud until Beryl's commanding voice called them off.

The road to the Kiln was mostly uphill in this direction. Jackal took his time, donning his brigand as he walked. Biro stayed a few paces ahead. The youth was no more than thirteen, still within his first year as a slophead, and still responding to the sworn members of the hoof with a mix of awe and dread. Fortunately, that also kept him from talking during the walk.

As they neared the Kiln, Jackal spotted a small encampment squatting near the gate.

"When did they arrive?" Jackal asked, peering at the half dozen horses and tents.

"Two days ago," Biro replied. "They are cavaleros from the castile."

Jackal almost mocked the slop for the obvious observation, but bit back on the abuse, choosing to educate the boy instead.

"They are cavaleros," he agreed, "but can you tell me if they are commoners or nobles?"

Biro stared blankly.

Jackal took him by the shoulder as they drew nearer the camp and pointed at the horses, hobbled and grazing on the sparse plain.

"Look at the quality of their mounts . . . not one is purebred."

Two men were standing sentry while the other four threw dice near their small cook fire.

"Noble-born frails rarely gamble with dice," Jackal continued, "and they wear a crimson sash to denote their privilege. These clods don't have that and their armor is poorer quality. But, they are usually the better fighters. Remember that."

Biro gave his rapid nod and swallowed hard.

Walking beneath the gate, Jackal entered the wall passage and began making the long circuit through the darkness. He could hear Biro's hand sliding along the wall behind him, the youth not yet used to traversing the black tunnel without that guidance. Jackal remembered when he had done the same, years ago.

"Why—?"

Jackal whirled on Biro before he could utter another word, shushing him harshly.

"Never talk while inside the wall!" he whispered. "You need to have your ears open for riders in both directions. I don't want to get trampled because some slophead couldn't keep his tongue from flapping."

To the youth's credit, he said nothing more, not even to answer.

Jackal continued to lead them through, quickening his pace. When he was Biro's age, he feared being inside the wall, constantly worried the Kiln would come under attack and the gates would be closed before he could run the circuit, the ovens heating the passage until he cooked in his own skin. All slopheads needed that fear, it kept them alert and alive.

But that was not the reason Jackal began to hurry. Commoner cavaleros at the Kiln meant that Ignacio was paying the Grey Bastards a visit, and that, no doubt, was why Jackal had been summoned.

"Get my hog saddled," he told Biro as soon as they emerged into the light of the compound. The youth ran for the stables. One way or another, Jackal figured his punishment was over and he meant to ride as soon as possible.

He entered the meeting hall and made straight for the Claymaster's solar. As expected, he found Captain Ignacio within, slumped in a chair opposite the chief's desk. Balding and homely, with pockmarked skin and rheumy eyes, Ignacio was every bit the common soldier. He was probably of an age with Bermudo, but could pass for his noble counterpart's father, the hard life of a peasant etched into every wrinkle of his swarthy face.

"Jackal," Ignacio said with a nod.

"Captain."

The Claymaster looked up and his mouth curled. Behind him, a pair of dusty ceramic jars rested upon a laden shelf. They were old sapper pots, an alchemical device used in the Incursion to blow holes in orc defenses. As a slave, the Claymaster had crafted them, shaping the pottery and filling the jars with the volatile substances that made them so damn dangerous. The two relics on the shelf were empty, inert, but Jackal always glanced at them when in the Claymaster's solar as a reminder of the chief's sudden turns in temper.

"I am starting to wish you were drowned at birth, Jack."

Jackal said nothing, waiting on the bad news.

The Claymaster waved a linen-wrapped hand at Ignacio. "Tell him."

The captain looked at Jackal, his tired expression rimmed with frustration. "Cavalero Garcia's horse returned to the castile."

Jackal struggled to keep his face placid.

"I found that interesting, Jackal," the Claymaster said, his tone dangerously light. "I found that very interesting, considering you told me that horse was going to be given to the Sludge Man along with the cavalero's body."

"I'll ride out now," Jackal said. "Talk to Sancho. Find out what happened."

"I already did." Ignacio sighed. "The whoremaster did what you asked. He sent a bird to the Sludge Man and he came the next day, took Garcia and the horse. But that horse turned up outside our gate."

"Jack? Care to voice a thought as to why that is?" the Claymaster asked.

Jackal shrugged. "Ask the Sludge Man."

The Claymaster's eyes darkened beneath his bandages. "You going to pass all your mistakes off to him?"

"No, chief."

"I sent a bird. Soon as Ignacio arrived and told me about this increasing pile of hog shit. Waiting on a reply." The Claymaster hooked a finger in the air from Ignacio to Jackal. "The rest."

The captain issued another weary breath. "That man you killed was the son of some shrew up in . . . Vallisoletum, I think. A marquesa or the like." Jackal gave no reaction. The names belonging to Hisparthan towns and titles meant even less to him than they did to Ignacio. Yet the captain's abiding weariness was chased away as he continued, the worry in his words giving him a rare vitality. "It's said she has a fortune. Influence at court. What she don't have is more than one son. You understand what I'm telling you?"

Jackal refused to let the captain's anxious tone affect him. "He couldn't have meant much to her if he was sent down here."

Ignacio huffed. "I don't know what the man did, but exile to the Lots could be a mother's love and money at work if the alternative was execution. Mother Marquesa might not be pleased with saving her son from the headman only to have him die during his first fortnight in the Lots."

Jackal looked at the Claymaster. "Do we care about this? Rumors and royals have no place in the badlands."

"Bermudo cares," Ignacio said, leaning in his chair to regain Jackal's attention. "The story you fed his new cavaleros, about Garcia attacking his captain and deserting? The fable fit the man's character, so none in Hispartha would likely look further. But. Now the horse has returned. From centaur territory. Where you said he fucking ran!"

"A place even thicks don't leave alive," Jackal realized aloud.

"Much less some fop's stable-raised prize stallion," the Claymaster snarled. "Your tale's come apart, Jack."

Ignacio clicked his tongue. "Bermudo's hounding those newcomers to tell the truth of what happened. For now, they are more frightened of you than him. But how long can that last?"

How long was right. Ignacio kept referring to Jackal as Garcia's killer. That meant the young cavaleros really were holding the truth back. If even one of them had let slip it was a female half-orc that put a bolt through Garcia's brain, Ignacio would have known exactly who they meant and told the chief. The Claymaster would be handling this very differently with that knowledge.

"The horse disproves nothing on its own, but you mark me, Jackal, if that body is discovered and Bermudo can use it to help himself, he will."

"Like paying for passage back to Hispartha by entertaining the marquesa with my hanging?"

Ignacio directed a crooked grin at the Claymaster. "I thought you said he was a fool."

"That don't make him stupid," came the reply.

"Why would it come to that?" Jackal asked the chief. "You can't tell me you would hand over one of your own to appease some noblewoman."

The Claymaster's eyes lit with anger. "Hispartha sets foot on my lot and demands anything, I'll put every last frail they send in the dirt. But it better not come to that. If it does, you won't need to worry about hanging, Jackal. I'll fuel the Kiln's ovens with your unthinking carcass."

Jackal hadn't stopped thinking from the moment he entered the room. He turned to Ignacio.

"Can you keep those cavaleros from talking? Keep their fear alive?"

Ignacio found that funny and wheezed a laugh. "Keep them from talking *and* alive? Maybe you are stupid. Me and my men don't linger much at the castile. We got duties that keep us away. Like patrols. And running bad tidings to the hoofs of half-orc riders that stir up shit."

Jackal didn't need the reproach of this tired, useless man. Besides, Ignacio's talk of patrols reminded him of something.

"Bermudo came to the brothel that morning looking for you," he said. "Thought you'd been there with us. Why was that?"

Ignacio's mouth stretched with annoyance. "To dump those milksops on me. You think he shows them the way of things here? No. Passes that pleasure to me."

"We're losing the trail," the chief said. "Captain ain't here to make a remedy, Jackal. You are."

"Then I'll head back to Sancho's and track from there. If Garcia's body is—"

"No," the Claymaster cut him off. "I already sent Oats and that bitch you two voted into this hoof to do just that."

"What do you want me to do?"

"Go to the farrowing shed."

Jackal nearly protested, but his mouth locked shut. Something told him this wasn't more punishing chores. Maybe it was the dead tone of the chief's command or the way Ignacio became very still, maybe it was the recollection that the hoof had no sows close to birthing a litter. Whatever it was, the command left an uneasy feeling in his gut.

Without a word, Jackal left the room. He could hear the discussion continuing as he went down the corridor, Ignacio broaching the subject of payment.

Despite the name, the farrowing shed was a sizable building a little removed from the stables and breeding pens, tucked beneath the wall. Jackal ducked into the low, long structure. As he suspected, the birthing stalls were empty. He made his way down the central aisle, through the gloom, his boots silent in the thick carpet of straw spread over woodchips and sawdust.

Hogs were the soul of a hoof, the strength. Without them, patrolling the Lots, engaging the thicks, would be nothing but protracted suicide. The sows that came here to deliver the next generation of mounts were provided comfort, quiet, and care. The Claymaster did not allow slop-heads inside the farrowing shed, trusting only Grocer, and whatever sworn brethren were requested to assist him, to bring piglets into the world. Jackal had little talent for farrowing. He lacked the patience. The only time he'd been asked to help, Grocer had expelled him from the shed. Oats had replaced him, and five healthy barbarians were soon suckling at their coddled mother's teats.

The aisle led to a single room at each end. Jackal doubted the Claymaster had sent him here to inspect the shed's supplies, so he went left, making for a door that only unfortunate sows ever entered, the ones that no amount of calm and expertise could save if the farrowing took a bad turn.

The mercy room.

He opened the door, releasing muffled sounds of pain and panic. The shed was always kept clean, but the reek of sweat and piss, both gravid with fear, struck Jackal's nostrils. He widened the opening to reveal Hoodwink's unsettling profile. The pale mongrel did not turn at Jackal's intrusion, but continued to stare, unblinking, at the wall behind the door. Hood's hairless skin was the color of dirty linen without even a tinge of grey or green. Behind his back, the other Bastards wondered if he was an albino, but his eyes lacked the strange pink hue found in those with the affliction. No, they were empty, black pits.

Six whimpering men, naked and chained, knelt before that pitiless gaze, the gags in their mouths stained with snot and tears. Before those ugly drippings reached the cloth, they left a shiny trail through the mustachios worn by every one of the prisoners.

Bermudo's new cavaleros.

Jackal ground his teeth to keep his jaw from falling slack. Ignacio had delivered more than news.

The men recognized him, too, and all began squirming with renewed vigor. Desperate noises pushed past their gags. Were they pleas or protests? Jackal could not tell. He'd spared them once. But only the woefully ignorant would believe he was there to do it again.

He stepped next to Hoodwink, but faced the opposite wall, turning his back to the doomed men.

"Have any of them spoken?" he whispered.

Hoodwink turned his bald head. "As you hear."

The lowing sobs continued. "Claymaster's mad if he thinks this is the way," Jackal said.

Hoodwink replied with nothing but his dead stare. There wasn't even a flutter of consideration. Every time Jackal looked at this scarred killer, he was reminded of a snake in the act of swallowing its prey. Slow, silent, remorseless, fixed on its cold purpose

Jackal searched for another path, his thoughts racing and going nowhere. The Claymaster had made his choice. Ignacio had played his part, tricked these men into a trap. They didn't know the Lots, likely had no idea where they were even once the Kiln was in view, as blind and vulnerable as the piglets born in this shed.

And Jackal could not save them. The Claymaster claimed he would give Hispartha nothing they demanded. He might not have known, but he lied. He would give them Fetching. If one of these men ever identified her as Garcia's killer, they would be providing the chief with the chance to be rid of her, absolving the hoof at the same time. Bermudo would have his hanging, the marquesa her vengeance, and the Claymaster would be free of the woman he never wanted in his ranks. Oats and Jackal would not have the votes to prevent it.

Unlike the death mask of his fellow executioner, Jackal's face must have betrayed his intent, for Hoodwink spoke, his thin voice at the edge of hearing.

"Work fast."

Jackal turned and held out a hand to the men. Six pairs of eyes, rolling with white fright, bulged up at him.

"Calm, now. We are just going to remove your gags." He almost choked on the lie and had to bite back a scream as relief lulled the men into silence. Their faces remained stretched and uncertain. Jackal moved around behind the rightmost man. Hood slid to the other end of the line. The head beneath Jackal's gaze was trembling, the hair drenched. The flesh at the back of the neck had darkened while under Ul-wundulas' hot care, a crescent border separating the paler skin below. Jackal fixated on that line while he drew his knife.

The man next in line was watching, craning his neck to see what his future held.

Jackal met his eyes and the deception was uncloaked.

The man pushed out a stifled wail, nearly drowning out the squelching thuds of Hoodwink's dagger punching into exposed flesh in rapid succession. He dropped each man with a single thrust through the back of the neck, moving with brutal efficiency. Four cavaleros were dead before they realized what was happening. The fifth, the screamer, was too focused on Jackal to notice his end approaching in Hood's crimson-speckled hand.

But the sixth man did.

He lurched forward, the need to live making him fast as a hare, clumsy as a drunk. His first step propelled him away from Jackal, his second brought him fully to his feet, but he tripped on the third, head and shoulder bashing the door closed. He rolled over, awkward with his hands shackled behind his back. Spine against the door, he pushed up on his heels, shoulders and chains sliding on the wood. His stricken face was defiant, an earnest, untenable warning against pursuit.

Hoodwink's dagger flew into his chest just as he regained his feet, the blade slapping into the man's heart. His defiance broadened to confusion as his legs gave out, dragging him to his rump and lifelessness.

Jackal had not made a move. He turned to find Hoodwink standing beside the last living cavalero, a hand pressing down on one shoulder to keep him in place. He needn't have bothered. The man's mind was gone. He was still screaming, howling through his gag until his breath gave out, then filling his lungs and doing it all over again.

Hoodwink's stare was fixed on Jackal, calm and expectant.

Chapter 6

THE FEEL OF A THROAT PARTING BENEATH SHARP STEEL WAS still in Jackal's hand. The blood was washed away, but that sickening resistance lingered. Jackal clenched his fist tight to banish the phantom sensation and entered the hoof's supply hall.

He found Grocer there, as expected, the old coin clipper muttering orders at a pair of slopheads and watching their every move with ingrained distrust. Since Warbler went nomad, Grocer was the last founding member of the hoof left other than the chief. It was widely known, but never said aloud, that the quartermaster was actually a frailing, the product of a half-orc mother and a human father. Thin, stingy, and cunning, he managed his hoard of supplies with ill-tempered efficiency. He was so covetous that he never cut his hair and it fell past his bony ass in a grey-streaked mass of twisted locks. Still, Jackal had seen the aging cuss in a knife fight and would not cross him without damn good reason.

"I have no liniment to spare, Jackal," Grocer told him as he approached the supply counter.

"Liniment? I'm not here for that."

Grocer sneered. "Aren't you? Figured your nipples would be raw from teat-feeding all those whelps at Beryl's."

The old coot had a good laugh at his own jest, all the while directing his minions to move various sacks and barrels. It was obvious he was ignorant of the cavaleros. The Claymaster had taken pains to limit knowledge of that skullduggery.

Hood and Jackal had not moved the bodies until night fell over the fortress, taking them away from the farrowing shed in the wheeled cart used to transport deceased hogs. They burned the corpses in the Kiln's ovens, tossing them onto the fires the same as cordwood. Jackal wasn't happy about joining the company of Hoodwink and Ignacio, the chief's loyal dogs. And he didn't plan on lying down with them for long. After a sleepless night, he had made up his mind and gone to the supply hall before the chief assigned any further tasks.

"I need one of the Sludge Man's birds," he told Grocer. "Claymaster wants to send another message."

Grocer eyed him for a moment before stalking back into his stores. Jackal could hear the old coin clipper berating the unseen slopheads that drew the duty of helping him. Years ago, Jackal had loved his tenure in the supply hall and grew to love Grocer too. It was an affection he had not held on to during his time as a sworn brother. These days, he just found the aged frailing tiresome. Grocer returned with a wicker cage containing a docile squab. Jackal took it from his resisting fingers.

As he left the supply hall, the old mongrel's voice called after him.

"I want that cage back!"

Not bothering to respond, Jackal began making his way across the yard.

Fuck the Claymaster.

And Ignacio.

And their schemes.

Jackal had just been cornered into the butchery of half a dozen men. It was a trap he helped fashion, but stumbling into it and staying in it were two different mistakes. He needed to know why that horse returned to the castile. If Garcia's body turned up as well, all the killings would count for nothing. Jackal needed to know the corpse had made its way to the Sludge Man. The Claymaster may have sent a message, but whatever answer the Sludge Man returned was not likely to reach Jackal's ears. He wouldn't trust one the chief provided anyway.

No, he needed to go to the source, to the Old Maiden Marsh, and speak directly with the Sludge Man. It was a vast amount of wetland to cover, and no one knew exactly where the bog trotter lived. Jackal could have used some help, but the only riders he trusted implicitly were already off at the chief's bidding. Oats and Fetch could be away for days more, and he couldn't wait. He needed to be gone before Grocer made mention of the bird.

It was a grievous defiance, one that would likely cause the chief to call for his ousting from the hoof. Let him try. He was allowing orcs to live, executing cavaleros, and hiding it from the hoof. Jackal would turn any attempt to get rid of him into his bid for leadership.

He was just entering the shadow of the Kiln's great chimney, the last black vestiges of the men he'd helped murder still leaking into the sky, when he spotted the wizard. He was sitting in the shade, his chubby form resting upon a small carpet. As he drew closer, Jackal saw his eyes were closed.

"An errand of great import, friend?" the wizard asked as Jackal passed.

Jackal stopped and looked down to find the fat mongrel looking at him with a lazy grin.

"No," Jackal told him.

"Wonderful!"

The wizard stood, agile in spite of his bulk. He was a good bit shorter than Jackal, but his turban made them appear of an even height.

"I beg to accompany you."

Jackal snorted, slightly taken aback. "Beg all you want. No." He kept walking.

"Brave," the wizard said, catching up. The movement caused the gold beads dangling from his chin braid to swing. "But I have heard it is dangerous to go alone into the Old Maiden Marsh."

Jackal stomped to a halt. Had he already been discovered? Could the wizard divine his thoughts?

"How do you know where I ride?" he snarled, leaning down threateningly.

The wizard's smile only broadened. He placed the heels of his hands together and gestured at the caged bird in Jackal's hand.

"This small, feathered soul would return there this instant were you to release him. Simple creatures follow familiar instincts, my friend."

"You know the marsh?"

"I know the bird. Alas, like much of Ul-wundulas, I have not seen the Old Maiden. But I wish to, so I shall come."

"The fuck you will," Jackal said, turning away.

"I think you know I walk where I wish."

Jackal stopped. The wizard's voice retained a courteous, nearly fawning quality, yet there was a threat buried in the thick folds of politeness. Turning back around, Jackal met the shorter half-orc's dancing eyes.

"Yes, you do," he said, putting menace in his own tone. "That was a crafty trick, showing up in the passage."

"Truly, I did not intend to cause a stir."

"I just bet you didn't. You got a name?"

"Uhad Ul-badir Taruk Ultani," the wizard said with a small dip of his chin.

Jackal blinked. "That name is a fucking nightmare. I'm going to call you Crafty."

The wizard smiled. "This is what you would call a 'hoof name'?"

"This is what I call a name I can say. And as far as I know, you aren't in this hoof yet, because I don't recall a vote."

"Indeed, this is so," the wizard said.

Jackal smiled. If he took the Tyrkanian along, he would be depriving the Claymaster of his favored guest. That was good. He was also giving himself time to take the measure of this stranger. That was better. If the wizard's powers extended beyond surviving being cooked in the Kiln tunnel, he could be useful in the marsh. If not, his flabby body would make a heartier meal for a rokh than Jackal's. Outrunning him wouldn't be difficult.

Jackal clapped the soft flesh of the wizard's shoulder. "If you're not in the hoof, that makes you a hopeful! A slophead. So come along, Crafty, and see the Old Maiden Marsh."

The wizard's plump face beamed. "Much gratitude! Do you think your Claymaster will approve?"

Jackal shook his head as he turned to go. "I don't much care. Besides, you walk where you wish, remember? Let's see if you can ride there too."

After going back to roll up his little carpet and tie it to a shapeless bundle of bags, Crafty slung the whole affair across his body.

"Might I know your name, friend?"

"Jackal."

"Ah!" Crafty held up a finger. "So named because you can eat anything, have an odious laugh, and mate even with ugly women!"

Jackal ground to a halt, his fist clenching, but as he spun on the wizard he saw the mischievous grin on his face. So, a sense of humor. And a good one.

Jackal smiled and relaxed. "You got two out of three."

They found Biro waiting at the stables. The youth worked quickly, getting Hearth ready to ride. Jackal gave the slop a nod of approval after giving the hog a quick inspection.

"Saddle one of the scouts' hogs," he told Biro as he mounted. "Our new friend is coming along with me."

The youth moved to obey, but Crafty stopped him with a gentle touch on the arm.

"No need for the saddle, I am thinking."

"You ride bareback?" Jackal asked, not sure whether to be impressed or doubtful.

"You think it unwise with these beasts?"

"You've never ridden a barbarian before?"

Crafty seemed amused. "Such an interesting name for the animal. No, I have never."

Jackal clamped his teeth and decided to say nothing more.

Biro brought a hog up from the pens. It was one the hoof used to train slopheads, but a solid mount. Biro, for all his youth, was no fool and had selected a larger hog for the corpulent wizard.

"Much gratitude," Crafty said to the boy. Biro released the hog's swine-yanker and stepped away. Jackal watched while Crafty leaned in close to the barbarian's face. He stood there, hunched over, for a long moment, then straightened. Without apprehension, he went around and easily swung his large frame astride the beast.

"I am prepared," he announced, smiling.

"We'll soon find out," Jackal said, and guided Hearth out of the stables.

They left the Kiln through the tunnel and soon emerged beyond the walls. Jackal turned their course north and for the first few miles kept one eye on Crafty, watching him ride. The fat sack had a terrible seat, his balance was horribly off, and his feet dangled far too low. By rights, he should have fallen off already, yet somehow, he stayed on the hog's back, that same dreamy grin still splitting his broad face. Jackal had seen a dozen slopheads with more natural affinity for riding dumped into the dust within minutes of mounting a hog, but this silk-swaddled sand eater was still aloft when they reached the River Lucia. And all without a saddle.

Jackal gave up wondering about the stranger and focused on leading their journey. He followed the river's course westward for several hours until he reached the confluence of the Lucia and the smaller Alhundra. Here, he turned southwest, keeping the Alhundra to his right. It was not the most direct path, but it ensured they stayed well clear of centaur lands. This journey was going to be treacherous enough without running into a band of horse-cocks drunk on wine and the words of their crazed oracles. Without trusted companions, Jackal would be easy prey for even a small group, be they 'taurs, Tines, or thicks.

Jackal kept Hearth at a mile-eating pace, certain he would soon be slowing for Crafty, but the wizard never fell behind. Indeed, within hours he had grown even more adept on the hog and was now riding beside Jackal. He surveyed the land with a keen interest and a look of appreciation, the fervor in his eyes undiminished by the glaring sun. Now knowing that Crafty's fat ass wasn't going to go spilling onto the ground, Jackal slowed Hearth to a trot.

"Why are you here, Tyrkanian?" he asked.

The wizard gave a small hum. "I was born in Al-Unan." When Jackal failed to see the point, Crafty gave him a little wink. "Which is a land separate from Tyrkania, though I was educated there."

"None of that answers my question."

"No," Crafty agreed. "I simply wanted to see this." He swept a hand out across their surroundings. "Ul-wundulas! The Lot Lands, much-contested doorstep of great Hispartha. That infantile kingdom sits above. Below, Dhar'gest, its vast deserts and strangling jungles conquered by the black grip of the orc. They peer hungrily northward, across the Deluged Sea, to the soft lands of man. Hispartha, Anville, Guabia. Yet the water thwarts the savages, for shipbuilding is a mystery to them. Indeed, the drowned homeland of the elves wards a quarter of the known world from its enemies of yester-age. Yet, the orcs have one crossing. One place where Dhar'gest puckers to nearly kiss Ul-wundulas."

"The Gut," Jackal said.

The wizard patted the side of his broad nose with a finger. "Little more than two leagues of sea. Nothing the muscles of an orc cannot swim with ease. And they do. Arriving here in the famed badlands of Ul-wundulas, site of their last defeat, where mongrels ride hogs and none bend a knee!"

Jackal was unable to suppress a bark of laughter. "Sounds like you've studied a map and read some books. Now that you are here, you can see this land for what it is. A nasty old quilt. Ugly, hot, dry, infested, and made up of many clashing patches."

"And yet, you love it," Crafty observed.

"Most days," Jackal admitted. "There are no kings here, true enough. No sultans or caliphs. Just us. The hoofs. Free to ride."

"This is what I heard, even in my homelands. From boyhood, I was told we half-orcs have a place in the Lots. This I have long yearned to see, before it is gone."

Jackal stared hard at the wistful look on the wizard's face. "Gone? The Lots aren't going anywhere. Not so long as the Grey Bastards and the other hoofs remain. We keep the thicks culled."

"Ah! But are there not other threats, friend Jackal?"

"What? Like the centaurs?" Jackal shook his head. "They're dangerous, but they can't bear to leave their temples and orgies for very long. Stay clear of those, and the nights of a Betrayer Moon is all the threat they pose. And if you mean the elves, they hate the orcs worse than we do. They may have different blood, but the Tines are a hoof, just like the Bastards. So long as the Lots' boundaries are respected, we have no quarrel."

"But no alliance either."

Jackal got the impression he was being tested somehow. It was annoying, considering he had brought the easterner along to find out *his* motives.

"So you're not here to join the Bastards," Jackal said. "You're just passing through on, what, some damn pilgrimage?"

"Of a sort, yes," Crafty replied softly. "Of a sort."

Jackal could not seem to get the upper hand with this stranger. Indeed, the more he discovered about the wizard, the less he knew. He had certainly named him well. Jackal was not too proud to admit that

Crafty was far more intelligent than he. Still, Jackal had also been aptly named and his own cunning, however low, had not failed him yet.

The scrublands on either side of the river began to house more frequent stands of trees. After a wide, lazy bend, the Alhundra turned almost directly south, flowing and falling over rocky outcroppings as the ground descended over languid miles toward the wetlands.

Jackal decided they should camp as the sun began to set, finding a grove of alder not far from the riverbank. Not wanting to risk a fire, he ate figs while Hearth dined on acorns out of his hand. Crafty merely drank from an earthenware bottle he produced from his bundle of belongings.

"You're kind of a fat fuck not to be hungry," Jackal said, seeing if the wizard would take offense, but whatever he was, Crafty was not prickly. He merely smiled that smile of his.

"Perhaps Ul-wundulas will transform me into something akin to you, friend Jackal. An impressive specimen of the half-orc, festooned with hard muscle! Truly, the human patrons of the pleasure houses in Ul-Kadim pay richly for well-formed mongrel males such as you."

"I thought those places only allowed men to pay for flesh," Jackal said.

Crafty gave him a knowing nod. "They do."

Jackal grimaced, which caused Crafty to laugh.

"So, in Ul-wundulas you are free but not enlightened! Do not the elves love as they will?"

"I wouldn't know."

Crafty smiled at his discomfort. "I shall shift the winds of our talk, to spare you. This Sluice Man we seek, he is important?"

"Off-putting is what he is," Jackal said. "And it's Sludge Man. He single-handedly holds one of Ul-wundulas' most vulnerable borders against the orcs, so he's valued in the Lots. When we reach the wetlands, you'll see. No hoof could ever dwell in the marsh. Thwarts the hardiest hogs and best riders. The Sludge Man . . . he's a hoof unto himself."

"One man does this?" Crafty asked, sounding impressed. "How?"

It was Jackal's turn to smile. "You'll see."

They passed the rest of the night in silence. Trusting the hogs' keen senses to alert him to any danger, Jackal lay down upon his blanket, but he slept little. Dawn came quickly and saw the pair riding once more.

The Old Maiden Marsh began some forty miles from the sea, a massive swath of flat land dotted with thickets, choked with bogs, and lacerated by shallow streams. Before the Orc Incursion, the wetlands had been used as a hunting preserve for the kings of Hispartha. The manors and castiles that had once dotted the borders of the marsh were torn down by one side or the other during the war, but Jackal spotted a few pitiful ruins as he guided Hearth across the most passable mud flats. He pointed them out to Crafty, who nodded appreciatively.

"At war's end, the Crown withheld the marsh during the lottery," Jackal told him. "Whichever king was alive back then wanted to restore it to the royal family. Several of his cousins foolishly tried to resettle the area, but were run off within months. Orcs still use the marsh to sneak deep into the Lots after they've swum the Gut, though even they often find the wetlands impassable. There's much that lives in the Old Maiden that makes even a thick think twice before entering."

"Yes," Crafty said. "I have heard many of the Old Maiden's natural inhabitants are quite formidable. Rokhs, yes?"

"Keep one eye on the sky."

Following his own advice as they continued, Jackal remained watchful for the huge, predatory birds. The rokhs nested in the wetlands, but their need for prey took them far beyond its borders. A single rokh was capable of lifting Hearth in its talons, soaring high enough to let the hog fall to his death before swooping down to feed. A few well-aimed thrumbolts could drive the massive raptors off, but without others to assist, Jackal wondered if he could shoot fast enough. As for Crafty, he did not appear to carry any weapons.

By noon, the hogs began to have difficulty with the increasingly soggy ground. Jackal realized they would need to be left behind. Hearth could power through the mire with brute force and stubbornness, but the slophead hog, with Crafty's weight atop him, would have a tough time. Jackal led them to a thicket of pitiful pines and removed the messenger bird's cage from the saddle, hanging it on his own belt beside his quiver. He dismounted and Crafty followed his lead.

"The trees," Jackal motioned above, "scrubby as they are, will help protect the hogs from any circling rokhs. Think your wide butt can handle a march?"

Crafty gave a single smiling nod.

"Give those feathered fucks the tusks if they try and swoop in here," Jackal told Hearth, knuckling him between the eyes.

"And you do likewise," Crafty told his own hog with an instructional wag of his finger, "to those fucks with feathers."

Jackal left Hearth untethered, knowing he would stay put for at least a day before hunger whittled away even the best training. He wasn't certain the slop hog would be so patient, but he couldn't worry about that now. Jackal offered Crafty one of his javelins to help steady his steps through the marsh, but the wizard waved it off. Favoring a loaded stockbow in his hands, Jackal put the javelin back in the saddle quiver and struck out. Armed with the thrum, his tulwar, his knife, and one caged bird, Jackal ventured into the Old Maiden on foot with a mysterious fat wizard.

All because he had lied to protect a cock-punching ingrate.

"Shit on you for a friend, Fetching," he said under his breath.

CHAPTER 7

JACKAL AND CRAFTY SPENT HOURS PICKING THEIR WAY FROM one small, soggy island of yellow grass to the next, often wading knee-deep in murky channels to reach the next spot of solid ground. They headed deeper into the marsh until no more trees were in sight. Then, Jackal released the bird.

The squab took flight frantically at first, but settled as it rose. Jackal kept his gaze fixed on the bird until he could see it no more.

"Due west," he said. "Directly into the Old Maiden's heart."

"You think the Slug Man lives within?" Crafty asked.

"Sludge Man," Jackal corrected, "and yes, I know he does. Just not exactly where. Between here and the ocean is nothing but countless miles of quagmire and salt marsh."

"Then let us have hope he does not live on the coast," Crafty said with good humor.

Jackal breathed his agreement and followed the direction taken by the squab.

It was late spring, the heat of the sun adding weight to the muggy air. Swarms of biting flies coalesced in humming clouds over the deeper pools. Occasionally, small groups of wild boar could be seen picking their way through the marshland.

"Let's keep our distance," Jackal told Crafty, pointing at the pigs. "Those are the rokhs' favorite prey."

He need not have worried so much about the birds. An hour later, they saw the first sludge.

It crawled off to their left, easily within thrumshot, tracking them. The thing was nearly the size of a bull, but was still difficult to spot when not in motion, appearing to be nothing but another dark, putrid pool amongst the marram grass. Its black, glistening form slid atop land and water with equal fluidity. Sludges reminded Jackal of giant, featureless leeches made of tar. He shuddered and stopped, searching the marsh for more of the creatures. To his increasing unease, he found another an equal distance to his right and two more behind.

"You got anything like that back in Tyrkania?" he asked Crafty.

The wizard was motionless, studying the creatures with no hint of trepidation.

"No," he said. "Not enough water for them to survive, I am thinking."

"The old-timers swear the things didn't exist before the war."

Crafty knelt on his haunches, his hands toying idly with some marsh grass as he watched the sludges.

"No doubt they are correct," he said. "These are the loathsome result of spells. The accounts of the Incursion I have been fortunate to read claim that it was here the elves first came to Hispartha's aid. Their shaman unleashed fearsome amounts of magic in their attempts to stop the invading orcs. Yet, the orcs have their own sorcery. Perhaps these . . . sludges are the children of so much conflicting energies mating over fields of death."

Jackal did not know, nor did he care to. The presence of the sludges meant only that he was likely close to his destination.

"Let's keep moving," he said.

The creatures continued to shadow them throughout the day, never drawing nearer or farther. Near dusk, two more of the fuliginous blobs appeared ahead. Now Jackal and Crafty were completely surrounded. Jackal had the unnerving suspicion they were being led, herded.

A cluster of five low structures took shape ahead, rising out of the muck on stout beams. Crude walkways of rotten planking, supported on similar beams, crisscrossed the marsh surrounding the buildings. Jackal and Crafty's laborious steps brought them directly to one of these precarious constructions, leading straight across a sizable lagoon toward the largest of the four buildings. As they traversed the creaking, moss-slick wood, the sludges continued to follow, keeping to the waters, drifting unctuously across the surface. Jackal stopped in the middle of the walkway.

"Sludge Man!" he called. "It is Jackal of the Grey Bastards!"

There was no response. No movement. The sludges had paused when he did.

Continuing across, Jackal reached the main hut. The roof was thatched with swamp grass, the walls made of woven reeds. There was no door, so Jackal leaned cautiously through the threshold. A few fishing nets hung from the ceiling, in desperate need of repair, and a cold fire pit skulked beneath a hole in the thatching. Otherwise the hut was empty.

Jackal did not know what he expected to find. If the Sludge Man's creatures had turned on him, there would be nothing left. Ducking out of the hut, Jackal saw Crafty still watching the six blobs floating near the center of the lagoon.

"They have no eyes," the wizard said. "Yet I feel distinctly that they watch us."

Jackal hated to agree. There was a horrible, mute patience to the creatures.

Crafty cocked one eye over his shoulder. "You say this man we seek, he controls them?"

"No one knows exactly how, but yes. They seem to obey him. They can fully consume whatever they envelop. Makes for a good way to get rid of corpses."

"Much need for such a service here in Ul-wundulas, friend Jackal?"

Ignoring that, Jackal tapped Crafty on the shoulder, urging him away from the main lagoon.

"Let's check these other sheds and be on our way before those things decide your lard-covered bones would make a good meal."

Crafty pointed to the two buildings to the right of the main hut. "I shall inspect these."

Jackal nodded and began making his way to the remaining pair of sheds to the left. They were barely half the size of the Sludge Man's domicile and, being made from the same waterlogged materials, also lacked doors. Leading with his stockbow, Jackal looked within the first shed and found nothing. Nothing stored, no refuse, nothing. It was not the same with the second. It held a tattered hanging on the wall opposite the door, some torn and mildewed tapestry depicting a goat on a black shield. Beneath this curiosity sat a pair of large chests, the wood waterlogged, black and rotten, the iron fittings barnacled with rust. The distorted lids could not properly close and Jackal lifted one with the toe of his boot to find coins nested within, a fortune in gold and silver begrimed with silt. Perhaps it was the unexpected sight of such treasure, but Jackal sensed that his presence intruded. The building retained the tense, whispering air of a dwelling, the walls imbued with the breath and motion of an inhabitant.

He spun at a touch upon his shoulder and nearly loosed a bolt into Crafty.

"Hells," Jackal cursed quietly. "Make more noise when you walk."

"Come," the wizard said, his face placid. "You must see this."

"What?"

Crafty turned without a response and led Jackal back across the gangplanks, again passing the main hut as they approached the other set of sheds. The sludges remained in the lagoon, their forms pulsing ever so slightly upon the dark water. The wizard stopped and nodded toward the nearest shed. Even before he entered, Jackal noticed this particular building, though no larger than the others, was more solidly constructed. It still had no door, but the walls were made of mudbrick, as was the domed roof.

Jackal stepped within and lurched to a stop.

A sludge had attached itself to every wall save that of the entry, its black mass curving upward to partially cover the ceiling. A naked woman was imprisoned in the oily substance. Her hands were encased up to the wrists and hung from the ceiling, while her feet were held in the wall behind, causing her to dangle forward, her spine bent cruelly. Her head hung low between straining shoulders, a tangled mass of filthy hair hiding her face. The flush of her flesh and the rhythmic pulse of her belly signaled she still lived.

Jackal removed the bolt from his stockbow and slung the weapon over his shoulder. He took a slow step farther into the room, wary of any motion from the sludge. Other than the slow, incessant rippling across its surface, the creature did not stir at his trespass. Another cautious step brought Jackal within reach of the captive and he carefully cupped her unseen face in his hands, raising her head while he squatted slightly. The woman's eyes were closed, her tanned skin feverish to the touch. She whimpered ever so slightly, but did not awaken. Whether this was caused by the sludge or the more mundane hardships of captivity, Jackal could not guess. She was slim, but well muscled, not emaciated from hunger, and though her skin was grimy, there were no obvious wounds. The creature did not appear to be harming her, merely acting as a living restraint.

As Jackal slowly released her head, his fingers brushed against her ears. Frowning, he moved her hair away to confirm with his eyes what his touch conveyed. The prisoner's ears were pointed. Jackal backed slowly out of the shed.

He found Crafty sitting with his back to the wall of the building, facing the lagoon. A strange, sizable brass bottle with a bulbous base was standing upon the planks beside him, and the wizard was busy retrieving other oddments from his belongings. His motions were sure and practiced, his eyes never leaving the sludges in the lagoon.

"That girl is an elf," Jackal said.

"Yes. I saw."

Crafty continued with his puzzling chore, now opening a compartment at the top of the bottle and filling it with what looked like a bunch of dried herbs and some dark powder. Next, he poured some liquid from a skin into another part of the bottle. Finally, he affixed a thin, serpentine brass tube into a shunt near the bottom of the curio. Jackal watched all this with growing aggravation.

"She could be a Tine. The elves don't tattoo the members of their hoof, so I can't be sure. What the fuck is she doing here?"

This last he said mostly to himself, but Crafty answered anyway.

"Clearly, she is of some use to the demon you seek."

Jackal glared. "Demon?"

Crafty now had the thin tube between his lips and his plump cheeks worked rapidly for a moment. Vapors soon leaked out of the wizard's nostrils and snaked out between his lips as he removed the pipe. Jackal wrinkled his nose at the cloying odor.

"Yes," Crafty replied. "This Sludge Man. Indeed, even his name is a lie, for he is no man. Of this, I am now certain."

"Oh, no, he's a frail. Just one with a few weird talents and some deadly pets. We need to get this girl out of here, but I don't know how to begin freeing her."

"In a moment," Crafty offered, "you may be able to inquire of her captor."

Following the wizard's gaze, Jackal saw another sludge approaching from across the lagoon. This one was larger than the other six, forcing them to slither out of the way as it passed. The big sludge made directly for the landing that Jackal and Crafty occupied. Knowing it would be of no use, Jackal unslung his stockbow and loaded a bolt. Beside him, Crafty continued to sit and suck upon his complex pipe, exhaling the vapors without apparent care.

As the big sludge reached the edge of the walkway, it changed fluidly from a crawl to a cresting rise. Now nearly vertical, the creature stretched upward until it equaled Jackal in height. He could have reached out and touched the thing, it was so close. His own image was reflected back at him from the shiny, black surface. A protuberance began to form at the top of the sludge, the membrane puckering as a round shape began to emerge.

It was the head of a man.

The eyes came clear of the sludge already open and staring directly at Jackal.

The Sludge Man rose from the body of the creature, his pale, rounded shoulders quickly following a face molded with hostility. No trace of the sludge remained on his skin, but was birthed clean and corpse-white. Once his bare torso was free, the Sludge Man ceased rising. The sludge continued to embrace him from below his sizable paunch, holding him up to weave unctuously above the planking.

Beneath his wild, thinning hair the Sludge Man's suspicious eyes narrowed. His mouth hung open, his tongue sliding in front of his lower teeth, causing his bottom lip to protrude stupidly for a moment before he spoke.

"Why are you here, half-breed?"

The Sludge Man's voice was deep, full of danger, and possessed a thick, mumbling quality.

"To find you," Jackal said. "And to find out why you broke faith with the Grey Bastards."

The sludge dipped slightly and leaned so that the Sludge Man could get a better look at Crafty, sitting behind Jackal. After a moment's scrutiny, the column of living muck straightened once more.

"The Hisparthan is gone, half-orc," the Sludge Man told Jackal. "My lovelies ushered him into the black parlor. The faith is sundered only by you, who come unwelcome to our suzerainty."

Jackal sighed in relief. That was it, then. Garcia was gone. All evidence of Fetch's deed lost to the mire. "What of his horse? Why did it return to the castile?"

The Sludge Man's frown deepened. "The fat man bequeathed to me the corpse the Grey Bastards made of a man. There was no steed offered or accepted."

Jackal's mind began racing. Why would Sancho have withheld the horse? The whoremaster had always been a friend to the Bastards.

The Sludge Man dismissed his obvious confusion. "The devious bawd is a problem for your coterie. I have received recompense for my aid and am well satisfied."

"Recompense? Was that the chests of coins or a damn elf girl?"

"Neither are the concerns of a mere liegeman. You are not privy to the inveterate dealings of your captain. Your ignorance is rendered by your lack of import."

Jackal swallowed a snarl. He had met with the Sludge Man only a handful of times, and never alone, but the arrogance of the frail never failed to amaze him. He was an ugly, naked, inbred marsh dweller, but he always spoke as if he were some damn king. He and the Claymaster had conspired for years, the exact nature of their arrangement murky. The king's ransom in those chests was more wealth than the hoof could provide in a lifetime, much less for the disappearance of one body. That left the elf. Was that how the chief kept the Sludge Man as an ally? Providing stock for his twisted pleasures? If so, it was more evidence that the Bastards needed fresh leadership.

Taking a deep breath, he rallied his patience.

"Sludge Man. This girl you hold could be a Tine. Do you want the entire elven hoof riding into the Old Maiden to take her back?"

"Elves are not half-thicks," the Sludge Man returned. "They do not come willingly here."

"You can't keep her."

The Sludge Man's eyes widened. "You add to your effrontery, soot-skin! You will not command me nor take what was traded. My beautiful vassals shall sup upon your flesh until you are naught but bones. These we will return to your blighted master as evidence of our displeasure."

Jackal focused beyond the Sludge Man and saw his creatures begin to advance, though slowly. They were difficult to see, for the surface of the lagoon was now covered with a low, thick carpet of fog. In fact, the stuff was everywhere, gathering quickly. Puzzled, Jackal looked at his feet and saw the vapors flowing past him to cascade over the edge of the walkway, heavy with moisture and moving with a queer vitality. The Sludge Man seemed equally perplexed, his gaze now directed beyond Jackal to where Crafty sat.

The fat wizard retained his relaxed posture. The vapors roiled out from his nostrils and escaped from between his lips. His pipe and the strange vessel attached to it were brimming over with the mist that now filled the lagoon. The sludges were no longer moving.

"Interlopers," the Sludge Man accused. "You couple the insult of your presence with eastern devilry."

"Devilry?" Crafty asked, amusement in his smoke-laden voice. "Truly, you are the only devil here. Beneath this human mask you wear, what cursed face is yours, *djinn*?"

"Foreign words!" the Sludge Man spat. "Keep them behind your teeth, mongrel. You pollute my servants with your primitive crafts."

Jackal kept his eyes and his stockbow pointed at the Sludge Man, but he heard the sounds of Crafty standing.

"Oh, yes," the wizard said. "They are quite inert. Friend Jackal, I believe you will find the maiden now unbound. Perform a kindness and bring her from within."

Jackal took one step toward the shed and heard a bellow of rage.

The Sludge Man leapt forward, his legs erupting from the oily trunk that had encased them. Jackal jerked the tickler on his stockbow and sent his bolt flying. It caught the Sludge Man in one fleshy thigh, but he took no notice.

Naked and screaming, he barreled into Jackal, backhanding him across the jaw before landing upon the planking. Blinded by pain, Jackal was sent sprawling, rolling upon the uneven boards. Somehow, he managed not to spill into the treacherous waters of the lagoon and regained his feet before his vision fully cleared.

The Sludge Man had Crafty seized by the throat, throttling the wizard as he lifted him into the air. Jackal's stockbow was still in his hand. Snatching one of the few bolts that remained within his quiver, he reloaded the thrum and jammed the stock into his shoulder, sighting quickly and pulling the tickler. The bowstring snapped forward, sending the bolt shrieking into the Sludge Man's ribs. His aim was true. Such a shot should have transfixed a lung before lodging in the heart. It would have killed the biggest orc. The Sludge Man did not so much as grunt. He continued to choke the life from Crafty.

"Fuck," Jackal said.

The wizard was right. This was no man.

Discarding his stockbow, Jackal drew his tulwar and charged. He brought the curved blade up on the run and brought it down in a vicious slice meant for the Sludge Man's outstretched arms, but the demon swung around with terrible speed, bringing Crafty into the blade's path. Jackal checked his strike, wrenching the sword away with such desperation it flew from his hand. His forward momentum brought him crashing into the suspended wizard. He careened off Crafty's broad back and fell once more to the planks. Snarling, Jackal sprang up, bull-rushing the Sludge Man as he rose. His shoulder barreled into the bog dweller's stomach and he wrapped his arms around the man's body. He may as well have charged a tree. The Sludge Man rocked slightly at the impact, but kept his feet as well as his hold on Crafty. Jackal was now wedged between the hanging wizard and the Sludge Man.

Yelling furiously, Jackal threw all his weight backward, hauling on his foe with every muscle in his body. He felt the balance tip and they all fell. Jackal was crushed between ally and adversary, but he heard Crafty gasp for breath as the Sludge Man's grasp was broken. Keeping his own hold, Jackal rolled and tossed the Sludge Man into the side of the shed, then scrambled to his feet.

The bog dweller was faster.

He was up before Jackal found his own balance, rushing in with fists flying at the ends of long, pale arms. The Sludge Man was a big-boned bag of meat, with hardly a hint of defined sinew, but Jackal dodged his blows desperately, knowing that just one might cave in his skull.

The narrow walkway afforded little ground to maneuver. Jackal could not dance away forever. He waited for the Sludge Man to overextend, then darted in, pulling at the striking arm and bringing a knee up into the man's stomach. The fletching of the bolt still protruded from the Sludge Man's side and Jackal hammered it deeper with the heel of his hand. The Sludge Man made a wet grunt and turned on him, a hand darting out to seize his throat. Jackal managed to swat the hand away, but the Sludge Man planted a foot into his chest and kicked the breath from his body. The walkway catapulted up to meet him and he swam in a puddle of nausea. The sickness rising in his throat was quickly banished by the scream forced from his lungs when the Sludge Man stomped down on his left forearm, shattering the bone.

Jackal rolled upon the planking, convulsing with the agony. He heard whimpers of pain and knew they were his own. Fighting not to pass out, he looked about.

Crafty had risen to his knees, still sucking raggedly at the air. The Sludge Man was stalking toward him, intent on finishing the wizard, his back now turned. Out in the lagoon, the sorcerous mist was thinning and the sludges were beginning to stir. The large one closest to the walkway, the one that had vomited out its master, still stood nearly vertical, motionless within the grip of the vapors leaking weakly from Crafty's upset pipe. Whatever the wizard had done, it would not last much longer.

Cradling his useless arm, Jackal choked on unrelenting pain. This was madness! The Sludge Man could not be harmed. They were going to die here, killed by some marsh demon wearing human flesh. Hells only knew what would happen to the poor elf girl, trussed up and exposed for this mudsucker's pleasure. Rage bubbled in Jackal's guts.

"Fuck that," he snarled.

Gritting his teeth, he rose and rushed the Sludge Man, keeping low. The sound of his boots pounding on the planks alerted the demon, but not in time. The big man had only half pivoted when Jackal bulled into him.

Jackal slammed his lowered shoulder into the back of the Sludge Man's legs. Taken off-balance, the Sludge Man fell backward as he was lifted from the ground, his buttocks and lower back pressing heavily into Jackal's neck and face. Broken arm screaming in protest, Jackal hooked it around his grappled foe's neck, bending his back across his shoulders. The Sludge Man began to struggle, digging into Jackal's cracked bones with his powerful fingers. Pain and vomit flooded Jackal's mouth, but his good hand was thrust between the brute's kicking legs and he seized the soft flesh of the Sludge Man's genitals. He gripped down hard and heard a squeal of pain. The Sludge Man's struggles became desperate, flailing.

"Does that hurt?" Jackal taunted. "Demon or no, some parts are needed. Why else keep a naked girl bound and alive?" He released the Sludge Man's fruits just long enough to make a fist and began blindly battering the now pulpy organ. With each blow he screamed triumphant abuses. "You! Bog! Sucking! Fuck!"

Whirling around on the spot, Jackal spun, gained momentum, and flung the Sludge Man into the lagoon. He broke the black surface of the waters with a slapping splash and disappeared beneath the foam of upset scum.

Reeling and breathless, Jackal found Crafty on his feet, the elf girl cradled in his arms, still senseless.

"Run!" Jackal screamed, and he stumbled after the fleeing wizard as they pounded across the gangplank, away from the Sludge Man's home. The sludges in the lagoon trembled violently as they passed, trying to rid themselves of the lethargy caused by Crafty's smoke. Jackal did not know how much longer the creatures would remain afflicted. He focused on moving as fast as he could across the marsh and did not dare look back.

Chapter 8

Crafty collapsed. He'd given a valiant effort, but the weight of the elf girl, coupled with the wizard's own bulk, had quickly exhausted him.

Jackal plodded to a halt as his companion sucked in lungfuls of humid air. He was hobbled by pain and had stumbled as many times as Crafty. They were both filthy and drenched from numerous spills into the bog.

Finally risking a look back, Jackal squinted at the marsh they had covered. He could no longer see the Sludge Man's compound. Nor could he find any sign of pursuit, all dead gods be praised. That meant nothing. Their progress had been torturously slow. Had they come a mile? Two? Less? It did not matter. They had not reached the hogs, and the hogs were life.

Jackal slogged his way over to the fallen elf. A low, exhausted growl rumbled in his chest as he hoisted her limp form out of the muck.

"Friend Jackal," Crafty protested. "Your arm . . ."

Jackal said nothing, too tired to speak. It took all his grit to get the woman up onto his left shoulder and drape his broken arm across her lower back. He would need his good hand to catch himself if he should fall, *when* he would fall.

They trudged on, no longer trying to run. The setting sun and the rising flies were incessant, both a plague on the eyes.

"Are you certain of the way?" Crafty asked after a time.

Again, Jackal did not answer. He knew the rough direction of the trees where they had left the hogs, but broken bones and a desperate flight from danger had properly befuddled his memory. It would have been difficult to backtrack even if he were calm and free from injury. The Old Maiden was an unvarying hell, all marram grass and stagnant pools. She took years to properly learn, years she spent trying to kill her explorers. Besides, Crafty knew the answer to his own question. Why ask if he were confident Jackal led them true?

Night fell, forcing an end to their steps. Even with the advantage of orc eyes, the chances of finding the hogs in the dark were narrow. Crafty helped Jackal lower the elf to the ground and they slumped down beside her. Insects replaced the light, deafening in their multitude. Jackal allowed himself to drift in the din, surrendering to the freedom of uselessness. They could not walk on, they could not fight. They would never see the sludges coming in the dark, their black bodies would be one with the shadows until it was too late. There was no more Jackal could do. It was an exquisite relief. He would live through the night or not; either way he could pass the time in glorious, unavoidable impotence.

Crafty was more industrious.

Jackal heard him rummaging in the bag he had miraculously retained. There came the sound of ripping silk. Wits dull with pain and exhaustion, Jackal was dimly aware of the wizard splinting his arm and coaxing him to chew on some bitter-tasting lump. The rest of the night passed in a flood of frog song and fever dreams.

Morning found them all alive. Jackal opened his eyes to Crafty squatting beside the elf girl, removing the leeches that had affixed themselves to her during the night. The wizard had also fashioned a rude garment from one of the many shawls that comprised his robes, and when he was done ridding the girl of bloodsuckers, he slipped the shift over her head, and belted it with a length of cord.

"She remains unconscious," Crafty said needlessly.

Jackal's mouth tasted awful. He bent to spit and saw the shadow. Cast by the morning sun, it lanced across the pale grass, lengthening more than widening, devouring Jackal's own silhouette.

"Down!" he shouted, and flung himself face-first to the marsh, rolling as soon as he hit.

A shriek of fury, a battering of feathers, and then the shadow passed over.

Jackal jerked his head up to see the rokh pulling out of its dive, flapping its great wings as it ascended. Crafty pushed himself upright, away from the prone elf he had shielded with his own body. The wizard needn't have worried. Jackal had been the intended prey. Why attempt the fattest calf when the injured one would do?

The rokh was climbing steadily, flying directly away. Soon, it would be lost to distance and glare, invisible until it chose to strike again. The giant raptor would come at them silently, as before.

Crafty was now searching through his shapeless bag, his head nearly buried in its depths.

"Keep your eyes up, dammit!" Jackal snarled, averting his own vigilance only long enough to look for some kind of weapon. There was nothing. No sizable logs or decent rocks. Nothing but bog water and vomit-colored grass.

Hissing in frustration, Jackal went back to searching the sky, especially to the east, where the sun was blinding. Hells, there was nothing he could do! Only now the thought was not comforting as it had been in the deep of night. With the morning came the will to live fueled by the illusion that survival was possible, that fighting would be worth a damn. It was a cruel lie. Twenty men could have sheltered in the shade of that rokh's wings. Even with a stockbow, a full quiver, and two good arms, Jackal would've been hard-pressed to bring the bird down. And here he was, scrambling for stones to throw.

Crafty continued to root around in his sack. For what, more smoke? No, their only chance was to leave the elf girl behind, give the rokh something even easier to eat than a wounded half-orc. The thought only made Jackal angrier, fanned the flames to fight. He still had a mouthful of teeth. Let the feathered fiend come! He would be standing here when it did.

The rokh didn't keep him waiting long.

He caught sight of it to the south, dipping one wing earthward as it came around for another pass. This would not be a plummet from the clouds. No, the bird was going to swoop close to the ground, lead with its beak. Hells, it wanted to be seen, trying to spook its quarry into running, for easier pickings.

"Whatever you're doing, do it fast!" Jackal called to Crafty over his shoulder.

The rokh was now gliding swiftly over the marsh, a natural, graceful hunter, certain in its ability to kill. As the distance between them dwindled, Jackal resisted the urge to flee, watching the bird grow in size with each pounding of his heart.

Two objects sped past Jackal's head, so fast they were nearly invisible, leaving only a whisper of air at the edge of hearing.

The rokh screeched as the thrumbolts struck. It lurched in mid-flight, abandoning its path with a frantic flapping of wings. Jackal turned and saw four hogs splashing through the marsh, two with riders. He knew their outlines well.

Oats and Fetching reloaded on the run, their bowstrings snapping as they loosed another volley at the retreating rokh. Hearth and the hog Crafty had ridden were with them, trundling through the morass and sending bog water flying in all directions.

Jackal was smiling widely by the time his friends reined up before him. Oats kept his stockbow pressed firmly into his shoulder and trained on the sky. Fetching had the butt of her weapon resting on her hip as she looked down at Jackal and shook her head.

"The Old Maiden certainly had her way with you," she said, her green skin flecked with pieces of wet grass. "You're supposed to ride through the marsh, Jackal, not let her sit astride your face all night."

There was no time to respond. Hearth trotted over and nuzzled Jackal so hard with a wet snout that he nearly fell over.

"Be glad that pig knows your scent so well," Fetch said.

"Ug led you to him," Jackal said, looking at Oats. It was not a question.

The big brute did not reply, but a smile appeared as he gave his own hog a rub between the ears. Ugfuck snorted.

From the ground, Crafty cleared his throat. "If one would help me get this woman upon my mount, I will tend her during our ride away from this place."

Fetching's lip curled. "So, you steal the chief's pet wizard and now the two of you are collecting naked, dead elf girls."

"She's not dead," Jackal replied. "And Crafty's right. We need to get clear of this damn marsh."

"Crafty?" Fetch asked.

The wizard dipped his chin. "Uhad Ul-badir Taruk Ultani, at your service."

Still aiming at the sky, Oats chuckled and shook his head.

"Crafty it is," Fetch said as she dismounted.

She could have easily lifted the elf girl by herself, but Jackal and Crafty both aided the process. The wizard climbed onto the hog's back and cradled the unconscious girl against his large body, keeping her curled in front of him as one would a child.

"What happened there?" Fetching asked, flicking her eyes at Jackal's injured arm.

"Later."

She looked as if she would press the matter, but Oats's gruff voice forced them to turn.

"Bird's coming back."

Fetching sucked her teeth. "Time to put a bolt through this vulture's eye."

Striding back to her hog, she mounted and slung her stockbow up. The rokh was coming in determinedly, its tiny brain unable to give up the hunt. As it sped closer, coming out of the sun, Jackal slung a leg over Hearth and plucked a javelin from the saddle harness. He wouldn't need it. Fetching was the best shot in the hoof and would make good on her boast. The rokh would fall with her bolt in its eye, and Oats was not likely to miss either.

The giant bird charged swiftly, pulling out of its dive to skim the marsh. It was well within bowshot, but Oats and Fetching held their bolts, waiting for the killing shot to present itself. With each flap of its impressive wings, the rokh sped closer, until Jackal was hard-pressed not to urge his companions to let loose. The beak opened, emitting a screech that seemed to come from everywhere but the bird. Its wings bunched, pulling back to catch the air on massive, colorless pinion feathers, allowing its talons to lead the charge.

Oats loosed his bolt and pierced the bird's breast, but it did not slow. Its claws opened, the talons long as scimitars.

"Fetch!" Jackal yelled. "Bring it down!"

The bog in front of the rokh erupted. Massive cascades of water burst into the air as a black shape shot upward. Hearth and the other hogs squealed, recoiling from the sudden violent disturbance between them and the bird.

Jackal's eyes widened.

It was the largest sludge he had ever seen. Leaping from the water, it spread out with horrifying speed and, for one terrible instant, the black mass shaped itself to match the rokh, fanning out with perfect symmetry to snatch the animal out of the air. In less than a heartbeat the raptor was engulfed by the viscous form of the sludge, which struck snakelike from the bog.

"RIDE!"

Jackal was not sure which of his friends screamed the word. It might have been him.

Hearth responded instinctually, turning around on the run and fleeing the unnatural creature. Jackal was forced to drop his javelin, grabbing the hog's mane with his one good hand. He clung as the hog raced across the marsh, skirting the mires and darting from one stretch of firm ground to the next. There was nothing for Jackal to do but trust his barbarian to find a safe path. Without two functioning hands, he could not risk taking hold of Hearth's swine-yankers, so he held on to the beast's bristles and focused on keeping his seat.

Crafty rode just ahead, struggling to keep himself and the elf girl upon his hog's back as it raced across the difficult terrain. The wizard was a fool for riding bareback and Jackal was twice the fool for allowing him to take charge of the helpless elf girl. Without a saddle, the fat conjurer could not hope to stay mounted, not with the panicked pace set by his hog.

Turning as he rode, Jackal cast a look back. Oats and Fetching were spread out on his flanks, not four paces behind. Beyond them was a living nightmare.

The huge sludge was pursuing, crashing through the marsh, a tidal wave of hungry black. Cresting and falling, the viscid monster surged over land and punched through the pools, parting the water with a fury. The thing was so wide, it would not need to run them down individually. If it caught them, they would all be dragged down in one swath, devoured by pitch-flesh.

Jackal waved his broken arm forward, signaling Oats and Fetching to catch up. Fetch drew up first and Jackal pointed at Crafty's back, wordlessly communicating the wizard's need for aid. Fetching kicked her hog to greater effort and began closing the distance.

Looking back again, Jackal saw the sludge was falling behind, but his relief instantly soured. The hogs could not keep this pace. They would tire long before the end of the Old Maiden. That sludge would continue to follow without faltering, without need for breath or rest.

Ahead, Fetching now rode alongside Crafty and was gesturing for him to hand the elf over. The wizard tried to comply, but was clumsy, hindered by uncertainty, uncomfortable with such a maneuver. Jackal grit his teeth, wishing for all hells his arm was not splintered. Fetching would lose patience, likely give up the attempt if she did not knock Crafty from the saddle out of frustration first.

After a harrowing batch of failures, Fetching managed to grab hold of the elf girl's makeshift garment and, with Crafty's unsure help, began hoisting her over.

The elf chose that moment to come around.

Jackal heard Fetching shout a startled curse as the girl jerked awake. She thrashed, confused and fearful, and sent a kick into the ribs of Crafty's hog. The barbarian lurched away, and the wizard lost his grip on the girl. Fetching tried to haul her the rest of the way with one arm, but was off-balance and lost her seat as her hog darted around a thick stand of reeds. Both women fell to the ground, rolling and splashing over the waterlogged turf.

"Go!" Jackal shouted, pointing at the elf.

Oats did not need to be told. He was already guiding Ugfuck toward the girl. Jackal rode for Fetching. She was already on her feet and facing him, her legs spread wide, bouncing slightly on the balls of her feet. As Hearth charged by, Jackal stuck out his injured arm, gritting his teeth and trusting Fetch to do the rest. She reached out and leapt. Jackal screamed through the pain as she vaulted up behind him. To their right, Oats had snatched the elf girl by the hair and tossed her belly-down over his saddle horn.

"What the fuck is that fat shit doing?" Fetching yelled in Jackal's ear.

Crafty was just ahead. On foot. He faced them, but his gaze was beyond. Jackal did not have to turn to know what the wizard looked upon. He could feel the sludge still back there, inexorable vengeance made manifest.

Jackal rode a few dozen paces past the wizard before he forced Hearth to turn.

"What are you doing?" Fetch demanded. "Ride on!"

Oats reined up beside them. The elf girl struggled feebly, but the brute held her firm with one powerful hand splayed across her back.

"Jack?" he said. "What are we doing?"

"We can't ride triple," Fetch said. "Not even Ugfuck could carry that sack of suet's extra weight."

Oats grunted. "She's right. We need to go."

Ignoring them, Jackal continued to watch the wizard.

Crafty's muck-sodden robes hung heavily about his ponderous frame. He did not turn to see if his companions were returning, but stood resolutely, watching the approaching sludge hulk. Occasionally, his right arm would raise and his head would tilt backward, as if he were drinking. Jackal glimpsed a sizable decanter in the wizard's fist, glinting in the remorseless sun.

"Brother?" Oats rumbled. "What are we doing?"

Fetching's breath was hot against his neck. "Hells, let's go!"

"No," Jackal said.

The sludge was upon Crafty now, rising as it surged near, dwarfing the wizard against a shapeless wall of black. The wave reached its zenith, crested, and began to fall, eager to drop upon the sorcerer.

Crafty took a single, stomping step, thrusting his arms back and his head forward. A swarm of cinders shot forth, accompanied by an intense sound of rushing wind. Wind that burned. Countless, flaming granules assaulted the sludge, striking the black membrane and halting its charge. Jackal and his friends winced as a blowback of scorching air hit them in an unseen wave. The horde of sizzling mites poured from Crafty and, as he rotated his head back and forth to cover the breadth of the sludge, Jackal saw they were being blown from the wizard's mouth. Cheeks puffed out, Crafty spewed forth the infernal specks, each a hellish mating of insect and flame. They flew directly into the sludge, thousands of them extinguishing themselves against its inky surface until it began to blister and boil.

The creature strove forward, desperate to reach the wizard, but Crafty's lungs were without limit. The battle between sludge and fire swarm was stalemated for a few dreadful heartbeats, but then Jackal saw the blackness begin to recede. The flesh of the sludge peeled back, flayed by a million tiny flames. Deep within the center, was the Sludge Man.

"Hells overburdened!" Fetching gasped.

Jackal set his jaw and watched as the sludge drew away from the man suspended inside its embrace. The Sludge Man's eyes were fixed on Crafty, the flesh of his face quivering with rage. He screamed as the burning reached him, an animal sound. His pale flesh turned pink and then began to singe. Red, angry scorch marks erupted on his face, his belly. Howling madly the Sludge Man recoiled, flinging himself deeper into the sludge as the entire mass retreated, sloughing away into the bog. Steam rose from the waters into which it sank.

Jackal, Oats, and Fetching sat motionless upon their hogs as Crafty turned and made his slow, steady way across the bogs to join them. In his hand was a dented copper vessel, thick with verdigris. After placing the decanter back in his sack, Crafty looked up and regarded them all with a friendly expression.

"How?" Oats asked, shaking his head slowly.

Crafty pondered this for a moment, before giving a large shrug.

"In terms you would understand?" he asked with a smile. "It's fucking magic."

Chapter 9

No one spoke until they were well clear of the Old Maiden Marsh. At last, Fetching called a halt at a grove of fig trees on the banks of the Alhundra. Fortunately, she and Crafty had managed to reclaim their hogs before they were lost to rokhs or sucking bogs. Every rider in their little group was filthy and weary, but sleep would have to wait. For now, answers were more important.

"Why was the Sludge Man out to kill us?" Fetching demanded as she dismounted, slapping her hog toward the river for a drink.

"Because we took her," Jackal answered, nodding at the elf girl as Oats hauled her off his saddle. Her legs gave out as soon as she touched the ground, but she crab-crawled swiftly toward the shelter of the trees, casting a wild stare at the half-orcs.

"Peace," Crafty told her in gentle tones, squatting down with his hands splayed. "None here will harm you."

"Who is she?" Oats asked, continuing to loom over the cowering girl.

Jackal motioned his friend away with a wave. He led Fetch and Oats closer to the river, allowing Crafty a chance to calm their rescued captive.

Jackal shook his head. "I don't know. But she might be a Tine. She also might be what the Claymaster paid for the Sludge Man's help."

"Hells!" Fetch swore, growing more agitated.

Oats's bearded face darkened. "You sure?"

"No," Jackal replied. "Not about any of it. But we have to find out. And we're not going to do that if you continue to stand over her like some bearded, fuck-ugly mountain."

The tension broke as Oats smiled. Fetching punched him on one trunk of an arm.

"Thrice-blood monster," she teased.

Oats sheepishly slapped her hand away, half spinning her. They all three grinned for a moment.

"Thanks for saving my hide," Jackal told his friends.

Oats grappled his shoulder. "We will until the day we don't, brother."

"Seems to me we ought to be thanking Ham Hocks over there," Fetching said, hooking a thumb at Crafty.

"I still want to know how he did that," Oats grumbled.

The wizard had managed to get a little closer to the she-elf and was now attempting to offer her a waterskin.

"Crafty is a separate mystery," Jackal said, "one that doesn't need solving right now. What did you two find out at Sancho's?"

Oats gave an angry grunt while Fetch answered.

"We couldn't get close, Jack. Castile soldiers were all over it."

"Captain Bermudo's boys?"

Oats nodded grimly.

"Shaft my ass!" Jackal spat. Bermudo was putting Sancho in his grip. He would be looking for his lost cavaleros too. They were greasy ash now, but it hardly mattered, the damage was done.

Fetch looked at Oats. "You should have killed him with that bucket."

Oats lifted his heavy brows. "Maybe. Maybe we should have killed them all in the first place. Woulda caused some fuss at the castile, but Ignacio could have smoothed it with enough silver in his palm. Hard to imagine this worse."

"What if I told you Ignacio lured those cavaleros to the Kiln, and the Claymaster had me and Hoodwink murder them?" Jackal asked.

Oats glanced at Fetching.

"Yeah," he said.

"That's worse," she agreed.

The thought of the commoner captain made Jackal pause.

"Sancho lied to Ignacio too," he said. "He told him he had given the Sludge Man Garcia's horse, as agreed."

"So?" Fetch shrugged. "Everyone in the Lot Lands knows Ignacio takes the Claymaster's coin. If Sancho is helping Bermudo against our hoof, he has every reason to lie to Ignacio."

"I know," Jackal said, frustration gnawing at the ragged edges of his exhaustion. "But if Bermudo squeezed Sancho for the horse, why not get Garcia's body too? It still doesn't smell right."

"Let's get back to the Kiln," Oats advised, "figure it out there."

That made Jackal let loose a short, bitter laugh. "That's the last place we want to be. I left without orders. The Claymaster will flay me alive."

Oats conceded by scratching at his beard. "Then what?"

"We be good little mongrels and do what we were told," Fetch said, her voice edged with venom. She bounced a hand off Oats's chest. "*We* had orders. To find answers."

"Then let's start with the questions in front of us." Locking his eyes on the elf girl, Jackal strode toward the fig trees.

Crafty cut him off halfway there, holding up his pudgy, ring-laden hands in a calming gesture.

"She remains quite frightened."

Jackal stepped around the wizard. "I just need to speak to her."

"That is impossible."

Jackal stopped and spun on his heel. "Why? You telling me a clever ass like you doesn't know the elf tongue?"

"Only a few words," came the reply. "Enough to convey friendship. But that is not my meaning. She does not speak. Entirely. Perhaps she never could. But more likely it is a result of her ordeal, I am thinking."

Jackal turned, frowning. The girl was watching him from the shade of the trees, her knees bunched beneath her chin. Her slightly slanted eyes were fixed on him. Keeping his steps slow and light, he made his way over, squatting down several strides away from the girl. She withdrew further into herself, her tanned, sinewy arms pulling protectively at her legs. Jackal placed her age a few years younger than his own. The eyes contained more reluctance than wisdom, the movements more fright than fight. Still, time spent as the Sludge Man's captive would have unnerved the staunchest sort. There was strength in this girl, despite her posture.

Jackal made sure not to smile, to keep his lower fangs as concealed as possible. Half-orcs were not rare in the Lots, but if this elf had lived an entire life of protected seclusion amongst her kin in Dog Fall, she might not be accustomed to the appearance of a soot-skinned mongrel. Despite the flattery of numerous whores telling him he was the comeliest half-breed they had ever seen, Jackal knew he was far from possessing the inherent beauty that manifested in elf-kind. Filthy and haggard from the swamp, he must seem more a demon to this poor girl than even the Sludge Man.

Scraping the dried muck off his left shoulder with his uninjured hand, Jackal pointed to the tattoo beneath the grime, the track of a swine's hoof wreathed in broken chains. He said nothing, waiting for the elf girl to look at the mark, and watching for her reaction. With her gaze lingering on the ink, she grew still, but her placidity did not stem from calmness. No, it was a detached acceptance, as if she had embraced her death while continuing to draw breath.

"Grey Bastard," Jackal said slowly, tapping his finger against the tattoo. "You know this?"

The elf's eyes returned to his, but otherwise she gave no indication she understood. Jackal pointed to the girl slowly, then formed his hand into a rough depiction of antlers, placing his thumb against his temple.

"Are you of the Tines?"

He did not even know if that was what the elven hoof called itself, but it was the best he could do. The girl remained silent, but there was no confusion upon her brow.

Abandoning the antler, Jackal ran his knuckles along the sides of his filthy hair, miming the act of shaving his scalp.

"Tine?"

There was the scantest flicker of comprehension in the eyes.

Jackal lowered his hand and sighed through his nostrils. Standing, he backed away, trying to give the girl a reassuring look, all the while watching her for any sudden act. He stopped when he reached Crafty, then used his head to signal Oats and Fetching over. All three looked at him expectantly.

"She's a Tine," Jackal told them, just above a whisper. Oats growled and Fetch swore, pacing a little circle.

Crafty watched their reactions, his mouth slightly open in puzzlement. "I am afraid I am not understanding."

"The elven hoof here in Ul-wundulas," Jackal explained, "we call them Tines, because of the stags they ride. They drew a rich parcel of mountains and highland forests during Hispartha's lot draw."

Recognition seeped into the wizard's plump face. "After the Incursion, yes? I recall from my reading."

"They hole up in a gorge called Dog Fall," Oats rumbled. "Mostly keep to themselves, but they don't suffer trespassers."

"On their land or on their women," Fetching threw in, giving Crafty a pointed look.

"Ahh, I see."

"No, you don't see," Jackal told him, leaning down until he was talking directly in the wizard's ear. "We all have to watch her close now. Because mark me, that point-ear waif will kill herself the moment we flinch."

He waited for the words to sink in, then straightened. Crafty's face was placid.

"And here I thought he'd be . . . nonplussed," Fetching snickered.

"No. No, not at all," Crafty replied. "It is reasonable. The elves are known throughout the known world as insular. Indeed, they are a race of refugees since their homeland was—"

"Put a cock in it, jowly," Fetching said. "Jackal, what are we supposed to do with her?"

Jackal did not have a ready answer.

Fetch did. "Best to leave her here. Put a knife in her hand and ride away. Tines might kill us all if they see us with her."

"Leaving her here alone is the same as cutting her throat ourselves," Oats said.

Fetching rolled her eyes. "So forget the knife and let her leap off a cliff the moment our backs are turned. Point-ears don't suffer to be sullied. You can't change that."

"What if we're wrong?" Jackal shook his head. "For all we know of Tine ways, she has to die in Dog Fall."

"Now you're just inventing shit," Fetch said.

"What if, Fetch? She's got water close at hand and the sun still rising in the east. She doesn't kill herself, she's going back to her kind. If she finds her tongue, what's the story she gives her people? That a gaggle of half-orcs saved her from the Sludge Man, sure. But how did she become his captive in the first place? Because I'm willing to wager her tale will involve a hairless, scarred mongrel the color of a snake's belly. Not many fit that description."

"You think Hoodwink was part of this?" Oats asked.

"If it was at the chief's order, who else?" Jackal replied. "Hood's reputation is well known amongst the nomads. It won't take the elves long to discover where he's lurking these days. And we took her from the Sludge Man. Sludge Man does business with the mongrel hoofs, all the Lots know it. And where was the girl being held when he picked her up? At Sancho's. Sancho! Another man known to be a friend to the Grey Bastards. Every turn of that girl's tale points to us. She talks, it's war. Do you think the Tines will care that the three of us saved this girl when they raid the Kiln? We'll just be three more half-orcs that need to be reckoned with. You both still want to let her go?"

"Hells, Jackal," Fetching shot back, "she's half a corpse already. No way she makes it to Dog Fall."

"We can't risk that. She needs to stay with us."

Fetch wasn't ready to let it go. "You don't think we have enough to handle?"

"We do. And we'll need her if we want to get it all sorted."

"She looks brain-addled, Jackal. What good is she if she can't talk?"

"I don't need her to talk. Just point. One look at Hood, she'll see who took her to Sancho's and no one in the hoof will be able to deny that the Claymaster ordered him to do it, risking a war with the Tines and showing he is no longer fit to lead! This is our chance. We can finally be rid of him!"

Too late, he realized what he'd said. Anger and fatigue and broken bones had put his caution to sleep. Fetch and Oats were rigid, neither looking at him. Jackal followed their gazes to where Crafty stood, regarding them all with mystified amusement. If he was spying for the Claymaster, he hid it well.

"Or you've just given him everything he needs to finally be rid of you," Fetch said, her quiet tone somewhere between regret and disgust.

Jackal looked hard at the wizard. "I don't think so."

"Are *you* brain-addled?" Fetch said. "He's been nested with the chief since he arrived. You can't trust him!"

"You said it yourself, we have him to thank for getting out of the marsh."

"He was also saving his own fat carcass!"

Tired of the argument, Jackal turned to Crafty. "Can we fucking trust you?"

"You can, friend Jackal."

"What else is he going to say?" Fetch demanded.

"What other choice do we have?" Jackal shot back. "He's heard. It's been said! Nothing for it now! What do you suggest, Fetch? That the three of us try to murder him here and now?"

"I will not be accepting that solution," Crafty said.

"There it is." Jackal's finger pointed at the wizard, but his gaze remained on his friends. "We all saw what he can do today. You feel up to defying that? Because I don't."

Fetch looked at him with an expression of pity. "I can't tell which one has you more bewitched, the little elf gash or the swaddlehead sorcerer."

Crafty cleared his throat. "If I may—"

"Quiet, paunchy!" Fetch snapped. "You don't have a say in hoof matters." Tearing out of her brigand, Fetching tossed the heavy vest in Jackal's face. "You need to remember who you are! A Grey-fucking-Bastard, in case you forgot. Sworn to the hoof! Not to the protection of some elf slut and not to some tubby Tyrkanian!"

"Keep your voice down," Jackal warned.

"Easy, you two," Oats said.

But Jackal was mad now, and took an aggressive step toward Fetch. She met him halfway, baring her teeth and pressing her forehead roughly against his. The heat from their breath danced in the tiny space between them.

"You think you're reminding me of something?" Jackal snarled, his voice low and menacing. "All this is for the hoof!"

"All of this is for you to lead the hoof!"

"Someone has to. The Claymaster's time is done. He stays and the hoof dies. You know it! Do you want to help me figure a way through or do you want to just keep trying to prove that there's something different between your legs? I need your brain on my side, Fetch, not another swinging cod!"

They remained pressed together for several moments, neither relinquishing the growing pressure. Jackal pushed and Fetch pushed right back, the sweat on their brows mixing. Their eyes were locked, hers burning. Jackal watched as Fetch gnawed on his words. At last, she grinned and drew back quickly. On her face was a look of triumph.

"You want a way through?" she asked. "Here it is, straight from the brain above my cunt. We kill the elf. Dump her back in the bog. No story told the Tines. No war. We are away from here on hogback, well and done. And before you balk at getting blood on your hands, consider if you're right. If it was the Claymaster that gave her over. What do you think he'll do when we show up with her and she starts pointing? You think he'll even let us reach the voting table? Or will we find ourselves in the farrowing shed with Hood? You think this is a chance, but I'm telling you it's the wrong one to take."

"Jack," Oats said slowly. "She ain't wrong."

Jackal did not bother looking at his big friend, keeping his glare on the one who truly needed convincing. Her jab about him fearing blood on his hands had rankled and he couldn't keep the bile from rising. "Yes, she is. It's our Fetch, swift as a thrumbolt and near impossible to sway once she's loose."

He watched Fetching squirm at his words. Her discomfort was subtle, well suppressed, but it was there. She wanted to embrace his opinion, take pride in his words, but she feared a trap. She knew him as well as he knew her.

"We killed a man," he said flatly. "And he deserved it. Now, six more are dead and a girl sold, all to help bury that first killing and all at the Claymaster's order. He thinks he's helping the hoof, but he's burying the Bastards along with Garcia, making an enemy of the Tines to stall making an enemy of the castile. We don't fix this now, there won't be another chance."

Fetch had quit listening, gnawing on his first words, unable to get them out of her teeth.

"*I* killed a man. Not you, not Oats. Me! I killed Garcia. And we wouldn't be standing here now if you had just allowed me that!"

"You're right. Me and Oats and Crafty would all be standing in the Kiln without consequence because the chief wants a wizard in the hoof far more than he wants a woman!"

That last cut her to hear, and cut him to say. Jackal steeled himself against the hurt in Fetch's eyes and the greater amount in his chest. She doused her pain so quickly, Jackal was unsure he had seen it all. Sharp as the truth was, she knew he was right. Fetch took a slow breath.

"Seems you get a say after all," she told Crafty. "Welcome to the family."

The wizard said nothing, but Jackal could feel his eyes on him.

"What's the move then, Jack?" Oats asked during the short silence.

"We go back to Sancho's," he replied. "Confront him with the elf girl. Make him squeal about the Claymaster's little slave trade."

Oats raised his shoulders in nonchalant agreement. "And Bermudo's soldiers?"

"We will figure that out on the ride. For now, we need to get that Tine girl looking less like a tortured prisoner, in case we're seen by her folk." Jackal looked to Fetching, tensing for another fight. "I need you to help her wash."

There was the barest flash of defiance, but Fetch's pride would not allow her to balk at so simple a task.

Without breaking eye contact, she unbuckled her sword belt and let it fall to the dust. "I could use a scrub myself."

"We all could," Jackal said, smiling, but Fetch ignored his feeble attempt to mend fences. She sauntered past him and approached the Tine girl. Hating himself for not trusting her, Jackal waited and watched as Fetch slowly made progress convincing the elf to stand. When they began making their way to the riverbank, Jackal thumped Oats on the elbow.

"Let's give them some room."

"Fetch is just as likely to drown that girl," Oats said, his heavy steps falling in next to Jackal.

"Crafty will watch them."

Oats grinned and lowered his voice. "I envy him the show."

"I think he would rather see you naked, Oats."

The big thrice ran a hand over his bald pate and fought not to look over his shoulder. "You mean . . . he's backy?"

Jackal chuckled quietly. "I really don't know. Maybe."

Oats was more intrigued than offended. "Makes sense. They say women rob your strength. Bet it goes with being a wizard, swearing off quim. Wonder if grappling with other cods makes him more powerful? You think?"

Jackal cast a look of exaggerated horror at his friend. "I am not going to help you find out if you're a wizard!"

With a scowl and a noise of disgust Oats shoved Jackal away, knocking him over. He landed hard, unable to properly catch himself with his broken arm.

"Shit, Jackal!" Oats exclaimed. "Sorry, brother."

Laughing through the pain to ease his friend's guilt, Jackal allowed himself to be helped up.

"You need to get that tended," Oats said, frowning at the splint.

"After we're done at the brothel," Jackal told him. "But first, I want to get the Old Maiden off of me. Help me down to the water. And don't get any more ideas!"

Oats snorted. "You ain't that pretty, Jackal-boy. If it came to it, I'd rather have the fat wizard. Least he's got tits."

Later, Jackal sat nude on a sunbaked rock overlooking the Alhundra, letting the heat of the day dry his skin. He was having some difficulty tying his damp hair back. He had not removed the bandage from his arm and the silk was now loose and sodden. Oats was still chest deep in the river, rinsing the muck from his beard and trying to get a look at where Fetching and the elf still bathed in an inlet pool screened by some boulders. Any other day, Jackal would have been out there with him, trying to spy something pleasing, but he was too damn tired, with no end to the toil in sight.

Keeping the Tine girl was likely a mistake. Going back to Sancho's was too. But Jackal saw no other options. Fetch was right. To confront the Claymaster, injured, with all his bets resting on a mute elf girl, would be a desperate gambit. It could undo every chance he had of replacing the chief. So, he needed to discover all that he could before facing the rest of the hoof.

A shadow fell across Jackal's back, and he felt his hair being gathered up by a pair of steady hands. Quickly, deftly, his wet locks were tied into a tail and allowed to fall down his neck. Craning around, Jackal squinted up at Crafty.

"I thought you were Fetch," he said, too weary to do anything but bluntly state his surprise.

He could sense the smile in the wizard's silhouette, hear it in his voice. "Would she truly be so quick to forgive?"

Shrugging, Jackal turned back to the river. "Why not? I am. She kicked me in the nut-basket, but do you see me holding a grudge?"

Crafty came and stood beside him. "Ah, yes. But you are both comfortable with violence, with physical pain. Today, friend Jackal, you launched an unfamiliar assault."

Jackal wished the wizard's words had left him confused. Instead, he found them all too clear.

"Shouldn't you be watching over our wayward elf?" he asked sharply. "See that Fetch's comfort with violence doesn't make an appearance?"

"And what do you suppose I could do if it did?" Crafty asked, a hint of sad amusement in his strange accent. "Kill Fetching for defying me? That would only make an enemy of you and the thrice-blood. Who gains from this? Not I. Not you."

"Then stop her without killing her," Jackal replied with little feeling.

Crafty laughed at him. "Because I am so potent a sorcerer that anything is within my power? There is so little you understand, friend Jackal. No, it is with sorrow that I must admit, the elf's life is a feather when weighed against the trust of your hoof. I must trust to your female friend's forbearance and her acceptance of the truths you used to wound her."

Jackal was feeling annoyed. And naked. It was difficult to find an advantage debating with a man when you sat at his feet without a stitch.

"Why do we matter to you?" he demanded. "The Grey Bastards. Why did you come to us? Why did you come with me into the marsh?"

Crafty eased himself down on the rock. His face and hands were completely clean, though Jackal had not seen him bathe. The wizard took a deep, satisfied breath and stared out across the river.

"Ul-wundulas truly is a marvelous country. And only you can guide me through it."

"There are seven other half-orc hoofs in the Lot Lands," Jackal told him. "Any one of them would have taken you in."

"None but the Grey Bastards would do."

Crafty said this whimsically, but something in the set of his jaw and the way he watched the water announced he would not discuss the matter further.

"I might have made you an enemy today," Jackal said after a long silence. "Fetching, I mean."

"The world is her enemy," Crafty replied, still facing the Alhundra. "It must be or she could not be who she is."

"And who do you think she is?" Jackal asked, knowing he sounded absurdly protective.

A languid smile appeared on Crafty's face as he turned.

"Someone capable of terrible greatness."

Jackal grunted. Crafty was not wrong.

"I am curious," the wizard ventured, "how she came to be counted amongst your brotherhood. It is rare, yes? For a woman to join a hoof?"

"It is impossible," Jackal said. "But she did it. Well . . . the three of us did."

"There is a tale there."

Jackal twisted his mouth. "Not much of one. It only takes two sworn brothers to propose another for inclusion in the hoof. Serving as a slophead helps, but isn't required. After that, it's a matter of votes. Oats and I put Fetching forward a few years back. She got the votes. That's it. She was worthy and earned her place."

"I am thinking that was because you trained her," Crafty said lightly.

Hells, this wizard didn't miss anything. Jackal peered at him sidelong for a moment. Crafty wore a patient, careless grin.

"Yes," Jackal admitted. "Though it was her idea, in a way. Oats and I just continued what another started . . . what Fetch could not let go of." He did not much feel like storytelling, but found himself talking all the same. Guilt guided his tongue, as if relating Fetch's accomplishments could somehow pardon him for his harsh words to her.

"There used to be an old thrice-blood in the Bastards. Warbler. He was a veteran of the Incursion, helped found the hoof, and was the Claymaster's most trusted rider. Oats's mother, Beryl, was his bedwarmer, though it is more truthful to say that he was hers. When he wasn't on patrol or doing something for the chief, Warbler was at the orphanage. Closest thing to a father any of us had. We called him Warboar, because his name was hard for the little ones to say. Of course, he doted on Oats, him being a thrice and Beryl's son. But you couldn't separate Oats from me and Fetch, not that Warbler wanted to. He taught us little things, more as we got older, about caring for hogs and weapons, about the hoof and the ways of thicks, their language. We were young, but he was grooming us to be Bastards. Two of us, at least.

"We were eight, maybe nine years old when he challenged the Claymaster for the chief's seat. Never really knew why, but he threw his axe. Others joined him, but not enough. The challenge failed. The Bastards who supported his bid retrieved their axes and begged the Claymaster's forgiveness. But not Warbler. As the instigator of the challenge he had to stand before the stump and allow the chief to throw an axe of his own. That's our code. The Claymaster showed mercy. I guess for the years he and Warbler had shared during the war, he allowed him to go nomad.

"Life continued without him, more or less the same for a few years. Until the day Oats and I walked to the Kiln to become slopheads, leaving Fetch behind in Winsome. She ran off that night. Beryl had to beg the Claymaster to send riders to look for her. They found her within a day. Oats and I got to see her. She told us she was going to find Warbler, so he could finish teaching her how to be a rider. Even then she was stiff-necked and we knew she would do as she said. So, Oats and I promised to teach her all we learned, to keep her from leaving. That was the only reason, just to keep her safe. I don't think either of us really meant it at the time, but what else could we do? Beryl may have suffered another run, but the chief wouldn't. No one was going to search if Fetch left a second time.

"It was nearly impossible those first years. Oats and I were all but fettered to the Kiln, but Fetch was patient." Jackal let out a small laugh. "Hard to imagine that now. Anyway, life wasn't the same without her. We both felt it, me and Oats, so what started out as an empty oath became a true purpose. We wanted her with us in the hoof. It was easier once we were sworn brothers. Fetch had not been idle during our time as slops and was a better aim with a thrum than either of us. But she couldn't keep a hog hidden in the thatching the way she did a stockbow, so her riding was poor. We were sneaking her out on patrols with us within a month of becoming Bastards. What took us nearly eight years to learn, she mastered in less than three. When it was time, Oats and I made our case for her. There were a few more members then and we had made friends. We won the vote and earned the chief's ire, but that didn't matter. We were whole again."

As if summoned, Fetch appeared on the bank, helping the Tine girl out of the water, both dripping. The delicate, rust-brown limbs of the elf girl contrasted sharply next to Fetch's green frame of curves and muscle. Quickly, they walked to the fig grove, where Fetching began rummaging in her saddlebags for dry clothes.

"She is beautiful," Jackal said, watching her. The women were far enough away for him to look without too much shame. Besides, he was nude. Surely that made his scrutiny less an intrusion.

Crafty followed his gaze and nodded once before looking back to the river.

With some effort, Jackal followed the wizard's example.

"But that is not the reason for her hoof name," he continued. "When she was voted into the Bastards, the Claymaster said that women were only good for two things. Fucking . . ."

"And fetching," Crafty finished blandly. He reached over and began unwrapping Jackal's soggy splint. When he spoke again, his tone was sympathetic. "And today you reminded her of that."

"No," Jackal replied, his mouth wrinkling with borrowed bitterness. "She's never forgotten it."

CHAPTER 10

JACKAL WAS THANKFUL DELIA'S ROOM WAS ON THE GROUND floor of the brothel. He did not relish the thought of a climb with a shattered arm. The injury continued to pain him greatly and the chills of a fever had begun to plague him in intervals. Crouching in the shadows below the window, he listened to the sounds of Delia entertaining two of Bermudo's soldiers, gritting his teeth as the grunts and groans of the frails intensified. Delia's own feigned moans of pleasure were muffled. Jackal tried not to think about what was occupying her mouth. Somewhere behind him, on the night-shrouded hill of boulders and scrub, Fetch was no doubt smiling wolfishly. Let her mock, long as she covered his damn back!

The moon was high by the time the heavy breathing subsided, replaced by the tense stillness of a room filled with slumbering occupants. Delia always waited for her humps to fall asleep before quietly removing herself to wash. She had done that with Jackal, in the early days, when he was still nothing but a mongrel paying for quim. But he had not felt her rise after coupling for nearly five years. He was more now than a sticky stink that needed to be scrubbed away at the first opportunity. That was the reason he had come to her window first, instead of creeping directly to Sancho's chambers and demanding answers with a knife under the slovenly whoremaster's chins.

Easing himself up, Jackal peered through the broken window slats and waited for the familiar shadow to detach itself from the crowded bed. As soon as Delia's silhouette appeared, he hissed sharply. There was little danger of waking the soldiers. Sancho's girls knew how to drain a man.

Jackal watched as Delia paused. She had heard. She left the room noiselessly, and Jackal crouched back down before hurrying along the brothel wall, making for the fence that enclosed the exterior bathhouse. There was no door from the outside, so Jackal waited until two soft knocks sounded on the far side of the wood before jumping up and grabbing the top of the fence with his good hand. Pulling upward, he hooked a knee over the posts and leveraged himself over. His splinted arm made the drop awkward and Delia was at his side before he could straighten.

"You're hurt," she whispered.

"Not much," Jackal lied, sweeping the wet gloom of the small courtyard for signs of others.

"None are about," Delia assured him. "This way."

She led him toward the low, rough-hewn timber building that Sancho had built for the girls and his patrons. Jackal found the bathhouse revolting, preferring the purity of a moving river over the stagnant soup contained in the half dozen tubs.

"Be like soaking in ball sweat," Jackal muttered, half to himself, as Delia directed him toward a bench.

"We fetch fresh water from the well, you oaf."

Jackal sat and stared at the nearest tub, making a face. "Still . . ."

Delia slipped out of her thin robe and poured water from a pitcher into a nearby basin. Taking up a rag, she ducked behind a wicker screen. Her voice drifted quietly from beyond the partition.

"So, why the skulking visit?"

Jackal did not respond immediately. He kept his eyes fixed on the entryway to the baths, his ears open for sounds of approach. Delia's ablutions were swift and she stepped from behind the screen, her red hair black with water. Jackal's mind conjured an unbidden image of Fetching and the Tine girl coming from the river, comparing Delia's beauty to theirs. He hated to admit it, but the human whore came up woefully short.

Though still in her twenties, a hard life of professional debauchery had taken its toll. The flesh of Delia's face showed subtle wrinkles at the mouth and brow, her breasts and belly just beginning to fall. Somehow she appeared both soft and underfed. Yet for all the imperfections dredged to the surface by unfair measure against Fetch and the she-elf, Jackal still felt his blood quicken at the sight of her familiar body.

He dipped his head so that she would not see the flare of lust, but was not quick enough.

"Is that all?" Delia teased. "A quick thrust to ease the pain of your injury that is 'not much'?"

She approached and swung a leg over the bench, placing her weight on his lap before bringing the other leg around. Straddling him, her wet hair tickling coldly against his nose, Delia lifted his chin with a finger.

"I wondered how long the cavalry would keep you out," she whispered. She must have chewed a sprig of mint, for her breath cooled the inch of air between them.

"And how long does Captain Bermudo plan on billeting his troops here?" Jackal managed to ask through his growing desire.

She flicked her tongue at the tip of his nose.

"Until the purse on their belts, or the one between their legs, has run dry."

Jackal wrapped his bandaged arm around the small of Delia's back and pressed her close, ignoring the painful pressure in his bones. With his good hand he pushed the wet locks away from her face then seized her lower jaw roughly, causing her to grin.

"Dammit, strumpet," he said without rancor, "I need no games. How long?"

"I do not know," she replied, taking delight in his touch. "Bermudo has them coming in shifts. Never less than eight men. A pair leaves every day or so, but not until they are relieved from the castile."

"Hells," Jackal swore. "Does he mean to make this a permanent barracks?"

Delia seemed puzzled by the question. "You knocked him senseless, Jack. Killed his man. What else would you expect he'd do?" She began to grind her hips into Jackal's lap, biting her lower lip.

Jackal's desire fled. He barely felt the inviting revolutions, the breathy kisses upon his neck. "Expect? Didn't expect him here that morning. Or that he would order us killed. Reckon I got no notion what to expect from *Captain* Bermudo. Or anyone."

Delia's motions ceased, a worried frown frozen on her face.

"Jack?"

"I think my chief used the brothel to deliver a Tine girl to the Sludge Man."

"What?"

"You didn't know?"

"Why . . . why would I know something about your hoof that you didn't?"

"You didn't see Sancho bring in an elf girl?"

Delia looked at him as if he had gone mad. "Elves don't whore, Jack."

"No. She was a captive. We found her in the Old Maiden."

"We?"

"Me and Oats and Fetch, and this . . . new recruit. We managed to get the girl out."

Delia's eyes widened. "You took her from the Sludge Man?"

Jackal nodded. "When I told him he couldn't keep her, he went mad. Madder than usual. He almost killed us all. The girl's safe, but . . ."

"Now you're stuck with a daughter of the Tines," Delia said, her head giving the barest of shakes. "Jack . . ."

"I know," he cut her off before the hopelessness in her voice infected him. "Worse than that, it may all be because the Claymaster arranged it. Has Hoodwink been here recently?"

Delia's brow knit. "That the ghost-looking one with all the scars?"

"Yes."

"Once or twice to collect from Sancho. But not in months. He never stays long, never takes a woman. Good thing too. He scares us."

Whores didn't frighten easily, especially in the badlands. It would take something like Hoodwink to do it. Jackal stared at the floor beyond Delia's waist. Was he wrong about all of this? Delia wouldn't have seen Hood if he didn't want to be seen. But gut feelings and suspicion weren't enough.

The dark thoughts must have shown on his face, for Delia hooked a finger under his chin and lifted his attention back to her face. "What are you going to do?"

"The only thing I can. Get to Sancho and carve the truth out of him."

"Fuck, Jackal!" Delia cursed, her voice rising a bit much for comfort.

Shushing her with a sharp look, Jackal slung her off his lap and crept to the door of the bathhouse. He waited until he was certain none had heard, then turned back to face Delia. She was standing now too, wrapped back in her shift and staring at him with something between alarm and anger.

"Have you lost your mind?" Her voice was again low, but she managed to punch with her words. She thrust a finger toward the brothel. "There are ten cavaleros sleeping within a piss stream of where you stand."

"Exactly," Jackal said. "Sleeping. Half are drunk and all are fuck-tired. I can get in and out before any of them roll over."

"For what?" Delia hissed. "To make Sancho admit he smuggled flesh for your chief? Safer to trust your gut and leave him be."

"I don't need him to admit to the elf. I need him to tell me why he chose to betray the deal, turn on the Claymaster."

"Turn on him?"

"Sancho let Garcia's horse loose. I figure he got spooked, but didn't have the stones to completely turn cloak. So he used the horse to get Bermudo's attention, gets the cavaleros back here without admitting he knows anything. Something made him decide it was better to throw in with the castile than with the Claymaster. I need to know what that was."

A ripple of confusion played across Delia's face, but settled quickly. "Jack . . . it wasn't Sancho."

Jackal stilled.

"It was Olivar," Delia told him.

"The stableboy?"

Delia nodded, a look of sympathy on her face, as if she were telling Jackal someone had died. "He wasn't used to handling a warhorse. It was too spirited for him. It took three of us to pull Sancho off when he found out. We thought he was going to kill Olivar, the beating he was giving."

Jackal's jaw clenched. So, not a betrayal, an accident. A fucking accident. Six men butchered and burned, all because Garcia's mount was as unruly as its master and bullied past a brothel's underfed stableboy. Jackal rubbed at his face, felt his mouth turn upward. He started laughing, had to make an effort to keep it contained to his throat.

"Oh, shaft my ass. This is . . . *fuck*."

Delia took a step. "Jackal, you need to get away from here."

"Can't," he said, his voice settling. "Sancho still has answers I need."

"You beautiful, brave fool." Delia said it almost to herself, her gaze drifting over him. After two more slow steps she was reaching up to take his face in her hands. "Listen to me. Greed and fear are all that Sancho knows. Bermudo's men are filling his hands with coin and his halls with swords. If he suspects the Bastards are coming for him, I'd say the arrangement works in his favor. You said it. Whatever his designs, the castile is now behind him."

"Frails on foals," Jackal scoffed. "The Grey Bastards . . ."

"No!" Delia snapped, shaking his face roughly, forcing him to focus on her. "Listen! You were born in the Lots, Jackal, but I have been to Hispartha. All the mongrel hoofs together could not stand against even one of the Crown's armies."

"Piss," Jackal replied, pulling away. "If they were so mighty, they wouldn't need us to guard their doorstep. They wouldn't rely on us to keep the thicks at bay."

Delia's face went slack. "You really believe that, don't you? You don't see Ul-wundulas for what it is."

"And what is it, Delia?"

"Scraps!" She leaned forward and whispered the harsh word with such force that spit flew from between her teeth. "A pile of guts and gristle and shit-smeared innards. The leavings of a feast, filth that can only be stomached by orcs and vultures and . . . jackals."

"That's what you think of me? A carrion-eater?"

Delia smiled bitterly, looking away. "It's what we all are. You, me, Sancho. Even Bermudo and the other well-born cavaleros. You know it. You said it yourself. I heard you the morning Fetching killed that fop. 'Fobbed off here to be forgotten.' That's what you told them. You think you are any better?"

"As you said," Jackal muttered, "I was born here."

"And you are going to die here, soon, if you test your luck tonight."

Jackal clenched his jaw with frustration. "I can't let the Claymaster continue leading us, Delia. I can't. We may have made a mistake killing Garcia, but he's making it worse with his madness. I need to unseat him. Sooner or later, I am going to challenge him. And that will be nothing but a test of luck if the others can't see what he's done. I can't show them without answers. Answers Sancho has. What else can I do?"

"I don't know," Delia replied, "but I can't let you throw your life away."

"What does that mean?"

"It means, I'm sorry."

Before he could stop her, Delia snatched a washing basin up off the bench and heaved it into a cluster of clay ewers on a far table. The pottery shattered and fell, stridently offending the calm of night. Jackal flinched at the tumult, then froze, staring at Delia.

"Go," she said.

Voices were already echoing hollowly through the walls of the brothel. The rushing footsteps would not be far behind.

Baring his teeth in a silent snarl, Jackal fled the bathhouse and ran to the fence. Scrambling up the side, he reached the top and found Delia had followed him out. She placed a hand on his calf and looked up at him imploringly.

"Keep the girl safe," she insisted. "Keep Oats and Fetching close to you. Keep yourself safe."

Meeting her gaze, Jackal nodded before dropping over the far side of the fence. He was sprinting as soon as his feet struck the dust. Rough voices sounded in the courtyard before he had gone a dozen strides. They questioned Delia, but the words were lost to the pounding of his blood as he ran for the cover of the rocks.

Fetching met him halfway, her stockbow covering his escape. As soon as he was past her, she spun and caught up, but said nothing until they were safely hunkered down amongst the boulders.

"Did you get to the flesh-peddling fuck?"

Jackal shook his head. "No. We need to get back to Oats and the hogs. The cavaleros might be following soon."

"Might?"

Jackal was not about to explain to Fetching why Delia had given him up. Instead, he motioned insistently for them to get moving, using the necessity of speed to avoid answering. They hurried through the night, hopping boulders and hot-heeling over scrubland. Skidding down the side of a gulch they reached Oats, standing sentry over the Tine and the hogs.

"What happened?" the big thrice asked.

"Woke the cavaleros," Jackal replied quickly, throwing a leg over Hearth's back. "We need to ride."

Fetching was already mounted, the elf girl sitting demurely in the saddle in front of her.

Oats frowned. "What about the mud plower?"

Jackal shot an aggravated look at him. "What?"

"The wizard," Oats clarified. "Don't you want to wait on him?"

Jackal cast a look around. In his haste to be gone, he had not noticed that one hog stood without a rider.

"Where did he go?" Jackal demanded.

Oats gave an innocent shrug. "Sancho's."

"The fuck?" Fetch said.

"He left not long after you two," Oats explained, his voice growing angry as he became defensive. "He said it was part of the plan. Figured you knew!"

"Knew what, Oats?" Jackal was nearly shouting. "That he was going to go off on his own mysterious errand while you sat here and composed poems for Ugfuck?"

"What was I supposed to do?"

"Try and stop him," Fetch suggested.

"He breathes burning bugs," Oats told her sharply. "I don't tangle with that!"

"Forget it," Fetching said. "Let's just go!"

Jackal was inclined to agree with her, but before he could make a decision, Crafty came skipping awkwardly down the side of the gully, his gut jostling beneath his robes.

"Apologies," the wizard said breathlessly as he approached. "We can be off now."

"What were you doing?" Jackal barked.

Crafty was now astride his barbarian and mopping at his brow with a silk scarf.

"Oh," he replied airily. "I went inside the pleasure house."

Oats issued an incredulous laugh. "Did you just duck in for a fuck?"

"Truly," the wizard said, fanning himself. "One does have needs."

Oats looked confused. "I thought you were backy?"

Jackal was neither amused nor bewildered. He just wanted to be gone. But Fetch's suspicions were screaming.

"That place was dead for the night," she said. "Who did you find willing to open her legs so late? Especially to a half-orc, when the cavaleros are lodging there to keep us out?"

"Eva," Crafty replied simply, his cheeks billowing out with every breath.

"Eva?"

Oats grunted a laugh. "Oh, *she'd* do it."

Jackal hesitated. Could the wizard truly have gotten into the brothel, found a willing woman, bedded her, and gotten out without being seen? There was certainly time; Jackal had waited under Delia's window for quite a span.

"Jackal!" Fetching's voice cut through his thoughts.

"We'll sort it later," he said. "We need to move."

"No need to rush," Crafty said, retrieving a skin from his bag and removing the stopper to take a long drink. "I took pains against any pursuit during my leaving."

"More fucking magic?" Oats inquired, his face wary, but his voice appreciative.

"Friend Oats," Crafty winked, "there is little mystical about ten incontinent horses. If the frails, as you all say, want to give chase, they will be doing so on their own feet." Popping the stopper back into the skin with the heel of his hand, the wizard gestured. "Shall we?"

Jackal looked into the night. "Let's ride."

"Where?" Oats asked.

Jackal thought a moment. He needed to get his arm fixed, and quickly. He was going to need both hands if he had any hopes of wrestling this mess into submission.

"To Zirko," he said simply.

Oats's face went slack. "Brother, I don't know . . ."

"Are you loon-brained?" Fetching said. "That little shit won't help you."

"I have no choice!" Jackal snapped, his rage at Delia's actions boiling over. He held his injured arm forth, gritting his teeth as he spoke to keep from screaming. "I can barely feel it anymore, Fetch! It's gone too long. You want I should let Grocer cut it off? Because that's all there is left unless the priest helps me. You don't have to come, but I am riding for Strava."

Fetch's jaw hardened as he spoke, but her gaze softened a touch. "He'll demand a price."

"I know."

Fetching chewed on his response for a moment. "Take the Tine. I'll take point. Oats, rearguard."

The thrice nodded.

Fetching relinquished the elf, not bothering to hide her enthusiasm to be rid of the extra rider. The Tine was less pleased, clinging to Fetch's saddle for a moment. The trepidation was brief, however, and a few gentle words from Jackal, coupled with the less-than-patient shoves from Fetching, succeeded in bringing her over to Hearth's back. Using his injured arm to hold the girl steady about her narrow waist, Jackal took hold of the barbarian's mane with his other hand and put heel to hog.

Behind him, he could hear Crafty and Oats jesting back and forth.

"So . . . you *do* favor women?"

"What is the expression here? 'Any port in a storm?' I think you understand."

"Ah. Well . . . you need a new saying, then. Like, 'Any ass in the night.' Because it's all the same in the dark, yeah?"

"Well, not all the same. I am certain I would have known if it was the buttocks of, say, a strapping thrice-blood."

"Rein up there, wizard. I ain't backy. Though if I was, you can be sure I wouldn't be the . . . backy one, or whatever."

"No, I am certain that is true."

There was a long pause, then Oats's voice rumbled again, his words slow with bemused pondering.

"Eva does like it between the cheeks, though. Course, it's extra."

Crafty giggled. "Butt of course!"

Kicking his heels into Hearth, Jackal rode farther ahead, trying to leave Oats and Crafty's laughter behind. Fetching was somewhere in the night, scouting far enough ahead that she was lost from view. Jackal quickly settled into the rhythm of riding double and tried to keep his attention on the shadowy landscape for signs of trouble, but his head swam with the effort of unraveling the events of the past days. Thinking was difficult. Now that he had voiced the truth about his arm aloud, it seemed the wound was quickly worsening, eager to lend his words credence. Every one of Hearth's steps sent a pulse of pain through his swollen arm, but the pain was better than the creeping, queasy numbness. Sickened and sweating, Jackal rode through the night, his every effort soon bent to staying in the saddle.

Chapter 11

THE HALFLINGS LIVED IN THE TOMB OF THEIR GODS. LITTLE more than a large hill of rotting dirt crowned with a crumbling tower, Strava was a canker on the already unfortunate face of the flatlands. The entire construction was a decrepit, colorless sight, yet its stunt-limbed stewards revered it as a holy place.

Jackal likened religion to madness. He had heard that in the north, in the great cities of Hispartha, there were more temples than well-fed children, that a hundred faceless gods received the wealth of the nobles and the fearful pleas of the peasants. He found that difficult to imagine, but Delia, Ignacio, and others had assured him it was true. Thankfully, such belief was all but unknown in Ul-wundulas. Perhaps the badlands were gods-forsaken, but Jackal preferred to think that the Lots were home to those who had no need of invisible old men, dog-headed demons, and sour-faced crones. Here, faith was better placed in a strong mount, a loaded stockbow, and a few solid companions.

Currently, Jackal had two of the three. His stockbow was lost to the marsh, but at least Hearth was beneath him and his friends were at his side. They all stared with reddened eyes at Strava, squinting against the sun that rose beyond the jagged tower. The ride had been long, and close to centaur territory. Fortune was smiling, however, and no horse-cocks came galloping out of the shadows, bellowing for blood.

"Remarkable," Crafty said, shielding his eyes with a hand at his brow as he peered at the tower.

"Give me the Kiln any day," Fetching groused. "I hate this place. Like a damn carcass, all those little black shits wriggling in and out."

"All right," Jackal cut in. "I need help here, so no more insults. That includes 'little black shits.' Oats, who is their god? I don't want a stump because you two pissed on our tongues."

"Belico," Oats answered dutifully, "but they also call him . . ." The thrice's face scrunched, struggling to recall the name, but Fetching came to his rescue.

"The Master Slave," she said, her voice adopting a bored tone as she recited facts quickly. "He was human a thousand years ago, and a great warrior. Fought some gods and won, but he could not have done it without his stumpy servant."

Jackal gave her a pointed look.

"Without his *halfling* servant," Fetch corrected herself begrudgingly.

"And the servant's name?" Jackal pressed.

Fetch looked at him like he was dull-witted. "Zirko. They're all named that."

"Just the high priest," Jackal told her. "Oats?"

"Belico asked the first Zirko how he could reward him, and the little fucker—"

Jackal threw up a hand. "Hells . . ."

"Sorry," Oats said, trying not to grin. "Zirko asked for . . . a wife. To return home. And a people of his own."

"That is not correct."

It was Crafty who had spoken and all eyes drifted toward him.

"Wife. Home. People," the wizard repeated, his gaze never leaving the distant tower. "These Zirko took for himself only after he was granted his true reward. The gift he requested from Belico, so the halflings claim, was 'Master, I would have you now be as I was.' With those words, the diminutive slave placed a god under his command."

Jackal nodded. "You want to finish?"

Crafty faced him then, his thick cheeks gathered up above a smile. "Do you truly think I do not know the rest, friend Jackal?"

"I figure we are about to find out," Jackal said, staring the fat wizard down.

With a shrug, Crafty turned his attention back to Strava.

"Belico granted his faithful slave's wish, and put his power at Zirko's service. Zirko took the most beautiful of women as wife. She was not stunted, yet the new prophet declared that all her children would be as their father. From Zirko's loins flowed the halfling race."

"And all the stumpies praised his balls, ever after," Fetching scoffed.

"Indeed," Crafty replied, oblivious to her mockery. "They call him the Hero Father, but it is Belico that they chiefly worship, and he only that they recognize as a god."

Fetch stretched her back in the saddle and expelled an impatient breath. "We all caught up on waddler religion? Good. Let's ride. Get this done."

Kicking at her hog, Fetching rode forward, winding through some scrub before heading directly across the plains toward Strava.

"I don't think the halflings like being called waddlers," Oats said, purposefully needling Jackal. Grinning, the big mongrel clicked his tongue at Ugfuck and rode after Fetching.

Jackal went more slowly. Sometime before dawn, the Tine girl had fallen asleep and he did not wish to wake her if he could help it. Her head rested against the arm he was using to guide Hearth, while his other held her steady in the saddle. After hours of this, his limbs were cramped, the muscles screaming at him for a change in position. He endured the growing physical discomfort in order to have some peace in his mind. When she was awake, the elf's mute placidity was unnerving. Jackal hated that she feared him. It was prideful, but he had freed her from a true terror and felt that her continued dismay somehow linked him to the Sludge Man's depravity.

"Truly it is a wonder," Crafty's voice broke through his brooding.

Jackal turned and found the wizard riding beside him. Crafty motioned at Strava.

"It is said that before he ascended to godhood, the warlord Belico commanded his remaining men to ride to Ul-wundulas, the only land he had not trodden. Along the way each man was to fill his helm with earth and drag a stone upon his shield. In this way the mound was raised and its tower constructed, with the conquered bones of distant lands."

Jackal grunted. "I've heard the legend before."

"Indeed," Crafty replied amiably. "I am impressed with your knowledge, friend Jackal."

"It's important to know enough about the halflings' religion to avoid offending them," Jackal said. "Folk who hold to gods are often prickly."

"Prickly. It is a good word. One which describes you these last hours, I think."

"You got something you want to say, wizard, say it."

"You fear to trust me."

Jackal turned to look at Crafty. His pudgy face was still smiling behind his manicured beard.

"You don't give straight answers," Jackal told him. "Not about why you rode with me into the marsh, and not about why you went into that brothel. You didn't bugger any whore last night, no matter what you claim."

"This is so," Crafty admitted calmly.

"You want to take a run at the truth?" Jackal asked, his sour mood turning the question into a threat.

"I went in to ensure you came out. That is also the reason I went with you to the marsh. Both are the truth."

"If you make me ask *why* at the end of every one of your statements, Crafty, I'm going to knock your fat ass off that hog."

The bead dangling from the wizard's beard braid danced as he chuckled. "I simply want what you want, friend Jackal. You leading the Grey Bastards. And before you strike me, the *why* of the matter is, I too wish for something. My hope is that you, and the hoof I will help you claim, will help me when the time comes. But today, I am at your service. I hope that will suffice and keep your pricks from my flesh."

"Prickles," Jackal corrected, smiling despite his best efforts.

He let the matter drop, trusting in his gut. It had told him Crafty was hiding something about the brothel and been right. Now it was telling him the wizard was being truthful, if not entirely forthcoming. Jackal did not know what Crafty wanted from the Bastards, and right now, he didn't care. He had sworn no oaths, made no bargains, and was not beholden to aid the wizard in whatever ambitions he pursued. For now, Jackal had a powerful sorcerer on his side, one who wanted to help him replace the Claymaster. Best not to check the hog's tusks too carefully. His most immediate concerns were ahead of him, where a cadre of horsemen was converging on Fetching and Oats.

"Are those . . . ?" Crafty began.

"Unyars," Jackal confirmed. "The descendants of Belico's army.

They are fiercely loyal to the halflings. Come on. We better catch up before Fetch says something that will earn her an arrow in the lungs."

No longer concerned with the elf girl's slumber, Jackal urged Hearth into a quick trot. The jostling woke her. As her head came up off his arm, her weight no longer pressed against his torso, which was both a relief and a disappointment. Jackal could not see her face, but he could sense her taking the situation in quickly, her attention fixing on the eight riders now surrounding Oats and Fetching. As always, the Unyars had their recurve bows in hand, but Jackal was relieved to see no arrows nocked.

He slowed Hearth's pace as he drew near, carefully riding between the horses to join his companions. Crafty followed his lead.

The Unyars' horses allowed them to sit taller than the half-orcs upon their hogs, and the men stared down with their keen, slanted eyes. They were a stocky breed, shorter than the average Hisparthan, their tanned skin tinged with yellow. Their broad chests were covered with scale armor, and their belts hung heavy with full quivers, stout throwing axes, and curved swords. Jackal found their leader by the presence of the trumpet hanging from his saddle horn.

"We are members of the Grey Bastards," Jackal told the man. "We come to you, humbly, to seek the wisdom of Zirko, high priest of Belico."

The Unyar swept the group with his unblinking gaze, lingering for a moment on the elf girl. The sight of her caused the man to pull uncertainly at his long, wispy mustachio. Jackal pretended not to notice, and waited with an open expression.

At last, the leader hissed and pulled his mount's reins around. His riders turned their own steeds toward Strava, herding Jackal and his companions across the plain. It was always unsettling to be escorted by these horsemen. Their skill at mounted archery was nearly as legendary as their divine warlord. Just these surrounding eight men could fill Jackal and his crew full of arrows, killing hog and rider, in seconds.

The Unyars were the oldest hoof in the Lots. They had dwelt in Ulwundulas for centuries before Hispartha claimed the land. The hill and tower of Strava were already ancient when the first armies marched down from the north. Halfling pilgrims of Belico had long wandered the world in search of relics from their god's time as a man, and Hispartha's kings had hosted them many times. So they decreed the shrine would benefit from Hispartha's protection, but was not governed by its laws. During the Orc Incursion, the Unyars made for indispensable allies, acting as skirmishers and harrowing the thicks across the plains. But their loyalty lay with their god and the halflings who served as his priests. They kept their home safe, first and foremost. No orc army ever came close to reaching Strava. At the end of the war, Hispartha exempted the lands surrounding Strava from the lot draw, in order not to anger Belico and his devotees. The halflings and their Unyar protectors were a neutral, if not wholly unbiased, presence in Ul-wundulas. Only the centaurs made war on them, and only during the Betrayer Moon, when all were prey.

Soon, Strava loomed above. Gazing up, Jackal had the dizzying perception that the tower was tumbling over, the moving clouds behind adding to the illusion. It may once have been square, but the winds of centuries had gnawed at the stones, countless rains dissolving the mortar. Up close, the entire thing looked ready to collapse, as did the desiccated hill on which the tower sat.

A sprawling village lay about the base of Strava, huts and horse corrals radiating from the hill. Human children herded goats and thin, grey steers from pens, while women continued the various chores that had occupied them since dawn. One in every three seemed to be fletching arrows. All the men with two good legs and a straight back were ahorse, riding off to hunt or patrol, or acting as sentry near the tower. Of the halflings, there was no sign. All would be inside Strava, within the tower or beneath the hill.

The riders escorted the hogs around the western slope and led them to an empty corral. The size and shape of the pen, as well as the small stable at one end, gave it the appearance of a training yard. The troughs outside the stable were full and the hogs went to them eagerly. The Unyars waited while Jackal and the others dismounted, and the leader gestured for them to shelter in the shade of the stable roof. Several women entered the corral, bearing jugs and wooden platters covered with linen. These proved to be full of goat's milk and meat. Just as soon as they had set the victuals down upon the ground, the women left. The horsemen tarried only a moment longer. The leader nodded once to Jackal, then followed his men.

"Think we're in for a bit of a wait," Oats declared through a mouthful of roast goat.

Jackal merely nodded as he stretched his legs, keeping an eye on the elf. She went and stood in the back of the shallow stable, in the deepest shadows. Crafty followed her in, offering one of the jugs. She took it without hesitation and drank deeply, but with care, not spilling a drop down her chin. Jackal felt a bump at his good arm and looked to find Fetching nudging him with a platter. Seeing the grease-slick meat, Jackal's hunger awoke and he took a heavy piece between his fingers.

"Courteous of them not to put a guard on us," he said before taking his first bite.

Fetch snorted. "You know better than that, Jack."

He hummed agreement and nodded. He did know better.

They spent the morning resting in the shade. Oats tended to the hogs, inspecting each one carefully before finding a spot in the stable to lie down upon his bedroll. Within seconds, the brute was snoring, drawing a well-used glare of annoyance from Fetching. Crafty sat with his back to the wall, his thick legs drawn up beneath him and his eyes closed.

"You got her?" Jackal asked Fetch, cocking his head at the elf, now curled up with her back turned.

"Sleep," Fetch insisted.

Giving her a grateful squeeze on the knee, Jackal lay back against his saddle and was asleep before he could take a second deep breath.

He awoke gently, slowly, his eyes regaining focus upon a small figure kneeling at his side. The bandages were free from his broken arm, though he had not felt them being removed, and the figure was probing gently at his bones with stubby fingers the color of richly fertile earth.

"Apologies," Zirko said without taking his eyes away from his task. "I tried not to wake you."

Jackal said nothing, watching the halfling as he worked. His long, twisted black locks were kept away from his face by a band of heavy, undyed linen. Limpid green eyes danced, accompanying his hands in the inspection.

"This is a bad break, Jackal of the Grey Bastards," Zirko said at last, his voice surprisingly deep for one so small. "And you have not been kind to it. Two moons, perhaps more, before it will mend, and even then, perhaps not straight."

"That's why I'm here," Jackal replied. "I need it healed now."

Zirko blew a heavy breath from his nostrils. He looked Jackal in the eye for the first time, searching his face. The halfling said nothing for a long while. At last he stood and walked to the edge of the shadows, which had grown long. The sky above the corral was instilled with the colors of dusk.

Jackal sat up and glanced around. Everyone was awake, and he got the embarrassing notion that he was the only one who had slept through the high priest's arrival. Oats squatted on his haunches, clearly not wanting to loom over Zirko, whose head wouldn't even reach the thrice's crotch.

The halfling appeared to be pondering, his back turned. His robes were simple and unadorned, as were the sandals upon his feet. At his side hung a wide, straight-bladed thrusting sword, fashioned in the style of the old Imperium. Knowing the halflings, it was probably *from* the old Imperium. Waiting at the far side of the corral were two other halflings, their skin and hair as dark as the high priest's, their garb equally austere. Eventually, Zirko turned around again, his hand stroking at the ring of close-cropped beard surrounding his protuberant lips.

"I am trying to recall the last time a half-orc placed himself in the hands of Great Belico."

Oats answered. "It was that member of the Cauldron Brotherhood, wasn't it? The one who took an orc spear in the gut. Can't remember his name."

"Rinds," Fetching said.

"That was him," Oats agreed.

Zirko held up a finger in a show of remembrance. "Ah, yes. And he has stood with us here every Betrayer since, in addition to the traditional rider provided by the Cauldron Brotherhood. I wonder, will your Claymaster be as incensed over this as the Brotherhood's chieftain? The mongrel hoofs have often chafed at giving up one rider. Two is often unthinkable."

Jackal tried not to grimace.

It was all part of an arrangement made at the end of the Incursion, long before he wore a brigand. Every half-orc hoof sent a rider to stand with the Unyars against the centaurs during their unfathomable rampages. In exchange, Zirko gave them warning of the arrival of the next Betrayer Moon. The diminutive priest had done what Hispartha's keenest star charters could not, and discovered the secret to predicting the moon's chaotic shift.

Since the horse-cocks first came to Ul-wundulas from the broken islands of the Deluged Sea, they had celebrated the Betrayer in an orgy of bloodshed. As a boy, Jackal had wondered if the moon's suddenly changing face had occurred prior to the centaurs' migration, but none had ever been able to tell him. The Betrayer, and the centaurs, had been residents of the badlands centuries before he began asking questions, and were long-accepted evils. And evil they were.

There was no strategy in the centaur attacks, no goal other than slaughter and rapine to please their heartless gods. The raids were brutal, unpredictable, yet more often than not, the Kiln was left completely unmolested, the ill-omened moon giving way to dawn without one sighting of even a single 'taur. But for every settlement ignored, another was set upon without mercy. A hoof going without Zirko's warning trusted to luck. And luck had been fickle in the past.

Just six years ago, the Rutters had refused to send a rider to Strava to fight during an impending Betrayer. The following summer, Zirko sent them no message of the next coming Moon. The Rutters were caught unawares and, though their stronghold held, their neighboring village was reduced to ash and corpse flies. The hoof tried to recover, but Ul-wundulas was a harsh land. With no crops, no bedwarmers, no children, the Rutters had been forced to disband, its members absorbed by the remaining hoofs. Polecat had been a Rutter before he rode with the Bastards.

"I need this, Zirko," Jackal said. "If I must stand with you every Betrayer, if that is your price, then say it."

This seemed to sadden the halfling. He dipped his head and smiled morosely.

"How small and covetous we must seem to you," Zirko said softly. When he looked up again, there was a softness in his face Jackal had never seen before. The expression was almost self-pitying. "I know you think us niggardly. But the burdens of my people, and the demands of my god, are unknown to you. And they exist above your inner, shallow judgments. You do not know what it is we sacrifice each time we petition our god to heal an unbeliever."

"Sacrifice is served with every meal in the Lots," Jackal replied. "We all bleed here. That I *do* believe."

"And why should we entreat our god further for you, half-orc?" There was no malice in Zirko's response, just a grim curiosity.

"Only you can answer that," Jackal told him. "As you say, I am ignorant of your burdens. But that does not mean I cannot help alleviate them, given the chance."

The high priest stood calmly, taking in the occupants of the stable. At last, he motioned for his attendants. The pair of halflings crossed the corral, taking up position on their master's flanks. Both were female, their coarse black hair shaved short, almost to the scalp.

"I wonder, Jackal," Zirko mused, "are you willing to receive my god's help without first knowing the full cost? I tell you now, standing with us against the centaurs shall not be all the Master Slave demands."

Fetching breathed in sharply, preparing to cast a barb, but Jackal turned and silenced her with a look. He looked Zirko dead in the eyes.

"If it means my arm whole again," he declared, "then, yes."

"Aw, hells," Oats groaned.

"Very well," Zirko said. He turned and retrieved several objects from his attendants. They were three ceramic jars, the largest barely the size of a proper cup. The halfling priest set them upon the ground in front of Jackal, in descending order of size.

"Fill this with your urine," Zirko instructed, pointing to the largest vessel. "The next with blood. And the last with your seed."

Jackal frowned, but it was Oats who voiced the question.

"Is that the payment?"

"No," Zirko replied simply, still watching Jackal.

"But it's required?" Jackal asked.

The little man flashed a white smile. "Oh, yes. The hardest of these to give says a great deal about a man, yes?"

Without further comment, Zirko left the stable and headed across the corral. His attendants stayed behind, waiting expectantly.

"Shit," Jackal swore under his breath as he stood. Turning around, he found Fetching standing very close. She wore a small smile beneath hungry eyes.

"I figure," she said throatily, "you can manage the first jar on your own. But I would be willing to help with the other."

She took his good hand in her own and began guiding it to one of the full breasts beneath her linen shirt. Not caring that the others were watching, Jackal opened his fingers eagerly. He grunted as pain sliced down his palm, and snatched his hand back. Fetching had moved so fast, he had not even seen her draw the knife.

"There you are," she said, laughing freely. "No need to thank me."

Oats was chuckling too. Clenching his fist and his teeth, Jackal glared at both of them.

"Better not waste it, brother," Oats advised, eyeballing the jars.

Squatting down, Jackal squeezed blood from the wound into the middle vessel. He could feel his pulse throbbing in his hand as the crimson flow quickly filled the jar. Crafty offered him a bandage and Jackal began wrapping his lacerated palm.

"Two bad hands is going to make pissing a challenge," Oats offered sympathetically, "and that last jar a damn nightmare."

Jackal gave Fetch a withering look. "You really are a cunt sometimes."

"Shit, Jack," she replied, looking genuinely guilty. "I didn't think about that." When no pardon was forthcoming, and all she continued to receive were condemning stares, Fetching shrugged deeply and raised her voice. "Sorry! What the fuck do I know about milking a cock? I don't think about it all the time like you two."

"Perhaps we should give friend Jackal some peace," Crafty suggested, motioning toward the quickly darkening corral.

The wizard coaxed the group out of the stable, giving the Tine girl a kindly smile as she passed. Jackal tried not to look at her, out of some boyish fear that she might have understood why he was being left alone. Zirko's attendants removed themselves farther as well, but he noticed they continued to face the stable.

Despite a youth spent throttling his cod, Jackal struggled. His injuries hindered him, of course, but the greatest difficulty resided in his mind. He conjured the feel of Delia on his lap in the bathhouse, but the initial swell quickly receded. Jackal found himself wishing he had joined Oats in spying on the she-elf bathing. He imagined what he had missed, but that brought up thoughts of Fetching and his newly sliced hand, which made him recall her kicking his nuts. This withered him almost completely. Fortunately, the memory also dredged up his interrupted encounter with Cissy, her buttocks bared atop a barrel and her desire for roughness. In his mind's eye, he did everything Fetch had prevented, his fantasy going further than even Cissy might have allowed.

When the third jar was out of the way, pissing in the biggest became only a matter of time.

The halflings took the vessels away, to what purpose Jackal did not know, and tried not to dwell upon. Oats and Fetching were still amused by the whole ordeal, but their grins and jibes masked a deeper concern for what unknown bargain Jackal had just struck. Crafty, however, remained worryingly blank.

As night fell fully and the moon rose higher, there was no sign of Zirko or any of his servants. A trio of Unyar women brought food and water, but otherwise, the corral became an unguarded cage.

Eventually, Oats joined Jackal at the fence, where he had taken up a torturous vigil of Strava's star-banishing shadow.

"Fetch and I are gonna sleep," the thrice said quietly. "Crafty's got the point-ear."

"Good." It was all Jackal could think to answer. He waited, knowing his friend had more to say.

"We have to return to the Kiln tomorrow, Jack. Gotta let the hoof know we're all still alive."

"Yeah," Jackal agreed slowly. "At sunrise, you and Fetching go. Crafty and I will follow with the girl when we can."

"You really going to bring her back? What's the chief going to do when he sees?"

"Exactly," Jackal said. "What? His reaction will tell us something. Hopefully enough."

"And if his reaction is to kill her? And you?"

Jackal had been thinking on that. "He doesn't have to know what we suspect. Hells, all he'll know for certain is what we tell him. Sludge Man tried to kill us when asked about the horse. We put him down and rescued his elf slave. Whatever more there is will be for him to betray. We just have to hope he does and we are quick enough to take advantage."

A rumbling sigh poured out of Oats. Briefly, he pawed the back of Jackal's head, giving it an affectionately rough shake before walking back to the stable.

Hearth trotted over, rooting around noisily before settling down in the dust. Soon, the hog was grunting and snuffling in his sleep. Jackal sank down to the ground, exhausted to the point of feeling sick. His broken arm had been completely taken over by the frightening numbness. Concentrating on the dull, dead feeling made Jackal nauseous, so he tried to put it out of mind. He lay back on Hearth, his head and shoulders resting against the hog's barrel of a belly. The rhythm of the barbarian's breathing quickly pulled Jackal's eyelids down.

Chapter 12

Jackal awoke coughing. The air was musty, heavy with a mixture of unpleasant odors. Hearth must have moved on in the night, for Jackal was flat on his back. Blinking against the lingering confusion of sleep, he sat up, nearly gagging on the morass sinking into his lungs. The stench of smoke was strongest, with foul undercurrents of rust and decaying leather.

Zirko stood before him.

"You have grown strong, Jackal of the Grey Bastards."

It was damn dark, the sky devoid of moon and stars. The high priest was visible only because of the torch in his hand.

"You remain companioned with a thrice-blood and that singular female," Zirko continued, "yet now you add a wizard and an elf slave to your followers. Some would call that madness."

Squinting against the glare of the torch and his own befuddlement, Jackal stood.

Zirko turned and his light revealed the stone arch of a low tunnel just behind him.

Jackal recoiled as his perception was violently altered. He had thought himself in the corral, under the vast openness of the sky, yet now he realized he was underground, hemmed in by rank dirt and threatening rocks. The oppressive air, allied with the reek of a thousand old graves, began to drown him. Spitting and coughing, fighting not to retch, fighting to breathe, Jackal struggled amidst the undeniable leaden blackness.

Zirko's voice reached through the panic.

"There were many who deemed Belico mad when he rode out to conquer his neighbors with only two brothers, fourteen men, and one dwarfish slave."

"Where . . . ?" Jackal sputtered before succumbing to dry heaves.

"In the end, none dared call him madman. Warlord. Scourge. God. These were the words now on the tongues of the world."

Snarling furiously against his own weakness, Jackal forced his body to obey.

"Where have you brought me?" he demanded.

"Come," Zirko gestured toward the tunnel. "Allow me to show you."

Clammy with sweat, but breathing easier, Jackal took a step toward the halfling. Zirko waited patiently until he was within a few steps, then entered the yawning mouth. Jackal had to duck to follow.

The dragging torchlight shone raw inside the narrow throat. Timber and mortared stone held the earth at bay, though the struggle was an old one and small avalanches of dry soil fell through fissures in the brickwork. They walked in silence for a long time, and Jackal's legs began to burn from the effort of propelling him while holding a squat. Numerous passages intersected with theirs, sinister gullets of shadow opening irregularly from left and right. Zirko made several turns and Jackal soon despaired of ever finding his way back to the sky.

Occasionally, they passed other halflings in the side tunnels, each halting and bowing their head as Zirko went by. Every one bore a torch and some other oddment, held carefully, reverently. Jackal noted weapons and armor ridden with rust or verdigris, some little more than misshapen lumps. Several held silken bags or small coffers, their contents a mystery. Most, however, carried bones. After witnessing the fourth halfling cradling a skull to his breast, Jackal avoided looking into the other tunnels and focused on Zirko's back.

At last, they emerged into a roughly circular chamber. The ceiling was domed, allowing Jackal to stand upright. The chamber might have once been quite sizable, but heaps of refuse piled against the curved wall intruded far onto the floor, choking the space. Treasure lay alongside trash; broken pottery scattered amidst golden urns, dry-rotted saddles perched atop gaping chests of coins, broken bows lying on burst sacks of gems. Atop it all was a grubby film of dust and patina and smelly age. In the center of the spoiling hoard lay an angled stone bier supporting the skeleton of a man. Fully dressed in moldering armor and surrounded by pitted weapons, the reclining bones faced the tunnel.

Zirko picked his way through the debris and stood next to the bier, holding his torch aloft to better bathe the remains in flickering light.

"This was Attukhan," the halfling said, his voice hushed with respect. "One of the original fourteen men with the courage to join Belico."

Jackal lingered at the mouth of the tunnel and said nothing.

"Your humors tell me that you share much with Attukhan, Jackal," Zirko went on. "Courage, ambition, a thoughtless confidence that some would call foolishness. It will be a good match. I pray you are worthy of it."

"Worthy of what?" Jackal ventured.

Ignoring the question, Zirko motioned at the contents of the tomb with a languid finger. "Do you know how long it took my people to find all this? How many halfling pilgrims wandered the world, tirelessly seeking the objects Attukhan possessed in life? How many returned empty-handed, their faith in splinters? How many . . . did not return at all?"

Jackal shook his head.

Zirko smiled. "No. And nor do you care. Why would you?"

Carefully, the halfling reached toward the bier with his free hand, winding his fingers beneath the skeleton's left vambrace, and lifted the forearm bones free.

"Perhaps," Zirko said, holding the bones close to his chest, "it is enough to say that your request requires something most precious."

"I told you, I was willing to pay the price," Jackal declared.

"Because you do not know what it is. You find charging into unknown danger simple, perhaps even comforting. But I wonder, would you be so bold staring it full in the face?"

Jackal felt his patience unraveling. "You asked if I would make a blind bargain and I agreed. Now you question my grit! Heal me or don't, priest, but spare me your insights into my nature."

Zirko took a deep breath. "Did you know that the first Zirko was born in the south? In Dhar'gest, that the orcs now claim?"

Jackal had heard something of the sort, but did not remember it until now. He was growing tired of questions, and was in no mood to voice an answer. The high priest did not appear to expect one.

"Before he was taken by slavers and sold to the Imperium," the halfling related, "Zirko was the stunted son of a lion hunter. His father traded him to the flesh markets when it was obvious he would never grow taller than a boy. Years later, he was given to a minor steppelands chieftain in tribute for some small service. He would eventually help that chieftain attain godhood. Yet still, what he wanted most was to return to the veldts of his childhood.

"When at last he did return, Zirko was the patriarch of his own tribe, the leader of the Unyar horsemen, and prophet of the god worshipped by both man and halfling. His former people, however, would never see his splendor. During Zirko's long years as a slave, the orcs had overrun his homeland. Calling upon the Master Slave, Zirko bade the god destroy the slaughterers of his birth-kin, but Belico, fresh in his divinity, could not combat the ancient powers fed by the sacrificial fires of the orcs. Zirko was forced to flee north, across the Gut, and came here to Ul-wundulas. During the journey, he commanded the Unyars to fill their helmets with dirt and drag stones upon their shields, so that he could build Strava from the soul of his home."

Jackal realized too late that he was grinning.

"Is something amusing?" Zirko asked mildly.

"No," Jackal told him. "Sorry. Crafty had the story wrong. I was looking forward to gloating."

Zirko chuckled. "To sorcerers, all knowledge is a weapon. In their haste to fill their quiver, they often do not look to see if the shafts are straight."

"So why tell me?"

"In order for you to understand the price," Zirko replied, his smile vanishing. "I have no desire for trickery. I simply could not speak terms in front of your companions. Your hoof sister was likely to try and kill me were she to hear the cost of my help."

"Name it, then."

"There are two prices. The one you must pay to me, you already know. The second is due to mighty Belico."

"Speak, priest!"

"For me, you must stand with us here at Strava every Betrayer Moon. Do you agree?"

"Done."

Zirko fixed him with a dubious squint. "You answer quickly, Jackal. I thought loyalty to one's hoof was absolute. You would abandon your brothers on the night they will likely need you most?"

"They are Bastards," Jackal said. "They can endure a few nights without me."

"But can you endure a life without them?" Zirko asked quietly.

Jackal hesitated. Something in the halfling's voice made his guts go cold. The little black man looked around slowly, calmly taking in the uncountable litter of relics.

"My namesake never relinquished his desire for vengeance. After long years, Zirko had a revelation. As a god, Belico could not contend with the orcs, but as a man there was no army that he could not defeat. So, my pilgrims dedicate their lives to collecting the vestiges of Belico's host, bringing them all here to his temple. When he witnesses the power of his mortal life assembled once more, he will return to flesh and bring his men back from death. Belico will ride again and spill orc blood until there is none left to stain the world."

Jackal saw the disturbing passion of belief spread throughout Zirko's entire body as he spoke. His short stature no longer mattered. At the center of his own zeal, the halfling was a formidable, controlled storm. Had he been surrounded by thicks, the priest would have cut them all down with ease, Jackal had no doubt. The thought of a hundred temples in Hispartha was suddenly not so difficult to imagine, if this was what faith in the faceless could do to even the smallest man.

Holding the bones out at arm's length, Zirko approached.

"I will give you the arm of Attukhan. But you must pledge, here beneath holy Strava, that if the great god Belico returns while you still breathe, you will ride beside him in place of the champion whose bones made you whole. You must swear to renounce all loyalties and serve only the whim of the Master Slave. This is the price demanded by my god."

Jackal took a long time to answer, though he no longer felt any reluctance. This was a bargain that would never need to be honored. Gods were fables and men did not return from death. But Jackal took a moment to ensure his relief did not show. It was clear that Zirko believed what he said, but even lost inside his god's fervor, the priest was no fool. Too quick an answer might tip him off to Jackal's dubiety.

"I swear," Jackal said solemnly, "that if Belico returns during my life, I will serve him."

Zirko's torch began to gutter. In the flickering, failing light, Jackal saw the halfling open his hand and allow the forearm bones to fall to the floor of the tomb. They were both snapped in two. Blackness spilled down from the dome, charging the weakened flame and snuffing it out. Jackal was blind.

And then he opened his eyes.

The morning sky was newborn, still jaundiced before a proper sunrise. Hearth was warm and bristly against Jackal's skin. Groggy and stiff, he rolled and pushed himself up off the ground. Hearth went right on sleeping, only kicking a little at the disturbance. Looking across the corral, Jackal saw Fetching and Oats already saddling their barbarians. It looked like Crafty and the Tine girl were still asleep.

Jackal was halfway across the corral when he stopped, realizing what he had done. Out of old habit, he had placed both hands on the ground when he got up, pressing his full weight upward. Holding up his left arm, Jackal peered at it, flexing his fingers. There was no pain, no awful swelling or aching pressure. No nauseating numbness. The damn thing felt fine. Unwrapping the splint, Jackal scrutinized his arm further. His flesh was a little sour-smelling from sweating under the bindings, but otherwise normal. Shaking his hand rapidly at his side as he walked, Jackal came up behind Oats.

"We're riding out," the brute said, too busy with Ugfuck to turn around.

"We're all going," Jackal said.

Oats turned slowly, frowning, and Fetching looked up from her hog. Jackal raised his arm, showing them the back of his hand and wiggled his fingers.

"Well, that's done," Fetching muttered, and went back to securing her javelins.

Oats's face went slack with relief and puzzlement. "When the . . . ? What did he ask you for?"

"Nothing," Jackal replied. "Going to be spending every Betrayer here, like he said."

"Huh," Oats grunted. "Claymaster's going to piss venom."

"Let's go home," Jackal said, ignoring the last remark and clapping the thrice on the shoulder. He whistled shrilly across the corral, waking Hearth. The hog clambered to his hooves and trotted over. Jackal wasted no time getting him saddled. Crafty came and stood by just as he was giving the girth strap a final tug.

"So," the wizard said, "I gather a pact has been made?"

Jackal gave him a grin. "As solid as the one between you and me. Oh, and you were wrong about the helms full of dirt. It wasn't Belico who ordered the Unyars to do that. It was Zirko."

"Well, he would know," Crafty replied with airy amusement. "He was there."

Jackal threw out a small laugh. "The first Zirko was there."

"As you say," Crafty returned, already walking toward his barbarian.

"Fat-ass doesn't like to be wrong," Jackal told Hearth, still chuckling. Looking up he found the elf girl waiting within the stable, watching the preparations.

Fetch's spare riding leathers were too big for her, cinched about the waist with a length of dirty rope. The shirt was not so bad, though the elf filled it out far less than its owner. Jackal found himself noticing her hair. She must have allowed Fetch to cut it at the river, too foul from the swamp to properly clean. Injury and a worried mind had kept Jackal from noticing before, but now he was struck with the vibrant color, so black it was nearly blue. The way Fetching's knife had hacked it to just below the elf's jaw, gave her a ragged, wild appearance.

Realizing he was staring, Jackal turned away and mounted up.

"Oats," he called, "you got the point-ear."

Once the Tine was up on Ugfuck's back, they all rode out of the corral, finding a troop of horsemen waiting for them. Zirko was with them, astride an ass. Jackal and the others reined up.

"The Unyars will see you safely away," the priest told them.

"We thank you," Jackal replied, dipping his chin respectfully.

As the horsemen began escorting the hogs away, Zirko raised his hand toward Jackal.

"One last word before you go."

The troop did not stop, making it clear that the priest wanted time alone. Oats and Fetching stalled.

"Go on," Jackal told them. "I'll catch up."

Zirko waited until all the riders were out of earshot before speaking.

"I trust I will see you again."

"The Betrayer Moon," Jackal said. "So long as you warn of its coming, I will be here."

"Good," the priest replied. "Strava will be the safer for it. Take this too."

From a pouch at his belt, Zirko produced a leather packet and tossed it to Jackal.

"Tea leaves?" Jackal asked, sniffing the contents.

"They will help with the nausea."

"I don't feel sick."

"Not for you," Zirko said. "For your elf woman. Another month and she will need those brewed each morning."

Jackal felt his jaw go slack. "You think she's pregnant?"

"I know what she does not. Not yet."

"Fucking Sludge Man!" Jackal snarled.

Zirko clicked his tongue. "I am afraid her time is less than seven moons away. That is not the seed of any man in her belly."

"That filthy bog trotter is no man . . ."

Jackal trailed off, his brain coming to grips with what the halfling just said.

"Seven months? You mean . . . ?"

Zirko dipped his eyes in response.

Jackal ran his newly healed hand through his hair. The poor girl was carrying a half-orc.

Chapter 13

Hobnail was the first bastard they saw after riding through the Kiln's tunnel. He didn't raise his stockbow or an alarm, nor call for the slopheads to put Jackal in chains. His voice contained relief rather than rancor.

"Fuck all the hells," he swore, jogging over to help wrangle their hogs. "We figured you all for dead. Where's Oats?"

Jackal managed not to cast a surprised look at Fetching. They'd been preparing for a confrontation, not an easy welcome.

Hobnail took his hesitation for grave news. "Shit. Don't tell me he's—"

"Oats is well," Jackal cut in, swinging down from the saddle. "He's back at Winsome. Long overdue visit with his mother."

It was the truth. Oats hadn't been happy about it, but the Tine girl had to be left somewhere and Jackal could think of no better place than Beryl's. He was not about to bring her into the Kiln, not yet, and he couldn't leave her completely unguarded. That meant Oats got to play watchdog while being badgered and overfed.

"Well, you are long overdue a report to the chief," Hobnail told him, holding steady to one of Hearth's swine-yankers. "He was a cunt hair away from sending the hoof looking for you."

Jackal noticed that Hob's gaze drifted to Crafty while he spoke. So, the Claymaster was worried about his potential wizard. Likely the source of all the forbearance. Whatever the cause, Jackal wasn't going to waste the chance.

"Where's Mead?" he asked, hoping to all hells he wasn't out on patrol.

"Mucking about with the ovens, I think," Hob replied, looking perplexed. "You not hear me? Chief wants a word."

"I heard," Jackal said.

He nodded to Fetching and she hurried off toward the Kiln's central keep. Mead spoke the elf tongue. The notion was for Fetch to bring him to Winsome, to see if he could coax the Tine into talking, give them any clues toward the chief's hand in her capture. Mead had carried a stiff cod for Fetching ever since he was a slophead, so he wouldn't need much convincing to help. If he could provide a few more answers before Jackal went to the Claymaster, all the better.

Hobnail leaned in and grabbed Jackal around the elbow. "You going to tell me what the fuck is happening?"

Though not a thrice, Hob was big and wore a beard that he dyed red with rose madder. He stuck his face close, eyeballing Jackal with a burning look. Refusing to be cowed, Jackal grinned.

"You'll find out at table, Hob. Along with everyone else."

Hobnail released his hold, his face going slightly slack. "You're calling us together?"

Jackal gave Hob's shoulder a reassuring thump. The larger mongrel was off-balance with confusion. Best to keep him that way. Jackal kept his own questions coming.

"Any brothers out riding?"

Hobnail shook his head. "Only a few slops."

That was disappointing, but Jackal tried not to show it. He had been hoping at least one of the Bastards was ranging. There could be no table meet unless all the sworn members of the hoof were present. Now, any stalling that could be achieved would fall on Oats, Fetch, and Mead, but the Claymaster could order them to return from Winsome. And that's precisely what the plague-ridden tyrant would do, soon as he learned they were gone. Fortunately, Jackal had a shiny trinket to dangle.

By now, a group of slopheads had converged on the hogs, bringing skins full of water and wine to offer to the returning riders. Jackal accepted one, made sure it was water, and took a long pull. He waited until the slops were making enough of a fuss before giving Crafty a pointed look. The wizard gave the barest hint of a grin and sidled up next to Hobnail.

"I would like to offer apologies to your Claymaster for taking so unexpected a leave," Crafty said. "Would you take me to him?"

"Sure," Hob said, clearly uncomfortable addressing the stranger. He gave Jackal an almost apologetic look. "Chief is gonna want to talk to you, too."

"Just going to see to my hog, first," Jackal told him, motioning at the slops. "Can't damn well leave him with these twat lips."

"Don't I know," Hobnail agreed, and mock-lunged at one of the hopefuls, causing the youth to flinch. "See you in a small while, Jack."

As Hob led Crafty away across the yard, Jackal heard the wizard chatting amiably.

"Hobnail? So named because you are blunt, yet keep your feet in difficult situations?"

"Uh . . ."

"Or perhaps it is simply the shape of your penis which gave rise to the name?"

Grinning, Jackal hurried in the opposite direction, leaving Hearth in care of the slopheads. Despite his prejudices, he didn't have time to waste in the stables. On his way to the supply hall he saw Fetching and Mead riding toward the gatehouse tunnel.

Good. They would be in Winsome soon.

Of course, it all hinged on the Tine girl actually talking, but that was out of Jackal's hands. Mead was younger and soft-featured for a half-orc. The Bastards had always given him shit for wearing his hair in the Tine fashion, but perhaps today that affectation would prove useful, help the point-ear to trust. She best start getting used to half-breeds, if Zirko's prediction were true.

Jackal hadn't told anyone about the halfling's revelation. If the elf truly was pregnant, and if she was carrying a thick's get, that knowledge would only twist things into more of a vipers' nest than they already were. Besides, if Zirko was correct about the girl not knowing, the last thing she needed was to hear it from a bunch of half-orcs she viewed as her captors.

Jackal didn't know what would become of her, no matter which way his plan went. Even sitting in the chief's seat, he could not prevent her from taking her own life. Likely he would have to bargain her back to the Tines to make amends. He was using her, same as the unknown orc that raped her, same as the Sludge Man. It wasn't right, but neither was ending the lives of naked, pleading men in chains. All of these evils had been handed to him. The only way to end it was to snatch everything away from the one that gave them over.

There was no doubt that Crafty would be able to keep the Claymaster preoccupied, especially if the chief's inevitable questions and aggravation inadvertently caused the wizard to suddenly become offended, forcing a scramble of apologies and fawning to ensure the hoof did not lose its prospects for sorcery.

Jackal's grin widened as he entered the supply hall.

"Look who finally comes slithering back," Grocer droned from his usual place behind the counter. "Got the birdcage you stole?"

"Sorry. The Sludge Man was smitten with it. Gave it to him as a gift."

Grocer blew out a disgusted blast of air. "Damn that bogfucker! I had that cage for twenty-two years. Old Creep made it, back before the thicks split his skull. And you just go and give it away—"

"Grocer," Jackal cut the curmudgeon off, "who gives a shit?"

The old mongrel's face curdled and he glowered. "Did you at least bring the Claymaster back his sand-sucking spell weaver?"

"Uhad Ul-badir Taruk Ultani?" Jackal said easily.

Grocer's wrinkles soured further. "Damn foreign-sounding gibberish . . ."

"Just call him Crafty," Jackal said impatiently. "Yes, he's here. I need new gear. Full kit, except for brigand and javelins."

The quartermaster really got offended now. "You trade everything with some whore? Serves you right, you being the one who caused us to have to pay for cunny now."

"Like you have any quick left in your shriveled cock, old man. So miserly, you couldn't bear to part with your spend, even if you could get hard."

Jackal was practiced at giving as good as he got, and made sure to put just enough levity in his insults to push back without offending.

Grocer chuckled darkly. "Why do you think I piss in the beer? Can't stand to waste it, and you young bucks don't notice the taste."

"We notice. We just like it. Now get me a fucking thrum and a thick-slicer. I've felt naked for days."

Sliding off his stool, Grocer skulked to the back to gather the gear. Neither he nor Hobnail had said anything about Jackal being gone without orders. Both had displayed curiosity and frustration at his absence, not anger. And Jackal reckoned he knew why. The Claymaster had not revealed one of his riders left without his consent. To do so would be to admit his hold on the hoof was slipping. Which meant Jackal's footing was stronger than he dared hope.

"Here," Grocer said begrudgingly when he returned, laying a tulwar, stockbow, two daggers, and a full quiver on the counter. "That's the last you get from me this year, so better keep hold of them."

Jackal laughed off the empty threat as he buckled the weapons on. Whatever happened now, at least he would be armed. "Anything interesting happen while I was away?"

"Thicks made a run at Black Knuckle," Grocer replied. "The Cauldron Brotherhood saw them off proper, but they lost one of their own and four barbarians."

"Nothing in our lot?"

Grocer huffed derisively. "Well, Roundth claimed he saw a Tine sniffing around while he was on patrol, but his mouth's as full of shit as his skull."

Jackal froze for half a heartbeat. He tried to play it off as a momentary difficulty with his sword scabbard, but Grocer was quicker than Hob and missed nothing.

"Unless you know something I don't," the old mongrel said.

Securing his tulwar, Jackal looked up. "Just be ready to come to table."

Not waiting for Grocer's reaction, Jackal shouldered the new stockbow and left the supply hall.

The possible presence of a Tine on the lot changed everything.

He grabbed the first slophead he saw and asked after Roundth. When the youth pointed at the bunkhouse, Jackal took off running. This was why he needed time, to catch up, to figure out, to make sure he went to the table meet with as few blinders as possible.

The moment Jackal entered the dim building it was clear, from the grunts and moans, Roundth was not sleeping. Each Bastard had his own chamber, and though the stucco walls were thick, the plank doors were thin. Not that Roundth bothered to close his door.

Jackal leaned around the jamb and immediately clenched his eyes with mild distaste. He was hoping to catch Thistle in a pleasing and compromising position, but he was served a healthy view of Roundth's pumping backside, replete with sweat.

"You could plant the flag of Hispartha in the crack of your ass, Roundth," Jackal declared.

"That you, Jack?" Roundth asked, not bothering to miss a stroke.

Thankfully, Thistle had a bit more self-respect, fussing and pushing at her single-minded lover until he ceased his plowing. With a heavy, exasperated breath, Roundth disengaged his namesake and sat back on his heels upon the creaking bed. He turned to face the door, breathing through his mouth.

"Glad you're back. You're still pretty. Now go away."

Jackal tilted his head to the side so he could give Thistle a wink. "I'm not the pretty one here."

"Go charm someone else, Jack," the woman said. She managed to suppress her smile, but could do nothing about the blush. Thistle was a heavier woman, but one of the prettiest frails Jackal had seen, and blond, which was rare in the Lots.

"Why?" he teased. "You're already stripped down and in bed. The hard work is done."

"I'm right here," Roundth complained, pushing some of the strewn covers at Thistle so she could cover up. The woman made an effort, but as the hoof loved to say, she had the largest breasts in Ul-wundulas. She served as wet-nurse for Beryl's orphans and was amply equipped for her duties. Roundth had taken to her the moment she came to Winsome. He liked larger women, which was a mercy, considering his famed proportions. Jackal was fond of Thistle. Not many human women would agree to feed a gaggle of half-orc infants from their own body.

"Darlin'," Jackal said, "would you mind giving me and the battering ram here a moment?"

With a final, resigned exhalation Roundth nodded at Thistle. "Just wait in the commons."

"Nooo," Jackal chided, seizing Roundth's arm and dragging him off the bed. "She can stay and *we* will go. What's the matter with you?"

Unprepared for the sudden tug, Roundth lost his balance and fell off the bed in an awkward, naked tumble. Jackal kept hold and headed out the door. Cursing, Roundth managed to get his feet under him and careened into the corridor. Jackal let go just long enough to put him in a headlock and they scuffled until reaching the bunkhouse common room. Roundth struggled free and stepped back, the smile on his face chasing away most of the irritation of having his fun interrupted. Roundth was short for a half-orc, but his nearly black skin, sizable tusks, and ghastly wide cock hinted at a thrice somewhere in the female line.

"What is it, Jackal? And it better be good." Roundth did not bother to cover up, just stood unmindful of his erection.

"I need to know about the Tine you saw."

"*That* couldn't have waited? Hells, it was one damn elf."

"And you're sure?"

"I don't know anything else that rides a harrow stag."

With a shake of his head, Roundth started to head back to the corridor.

Jackal put a hand on the shorter half-orc's chest. "I need to know about it. It's important."

It was his tone, more than his hand, that stopped Roundth.

"Sure, Jackal," he said, stepping back again. "Um. I was riding near Guliat Wash. Chief had us out solo, on account of you, Fetch, and Oats being gone. I stopped to water my hog and as I was mounting back up, I saw it on the other bank, higher up the gully. Damn big stag with those shimmering damn antlers and there was a rider, right on its back. Fucker was watching me. I called out, demanded what he was doing on our lot, and started riding across the water. By the time I got to the other bank, there was no sight of him. But the tracks were there, right where he was waiting. I know, I know, you think I was heat-sick or some shit but—"

"No," Jackal interrupted, "no, I believe you. When was this?"

Roundth's eyes looked at the ceiling as he thought. "Two days ago. It's one rider, Jack! Nothing to worry about."

Jackal didn't say anything. One rider, not enough to worry about. That was exactly the point. One rider was not a threat and easily ignored, but more than enough to look around. The Tines were searching for her.

"Can I get back to it now?" Roundth asked, gesturing down the corridor.

"Yeah," Jackal replied.

Roundth was halfway back to his room when Jackal called after him.

"I need a favor."

Roundth turned around, but continued to walk backward, making a face that demanded haste.

"Give Thistle a ride back to Winsome when you're done," Jackal told him. "Tell Fetch and Oats I need to see them. Right away. Ride back with them. And tell them to bring the girl."

"Girl?"

"You'll see when you get there."

Rolling his eyes as he spun on his foot, Roundth waved acknowledgment and jogged to his room. The moans started up again before Jackal could leave the bunkhouse.

Shit.

Stalling further was pointless. They could not keep the elf in Winsome. Her people were looking for her. If they were already scouting the Bastards' lot long before Jackal and his companions brought her through, it was very possible a Tine outrider had seen them coming home. And they would not have missed the elf woman riding captive on a barbarian. A lone scout would not have been foolish enough to confront four half-orcs, but if a message got back to Dog Fall, there could be a raiding party of angry point-ears riding for the Kiln even now. There was no choice but to reveal the Tine girl. And be ready to adapt to what happened next.

The Claymaster's head snapped up when Jackal pushed into his solar. Crafty lounged in the chair opposite the desk, a languid smile ornamenting a mouth that stopped speaking at the intrusion. It was the scene Jackal had conspired with the wizard to design during the ride from Strava. Crafty was relaxed. From beneath the bandages, the chief's eyes were heavy with thought.

Jackal clenched his jaw against a gloating smile.

Seeing his submerged relish, Crafty gave Jackal a tempering look. "Ah, here he is. I was just describing our shared adventure, telling how that devil the Sludge Man attacked us. There was nothing but to defend ourselves." He spoke to no one in particular, carelessly tossing his words into the room, yet they were laden with messages.

Drumming his swollen fingers on the desk, the Claymaster stewed. Finally, his far-staring eyes focused on Jackal.

"Wouldn't have needed to defend yourselves if you'd stayed out of the marsh. But this mongrel's stones swell at the thought of defying me. Don't they, Jackal?"

"I was angry, chief," Jackal replied, and meant it. "Doesn't sit well when my hoof is in danger. I couldn't let it rest. Had to know Garcia's body wasn't going to come back to bite us. But he's swamp scum now."

The Claymaster nodded. "Fucking frails. If Bermudo thought he could bring down this hoof with nothing but a lost horse and a greasy gash peddler, he has no notion of who we are. Now that we're whole, we can decide how to show him."

This wasn't the chief Jackal expected. He had prepared for him to rage, to scream and fret uselessly. But the mongrel sitting behind the desk sounded like the old Claymaster, the one from Jackal's slop days, the formidable leader who had forged the most famed hoof in the Lot Lands.

The Claymaster peered up at Jackal, a sudden glint in his eyes. "When is Oats coming back with this point-ear cunny?"

Jackal nearly choked, and had to prevent his eyes darting to Crafty. That was not a detail he was supposed to reveal. Jackal had wanted to ambush the Claymaster with the sight of the elf. But his snare had been sprung early.

"I sent Fetching to go get them," Jackal replied, recovering quickly enough to keep from stammering. "Mead went with her. Roundth is joining them on the ride up. I heard about his Tine sighting, figured more thrums around the girl the better."

"That why you bust in here?" the Claymaster asked, his voice gaining a little heat. "You think we're about to get a visit?"

Jackal's eyes drifted to the sapper pots on the shelf. "Chief, we were careful on the ride back, but if a Tine doesn't want to be seen it won't be. If they saw us with that girl, they know she's here."

The Claymaster knuckled the desk and pushed his misshapen bulk to standing.

"Let's go."

As they followed the Claymaster out of his solar, Jackal shot a scowl at Crafty and received a wink in return. In the taproom, two slopheads watched them pass with expectant faces.

"Get up on the walls, you bare-balled whelps!" the chief barked as he stomped past. "I want every last slop with a spear in hand and walking the rampart. Go!"

The young half-orcs ran for the door, leaving it open behind them. The Claymaster stepped out into the heat of the yard. His tumid body, heavy with age and swaddled with wrappings, seemed to shrink under the harsh glare. Still, he did not seek shade, but stood upon the hot dust and surveyed the fortress he had built.

"Tines will try to sneak over the walls," he muttered, "not assault them head-on. If they come, it will be at night. That gives us some time. This girl? She trouble?"

"No," Jackal replied. "She was frightened, at first. Now she's just . . ."

"Resigned," Crafty offered.

The Claymaster grunted. "Good. Then it shouldn't take more than a pair of slops to watch her."

"Perhaps that duty should be mine," Crafty said.

"Fine. We need the eyes on the walls anyway."

"What about Winsome?" Jackal asked. "Should we bring them inside?"

"They won't attack the village," came a thin voice from behind.

Jackal turned and found Hoodwink leaning against the wall of the meeting hall, right next to the door, keeping to the shadows cast by the building's roof. He had not been there a moment before, Jackal was certain.

He wore a loose, deep cowl, as was his custom when forced to be in the sun. This garment, along with Hoodwink's unnerving tendency of rarely blinking, gave rise to his hoof name.

"It's not their way," he finished.

"Hood's right," the Claymaster said. "Elves aren't 'taurs. They'll leave Winsome be."

From across the yard, Grocer was approaching, his thin, sinewy frame carrying him swiftly despite his age. From the direction of the stables, Hobnail and Polecat were coming as well. The three converged on the Claymaster.

"My slops just got pulled to the walls," Grocer said. "What we got?"

"Table meet," the Claymaster said. His eyes were fixed across the yard, toward the unseen gatehouse tunnel blocked by the bulk of the keep. Soon, as if he willed them to appear, Oats, Mead, Fetching, and Roundth rode up. Jackal saw that Fetch bore the Tine girl. The riders reined up in front of their waiting brethren.

Hob, Grocer, and Polecat all stared at the captive elf, puzzlement manifesting in unique ways on their faces. Even Roundth still seemed a bit surprised, though he'd had the entire ride from Winsome to grow used to her presence. The chief gave no reaction. Why would he? Crafty, damn him, had thwarted any chance of catching him off guard. As for Hood, Jackal did not bother to look. A viper would flinch before that mongrel.

"Pen your barbarians," the Claymaster ordered, "then get your asses to table. We got some lip service to attend. Fetching, give that girl over to the wizard."

Crafty approached Fetch's hog and slowly raised his arms to help the elf down. She complied, but her gaze was darting around, taking in the surrounding fortress and the new faces. Her eyes kept returning to the Claymaster, Jackal saw. Was it his deformities unnerving her or something more? Could it be recognition? The chief returned the stare, but his gaze suggested nothing but the sizing up of a new hazard. Yet he was not alone in his scrutiny. Polecat was already stripping the Tine girl with his eyes. Now over his initial confusion, the hatchet-faced lecher bore a naked interest, the corners of his mouth beginning to twitch upward.

Jackal stepped up to Crafty, purposefully blocking Polecat's view.

"Take her to the bunkhouse," he told the wizard, loud enough so the others could hear. "There's food in the commons. If she wants to sleep, my room is the second door down on the right."

Up on her hog, Fetching clicked her teeth. "Across the hall is my room, Crafty. Best for her there."

"My room!" Jackal insisted, throwing a warning look up at Fetch.

She grimaced at his outburst, confused and affronted. Mixed laughter bubbled in the air around them.

"Watch out, brothers!" Hobnail hooted. "Our two prettiest are snapping over the new meat."

"Don't fret, Jack," Polecat wheedled, "I hear elf girls hunger for quim *and* cock. Likely she won't mind being a bridge between you."

Roundth guffawed from his hog and next to him Mead was trying to swallow a snicker.

A bellow from the Claymaster quickly silenced the jeers.

"Enough! I said get those hogs stabled and I meant now! We got a long talk in front of us, so let's get to it!"

The riders spurred their hogs toward the pens as Jackal's chuckling brothers ambled back into the meeting hall. He stood outside, watching Crafty lead the Tine girl away. She took one look over her shoulder and their eyes met before Jackal could turn away. He had saved her from the Sludge Man and brought her to the mercy of the Grey Bastards.

And mercy was not something this hoof was known for.

Chapter 14

THERE WAS A LONG SILENCE WHEN THE CLAYMASTER FINALLY stopped speaking. He looked around the table, reading the reactions, the axe-scarred wood of the voting stump framing his humped back. Other than the premature revelation of the elf's rescue, it seemed Crafty had fed the chief the story they had planned. He was supposed to leave out the convalescence at Strava, but Jackal's confidence in the wizard's discretion had withered. However, if the Claymaster knew that Jackal had bargained aid from Zirko, he said nothing about it to the hoof.

Polecat was the first to speak.

"So . . . we think Sancho sold point-ear quim, but don't know for sure because he's playing host to cavaleros looking for the one Jack killed, he's leech food thanks to the Sludge Man, but *he* went berserk because we took his Tine plaything away, and now we got her people on the sniff, looking to take her back and level some blame?" Polecat's tongue searched the inside of his mouth and he shook his head. "What in all the hells am I missing? Because I feel like we're hip deep in hogshit that should hardly have messed a boot."

The heads around the table bobbed in agreement. Jackal remained still. He didn't much like Polecat, but in that moment he could have embraced the former Rutter. Those were the questions that needed asking, needed answering. He had to prod his brothers toward the truth and hope they sniffed out the falsehoods. Already, it was happening, but Jackal was careful not to trumpet his thoughts with even the smallest body language.

Next to him, Oats's large form held a similar tension. On Jackal's other side, Fetching lounged in her chair, seemingly uninterested in anything that was being said.

"Whatever more there is we will get from Sancho," the Claymaster said.

From the other end of the table, Hoodwink's bald head turned. He received a nod from the Claymaster. Whatever more there was would be buried along with Sancho's gutted carcass.

Jackal could not allow that.

"The brothel is crawling with Bermudo's men," he said. "Let me go with Hood. Watch his back."

In reply, the Claymaster only glanced down the table at his favorite errand boy. Jackal followed his gaze to see what the answer would be. The black pits in Hoodwink's skull bore into him, and for one horrible instant, a twinkle of life appeared.

"You can come."

"If," the Claymaster amended, "we don't need you elsewhere. We're going to want every thrum close to home if we got castile cavalry or Tines knocking at our gate."

"You think that's likely?" Hobnail asked.

"I'll send word to Captain Ignacio," the Claymaster replied, "find out what he knows about his noble counterpart's intentions. The castile won't be a problem so long as Ignacio and the commoner cavaleros are on our side. At the very least, they won't ride against us, and Bermudo doesn't have the numbers to take us with just his blue bloods." The chief paused and took a long, deep breath. He looked directly at Mead. "As for the Tines, I'm not the one to say."

Mead grew visibly nervous, but no more than any other fresh Bastard would under the chief's attention. Jackal couldn't recall being spoken to directly by the Claymaster during his first year as a sworn brother.

"Well . . . I talked to her," Mead ventured. "And I didn't have a lot of time, so . . . I mean, she's scared."

"So you didn't find out shit," Grocer said.

Mead fidgeted and made a hopeless gesture. "I got her name."

Jackal found himself leaning forward. Thankfully, the others were too busy berating Mead to notice.

"Well, I call that a victory," Roundth said, roughly pawing Mead's head. "Our backy little elf-speaker managed to coax a woman's name out of her."

"Now, remember, boy," Polecat joined in, "when you bend her over, you won't see a pair of balls hanging down. Don't get confused."

Mead adopted the tense smile and slow nod long proven to help weather such sport. Oats's laughter made Jackal aware of his lack of participation. For appearances, he leaned farther over the table and grabbed a fistful of Mead's Tine mane.

"Don't worry, she'll show you what to do. You did know that's why the point-ears wear their hair like this, right? So their women can guide the head!"

The brotherhood erupted at the jest as Mead knocked his hand away. Jackal sat back, receiving an approving back slap from Oats. Fetching remained withdrawn, idly spinning her voting axe on the table. When the laughter died down, she looked across at Mead.

"But she didn't exactly speak."

That brought the laughter to a puzzled end. The hoof peered at Mead.

"No," he agreed with Fetch. "She gave a call."

Hobnail looked disturbed. "A call?"

Mead hesitated a moment, not wanting further attention. "A bird-call. It was perfect . . . unmistakable. A starling. So, I asked if that was her name. And . . . she nodded."

"Starling." Polecat wrinkled his nose. "That doesn't sound . . . elf-ish."

"Well, that's not how'd she say it if she could, fool-ass," Mead said, happy to retaliate. "But it's what it means, in her tongue. You mongrels would sound like that halfwit stableboy at the castile if you tried to say it."

"The one that got kicked by the donkey?" Oats asked. "Fuck you, Mead, he can't help the way he sounds!"

Seeing the brute's frown, the younger half-orc raised his hands apologetically.

Hobnail snorted. "Oats. Champion of simpletons everywhere."

"I get out of this chair and hit you, Hob, you'll be one of 'em," Oats said.

The Claymaster was not amused. "Shut it, all of you. Mead? You telling me that right now we don't know anything else about her?"

"I will talk to her again, chief. With more time . . ." Mead trailed off as the Claymaster lowered his bandaged head into a swollen hand, rubbing at the rheumy eyes nestled within the stained linen. It could have been a gesture of frustration. Or relief.

"We may not have more time," the chief said, still cradling his face. "That Tine Roundth saw points strongly to the elves looking for this girl. If they spotted her coming in, we could have trouble by tonight. That means we stay vigilant. Slops on the walls, Bastards in the yard riding circuits. Meantime, we have to decide what to do with her."

"I say we chain her up outside the Kiln," Grocer said. "Let her people take her back. Mead can sit out there and be ready to gibber at them if needs be, tell the point-ears we didn't harm her. Simple as that."

Hobnail and Roundth nodded at this.

The Claymaster pondered.

Jackal, too, was weighing the outcome. The chief wouldn't let her go back. He'd kill her rather than risk what she might reveal. Another innocent killed. Jackal found his little finger touching the handle of his voting axe.

Starling. Mead had said her name was Starling.

"We can't let her go yet," the Claymaster decided. Jackal's hand twitched away from the axe haft. "She might be the only proof we have of Sancho's scheming. If the Tines want our blood for this, I need the girl to be able to point to the whoremonger and place the blame where it belongs. We give her back now, we lose that chance."

"Not gonna have that chance anyways if they come tonight," Grocer pointed out.

"We'll handle that if it happens," the Claymaster said. "But I want all hands here in case it does. Once we see daylight, Hoodwink will go invite Sancho to join us."

Jackal did not fail to notice his name was left out of that task.

"What about the Sludge Man?" Roundth asked.

"What about him?" the Claymaster pressed.

"Sounds like it ain't certain that the Tyrkanian killed him. If he *is* dead, that leaves the Old Maiden wide open. If he's not, that leaves him with powerful ill feeling for us. I mean . . . which do we hope for? Thicks coming through the marsh or the Sludge Man seeking vengeance?"

"That's a saddle made of thorns," Hobnail agreed.

Jackal waited for the fault of that situation to fall on his head, but again the chief surprised him.

"Sludge Man slithers this way, we'll see him off. As for orcs, the hoofs will deal with them the way we always have. For now, you have your orders. Anyone unclear?" The Claymaster's head swiveled and he gave a satisfied grunt at the nods coming from his riders. "Get to it, then!"

Chairs squeaked on the floor planks as the Grey Bastards stood.

"You three," the Claymaster pointed at Jackal, Fetch, and Oats. "Wait a while."

Oats sat back down, while Fetching leaned on her chair back. Jackal continued to stand, waiting for the others to clear the room and close the doors.

"This wizard," the Claymaster began slowly, "tell me about him."

Oats blew out a bemused breath. "He's a genuine sorcerer, chief. Seen him do queer stuff. But he saved our hides in the Old Maiden."

"He's fat and can't ride for shit," Fetch threw in carelessly.

The Claymaster wasn't listening. His ugly, half-concealed face was fixed on Jackal.

"Oats is right. You would have been short three Bastards if Crafty hadn't come with me to the marsh. I believe he wants to help the hoof. But I can't figure out why."

None of that was a lie, but it contained little truth.

The Claymaster seemed amused by his answer. "Well, you convinced him to ride with you, Jackal. Gave him a hoof name. Now you credit him with saving your life. Sounds like a brother to me. I'm thinking of putting his name forward as a Grey Bastard."

That caught Jackal off guard. He hesitated, but his friends were quick to respond. They spoke almost at the same time.

Oats slapped his large hand on the table. "Damn right!"

"Fuck that!" Fetching exclaimed, springing upright.

The Claymaster gave them each a glance, but his eyes immediately returned to Jackal. The chief waited, patient as a spider.

"I think it's too soon for that," Jackal told him, trying to sound casual. "The others should get used to him first."

The Claymaster was silent for a long, uncomfortable span, his grin creeping all the while.

"Hells," he said at last, sounding pleased. "I guess I'm not too old to be surprised. Because I cannot remember a time you three weren't of one mind."

Savoring his little victory, the Claymaster dismissed them with a wave of his swollen hand.

Out in the yard, Jackal let his anger rise to the surface.

"What the fuck was that?" he demanded, whirling on his companions.

"It's called an ambush," Fetch replied, striding past him.

"And you two blundered right into it!"

"Only because we were led there, Jack."

Seething, Jackal quickened his pace and cut Fetching off.

"If you had been following my lead you would have kept your mouth shut," he told her.

Fetch's hand darted out and caught Jackal's stockbow strap. She pulled him roughly forward and her words were delivered on a forked tongue.

"I don't speak only by your leave, Prince Jackal."

Shoving him away, Fetch continued on. Only a restraining hand from Oats prevented Jackal from going after her.

"Leave it, brother."

Sick of being manhandled, Jackal threw off the thrice's grip, but he stayed put. He watched Fetching cross the yard and disappear into the distant bunkhouse. With a snarl, Jackal snatched the kerchief off his head and scratched irritably at his hair.

"And what were you doing?" he barked at Oats. "Shouting support for Crafty like that?"

"Didn't know it would get me hanged," the brute replied lightly. "And I don't see the trouble. Hoof needs new blood, and one that can do the things Crafty can won't hurt us."

"Unless it does!"

Oats crossed his massive arms in front of his huge chest. "You're more chummy with him than any. Now you don't trust him?"

"I trust him to help himself," Jackal said. "But I don't think he wants to join us."

"Then what?"

"I don't know. And now the chief knows I don't. He smelled the growing alliance, Oats. Between me and Crafty. Maybe the wizard even told him. He certainly told him plenty already. Our position in this hoof is getting unsteady, and fast."

Oats shook his head and looked down at the dust of the yard. "I know you want to be chief, and when the time comes, I'll throw my axe. But until then, brother, you best quit getting angry at us ruining plans you're making up as you go."

With that, the thrice strode slowly away, giving Jackal a heavy clap on the shoulder as he passed.

The brute was right. Jackal was trying to catch mute crickets in the dark. He needed them to start singing.

Oats was already speaking with Roundth, Hobnail, and Polecat when Jackal entered the bunkhouse. They were working out the patrol order for the night. Leaving them to it, Jackal went quickly to his own room and found Crafty within, but not Starling.

"She sleeps in Fetching's chamber," the wizard explained, seeing Jackal's frown. "I thought that more tolerable should elven . . . emissaries arrive to inquire on their missing maiden."

"I think we both know she's no maiden, Uhad," Jackal said, ridding himself of his stockbow and quiver, before slumping down to sit on the edge of his bed.

Crafty lowered his bulk down on the small room's single stool and rested his back against the wall.

"You use my name," the wizard said, cocking his head to the side. "Am I no longer deserving of an unimaginatively descriptive appellation?"

"That may be entirely your choice," Jackal replied. "The Claymaster proposed putting your name up for brotherhood. Seems you've made an impression."

Crafty smiled and twisted his beard braid around one pudgy finger. "You think I bargained with him behind your back. Told him of our rescued elf—which you would rather have related yourself—in exchange for further trust and whatever other mystery terms I may have set."

"Something like that," Jackal admitted.

"I assure you, that did not occur."

Jackal leaned forward. "You certainly told him more than I wanted. That occurred. Why should I believe the rest didn't?"

"I told your Claymaster everything he needed to know," Crafty replied. "Had it come from you, his rival, he would only have listened to the words you did not say and seen the trap. But for me, he was intent, eagerly hearing every flapping of my tongue, for he *wants* to trust me, so that I will trust him. This saved time. Often the best scheme is none at all. Your hoof is now in quite a scorpion pit. In order to survive, its current leader needed to be made aware of the dangers quickly. But that does not mean I betrayed his successor."

Jackal glanced at the closed door. Crafty was not making an effort to whisper. Any ear pressed to the wood could not have failed to hear their discourse. Jackal chose not to let that worry him. Let the word get back to the Claymaster that Jackal and the wizard were closeted away in conversation. It could only bring further fears to the old man's brain.

"Out of curiosity," Crafty said, lowering his voice with mock caution, "how would my joining the hoof transpire?"

"I thought you had no interest in being a Bastard?"

"I don't. But it would behoove me to know the process, no? You said it took two to propose a new member."

"Not when it's the chief putting you forward. The Claymaster's word is law. Unless . . . one of us disagrees. Any member can cast a vote against the chief's order by throwing an axe into a stump behind his chair. It is no different from any other decision he makes."

Crafty blinked slowly. "Symbolic. Yet not subtle."

"It's a challenge," Jackal stated. "An open display of aggression against the Claymaster's will. Once an axe has been cast, others may join the opposition. If the majority of the hoof disagrees, the chief's order fails or is amended by the brother who first threw."

"And if the vote fails?"

"All opponents retrieve their axes with no consequence . . . except the original. Whoever first throws against the Claymaster must stand before the stump and allow the chief to throw an axe. Refusal to do so is craven, and cowards are not tolerated within the hoof. A true Bastard will stand firm and accept whatever fate comes."

"And hope your Claymaster is feeling merciful," Crafty said with grim humor.

An image of Warbler appeared in Jackal's mind, the same as it did every time he came to table and saw the lone axe embedded in the stump.

"Only a fool would hope for that," he said.

"If . . ." Crafty said, drawing the word out very slowly, "I was to be put up for your fellowship and none dared oppose, what then?"

"You could refuse," Jackal told him, "but that would be a great disrespect to the Grey Bastards and you would never again be welcome here. You would be escorted from the Kiln, to the borders of our lot. To return would be a mistake."

Crafty looked impressed. "So, all the Claymaster must do if he wishes to be rid of me is embrace me."

"Unless a vote is cast against your inclusion and won. Then you have not refused, but simply been denied by the hoof. Like all of the slopheads who have not been found worthy, you could still remain under the protection of the hoof, so long as you were of some service."

"Like growing grapes in your Winsome town?" the wizard asked, his eyes dancing within his plump face.

"Or advising the new Claymaster," Jackal offered pointedly.

Crafty's white teeth shone. "And so here I am, between old and new. I wonder, what will be the outcome?"

"The same that always happens when two men wrestle with one knife," Jackal answered.

Chapter 15

Jackal waited sleeplessly for his watch to begin. The ceiling of his chamber kept beckoning his eyes to open and stare at the timber struts above, little more than wide bars of heavy shadow in the gloom. Crafty had long since departed to seek his own repose, leaving Jackal alone with a guttering candle and the choppy sea of voices in his head.

Several listless hours later, he heard the door of Fetching's room open and shut across the hall. His own opened a crack, admitting nothing but a voice.

"You're on girl-guard, Jack."

Not closing his door nor waiting for a response, Fetching withdrew. Her familiar footsteps dwindled as she left the bunkhouse to take her turn riding circuit in the yard. Jackal sat up in his bed and swung his legs over the side, letting out a breath. Oats had helped set the watch rotation, pairing Fetch with Grocer and Polecat, and himself with Hood and Hobnail. Clearly, neither of Jackal's friends wanted his company this night.

He took up his weapons, and slid out to Fetch's door. He eased it open.

Starling was asleep on the bed. A lone blanket lay rumpled on the ground where Fetching must have rested. This small evidence of kindness surprised Jackal, but he immediately cursed himself for a fool-ass. Fetch wasn't cruel by nature, just hard, the way a Bastard should be. They were all forged in the heat of Ul-wundulas, tempered by the pressure of the badlands and quenched in the brackish water of life in the hoof. Perhaps it was Jackal who was losing his edge, softening to brittle scrap. Fetch had lost no sleep over killing Garcia. Likely she would not have lost any over the cavaleros in the farrowing shed had she been tasked with their slaying. Would she have killed Starling at the river if he'd agreed? He didn't know. He only knew he couldn't.

Standing in the doorway, looking at Starling's slumbering form, he was seized with a need to wake her, gently, with soft touches and tenuous words, or roughly, with lusty snarls and a fistful of her hair. It didn't matter. Jackal wanted her eyes upon him, be they filled with trepidation or fear. If she had made him soft he wanted to prove it, to show it. Would she allow a mongrel hoof rider to touch her in comfort? It was doubtful. But her rebuke would permit him to retaliate. He could become what she thought him to be and delight in her fear, rid himself of all thought of her well-being with rough caresses, leaving her bruised and sobbing. For that was the mongrel needed to lead a hoof. A mongrel without mercy, one that slit throats, bartered flesh, took what he wanted from helpless girls.

He stood there a long time, despicable visions fomenting within his skull. So lost was he in vain hopes and dark fantasies that Jackal failed to notice exactly when the elf's eyes opened. She had not stirred, not even a twitch, yet two tiny glittering reflections of moonlight appeared in the silhouette above her sharp cheekbones. The pair of nearly imperceptible lights shone at him, unblinking. Jackal, already motionless in his brooding, froze. He felt ashamed as Starling's eyes lifted the rock of his mind and beheld the crawling things beneath. Unable to retreat, he simply stood and weathered the intractable motes until Starling rolled over to face the wall. He could see in the tension of her slim shoulders that the girl held her breath.

Revulsion bubbled in Jackal's guts as he shook off his musings. He took one step into the room, closed the door behind him, and lay down on Fetch's thin blanket on the floor, refusing to glance sideways at the bed lest the perverse demons arise again.

When Fetching returned, hours later, Jackal arose.

"All quiet," she reported, answering the question voiced only by his lingering. Passing her by without a word, he left the bunkhouse.

A slophead awaited him outside with Hearth fully saddled. Jackal mounted up and rode swiftly for the Hogback, glad to leave the waiting behind.

The Claymaster had commanded that the Kiln not be lit. Their supply of timber was low and keeping the walls filled with deadly heat was a waste of fuel against an enemy that would likely sneak over the parapets in small numbers. The Hogback was the most vital point to protect, as any raiders who made it into the yard could lower the great ramp and provide their allies a direct route into the Kiln. Ten slopheads stood guard around the works, five on the ground surrounding the hogs yoked to the gears, and five on the wall above. The Hogback was also the point of convergence for the circuit riders, as well as the place to relieve shifts.

Polecat and Roundth sat their hogs beneath the dark mass of the device. Jackal reined up in front of them.

"Bunk time," he told Polecat.

The hatchet-faced mongrel sighed with relief. "Fuck, finally . . . I got Cissy waiting in my bed. Luck, brothers."

Polecat urged his barbarian into a fast trot and was away. Jackal was both relieved and annoyed he had not known Cissy was in the bunkhouse. He might have visited Polecat's room before going in to guard Starling. It would have been foolish to leave the elf unattended, but the release would have been welcome. Cissy would likely not have minded.

"And my shift's just half over," Roundth said mournfully as Polecat vanished into the night.

"Better that than just begun," Jackal told him, then motioned at the slopheads. "And these poor shits are here all night."

Hearing this, the younger half-orcs all stood a little straighter next to their spears, trying to appear fresh and alert. Jackal recognized Biro, the slop who had escorted him back from Winsome, amongst the lower guard.

"It's nights like this that will be remembered if your names ever come up for brotherhood," Jackal told the slopheads. "Stay vigilant and keep a close watch."

The hopefuls all visibly recommitted themselves to their task and Jackal gave Biro a slight nod.

"You done inspiring the arrow fodder?" Roundth asked, playing his part in the delicate dance of supportive degradation used when addressing the hopefuls. "We need to dizzy these hogs."

"What pace did you and Polecat use?" Jackal asked.

"Piglets. Figured on Feathers next."

Jackal nodded. "Feathers, then Guard Dog. Figure out the rest on the third pass."

"Got it."

Roundth rode past and headed west along the wall. Jackal took the opposite way and spurred Hearth into a trot for forty counts, then into full gallop for forty. The hogs were well trained to these paces and picked up on the pattern quickly. Such practices made it difficult for skulking intruders to time the patrols, and also ensured the circuits met at certain points along the wall. With Feathers, Jackal and Roundth would pass each other at the tunnel gate first and again back at the Hogback. During his first circuit, Jackal would mostly watch the parapets above to see if the slops stationed there were walking the walls properly. Best to make sure their first line of defense was not slacking.

He and Roundth reached the tunnel gate with precise timing. Roundth was standing in his stirrups, balanced perfectly, and windmilling his exposed cock around in one hand as he passed. The damn thing was as thick as a floppy tankard. Jackal could not help but laugh. Such buffoonery was a tradition on overnight watches, something to keep spirits high. They never did it in presence of slops, however, so Jackal would have some time to invent a response.

The night was warm and dry. The moon was nearly full, but partially veiled by a march of cloud. The stars, however, held most of the sky, providing abundant light. The Tines would be hard-pressed to enter the Kiln unseen. Still, Jackal did not allow himself to become complacent. Elves were known to walk shadowy paths and the keenest ear could be deaf to their footfalls.

The Kiln's walls were nearly thirty feet thick at the base, making the yard within much smaller than the view from outside the stronghold would suggest. It did not take Jackal and Roundth long to ride full circle and cross paths again at the Hogback. They played no pranks, but Roundth grinned challengingly as he rode by. Jackal urged Hearth into the Guard Dog pace, which was slower and steadier than the previous pattern. This meant Jackal had until the stables to come up with some jest.

This circuit, he placed most of his attention on the interior of the fortress. The Kiln was designed so that the oval yard was mostly open ground, allowing for quick rides through the compound and giving intruders few places to hide. The center of the yard was dominated by the structure that gave the stronghold its name. Its round, bloated bulk was imperiously entrenched behind the curtain wall, crowned with its towering chimney. This keep essentially split the yard in two, with space to its east and west for three hogs to ride abreast. The northern half of the yard contained the meeting hall, Claymaster's domicile, and supply hall, along with the Hogback. The southern half was more crowded and home to the stables, breeding pens, farrowing shed, bunkhouse, slophead barracks, and the tunnel gate. When he reached the southern yard, Jackal took special care scanning the dark alleys between the buildings for movement.

It was important that no one roam about, to avoid false alarms. The slopheads were all standing sentry on the walls, with a few on duty in the stables to keep the Bastards' hogs tended and ready. Amongst the brotherhood, only the circuit riders were to be out, the others snatching what rest they could in their bunks. This also placed the meat of the hoof close to Starling should the elves make an attempt to reach her.

The sows and piglets were all bedded down in the breeding pens, content in their hovels and filling the warm air with a familiar, earthy stink. Passing the stables, Jackal peered in without easing Hearth's trot and was pleased to see a pair of slops brushing down a barbarian while a third stood guard outside. His mind had been on the patrol and Jackal realized he had forgotten to come up with a counter to Roundth's codwoggling. Looking ahead, he prepared to catch shit.

But there was no sign of his partner.

The Guard Dog pattern put the greater ground to cover on the westward rider, so it was possible Roundth had merely fumbled the pace. Jackal urged Hearth to quicken, passing the tunnel gate and coming around the southern loop of the wall.

Still, nothing.

Jackal breathed a curse. If Roundth was pissing about, he was going to get a thrashing. Looking around, Jackal reined Hearth to a stop, giving Roundth every chance to spring a hogshit prank, but the thick-dicked mongrel did not appear. Swinging his stockbow around, Jackal yanked back on the string and loaded a bolt. Training the thrum at the interior of the yard, he kicked at his hog and set off to complete the circuit at speed.

The slopheads manning the Hogback were confused to see him return alone.

"You haven't seen Roundth?" he demanded of the group, and was answered with shakes of the head. He bit back another curse.

"Should I run and rouse the others?" Biro asked, ready to be of service.

"You stay where you are," Jackal growled. "No one moves from this spot, understand?"

The second round of nods was still bobbing when he rode off, cutting directly across the yard. He passed the meeting hall and Claymaster's domicile, and only briefly considered waking the chief. The old man's bellowing and blame seeking would only slow Jackal down. Better to handle this quickly.

When he reached the keep, Jackal pulled Hearth to the right and headed for the western part of the curtain wall, back to Roundth's first half of the circuit. The whitewashed walls of the supply hall shone ahead, lonesome and quiet. Jackal was about to ride by when Hearth grunted in complaint and pulled stubbornly toward the building. Knowing when to trust his hog, Jackal gave the animal its head. Hearth trotted around to the back of the structure, where the shadows lay thickest. Roundth's hog stood in the darkness, still and nervous. The barbarian's saddle was empty.

Jackal eased Hearth closer and dismounted, covering the eaves of the supply hall with his stockbow as he carefully approached the hog. Other than a spasmodic quivering at the shoulder, the animal was completely motionless. Jackal knew it was hurt. With soothing noises, he came around and gently took hold of one of the beast's swine-yankers. He pulled just enough to turn the hog's head away from the building wall, squatting as he did so. Leaning to get a view of the hog's other side, Jackal hissed. A deep gash yawned wetly in the barrel of the animal's belly, sagging intestines plugging the wound so that there was little blood. As soon as he released the tusk, the hog buried its face back against the shadowy plaster, resuming its spooked stillness.

Inspecting the saddle harness, Jackal saw that all of Roundth's javelins were there, as was his signal horn. Whatever had happened, it was swift.

Jackal resisted the urge to sound his own horn and raise the alarm. That would only bring everyone running to his aid, which was little use. The enemy was not here, just the evidence that they were within the walls. Drawing the slopheads away from their posts could only help the intruder.

Searching the dust, Jackal found the animal's blood trail. It appeared to lead around the other side of the supply hall. Leaving Hearth with the other barbarian, Jackal followed the splatters, his stockbow pressed into his shoulder. He stalked around the corner of the hall and continued to allow the blood to guide his feet. Soon, he found himself at the curtain wall. He could see the tracks made by the patrol riders, the freshest left by Hearth when he and Jackal had ridden by at a gallop in search of Roundth before checking at the Hogback. The blood would have been impossible to see at such speed, even with half-orc eyes.

Thinking quickly, Jackal shot a look upward, craning his neck to view the rampart. He began a silent count. When he reached eighty and there was no sign of a slophead patrol, Jackal growled and rushed for the nearest stair, taking them two at a time until he reached the battlements. Whirling in either direction, he quickly ensured the wall was clear of foes. Nothing moved, but the rampart was not entirely vacant. A body lay along the wall-walk to the south. Jackal rushed over to find a young half-orc sprawled with a spear still clutched in lifeless fingers. His head was wrenched at an unnatural angle above his shoulders.

Jackal ran to the outward-facing edge of the wall and stole a look over the parapet. Below, the starlit scrub of Ul-wundulas was mute and empty. There was no Tine raiding party scaling the walls. At least, not here.

Jackal hesitated. If he ran north along the wall he would reach the Hogback, the most likely spot for an assault if the elves wished to bring larger numbers into the Kiln. But south lay the bunkhouse and the object they sought.

Starling.

Jackal stuck two fingers in his mouth and let loose a shrill whistle before breaking into a sprint. He ran south.

Glancing down, he saw Hearth racing through the yard below, keeping pace with Jackal's progress along the wall. His boots pounded the planking, his stockbow clutched in both hands at the ends of his pumping arms.

"HALT!"

A challenge rang out ahead of him. The voice was loud, yet twanged with uncertainty. Jackal answered the slophead in a voice made of iron.

"Keep to your post! We have intruders within the walls! Keep to your post!"

He sped by the sentry without stopping, ignoring the half-leveled spear. To his left, the mass of the keep seemed to crawl by and Jackal pushed himself to run faster. He lost Hearth for a moment, as the hog was forced to travel closer to the wall to pass the great central structure. Two more sentries issued challenges and were answered as the first. As soon as he cleared the keep, Jackal again caught sight of his mount and his destination.

The bunkhouse was a long, narrow three-story building that rose to almost half the height of the rampart. The span of empty air between the two, however, was daunting. Not wanting a loaded thrum in his hands during what he intended, Jackal jerked the tickler of his stockbow, launching the bolt out over the wall into the night. Keeping his eye on the roof of the bunkhouse, he darted left, angling his steps, and jumped.

There was a heartbeat of weightless wonder. Jackal nearly choked on the next heartbeat as his leap quickly transformed into a plummet. His feet smote the roof a handsbreadth from the edge, shattering tiles as his legs buckled, the shards piercing his knees. He fell forward, catching himself as tiles began to slide out from under his scrabbling boots, falling to the yard below. Finding his balance, Jackal stood and slung his stockbow behind him. He moved over to an unspoiled section of tiles and lowered himself slowly over the lip of the roof until he hung from his fingers. The windows of the bunkhouse were little more than arrow slits, but they made decent handholds. Kicking forward, he reached out with his right hand to grab at the nearest window and managed to hook the upper sill. The rest of the descent was a simple matter of crawling down from window to window.

Hearth awaited him at the bottom, falling into step beside Jackal as he made his way around the bunkhouse, reloading his stockbow on the move. The door was flung open just as he reached it, revealing Hobnail and Oats with thrums leveled.

"Hells," Hob swore, stretching his fingers away from his thrum's tickler. "What the fuck are you doing? Trying to die?"

"They haven't been here yet," Jackal said. It was not a question. He spun to cover the yard behind him.

"Talk to us, brother," Oats urged.

Jackal backed up a pace, but continued sweeping the shadows. "The Tines are inside. At least one slop on the palisade dead. And Roundth is missing."

"What?" Hobnail demanded. Roundth was his ranging partner.

"Found his hog hiding behind the supply hall. Nearly gutted."

"Fuck!"

Jackal felt Hob try to run out, heard Oats hold him back.

"Not alone," the thrice rumbled.

"Then you two fucking come on!"

A tense silence settled behind Jackal. He could sense Oats looking to him. Turning, he found he was right.

"Take Grocer and go," Jackal told Hobnail.

"I don't take orders from you."

Jackal spoke quickly. "It's not an order, Hob. It's the damn smart thing to do. Fetching and Mead need to stay here with the girl. Oats, you too. We are going to need our main strength here for when the point-ears do make a run for her. Is Crafty still here?"

"Took a room on the second floor," Oats replied.

"Good. Get him too. Hood and Polecat need to reach the chief, make sure he's aware and safe." Jackal turned back to Hobnail's simmering face. "That leaves Grocer to help you find Roundth."

"And you?" Hob asked through a mouthful of loathing.

"I'm going to the Hogback," Jackal told him. "Make sure the slops hold."

Oats shook his head. "Same rules. Not alone."

"I'm going to ride fast," Jackal said, already swinging a leg over Hearth. "And I won't be alone once I'm there unless something has gone very wrong. It's the best way to divide our numbers."

Hobnail hadn't cared to wait through the debate and was already back inside gathering the others.

"Let me go with you," Oats said. "Three on the girl is plenty."

"I need you here," Jackal insisted. "With Crafty at your back, you and Fetch can hold off an army. And you might need Mead if the Tines decide to talk."

"They've already killed a slop, brother. The time for words is burnt."

Jackal nodded grimly. "I know."

With that he punched his heels into Hearth and rode away before Oats could say another word.

Jackal rode directly east, past the lower curve of the keep. He needed to reach the Hogback with all haste, but the slopheads in the stables needed to be told of the danger and get a head start on readying the hoof's mounts. After, Jackal could cut up along the eastern wall and get a look at the stronghold's other half. The Tines had to be somewhere.

He could hear the hogs squealing before he reached the stables. Something was wrong.

Fearing fire, Jackal surged ahead. When the building came into view, he saw no flames, no smoke, but the slopheads were down. Jackal could see them in the glow of the lanterns, lying in beds of red straw. He rode his hog directly into the stable and jumped off on the move. One of the slops still moved. The poor youth was feebly struggling to keep his life from flowing out of his ruined throat. He was failing. Jackal knelt beside him, knowing there was nothing to be done. Their eyes met and the ebbing light in the boy's read the inevitable in Jackal's.

"How many?" Jackal asked.

Unable to speak, the young half-orc raised one finger, sticky with blood. The hand fell.

Gritting his teeth, Jackal rose, turning away from the body and sweeping the stable with his thrum. The surrounding stalls emitted a horrible chorus of screams and squeals from the hogs. The wood resounded with the strikes of hoof and tusk. The barbarians were crazed, fighting to be free of their pens. They were war mounts, bred for battle, the blood of three young half-orcs should not have stirred them to such fearful frenzy.

Icy realization seized Jackal's guts. It wasn't the Tines.

As if sensing his awareness, the orc stepped out from an empty stall at the far end. The large, curved knife in his hand dripped. His dark grey flesh was further darkened by smears of soot, applied for better concealment in the dark. He wore no armor, nothing that would glint in the night, just a simple leather clout about his loins.

Since entering the stable, Hearth had grown steadily agitated, the behavior of his caged kin building within him. The hogs sensed the greater predator, their natural inclination to flee replaced, through the careful selection of their forebears, with a need to attack. Seeing the orc forced Hearth to charge.

Jackal reacted quickly, dropping his stockbow and seizing the barbarian by the swine-yankers, stalling his rush. He could not allow him to be butchered. Digging his heels in and pulling back with all he had, Jackal was only dragged a stride or two before managing to stop the beast. The orc continued to stand at the rear of the stable, his long lower fangs bared with brutish amusement. Jackal needed to mount up, to get full control of Hearth, to ride out of this enclosed space. To do so was to flee, however momentarily, and the mocking smile on the thick's face would not allow him to.

Pulling hard on Hearth's tusks, Jackal forced him around to face the doors and gave him a hard swat on the haunch. The hog, long trained to the hand of his rider, trotted out of the stable.

Jackal's stockbow still hung from its strap, down by his left thigh, but the bolt had fallen free. The orc would close the distance before he could reload. Thicks were always bigger, but they were rarely slower. Keeping his eyes on the grinning beast, Jackal hooked a thumb under his thrum strap and freed himself of the weapon. He drew his tulwar and dagger, filling his hands with sharp steel. This only widened the thick's amusement.

"You won't die in the saddle, half-blood," it said in the foul tongue of orcs.

"No," Jackal replied in the same language, "I'll be balls deep in your eye socket."

He launched himself at the orc, robbing its chance to charge. It hunkered to receive him, so big its head remained level with his own. Jackal made a reaping cut with his tulwar, leading with the longer blade to force the orc to give ground, wanting to back it against the wall. But the orc gave no ground. Instead, it jumped straight upward on corded legs, throwing up one long, bulging arm to catch the lowest cruck. As Jackal's sword parted the air, the orc swung itself forward and released the beam, twisting its heavy body nimbly to land, reversing their positions. The large knife was already thrusting for Jackal's spine.

Allowing his missed stroke to bring him fully around, Jackal parried, and responded with a cut of his own dagger, whipping it at the orc's face. The thick snapped away, the muscles of its torso recoiling only to immediately spring back, driving a fist into Jackal's face. He rolled with the blow, avoiding the unconsciousness that hungered in the center of the colorful pain. The knife came again and it took both of Jackal's blades to stop its edge, leaving him open to a knee sieging the gates of his ribs. Losing his balance, he careened away from the assault, making a warding strike with his tulwar, preventing the orc from pressing the attack.

Nauseous and bleeding, Jackal backed up another pace. The wall of the stable was behind, his enemy ahead, empty pens to either side. The stable was wide enough for four hogs to ride abreast, but Jackal had little hope of darting past the thick, not with its frightening speed and reach. He had never faced an orc while afoot and alone. But he didn't need to win, just survive, survive long enough for the others to arrive. Hood and Polecat, Hobnail and Grocer, they should all be on their way to claim their hogs. Soon, they would arrive and feather this big throat slitter with thrumbolts.

Survive.

Jackal waded in to the waiting orc, flinging strokes with his tulwar, his dagger ready to counter. The orc had only his knife, but it was a serpent in his hands, darting with alarming speed to turn every attack. The edges of the weapons scraped and sparked, ringing amongst the drumming of the cloistered hogs. But for all the clashing of blades, the orc gave not a single step. It was a bulwark of muscle and murder, a spawn of panther grace and monstrous ferocity.

Through clenched teeth, Jackal grunted wordless challenges and fought. He held to a tenuous offense, preventing the orc from attacking yet unable to draw blood. For years, he had wondered what it would be like to fight Oats in earnest. Now he knew.

Hells! Where were his brothers?

Anger blossomed. Anger over the intrusion of his home, anger over the dead slopheads, anger over his inability to slay their killer. He slashed with both blades, forgoing all defense. The orc turned his tulwar, but neglected the dagger that raked across the brute's abdomen. Growling, the thick hammered his head down, trying to smash Jackal's face with his sloping forehead. Darting back, Jackal saved himself, but collided with the unresisting wood of the wall. Unwilling to be trapped, he rushed forward, pushing himself off the planking and thrusting with his sword. The orc slapped the blade away with his bare hand, but Jackal kept coming and punched his dagger into his opponent's thigh. With immediate vengeance, the thick slashed into Jackal's left forearm, his knife opening a vicious gash on the underside. He swallowed the pain, but his hand came away from his dagger, fleeing the injury. He chopped upward with his tulwar and the blade sunk into the orc's side, biting into its ribs before halting. The big knife screamed for his throat. With no choice, Jackal released his sword, snatching at the orc's wrist with both hands, wrenching the blade aside. The wind left him in a rush as the orc's knee struck again, punishing his guts.

Doubled over, world spinning, Jackal saw the knife coming again. He snatched desperately for his dagger, still protruding from the orc's leaking thigh, and pulled it free. He pushed the blade into the thick's descending wrist joint, arresting its stab, severing tendons. The cleaver fell from useless fingers, but the orc's other hand seized Jackal by the brigand, lifting him bodily, spinning him around before flinging him to the ground. All three blades now lay at the thick's feet and it stepped over them contemptuously to kick Jackal before he could rise. He found himself facing the doors, his fallen stockbow halfway between him and the exit.

Jackal rushed for the weapon, half crawling, hands scrambling in the straw as he tried to gain his feet on the move. He felt a grip on his ankle and was snatched back, his chin striking the ground before his vision went sideways. Hurled through the air by his foot, Jackal struck the door of a pen. Head swimming, he found himself on the ground once more. He tried to rise, but was betrayed by his addled senses and spilled over, rolling to a slump. At his back came a recurring, violent vibration and a deafening crash, over and again.

The orc had retrieved his knife, brandishing it in his uninjured hand as he lumbered toward Jackal. The grin was back.

Jackal was battered and disoriented, the contents of his stomach souring within his skull. His vision was blurred and his ears roared. But he had grown up in these stables, mucked them as a youth, spent long hours mending tack and harness beneath this roof. He knew precisely where he sat. The thick was towering directly in front of him when Jackal returned its grin.

"Orc. Meet Ugfuck."

Reaching up, Jackal grabbed the latch of the pen door and pulled, leaning away. Oats's massive hog came barreling out of the enclosure, screaming with pent-up rage. Ug struck the door aside, slamming it into Jackal and knocking him completely over. He heard a harsh, alarmed cry followed by an awful concussive splintering of wood. The stables resonated with the crash and the increased squealing of the hogs it encouraged.

Jackal got to his feet.

Ugfuck had the orc pinned against the opposite wall, gored on both tusks through the belly. The hog continued to press forward, shaking his head back and forth, worrying his tusks deeper as the orc punched feebly at his shoulders. His knife lay far away, fallen to the straw. Jackal walked slowly over and picked up his stockbow, fitting a bolt to the runnel as he returned to the orc. The thick, no longer struggling, was gagging on a feast of its own blood, beyond questioning. Jackal was in no mood to talk anyway. The orc raised its bald head and looked at him. Its eyes could have lit the Kiln.

Holding his stockbow low at the hip, Jackal aimed.

"What did I say? The eye socket?"

He pulled the tickler.

CHAPTER 16

ROUNDTH'S BODY WAS FOUND IN THE SLOPHEADS' BARRACKS. The orc's big knife had taken him up under the jaw, just below the ear. It was a wound dealt to render Roundth silent, yet suffering. Death had come at a cruel pace. The slops' barracks had been empty, all the hopefuls turned out for guard duty. The orc must have dumped Roundth on his way to the stables. Thankfully, the dying slophead had been right; only one thick infiltrated the Kiln.

One, and he had taken six lives.

Roundth, the three slops in the stables, the sentry Jackal had seen on the rampart and another they found in the morning, lying outside at the base of the wall, broken on the rocks. The orc had probably killed him first, snatching him over the parapet just before completing his climb.

Hoodwink and Polecat had arrived at the stable moments after Jackal put the intruder down. Hobnail and Grocer were seconds behind. They responded quickly, saddling hogs and riding to secure the Hogback, the Claymaster, and the keep, in that order. Oats, Fetching, and Mead were pulled away from Starling, leaving only Crafty to watch her. The threat of the Tines coming for her was nothing compared to a night raid of orcs.

Dawn broke with no further sign of the enemy.

The Grey Bastards rode out squinting against a fresh sun, each member in full kit, to sweep their lot. Winsome had slept soundly, unmolested and unaware of the bloodshed. Jackal breathed with relief when he saw Beryl and the orphans safe. The Claymaster quickly addressed the assembled town from his chariot, telling them of the thick assassin. As the chief spoke, Jackal kept his eyes on Thistle. She stood with a half-orc babe in her arms. Roundth was not mentioned by name when the Claymaster informed the villagers of the dead, but Thistle could see who was missing. The woman kept a strong face, and even withdrew a breast to nurse the foundling infant when it began to squall halfway through the chief's pronouncement. In that moment, Jackal felt frails to be an unworthy name for humans.

With final instructions for the villagers to come up to the fortress at sundown and stay the night within the walls, the Claymaster ordered the hoof onward.

They stayed together at first, patrolling several concentric miles around the Kiln. Then they split in half to expand the patrol, and split again once ten miles were secure. Eventually, they each rode alone, checking the farthest corners of their lands. The day's end found them all returned to their stronghold with the same report.

No orcs. No elves.

Jackal numbly unsaddled Hearth in the stables alongside his hoof-mates. The bodies were gone and the bloody straw swept out, but the place was now imbued with a nagging shame. No one spoke. They hung up tack and harness in silence, each member tending their mount in a bubble of weary brooding.

The aches in Jackal's body sang, emboldened by his lack of sleep. While hanging his saddle, his stinging eyes fell to his left arm, where the orc had slashed him. He held still, perplexed and staring. There was no wound. He had not wrapped it, nor given it any thought. There had been no time. He had ridden all day with no care of it, and now, as he looked at his flesh, he began to wonder if he ever received the cut at all. No, it had been there. He recalled the pain, the edge of the big knife splitting him open. Yet the grey-green skin of his forearm bore nothing but the pale shadows of old scars peeking through the dust of the ride.

"That arm still troubling you?"

Blinking, Jackal looked up to see Oats leaning over the partition separating their stalls.

"I'd bust Zirko's head if he gave you a bum healing," the thrice growled.

Jackal looked back down. Hells, it was the same arm. It hadn't even occurred to him. Was the halfling's hoodoo that potent, that it could continue to heal wounds days after conjuring? Jackal found he was too tired to care.

"It's fine," he told Oats, finishing with the rest of his tack.

They stood in silence a long time, wading in shared fatigue, shared grief. Their silent, sullen commiseration was suddenly interrupted when a crash resounded across the rafters. It came from Hobnail hurling a bucket into the tack room as he stormed out of the stables.

Oats shook his head in sympathy. "Would have been better if we had run into a couple of *ulyud* today. Given us a chance to even the score."

"There wouldn't be a score to settle if the chief hadn't let those orcs go at Batayat Hill," Jackal replied. "The thicks smell weakness on us now. It's made them bold."

"We're all thinking it, brother."

"And someone needs to say it."

"Maybe," Oats conceded. "But maybe, for once, it shouldn't be you."

"Who then?" Jackal challenged without much rancor.

The thrice's bunched shoulders shrugged atop the partition. "Looks like Hob has some things he'd like to say."

Jackal gave a noncommittal grunt. Hobnail had always been loyal to the chief. Not fawning, like Polecat, or dyed in the wool, like Grocer, but staunchly supportive. Roundth's death could certainly have swayed Hob's favor, but that did not mean he would support Jackal's designs for leadership. Hells, Hobnail may put himself up for the chief's seat, and that made him a rival.

But all of that could wait. There was a brother to burn.

Jackal walked with Oats out into the yard and made their way toward the keep. Beyond the structure, unseen, the Hogback was being lowered to admit the denizens of Winsome. Dusk had just begun to bruise the sky, and the slopheads were under strict orders to have every villager inside before full night.

The keep possessed only a single door, a tiny navel nestled within the belly of the structure. This lone iron portal made the bastion easier to defend from within. On the unlikely chance the curtain wall was breached, the keep was the Bastards' last defense. It was built over two wells and contained not only the furnace for the wall tunnel, but also the forge, baking ovens, and kitchens.

Jackal rarely came in here, preferring to take his meals in the bunkhouse or up on the palisade where he could feel the wind and look out over the lot. He and Oats entered the stuffy darkness and began making their way through a serpentine corridor until it debouched into the cavernous gullet of the furnace chamber. It was a vaulted, domed ring, circling the towering brickwork of the great chimney. Along the walls, stairs and ladders led up to gantries and scaffolds sprouting from the upper reaches of the furnace. Ovens of varying size clung to the base of the beast, some big enough to walk into without the need to duck.

Walking around the elephantine foot of the works, Jackal and Oats soon came to the one oven used for cremation.

Roundth lay upon a wheeled, wooden bier standing before the closed doors of the oven. The Claymaster had returned to the Kiln after the day's first circuit and prepared the body himself, washing away the grime and gore, dressing Roundth in his brigand and riding leathers. The chief stood beside the bier, awaiting his hoof. Hobnail was the last to arrive.

The Claymaster's head swung slowly, taking in each member. He was sweating from the flickering heat escaping from behind the oven's doors. Soot smirched his hands and the bandages across his face. He never allowed the slops to help him stoke a funeral fire.

Slowly, the chief began to speak. The words were familiar.

"The half-orc hoofs of Ul-wundulas began as slaves. There are only a few of us left who remember the chains, the lash. Hispartha kept us for pack animals, pit fighters, miners, anything that called for a strong back. They worked us, and many strong backs broke under their noble whims. We were the mongrel offspring of the frails' enemy and their own ravaged women. Hated, we were used. Those of us not killed at birth were destined for mass graves after a short life of servitude. And then, the Incursion came. Many of us were pulled from the mines and the arenas so that we could serve the war.

"The first Grey Bastards were potters, named not for our skin, but from the dry clay which covered it. We knew fire and heat and mud, until the day we rode into battle on the backs of hogs that knew only the yoke of the supply wagon. That day we became warriors. We were carving a path to freedom, though we didn't know it then. Carving it with swords fallen from the hands of our fleeing masters, carving it through the flesh of our orc fathers.

"And so, we are no longer slaves, no longer potters. We are a hoof and we own this land that is our Lot. We ride free, we fight free, we live and die . . . free."

The Claymaster paused, breaking his sweeping gaze away from the living to look down upon the dead.

"Roundth was a good rider. A loyal brother. A true Bastard. He lived in the saddle and died on the hog." Looking up once more the chief smiled beneath his bandages. "For any other that would be our parting salute. But I think we all know what this thick-dicked son of a bitch would have wanted said. He had guts. He had grit. Most of all he had—"

"ROUNDTH!!!"

The furnace chamber echoed with the simultaneous yell of the hoof. Jackal smiled as he shouted the word, as did every one of his hoofmates.

The Claymaster waved them all forward with a swollen hand. "Come say goodbye to your brother."

One by one the Grey Bastards filed forward and leaned down to kiss Roundth upon the forehead, some whispering private parting words, others lingering with a hand on his shoulder. Hobnail thumped the body playfully in the crotch with his knuckles.

"This log will fuel the Kiln for a week," he said with laughter in his voice and tears in his eyes.

"Let's send him on," the Claymaster said quietly. He stepped over and swung one half of the oven doors open. Oats got the other. The blistering heat poured from the roaring furnace, robbing the lungs of air. Jackal, Hobnail, Polecat, and Grocer took hold of the bier and pushed it into the blazing cavern. As the doors were heaved shut, they all had one last look at Roundth lying upon a bed of ascending fire.

The hoof left the chamber silently, leaving care of the furnace to the four slops waiting respectfully on the other side of the chimney. The bodies of the five hopefuls were also on wheeled biers. They would be burned by their own. Emerging into the twilight of the yard, the Bastards took a moment to watch the smoke drift into the purple heavens. Then they all began making their way to the meeting hall.

Jackal slumped down in his chair, adding his own sigh to the chorus of tired breaths let loose around the table.

"All right," the Claymaster said as he sat. "We're down a man. We're all ragged and we got another night to stay vigilant. Today's patrol told us there is no significant thick force nearby, but there may be another ash-smeared cutthroat skulking around waiting for us to sleep. So no one does. Except Jackal."

The mention of his name roused Jackal from his torpor. He looked up, frowning.

The Claymaster looked him full in the face. "You did good with that thick. Might have been a bucket more blood if you hadn't acted fast as you did, thought even faster. Slopheads said you kept them rooted. All good work. Get some rest, Jack. It's deserved."

The prospect of sleep made Jackal nearly euphoric, but the praise made him suspicious.

"Wouldn't be able to sleep, chief," Jackal told him respectfully. "Not when my hoof is standing watch without me."

This received a rapid drumming of approval from most of the table. The only fists not pounding were Grocer's, Hobnail's, and Fetching's. This was no surprise. Fetch had learned early on not to draw attention to herself while at table. The Claymaster continued to look at Jackal as the drumming subsided.

"Then don't sleep," he said flatly. "Keep both eyes on that Tine. Still need someone guard-dogging her on the chance her kin come looking."

"Crafty can do that," Jackal said. He wanted to keep an eye on Hoodwink. For all the chaos of the past day and night, he hadn't lost sight of his goals, one of which was to keep Sancho alive.

The Claymaster shook his head. "I got him doing something else."

That tripped Jackal up and his fatigue prevented him from hiding it.

Two men. One knife.

Fumbling for an alternative, Jackal almost suggested that Beryl could watch Starling, but kept his mouth shut. She would have her hands full dealing with the orphans tonight. Some would be excited spending the night in the Kiln, some scared. Either way, Beryl and the other women wouldn't have an easy time. Mead was a better choice anyway, Jackal realized as his muzzy brain recovered. At least he might be able to talk to her. Jackal leaned forward.

"I can mind her, chief," Fetching offered before he could speak.

"Did I fucking ask you?" the Claymaster snapped. "Jackal does it."

Fetch sat back, resuming her usual detached air.

"Jack? You hear me?"

"Yes, chief."

"Good. The slops have split the Winsome folk between their barracks and the upper floors of the bunkhouse. Just like on the Betrayer. That's how we are treating this. Do I need to remind you how the patrols work?"

"No, chief," Polecat said, giving lone voice to the general shaking of heads.

"Get to it."

Chairs scraped and the Bastards stood, ambling out of the room.

Jackal spent the first half of the evening in the slophead barracks, where Beryl and her orphans were lodged along with the Winsome families who had children. Starling was also there, sitting quietly by herself, an untouched bowl of stew beside her. Oddly, she sat on Oats's old bed, just below the one Jackal had once claimed. Hopefuls to the hoof weren't afforded their own rooms, so the barracks offered plenty of space for the little ones to play. They dodged between the rows of bunks, laughing and chasing one another until their play became boisterous enough to receive a warning hiss from the women, then the cycle would begin anew. Jackal watched the reflections of his childhood scamper about the big room where he had spent his adolescence. He ate Beryl's fondly familiar cooking and tried not to doze. It would have been a grand way to spend an eve if not for the pall of danger just outside the doors.

At last, the children were put to bed, two and three to a bunk. Cissy, Sweeps, and Beryl crept around, comforting or scolding where necessary. The barracks settled into a tenuous quiet. Jackal sat in a chair that afforded a good view of the room and the perfect shooting angle toward the doors. His stockbow was on his lap, unloaded. Beryl came and sat on the empty bunk next to him.

"How's my son?" she whispered.

Jackal grimaced with good humor. "Wish it was him that fought the orc and not me. He would have fared better."

"I didn't mean Oats."

Jackal tuned to look at her. Decades of raising children had inured

Beryl to fatigue. She fed off of it, an aged tree grown strong from a lifetime of storms. As their eyes met, one half of Jackal wanted to rest his head on her and succumb to sleep, the other half found a third wind in her presence. She stirred the boy to seek solace and encouraged the man to steel himself. They both wanted the boy to win.

Jackal sat up straighter in his chair, set his jaw, and checked the pull on his thrum.

"I'm fine. No hurts."

Beryl scrutinized his face. "I wouldn't say that."

Jackal nodded toward the bunk where Thistle slept. The little thrice, Wily, was at her tit, nursing languidly in slumber.

"How is she?" he asked quietly.

"She's taking it well," Beryl answered after a moment's consideration. "She wanted to sleep in Roundth's room, but I talked her out of it. No good would come of it."

Jackal accepted this silently. No doubt Beryl spoke from experience, as she did with most everything, though he could not recall her ever bedding down in Warbler's room after he was gone. Maybe she only considered it, her wisdom winning out over cold comfort.

As they watched, Wily awoke. He calmly unlatched from Thistle's breast and, without disturbing her, lowered himself down from the bunk, his chubby legs stiff in anticipation of the floor. Beryl opened her hands and gestured for him when the little mongrel's big eyes settled on her, but he turned his head sleepily and looked at Starling.

The elf girl was still awake, sitting at the head of the bunk with her back to the wall, lost in whatever private hell continued to cage her even after being freed. Wily had toddled halfway toward her before Starling realized he was coming. Oblivious to her confused tension, the little half-orc clambered up on the mattress and crawled drowsily forward.

"I'll get him," Jackal said, starting to stand, but Beryl gripped his arm, stopping him. Her eyes never left the distant bunk.

Had Starling glanced around, she would have seen she was being watched, but she seemed mesmerized by the child. She studied him with an unsure expression for a moment and he paused in his advance, waiting, his hands on her legs. Starling reached out slowly and gently grabbed the little one up under his arms. Wily surrendered trustingly to the half-lift, half-drag and settled comfortably when Starling cradled him in her lap. Within moments, he was asleep again.

"Well, that's fortunate," Beryl said quietly. "More likely to keep her own now."

Jackal snapped a look at her, his mouth beginning to hang. "How did you . . . ?"

Beryl rolled her eyes and expelled a half-offended breath. "Please, Jackal."

Zirko claiming it was one thing. Beryl agreeing was another.

"No one else knows," Jackal told her.

"That's what you thought a moment ago. Might not want to keep making that mistake."

"The Tines will kill her when they find out. Or she'll do it herself."

Beryl stole a glance back to Oats's old bunk. Starling's eyes were now closed, Wily resting comfortably in the nest of her arms and legs.

"She'll be less and less likely to do that as time goes by," Beryl said. "As for the Tines, Claymaster won't let them touch her once he finds out."

Jackal wrinkled his brow in disbelief. "He wouldn't risk a war over one mongrel baby."

"A mongrel baby that's half-elf?" Beryl chided. "Jackal, there's not much anyone in the Lot Lands wouldn't risk for that. Rare is valuable and what she's got in her belly is worth enough to die for." Beryl patted the bed she sat on and rose. "Now, get some rest."

Finding he could not argue with the look she gave him, Jackal complied. He tried to work out what the Claymaster could possibly want with such a baby, beyond a future recruit, but his exhausted brain dragged him into darkness before an answer appeared.

Chapter 17

A scream woke him.

Not knowing how long he had been out, Jackal rolled out of the bunk. All around, babies had begun to cry, children were whimpering, awoken suddenly by the same tortured howl. It came from somewhere outside, loud enough to pierce the walls of the barracks.

"Stay here," Jackal commanded several of the Winsome men, already alert with wood-axes in hand. "Bar the door behind me."

Starling was awake and wide-eyed, holding her hands protectively over Wily's ears, trying to shield him from the awful sound. It came in waves, bursting out of the silence in a bellow and drifting away, only to come again with renewed furor. Giving Beryl a reassuring look, Jackal rushed out of the barracks.

He loaded his stockbow just outside the doors and waited to hear the bar sliding into place behind him before breaking into a run. The terrible scream came again, offending the night, echoing from the north of the compound.

The Hogback.

Jackal quickened his steps, pushing himself until his legs and lungs burned.

The great ramp came into view. The Grey Bastards sat upon their hogs in the yard. The Claymaster and Crafty were afoot, standing near the end of the ramp, which was just beginning to rise off the ground. The agonized scream was coming from something writhing upon the ramp. Jackal jogged forward.

An orc was nailed to the Hogback, crucified to the wooden skeleton of its underbelly. The thick's head was angled toward the dirt, but slowly became level with the ground as the draft pigs pulled the ramp higher into the air.

Jackal was standing closest to Hoodwink.

"You caught another one?"

"No," Hood replied. His unblinking eyes were full of hungry glee, never leaving the afflicted orc.

Confused, Jackal looked again at the howling captive. Like the one he had killed, this orc wore nothing but a leather clout. Two gaping, raggedly circular wounds adorned its gut. Wounds like a hog's tusk would make.

"Hells," Jackal breathed as he saw the thrumbolt protruding from the eye socket. It was the thick he had killed.

The Hogback continued to rise, taking the orc up and out of sight as the ramp angled to face the sky. Nearby, the Claymaster craned his neck and placed a hand on Crafty's shoulder. The wizard seemed pleased. His teeth shone with starlight.

When the Hogback was perfectly vertical, the Claymaster signaled the slopheads to halt the draft hogs. Half the ramp was now a tower, swaying gently at its apex, high above the palisade. From the far side of the tip, the orc, now facing the badlands beyond the wall, screamed.

The Claymaster turned to face his hoof, his corrupted form radiating triumph. "Half of you, hit your bunks. Slops too. No need for all of us now."

"Not gonna get much sleep with that going on," Hobnail complained, pointing up to the unseen orc.

"Our friend will cease his baying in a moment," Crafty announced. "If we hear it again, that will be the signal his comrades are close, though I doubt they will dare come farther."

Fetch was the first to leave, giving the wizard a disgusted look before turning her hog and riding away. Grocer, Mead, and Polecat followed. Jackal could hear the rest discussing the remainder of the night's patrol, but he did not listen. Slack-jawed, he passed by the smirking Claymaster and approached Crafty.

"Friend Jackal," the wizard said with an affable little bow. "We can all rest easier now, no?"

Jackal raised an accusing arm skyward. "That orc was dead."

"Oh," Crafty gave a giggle, "he still is."

Jackal could muster neither response nor surprise. From the moment he revealed himself standing in the deadly heat of the walls, Crafty had done nothing to hide his power. The business with the Sludge Man, it seemed, was far from the height of the fat conjuror's potency. This newest display, the mastery and manipulation of the dead, only served to solidify something Jackal had known since boyhood.

Wizards were to be feared.

The garrison at the castile had kept one in residence since the end of the Incursion, his mere presence enough to prevent attack on Hispartha's sole remaining stronghold in Ul-wundulas. The elves were said to shit sorcerers, and though likely an enlarged truth, it was another reason not to intrude on Tine lands. But the half-orc hoofs had never been able to bring a wizard into their midst. The Claymaster had obsessed over attaining one for as long as Jackal could remember. Now that he had, would the chief reveal it to the other mongrel hoofs, or keep Crafty as a blade up his sleeve? A blade that had confided in Jackal that it would cut both ways. Of course, Crafty and the Claymaster had spent many hours behind closed doors. It had not escaped Jackal that the wizard may very well have been whispering promises in the chief's ear regarding his young rival. Doubtless, his true loyalties lay only with himself, with whatever designs he had come to the Lots to pursue. Jackal had chosen to trust that Crafty, being dangerously clever, saw no benefit in a tired, plague-wracked old cur leading the Bastards.

With a nod of feigned approval, Jackal left Crafty and walked to the nearest slop, instructing his hog be brought to him. The hopeful sprinted away. Ambling over to where Oats and the others still sat their hogs, Jackal inserted himself into the muttering.

"I'll be joining you," he told them.

"Good," Oats said. "We will do this in pairs. Hood, you and Hob—"

"No," Hobnail threw in, "I'll ride with Jackal."

Oats barely hesitated, taking the sudden demand in stride. "You good with that, Jack?"

Jackal nodded.

Hob's red beard quivered as he gnawed on a wad of inner anger. He wouldn't meet any eyes. Likely he blamed Jackal for Roundth's death. So what was coming? Was Jackal about to spend the patrol in more danger from his partner than an orc knife? Killing a fellow Bastard was strictly against hoof code, but it wasn't unknown. Ul-wundulas was full of free-riders exiled from their hoof because a personal feud went too far.

"Let's ride," Hoodwink urged Oats.

The thrice looked uncertain for a moment.

"He's right," Jackal said. "Go on. Hob and I will fold in. We'll decide our pattern when we first cross."

Before he rode off, Oats looked down, his face asking Jackal not to kick up any dust.

Hobnail remained silent and sullen as they waited for the slop to return with Jackal's hog. A few dozen strides away, Crafty and the Claymaster continued to stand beneath their unnatural alarum, commiserating in low tones. Soon, they moved off in the direction of the Claymaster's domicile. Jackal pushed down the worries that began to rise. If Crafty was playing him for a fool, there was little that could be done. Besides, the wizard was a formidable foe all by himself. He wouldn't need the Claymaster's help, or that of any other, if he wanted to harm Jackal. No, Crafty's inscrutable plots were less immediate.

When the slophead arrived with Hearth, Jackal mounted, purposefully slinging his stockbow. He wanted both hands ready if Hobnail tried anything. Kicking their hogs into a trot, they rode for the eastern bend of the wall, directly opposite where Oats had gone with Hood. Jackal made sure he was the interior rider, not wanting to be pinned between Hob and the wall. They made quick time and the cluster of silhouettes that comprised the stables and breeding pens soon appeared before them. Oats and Hoodwink rounded the bend. As they passed, Jackal held up his right hand, four fingers extended. Hood returned the gesture, acknowledging the Broom pattern. It was a quick-paced circuit for both pairs. Jackal did not want to be away from other eyes for too long.

"Afraid to be alone with me?" Hobnail asked, laughing in his throat.

"Just keeping the barbarians awake," Jackal replied.

Kicking his hog into the pace, Hob laughed again. They met Oats and Hood again just west of the Hogback. Oats signaled for Guard Dog, but Hob countered with Yoke, the slowest pace in the drills. Oats confirmed instinctively and Jackal issued curses in his head. They began the ponderous pace and Hobnail began checking over his shoulder to see when the other pair was out of sight. Jackal's hand drifted to his dagger.

"Relax," Hobnail groused, still glancing backward. "I ain't going to knife you, Jack. Need to talk. And I don't want to yell over wind and pounding hooves to do it."

Jackal kept his hand close to the dagger's grip. "Talk, then."

Despite his prompting, Hobnail said nothing for a long while. They were passing the slops' barracks when his lips finally parted.

"Roundth should never have died the way he did."

"There was nothing I—"

"Shut your quim and let me fucking finish!"

Jackal bristled, yet something in Hobnail's voice stopped him from his own outburst. There was anger in that voice, but it was adrift in a sea of shame.

"Roundth is dead," Hob droned, "because the Claymaster showed those thicks mercy at Batayat. He showed the orcs weakness and now they're testing us in our own fortress."

Jackal remained carefully still, keeping an eye cocked on the brother riding beside him, the brother echoing the very words he had spoken to Oats. Hob seemed relieved now that he had given breath to his dissension. The anger began to boil away the shame.

"The chief should have known better!" he barked. "He did know better . . . once. But no more."

"What are you saying, Hob?" Jackal asked slowly.

Hobnail reined his hog to a halt, forcing Jackal to do the same. Above his beard, the muscles of Hob's face twitched, fighting against a dangerous mixture of fury, pain, and self-loathing.

"I'm saying his time is over."

"Not everyone at our table would agree with that," Jackal replied evenly.

"Yeah, but you do! Your eye has been on that chair for years, we all know it. Hells, mine was too. But without Roundth I got no camp to start that war. The boys liked him, might have backed his axe. I'll never get the votes on my own."

Taking a deep breath, Hobnail met Jackal's eyes squarely.

"You killed the thick fuck that killed Roundth. That matters to me. You were the only one that raised complaint at Batayat. More of us should have spoken up."

Fetch had challenged the chief's decision too, but Jackal kept silent, waiting to see where the winds blew Hob's tongue.

"We need new blood at the head of our table, Jackal," Hob went on, "and we need it soon. So . . . you challenge the Claymaster and I'll cast my axe in favor."

Without waiting for a response, Hob kicked his hog onward, eager to put the declaration behind him. He said nothing else for the rest of the patrol, and Jackal did not press him. The words had been said, it would not serve to peck at them for further meat.

Hobnail's support changed everything. With it, Jackal had the majority of the hoof on his side. Oats and Fetch would back him. Mead too, long as his yearning for Fetching tugged him to follow her lead. That left the Claymaster only Polecat, Hoodwink, and Grocer. Cat and Hood were foundlings, one a former Rutter and the other an aloof free-rider, ostracized by every other hoof in the Lots. The chief had offered them both a place when they had none, accepted them into the Grey Bastards, though in Hood's case the vote had been close. Regardless, Jackal could not conjure that either would throw against the old man. As for Grocer, he had helped found the Bastards, and would never support any other claimant for leadership.

Still, Jackal had the vote, five to four.

There would be no more biting his tongue against foolish orders, no more weighing his next move against the petty jealousies of an aging, sick dog. No more schemes. There were a couple of slops that showed tremendous promise. Once in the chief's chair, Jackal could put their names forward for brotherhood, bolstering the hoof and ensuring he retained a loyal majority. He could decide what to do with Starling without interference and stop the struggle for Crafty's loyalty. At Strava, the wizard had claimed he wished to see Jackal in control of the Grey Bastards. The only way to find out for certain if the foreigner was in earnest was to make a grab for the chair.

But was it time?

Hobnail was right, the Claymaster needed to be removed soon.

Hells, he needed to have been removed years ago. But a one-vote advantage was a fragile bridge. If Hob changed his mind or Mead sided with the old guard, then Jackal was dead. The Claymaster would never spare him as he had done with Warbler. Those two had toiled together as slaves, struggled side by side against Hisparthan cruelty and, later, against the thicks during the Incursion. They were brothers for long years before they forged the Grey Bastards. Warbler had been the chief's trusted right hand for decades before their unknown disagreements led to the final, nearly bloody, break. Jackal had never been anything to the Claymaster but a contentious upstart. There was no love between them, nothing to stop the chief from burying an axe in his skull at the first opportunity.

To challenge and win was to lead. To challenge and lose was to die.

Dawn broke before Jackal reached a decision.

The patrol met for the last time at the Hogback and all four riders reined up, giving one another the tired nods of a job completed. Hoodwink left without a word, dismounting to walk his hog in the direction of the Claymaster's domicile. Jackal watched him go with niggling trepidation. There was no chance he could have overheard Hob's declaration, yet it appeared for all the hells like he was reporting to the chief. Which, of course, he was, but about the patrol. Shaking off his unavailing suspicions, Jackal found Oats waiting at his side. Hobnail had already departed for the stables.

"Find some food?" the thrice suggested.

"No," Jackal replied. "Find Fetch. I need a word."

Oats's brow furrowed. "Something happen?"

"Can't tell you in the middle of the yard. What say you find food for three, I'll find Fetch, and we will all meet up on the rampart, just west of the gatehouse?"

"All right," Oats said with a touch of chagrin, "but I hope you don't expect me to talk. I want bread and beer in my mouth, not words."

"Didn't Beryl teach you to listen *and* chew last year?" Jackal jabbed.

Without a word, Oats turned his hog, but just as he was riding away Ugfuck released a thunderous fart. Urging Hearth away from the malodorous assault, Jackal shook his head. He swore Oats had trained Ug to do that on command.

After seeing his hog installed in the stables, Jackal ducked into Fetch's room in the bunkhouse. She was not within. Mead was coming down the corridor, still sluggish from sleep.

"You seen her?" Jackal asked.

Mead regarded Fetch's door blearily. "No."

"If you do, tell her I need her up on the wall above the gatehouse."

Mead gave an agreeable shrug and continued on his way. Jackal had to stop himself from calling the youngblood back, get a feel for where he stood on the Claymaster. It would ease his mind to know for sure if he had Mead's support, but it was too risky. If word got to the chief that Jackal was considering a direct move against him, then the challenge could be crushed before it was even issued.

He remembered seeing Fetching's hog in its stall, meaning she was somewhere within the fortress, but Jackal did not want to go scurrying around looking for her. He told every slophead he passed to keep an eye out and repeated his instructions for her to meet him. Naturally, she was already waiting on him when he arrived. Only Fetch could make Jackal late to a meeting he had called.

She leaned against the parapet, her stockbow propped up beside her feet. The morning hosted a lively breeze and Jackal took a moment to tie his kerchief across his head to keep the hair from his face. Fetch's heavy twistlocks refused to be swayed.

"If you had been a deer I would have gone hungry," Jackal commented.

"Then you would make a shit hunter," Fetching returned, smirking. "Though I make it a rule to be difficult to track when I am summoned." She put a barbed emphasis on the last word that caused Jackal's mouth to twitch. "Must have had half a dozen slopheads chirping at me to come up here."

"How many did you punch?"

Fetch tried to hold a straight face and failed. "None! I kicked two. Well . . . one, the other managed to scamper out of the way."

Jackal grunted out a laugh and leaned next to her.

"So why am I up here, Jack?"

"Let's wait for the porridge bowl."

The slophead walking sentry on this section of the wall came by while they were waiting, his steps made uncertain by the presence of two Bastards along his route. Fetch and Jackal let him go by unmolested, eschewing their duty of giving all the hopefuls grief at every opportunity. Besides, the poor whelp met Oats coming the other way and was soon doing press-ups while the thrice threatened to pee on him. The verbal abuse was impressively clear, considering Oats held an apple clutched in his teeth. The afflicted slop failed to notice that the impending piss bath would be damn near impossible, considering Oats's arms were so laden with food he would never have been able to free his cod from his breeches. After the sixtieth quivering press-up, the slop was granted his reprieve and allowed to move on.

Oats was still chuckling from behind the apple when he approached.

"Hog's ass," Jackal accused lightly, rescuing a jug of beer and half a cheese wheel from Oats's hoard.

"You brought fucking onions?" Fetch groused, inspecting the contents of the sack she had taken.

Oats looked puzzled. "Whud?"

Freeing themselves of sword belts and quivers, they all sat down on the edge of the walk, their legs dangling down over the yard, and arranged the food between them.

"What are you wearing?" Jackal asked Oats, peering critically at the arrangement of loose cloth the thrice had draped about his head and neck.

Oats stopped gnawing on a lamb shank long enough to look affronted. "What's wrong with it?"

"You look like an Uljuk goat herder," Fetch declared without looking up from opening a pomegranate with her knife.

Popping an olive into his mouth, Jackal laughed his agreement.

"Well," Oats countered sheepishly, "I thought it looked . . ."

"Crafty?" Jackal offered.

"I was going to say cunning."

Fetch began breathing in laughter as she sucked on the fruit.

"I couldn't find a kerchief," Oats complained, "and I don't have hair to keep the sun off my skull like you two! Damn meeting on top of walls."

"Keep your voice down," Fetch whispered. "You'll scare the goats."

Jackal nearly choked on an olive pit.

They ate and laughed and jested, playing the small pranks and needling with the old teases, the ones invented in the orphanage and perfected in the hoof. The morning sun continued to rise, and the wind birthed by the dawn faded to a death-whisper breeze. Jackal did not mention his reason for bringing them here. Not yet. He basked in the comfort of having his friends sit beside him, each half-drunk with fatigue and breakfasted beer. Too soon the morning would be gone, too soon would he tell them his intentions and the mood would change, probably forever. If all went as planned, Jackal would be chief, elevated with the support of his friends. In backing his challenge, they would also be hoisting him above the reach of simple, pure companionship. Breaking bread and exchanging cuffs on that wall, Jackal found he was in no hurry.

Nothing lasts, however.

"So?" Fetching said, the word sailing on a belch. "Why we here?"

Jackal swiveled his head, looking from one side to the other, taking in his siblings' expectant faces. He took a final pull from the jug and set it aside, leaning forward to rest his elbows on his knees. A deep breath, meant to help propel a simple statement, froze in Jackal's chest.

In the yard below, a hog was riding toward the tunnel gate. It bore two riders. Both figures were familiar, but seeing them together, one held close in the restraining arm of the other, was alien and frightful. Unnatural.

Hoodwink and Starling.

"Where the fuck?" Jackal cursed, scrambling to stand, knocking the beer jug off the walk.

"Jack!"

"Brother, what are you—?"

Ignoring his friends' exclamations, Jackal snatched up his tulwar. He didn't have time to gather all his weapons and couldn't be bothered with loading a stockbow, not now. Reaching the yard before Hood's hog entered the tunnel was his only concern. Sprinting across the top of the wall, Jackal sent the slophead sentry sprawling on his way to the stairs. He descended them two at a time until he was halfway down, then jumped off the side to fall directly to the dirt. Hoodwink was nearly to the walls and Jackal surged to intercept him. He skidded in front of the tunnel mouth and tore his tulwar free, discarding the scabbard onto the dust. Hoodwink reined his hog to a stop. No doubt his face was expressionless, but Jackal was not looking at him.

Starling sat astride the barbarian, wilted, eyes downcast. She looked up slowly when the hog stopped, seeming to take no interest in Jackal's sudden appearance. Whatever she believed her fate to be at the hands of her captors, she was unmoved by it.

"What are you doing, Hood?" Jackal demanded.

"Taking her away," Hoodwink replied tonelessly.

"Where?"

The cadaverous eyes lodged in Hoodwink's face did not blink. Hells, did they ever? There was no response.

"WHERE?!"

Hood's hog squealed and recoiled slightly from Jackal's outburst, but neither of its riders reacted.

Still no answer.

Through the hot pounding of blood in his ears, Jackal heard Oats and Fetch draw up behind him. A hand reached for his arm, he was not sure whose, but he jerked away from the touch.

"You stay right there, Hood," Jackal managed through a jaw locked with rage. He lowered his tulwar and strode swiftly past the hog.

"Don't let him leave!" he called harshly over his shoulder.

Throwing the doors of the meeting hall aside, Jackal stormed through the common room, barely seeing the slopheads on duty. He pushed into the empty voting chamber and went directly to his place. Snatching the axe up off the table, he flung it into the stump behind the Claymaster's chair, the wood tolling his choice as the blade smote the wood.

Chapter 18

The air around the table was suffused with conflicting currents. Heavy lidded eyes lolled above clenched jaws, rapidly drumming fingers extended from slumped shoulders, flagons were drained quickly or left untouched. No one so much as glanced at Roundth's empty chair, or Jackal's full one. Stares bore into the surface of the table or were cast sidelong at the Claymaster.

A hoof survived on regimen. Riding drills, patrol patterns, protection runs, slop training. All of these were carried out in rigid order, day after day. Only the assured chaos that would follow if just one grinding task were neglected kept the tedium from birthing madness. Ul-wundulas demanded vigilance, constancy, and unfaltering patience. Even then, the land would conjure a test. A famine, an orc raid, the Betrayer Moon, all of these rose without warning, and a hoof's reaction must be as unvaried in peril as in peace. Threats were met swiftly and decisively. Brutally. It was the only way to live in the Lot Lands.

Time and again of late, the regimented existence of the Grey Bastards had been interrupted. Garcia. Batayat. Crafty. Starling. Roundth's death. And the hoof had not responded with the needed alacrity. The secure foundation of their regimen had been shaken by events, but their ability to respond with customary force had been denied them by the Claymaster. The chief's pox was no longer catching, but his scheming had infected them all.

Jackal saw it running rampant through all his hoofmates. Uncertainty was rife, yet all continued to look to the chief for answers, though his every word were another stone placed upon the cairn of the Grey Bastards.

Jackal was done allowing the chief's governance to afflict him further. No more.

No more underhanded ploys, no more conspiring whispers or grubbing for support. Jackal had told no one of what he intended. He had been robbed of the chance. But the Claymaster had also unknowingly robbed himself of his greatest advantage. His attempted disposal of Starling had forced Jackal's hand, but now there would be no time for the chief to shore up his authority. The challenge was made, with no time for either side to maneuver for an advantage within the brotherhood.

Jackal trusted Oats and Fetch completely, and he was confident Hobnail would keep his word. Otherwise why would he have revealed his support? Hob was not cunning enough to bait Jackal into a trap, the lie would have shown, and he was too mulish not to stand by his decision. Mead was the only true unknown. His affection for Fetching would play upon his choice, but he was also only a year removed from the slopheads and still might perceive the Claymaster as a frightful, absolute ruler. Hopefully, an erect cod would win out over childish fear.

Jackal relaxed in his chair and waited.

"A challenge has been issued," the Claymaster began, formally announcing what they all knew. "Jackal has thrown his axe in defiance of my decision to rid our hoof of the Tine captive. It's his right as a Grey Bastard to voice his reasons."

Jackal looked up at the chief, trying not to allow a bemused expression to take root on his face. Had the Claymaster truly misconstrued Jackal's challenge? Or was he giving him a chance to back away from the greater undertaking?

Fuck that.

"I threw my axe against you, Claymaster," Jackal said gravely. "Against you sitting in that chair."

The room became very still.

The chief's deep voice, restricted by the bandages, mumbled over the table.

"So you think to sit here, boy?"

"I do."

Grocer shot to his feet, his axe in hand. He scowled across at Jackal and raised his sinewy arm before chopping it down, burying the axe into the surface of the table, the sign of support for the current leader. No one else moved as the cups and flagons danced from the impact.

"It appears some aren't interested in hearing your reasons, Jackal," the Claymaster gloated.

Grocer remained on his feet, seething. Jackal ignored him and looked around the table.

Mead was clearly rattled, which did not bode well. Polecat was a bit slack-jawed. Jackal reckoned he saw despair in the former Rutter, as if he feared losing another hoof. Oats seemed to grow in size even as he sat there, unmoving, the strength of his resolve increasing in the face of turmoil. Fetch was typically sulky, and Hobnail's demeanor bordered on hostile. But his ire was directed at the Claymaster. Every word from the chief's lips seemed to pick at the raw ends of Hob's patience. At the far end of the table, self-sequestered in stillness and half-shadow, Hoodwink was an unnerving effigy.

"Well, Jackal?" the Claymaster prodded. "You going to say something or just sit there looking young and pretty?"

Jackal did not want to make some foolish speech, but it was obvious Mead and Polecat were straddling two hogs. He needed at least one of them.

"The Grey Bastards can make up their own minds about who they think should be sitting in that chair," Jackal said, addressing the Claymaster directly. "But from where I sit, Roundth is dead because you allowed five thicks to live. We need less orcs in the Lots and more Bastards, but you seem to have gotten that turned around. And the rest of us are going to follow Roundth if you keep on." Jackal swept the Bastards with a look. "He gave that Tine to the Sludge Man, brothers, risking a war with Dog Fall. Now he's trying to bury her, same as he had me and Hoodwink bury the new cavaleros from the brothel."

Hearing that, the Bastards stirred. Oats took a breath and held it. Hobnail's frown deepened as Mead searched every surrounding face, looking for clarity. Grocer looked as if he regretted planting his axe in the table instead of Jackal's face.

"But the trouble didn't get buried with the bodies," Jackal went on. "Bermudo is still seeking a way to end us. You can damn well wager the Tines won't vanish with Starling."

The Claymaster leaned forward, rested his arms on the table, slow as a grinding millstone. He didn't address the hoof. His response was for Jackal alone. "You believe that, don't you? That I'm the root of all the rot in the world. I don't know how the Sludge Man got that elf hussy, Jackal. Don't care. I do know how I got her. You. You brought her here. Same as you brought the trouble from the castile. You went into the Old Maiden without my leave, made an enemy of a strong ally, likely killed him. If the Sludge Man's gone that leaves the marsh unguarded. We'll have thicks coming through unchallenged in droves by high summer. Because of you. And yet you challenge me, want to replace me, for trying to rid us of the shit you hauled into our midst."

Jackal didn't believe the Claymaster's lies about Starling, but there was no sense in challenging them. He could not prove his suspicions. The time for that was over. All he could do was plant them in the heads of his brethren, hope they sprouted into doubt. But the chief had just sown his own seeds and they were many. Jackal had only his own conviction to scatter them.

"The wizard you've been wooing did for the Sludge Man, not me. Save for the shackled man you had me murder, the only corpses I've made were of those trying to make corpses of us! We have less enemies because of me, less brothers because of you. I want to see this hoof survive. I think there are those at this table who want the same."

The Claymaster's smile managed condescension even beneath the wrappings.

"Let's find out if you're right about that. Boys, cast your votes."

An axe came whirling by the chief's head, close enough to disturb the wisps of hair sprouting from between his bandages, and struck the stump. Hobnail had moved so quickly, Jackal had not seen him stand, much less throw. The Claymaster did not so much as flinch. But neither did Jackal when an axe came arcing over to embed itself in the table right next to his hand. Hoodwink had made the unerring cast without even rising from his seat.

"Two against me, two for me," the Claymaster said. "And, of course, I'm comfortable where I am."

The chief took up his axe in one swollen hand and lazily, effortlessly, hammered it into the wood before him, all without leaving his seat. With a display of almost laughable devotion, Polecat stood and followed the Claymaster's example.

Four to two.

Jackal felt pangs of doubt begin to take root in his chest. But then Oats rose.

"Sorry, chief," the thrice rumbled, and hurled his axe into the stump, the force of the toss opening several new splits in the old wood. From the other side of the table, a chair scraped back and Mead stood up. His voting axe was in his hand, and Jackal could see he was holding his breath. The toss went a bit wide, coming nowhere near the Claymaster, but it struck the stump behind him nonetheless.

Jackal smiled as a wild look appeared in the Claymaster's eyes. He had managed to hide any surprise he felt at Hobnail casting against him, but he clearly thought the youngblood's loyalty was his. What he had not seen, what he had refused to see, was the influence of a certain member of his hoof. Ever since her hotly contested admission into the Bastards, Fetching had been maligned and discounted. Most of the brothers had come to accept her, even love her. Not the Claymaster, never the Claymaster. Entrenched in blind ignorance, the chief treated her with open hostility when possible and dismissive scorn when she began adopting the reticence necessary while in his presence.

Looking to his left, Jackal saw she wore the guise now; the taciturn Fetching that only existed in this room, a false face she had created in order to weather the Claymaster's ire. It would no longer be needed. Hers was the last vote left to be cast and Jackal nearly screamed in triumph at the justice she had been handed. It was only right that her axe be the one to finally bring the chief down.

"Bury him, Fetch," Jackal urged softly.

She stood, her hand going to her axe idly, sliding it off the table edge. All eyes were on her, though she seemed unaware of the scrutiny. The axe hung in her hand, the flat of the blade flapping slightly against her thigh as she twisted her wrist in rapid motions. She seemed both lost in thought and gripped by a furious concentration. The room began to be charged with expectance. Jackal would not rush her, she deserved the moment.

The Claymaster was not so gracious.

"Throw the damn axe, you gutless quim!"

Fetching's head snapped over to look at the chief, the muscles of her neck tight with fury. The breath coming from her flared nostrils was audible. Close as he was, Jackal could feel her whole body vibrating. Her aggression slipped its chains and the axe came up over her head, hanging in the air for a heartbeat before the striking snake of her arm brought it down. The wood resounded alarmingly beneath the steel.

Jackal's horrified eyes fixed on Fetching's axe, lodged into the table.

"Hells overburdened," someone hissed, the shock rendering the voice indiscernible.

Jackal looked up from his chair at Fetch. He did not recognize her. It wasn't Fetching. Fetching would never have betrayed him. The stranger glared down at him, her body readying itself in anticipation of reprisal. But Jackal could not stand. All he could do was gawk at the stolen face of the one who had just killed him.

"Fetching, what have you done?"

Oats's voice, perplexed and strangled.

"She's just given me the vote," the Claymaster said, his own tones dull with disbelief. The old villain recovered quickly. "Jackal, your challenge has failed, five to four. You know the code of this hoof."

Jackal did know. He was now to stand before the stump, his axe thrown back at him by the Claymaster, his fate decided by his own blade in the hands of the one he had tried to supplant. Oddly, he could detect no pleasure in the chief's pronouncement.

He wanted to know why, why Fetch had done this, but he would not allow his last moments to be marked with mewling questions. Not daring to look at her, lest the need for revenge overtake his limbs, Jackal gained his feet. Oats was there, his bearded face seeking pardon for a treachery he had not committed. None of the other brothers would look at him.

"Wait."

It was Grocer who spoke. His pinched face was peering at the stump.

"Claymaster does not have the vote," the old miser said.

Jackal looked. Five axes protruded from the stump. And five were in the table. Where had the fifth vote come from? And then he realized.

"Warbler's vote stands," Oats proclaimed. "Hoof code."

"Only if he is still alive," Polecat added.

The Claymaster looked down the table to the only other Bastard still seated.

"Well, Hoodwink?" the chief asked. "You still have friends amongst the free-riders. What's the word on Warbler? He still breathing?"

Hoodwink raised his hairless head. "Yes. He is."

Oats released a relieved breath. Jackal, feeling the brink retreat, rallied. He looked at the Claymaster.

"We have a draw," he said. It was as needless a declaration as the chief's about the challenge, but Jackal needed to hear it out loud in order to dispel the duplicity that had torn the earth from under his feet.

"Noon," the Claymaster decreed, "inside the keep. Until then the opposing sides are to have no contact."

Jackal agreed wordlessly and gathered up his supporters with a sweeping look, a look that, unfathomably, excluded Fetching. Leading Oats, Mead, and Hobnail out of the voting chamber, Jackal left her behind.

"What happens now?" Mead asked when the four of them reached the privacy of the yard.

"Trial by combat," Hobnail told him.

There was more air in Mead's voice than words. "Jack is going to fight the chief?"

"How did your fool-ass ever become a Bastard?" Hob berated the younger half-orc.

"Let him alone," Jackal urged soberly. "Not like any of us have ever been here before."

"It's happened in other hoofs," Hobnail countered without much energy. "He should know the code."

Jackal took a step closer to the perplexed Mead. "Claymaster and I each choose a champion to fight the trial. That way the combat can't leave the hoof without any leader at all."

"This shit's to the death?" Mead asked, looking more spooked.

"Not always," Jackal told him.

"It was the last time the Fangs of Our Fathers chose a new chief," Hobnail declared.

Jackal gave him a sharp look. "We're not the Fangs. It's a bare-knuckle fight. Surely the Grey Bastards can declare a victor without caving in a skull or tearing a throat out."

"So . . . who are you going to choose, Jackal?" Mead asked.

Jackal turned to the only one amongst them who had not spoken.

Oats stood with his arms folded over his chest, his eyes burning at the sand beneath his feet. Feeling Jackal's gaze, the thrice looked up. They had known it would come to this, had planned and plotted and mused for years. The three of them. But now, only Jackal and Oats were standing here, their silence reiterating a hundred private talks. Everything had changed, and yet, nothing had. The possibility of a draw had always been there. Jackal would challenge, Oats would champion. He was the only thrice-blood in the hoof, the biggest and the strongest amongst the Bastards.

"Who do you think the chief will pick?" Oats asked, already preparing himself for the fight ahead.

Hobnail barked a short laugh. "Would have been me."

Jackal nodded slowly in agreement. Hob was the nearest to Oats in stature and brawn, without him the Claymaster was lacking in raw strength. But he had something else.

"It will be Hood," Jackal said, looking only at Oats.

His friend took this in resolutely, but there was a flicker in that familiar, bearded face. Jackal was sure he was the only one who caught it, so tiny was the reaction. He did not begrudge any trepidation. Hoodwink was not a foe to be taken lightly.

Mead had blanched. "Didn't Hood once kill an entire *ulyud* when he was a free-rider? Six thicks, single-handed. I heard he wasn't even mounted."

Hobnail cuffed him hard across the back of the head. "You see him do anything of the sort at Batayat? Or any of the other half dozen times he's ridden to stop a raid? Would have been useful! How can you speak Tine-tongue, Mead, and muck about with that alchemist's fire in the ovens, and still be so fuck-all stupid?"

"Yeah . . . no, I know. But it's different when he's with us. That's why the chief sends him out alone all the time. He's got ways when no one is looking."

"Well, everyone will be looking during the trial," Jackal said, wanting to put an end to it.

They had all heard the stories about Hoodwink, but anyone who survived years as a free-rider built up a reputation. Amongst the nomads there were only the dead and the famous. Sifting out the facts from the legends was pointless. What was certain was that Hood had been the chief's pet cutthroat since joining the hoof and there was no doubt he was dangerous.

Jackal drew Oats aside.

"Don't let the ghost stories get inside your head. He'll have speed and a few dirty tricks. Avoid a grapple and don't tire out. That pallid snake won't be able to take more than a few of your punches. Hells, none of us can. Pick your moment and put him down."

Oats listened intently, chewing on the advice. After a moment's digestion, he clapped Jackal on the shoulder, but his confident expression withered quickly.

"Why did she do it, Jack?"

All Jackal had for an answer was painful earnestness. "I don't know. We'll ask her once we are on the other side of this. Thank you . . . for standing with me."

Oats's powerful fingers clenched down. "Just a little ways to ride, brother. The hogs smell water."

Noon came.

The interior of the central keep was sweltering. It was always hot within, but Jackal felt as if he were trying to draw breath at the bottom of a boiling sea. This amount of heat could only mean one thing: the Claymaster had ordered the ovens lit.

"Why would he waste the timber?" Mead asked, with no small amount of wounded pride. The ovens had been his charge for the last year.

"A precaution," Jackal lied. "Help keep the fortress safe while we are distracted with the trial."

The true reason was more sinister. Fighting in this blistering air would be terrible. The chief was trying to give Hoodwink some kind of advantage. Was the gaunt-faced mongrel immune to heat? Jackal kept his suspicions behind his teeth. There was no need to burden Oats with unknown worries regarding the queer talents of his adversary. The brute walked at Jackal's right, already stripped to the waist. Oats looked prepared, formidable, he had even snatched some sleep in the intervening hours.

As Jackal's group entered the great chamber he saw no sign of any slopheads. What was about to happen here was for only the brotherhood to witness. The Claymaster and his entourage were already present. There was no cordoned-off arena, just a broad section of open ground beneath the great chimney. The two factions faced each other across the innocuous expanse of dirt.

"Your champion ready?" the Claymaster inquired.

Oats answered for himself, taking a full step forward and rolling his trunk neck around atop his corded shoulders. His attention was on Hoodwink, who seemed shrunken and sickly by comparison, lurking at the edge of the chief's cadre. Jackal tried to read that sunken visage, but came away, as always, mystified.

"No weapons," the Claymaster announced, sounding almost bored. "No yields. A champion is only defeated if knocked senseless . . . or killed. Understood? Then let's get this done."

The chief gave a quick, ushering wave, but Hoodwink did not move.

It was Fetching who stepped onto the fighting ground.

Jackal's throat constricted. He had been avoiding looking at her and had not noticed the change in her attire. Her riding leathers were replaced by loose linen breeches, cropped above the knee, her breasts wrapped tightly in the same material. A glistening film of pig lard shone on her exposed skin and through her bound hair. The set of her head, the way she bounced slightly on the balls of her bare feet, the far-away brushfire in her eyes, it all bespoke a Fetching ready to fight.

Oats had tensed when he first saw her, but now he took a furious step forward.

"FETCH! What the fuck game is this?"

She stepped lightly away from the bellowing thrice, her fists coming up in relaxed defense. Oats's hands remained by his sides, fingers splayed in pleading confusion. Just as suddenly as he had surged forward, Oats whirled and hurried away from her, his eyes agog with pained panic, his head shaking with disbelief.

"Jackal . . ."

Jackal caught his friend's face in his hands, feeling the fear-tight jaw beneath the beard.

"What . . . what," Oats stammered, "what is she . . . I can't . . ."

"Listen," Jackal tried to shake some focus into the near-crazed mask. "Listen!"

Oats's eyes settled on him, barely. Jackal lowered his voice to a near whisper.

"I don't know why. But it's here. You're letting her rattle you and that's what they want. They got no one who can beat you, so they're resorting to this. You can't allow this to change anything."

"I can't hurt her, Jack."

"Then put me in," Hobnail said from behind Jackal, "I'll put the rabid cunt down."

Oats lunged.

Jackal managed to stall the brute's charge, but it was the derisive laughter from the Claymaster's camp that actually stopped him. Throwing a warning look back at Hobnail, Jackal returned his attention to Oats.

"I don't want her hurt either," he assured, and was surprised to find he meant it, "but she put herself here. *She* put us here. Oats . . . she's trying to get me killed."

This last seemed to waken his friend, the truth of the words effective as a bucket of cold water. He calmed slightly, though Jackal could feel every muscle trembling, shivering from the frigid realization.

"I won't let that happen," Oats vowed.

Releasing his breath gratefully, Jackal lowered Oats's head down with his hands until their brows were touching.

"She's going to be fast. Remember. Don't tire out. Let her temper get the best of her and snuff her candle. When she comes to, we will both get answers."

Oats nodded, his forehead scraping against Jackal's, then he stepped away.

Fetch was waiting on him in the center of the trial ground.

These two had faced each other many times in training. Sword drills, grappling matches, half-lark fistfights. Black eyes and busted lips had been traded between them since Beryl's. Yet seeing them now, Oats's slab-thewed back drawing closer to Fetch's springy stance, Jackal found a souring dread in his belly.

Hobnail was already barking encouragement and, on the other side,

Polecat and Grocer urged Fetching on with zeal. Jackal had no voice. He barely dared breathe.

Oats advanced on Fetch, implacable as a mudslide. He was a good head taller and had the reach, but he kept his hands hovering beneath his chin well after he had closed the distance. Fetch slid to the right, tracing an agile semicircle to keep from being bulled over. Twice Jackal saw her left toes rise slightly off the dirt, but she held the kicks back.

They were both showing restraint, caution, using their heads instead of their bodies. Oats kept on pressing, forcing Fetch to keep scampering, tempting her to react.

Smart.

Eventually, she would get fed up with the rabbit game and her anger would surface, then she would do something stupid. Jackal stared hard at her feet, willing her to lash out. Fresh as Oats was, he would catch the leg easily and end this trial quickly. But Fetch was smart too. She moved with that natural, effortless grace that had been hers since adolescence. She used twice as much motion, but appeared to make Oats work twice as hard. Sweat was already dripping from his beard.

"Smash that cricket, Oats!" Hobnail yelled, forcing Jackal to reach over and silence him with a touch. That kind of talk was going to goad Oats into a mistake.

The brute ceased his advance and began merely pivoting to keep Fetch in view. She hovered dangerously close, well within the crushing purview of Oats's fists. Jackal saw her toes come up again. Oats did too. And that's why he missed the jab that Fetch sent darting into his face. She barely had the reach and her knuckles glanced off his cheekbone, but the punch was just as much a feint as the raised foot. Ducking under the hook Oats used to counter, the hook she must have expected, Fetching slammed a pair of quick strikes into his midsection and was away again.

Oats wasn't hurt, Jackal was relieved to see, but Fetch had touched him three times without coming close to reprisal and that fact was creased on the thrice's concerned face. Still, she could needle all day and not bring that tree down, while all Oats needed was one solid hit.

"Wait for it, brother!" Jackal reminded his champion.

The tilt of Oats's head showed he had heard and understood. He waded back toward Fetching, hunched lower, his head and face more within reach yet bulwarked behind his rippling forearms. He was a moving wall of bunched muscle, prepared to bring all his power down on a single mistake from his opponent, a mistake he now courted. This time he sent fast, compact jabs at Fetch, his big fists scattering her fluidity. She dodged and weaved, but there was an ugly, fitful quality to the motions. One jab nearly caught her and she was forced to buffet it aside with her own hand, upsetting her balance. Smelling the opening, Oats barreled through, bringing a tight elbow around to hammer Fetch's shoulder, then made a grab for her. For half a heartbeat he had her bound up, but his hands slid against the lard as Fetch contorted free, managing not only to break the grapple, but also land a departing strike to Oats's jaw with the heel of her hand.

Hells, she had moved so fast, Jackal was not sure how she had managed it.

Oats expelled a wad of blood along with a curse. Thankfully, he refused to get angry. Pressing the back of his hand gingerly against his teeth, Oats paused. Fetching had retreated several arms' lengths, and he watched her intently. Waiting, catching his breath, cooling off.

"That's the way," Jackal hissed to himself, biting the inside of his mouth to keep from smirking.

Oats was refusing the offensive. If Fetch wanted to come to grips, she would have to come to him. Every moment she delayed was another moment Oats gathered himself. He need not chase her all around the fight ground when he could simply wait for her to try to tackle the mountain.

"What's wrong, honey-clit?" Hobnail jeered. "You only know how to run one way?"

Jackal saw Fetch's jaw clench, the pride boiling into something dangerous. Dangerous and reckless.

You never were fit to be here!

The words were forming on Jackal's tongue, but they died before he could voice them. He could not wield such a lie, even in service of his cause. Still, he made no effort to silence Hobnail.

"Come on, you useless gash! Stop stalling and fight like a Bastard!"

A silent snarl twisted across Fetching's mouth, baring her teeth. She advanced on Oats, but it wasn't the headlong, foolhardy rush Jackal had hoped for. No, it was a straight-backed, purposeful stride.

Halfway, her fists came up, locking calmly just below eyes that were limned in chilling intent. Her first jab, swift as a striking snake, was met by an almost lazy swat from Oats. He caught the follow-up cross against his bunched arm, which he then sent out in a wind-punishing punch meant for Fetch's face. Snapping away, she came right back, her hip twisting as she launched a kick. Her long, powerful leg careened into Oats's side and Jackal just barely heard a grunt over the impact. Oats made a grab for the leg, but it had already recoiled, returning to place beneath its fast master to further fuel her assault.

The pair began to weave a storm of violence between them. Oats sent thick-armed blows revolving away from his savage torso, each an unfulfilled promise of a snapped bone. Fetching dodged and countered, her limbs a nest of pit vipers. The dull slapping of meat accompanied their breathy expulsions of fury. Oats blocked more than he avoided, weathering the knees and elbows of his swift opponent. He was able to send counter-blows less and less as Fetch's attacks reached a fever pitch. Bright droplets of sweat were spinning off of both champions, but Oats was clearly flagging more beneath the palpable heat.

A trio of punches made it past his guard, the first carving a path for the next two, and Oats's head rocked to one side and back again, blood now flying next to the sweat. A bestial growl tore from his throat and, abandoning all attempts at protection, the thrice lunged forward, driving his knee directly into Fetching's midsection. She folded up as she was lifted off her feet and pushed backward, a choking rush of air coming from between her lips.

Jackal shivered. Every blow to this point was nothing that would not have happened in the training yard, but the sheer brutality of the strike Oats had just delivered seemed to stop time. A threshold had just been crossed. Somewhere within a muffled void, Hobnail was crowing. Ropey spit cascaded from Fetch's pain-gaped mouth, but somehow she kept her feet when they again struck dirt. Unhappy with the result, Oats kept coming. He bulled into Fetching, scooping her nearly bent-double form in his arms to haul her into the air, flipping her into a head-dangling bear hug. Using the momentum of his charge along with prodigious strength, Oats prepared to toss his inverted foe over his shoulder.

From both sides, cries of alarm issued from the spectators as

Fetching hooked her legs around Oats's neck and used that same momentum to sit upright. She was now astride his shoulders, his face buried in her stomach, and she began raining elbow strikes down upon his bald pate. Blocked by the clinging body of his attacker, Oats could not properly bring his own arms up to defend himself. Flailing ineffectually as Fetching smote his skull, the brute finally halted and began twisting his body in an attempt to dislodge her. Having witnessed Fetch break many a hog to the saddle, Jackal knew Oats's attempts were useless.

"Bring her to the ground!" he yelled, hoping to be heard through Fetch's gripping thighs.

His voice, or instinct, must have gotten through, for Oats grabbed hold of Fetch's legs and threw his weight forward, slamming her shoulder blades into the ground. The maneuver had forced Oats to one knee and he tried to rise, but through the upset dust Jackal could see that Fetching held fast, now straightening her spine to hold her opponent to the earth. But Oats's arms were still free and he punched viciously into Fetch's kidneys, once, twice, and she let go, throwing her legs over her head into a back tumble to regain her feet.

Oats shot forward from his crouch and weathered a crosskick to the face in order to close the distance. His charge now a stumble, he swept his arm at Fetch's weight-bearing ankle and knocked her to the ground beside him. She rolled and planted an elbow in his ribs, trying to stand, but he caught her. The lard on her skin, now infused with grit from the floor, was useless. Oats had her seized by the neck and one wrist. He pulled her up and around until they were both on their knees, facing each other. Fetch's free hand struck defiantly across Oats's jaw, but he dissuaded a second blow by hammering his forehead into her face.

Jackal winced and muttered a curse when Oats did it again.

Fetching was bloodied now, her eyes rolling about unfocused. Oats let her go and stood. He loomed over her a little unsteadily, his fist balling up. Unable to stare directly at what was coming, Jackal looked around. Mead had his eyes completely averted. Hob was leaning forward, eager for the final blow. Across the way, the Claymaster's bandage-shadowed face looked firmly upon the impending end of his reign.

Oats hesitated for just a moment, then drove his fist down. Jackal narrowed his eyelids against the impact and immediately snapped them open.

Fetch had not fallen.

Her entire body had reeled beneath the resounding blow, but she caught herself, the knuckles of one hand dug into the dirt. For what seemed an eternity she remained there, motionless save for the heave of her ribcage as she sucked air through a mouth pouring blood. Jackal could not say whether Oats had pulled his punch or Fetch had borne the best he could give. Either thought was a heartbreak.

Craning around, Oats looked at Jackal, his bruised face riddled with conflict. All Jackal could do was nod.

Again.

Hells, Fetch. Are you going to make him kill you?

Oats clenched his eyes against the scourge of his task and turned back, raising his arm once more. He swung.

And Fetching erupted off the ground. Her powerful legs drove her upward and she caught Oats's entire arm, binding it in a locked hold. Before he could react, she sprang again, twisting herself around in the air to hook the back of one knee behind Oats's head, the other looping under his armpit. Using his arm as leverage, she threw him to the ground head over heels. His arm still locked in her grasp, and her leg now across his throat, Fetching straightened with every muscle in her powerful body. Jackal heard Oats begin to gasp, then choke. He tried to hit her with his free arm, but there was no force to be had. The bulging muscles of the thrice's torso bunched, working against the downward pressure. Inch by inch he began to rise, but inch by inch he strangled. Spit shot from between his clenched teeth, as Fetch grit hers and held firm.

Jackal stood transfixed as the frightening wills of his two most loved friends ground themselves to dust against each other. Oats's strength was monstrous. He labored with empty lungs and still managed to rise, torturously. Fetching punished him every bit of the way, her ability to constrain him a nearly unbelievable feat. Were he not seeing it now, Jackal would never have thought it possible. With nothing else to be done, he watched the nightmare.

Oats was nearly upright, Fetching turned nearly sideways to maintain control. Suddenly, she released him and rolled to her feet. With ragged breaths Oats managed to make it to his knees, but that was as far as he could go. He slumped back, sitting on his heels to weave drunkenly, his face seeming to search the far removed ceiling of the chamber.

Fetch paced before him, watching him. After a moment she hopped forward and sent a knee flying into the side of Oats's skull, just above the ear. Jackal felt his guts curdle at the sound. The only thing more painful than that sound was the sight of Fetch catching Oats as he fell and lowering his head gently to the ground.

CHAPTER 19

JACKAL STOOD BEFORE THE STUMP.

The hafts of the axes that supported his challenge stuck out around him, comfortless as an embrace from a corpse. For all the long hours Jackal had spent in the voting chamber, he had never seen it from this vantage. The head of the coffin-shaped table was within spitting distance, stretching out away from him as it narrowed toward the doors. The back of the chief's chair was within a single, mocking stride, yet forever unreachable.

The Grey Bastards were standing behind their chairs. Each tried to remain stone, but Jackal saw oily films of emotion playing upon the surface of the familiar faces. Sorrow. Shame. Disappointment. Wrath. Pity. That last was the worst, but thankfully, Jackal saw no pleasure. None were leering in anticipation of his end. Even the Claymaster, standing at the far end of the table with the doors at his back, was dour. Generously, he had allowed Jackal to stall this moment until it was certain Oats would not be following him in death.

The care of injuries usually fell to Grocer, but Jackal had insisted that Crafty tend to Oats as well. They brought him into the Claymaster's domicile and stayed closeted away for hours, hours that Jackal spent in the yard mere paces from the door. No guard was placed upon him. His hoof knew he would not run and dishonor himself. Besides, his worry for Oats was enough to shackle him to the fortress.

The Claymaster came and went several times, always bypassing Jackal without a word. Of Fetching there was no sign. Jackal kept dreading and wishing for her to appear, fearing what he might see, what he might do. But she never came. Even after Grocer emerged to tell Jackal that Oats would recover and then left to inform the rest of the hoof, she never came. She was present now though, in the voting chamber, waiting with all the other riders to watch the execution of one of their own.

Jackal stared hard at her, desperate to glean some answer before his vision darkened forever. But her swollen face, mottled with bruises, displayed nothing but a guttering anxiousness, as if she wanted the impending deed done and over with. Jackal did not share her impatience.

He did not want to die. Leastways, not like this. He kept yearning for the weight of a tulwar in his hand, so that he could unleash himself upon the room, try to cut Fetching down, the Claymaster, any who stood in his way. Part of him hoped they would all try to stop him, even Hob and Mead, who had tried to help him.

Would he have felt such undiscerning hatred if Oats had been in the room? Would his instinct to fight for his life have made an enemy of the one who had given the most in his bid for power? Jackal hoped not, and was grateful he would never know. Oats was laid up, his injuries rendering him unaware of what took place here. Jackal was glad his friend would be spared the display. His bearded face would undoubtedly have been a comfort, but a selfish one. In truth, Jackal did not want any in this room to be the last thing he saw. He would rather have gazed upon the sun-drenched freedom of the Lots.

But he stood firm, in this dark, remorseless chamber, and waited.

An icy twinge slithered through him as the Claymaster began to approach. This would be the last thing he saw. The hunched, diseased form of the old man he had failed to bring down. It was woefully fitting.

The chief came around the table and wedged himself between Jackal and the back of his retained seat. He leaned forward and reached an arm out to grasp the haft of Jackal's axe, now lodged just above his left shoulder. This close, the Claymaster reeked of stale sweat, damp bandages, and dried pus. Jackal's nose crinkled against the odors. Through the haphazard mask of wrappings, the chief's rheumy eyes crawled across Jackal's face. Despite his twisted back, the poxy mongrel was still equal in height. In his prime he must have been a monster. He stood there for a long spell, his hand resting on the axe handle, not yet removing it from the stump. When he spoke, his voice was low, his words meant only for the one he was about to kill.

"You always were too damn ambitious, boy. Never did understand your place."

"I'm in the place you always wanted me," Jackal returned.

The Claymaster grinned. "You're just going to keep thinking you are always right. Right to the end."

"Clearly, I was wrong about some things." Someone.

"I almost wish you had succeeded. I would have got to sit back and watch you break under the weight of being chief. The weight of discovering you don't have all the answers."

"Oats and I would have figured it out. All of it."

The Claymaster's face fell slightly. "Well, we will never know now."

"Don't seek revenge against him," Jackal said, not allowing the words to sound like a threat or a plea, just a last request.

"Jackal," the chief said, "with you gone, Oats is going to flourish in this hoof."

And then Jackal saw it, something he had missed for years, but was now made obvious by the closeness of his rival. Not even the stained linen wrappings could hide the hope Jackal saw in the Claymaster's face.

"You want him to lead after you," he said.

"The thicks respect power," the Claymaster said. "A thrice-blood at the head of our table proves we have it. You're clever enough, Jackal, and you make the women wet, but our enemies ain't whores and wet-nurses. They're orcs. You are not the leader the Grey Bastards need. Never have been . . . never will be."

Impotent fury frayed Jackal's patience and he leaned into the chief's face. "Then fucking pull that axe free and be rid of me!"

The Claymaster matched his aggressive motion, causing Jackal's nose to brush against the loathsome bandages. The chief's voice rose, now able to be heard by all in the room.

"I pull this axe free and you are dead, boy. Don't trust in some vain hope that this pustule-ridden carcass of mine is not up to the task of sending you to all the hells. I will bury this hatchet in your fucking heart if that is what you choose!" The Claymaster let the words hang there a moment.

Choose? Confusion curdled Jackal's anger.

The chief took a slow breath and withdrew a bit before continuing, his voice calmer, yet still pitched for the hoof to hear.

"I will give you a choice. A chance. Turn free-rider and you can live."

The energy in the room changed. Beyond the Claymaster, Jackal could sense his brethren silently react to this sudden offer of mercy. There were several perplexed glances exchanged. Fetching remained carefully motionless.

Jackal was equally surprised and he stood transfixed, trying to reason out why the chief would allow him to live. Then he had it. Killing him would only push Oats further away, lengthen the time it would take for the Claymaster to bring him to his side. Since childhood, Jackal had held sway over Oats, sway the chief coveted. That was the reason he had scorned Jackal all these years, jealous of the influence over the one he had earmarked to be his successor. Too late, it was all so damn clear! Well, Jackal wasn't about to help the Claymaster coax Oats into being his puppet.

Jackal lifted his chin and spoke so all in the room could hear.

"I am not some nomad," he said. "I will die as I am, a Grey Bastard."

Grocer, Polecat, and Hobnail nodded with approval. Mead's eyes brimmed with a mixture of horror and worship. Fetch's eyes were closed, her chin fallen.

The Claymaster leaned in once more, his voice again dropping to a conspiratorial whisper.

"You better think hard on that decision, boy. And fast."

"Oats may one day be chief," Jackal hissed back, "but it will be because he wants to grind you beneath his heel, to avenge himself on you for killing his friend, not because you tempted him like a dog with promises of more meat."

"Very well," the Claymaster said, his smile turning malicious. "You won't do it for yourself. But what about the Tine girl? What do you think happens to her when you're dead? Go nomad and you have my word you can take her with you, ride where you will. Stand here all prideful and die, and I swear on every god who craves bloodshed that I will turn that elf quim over to Polecat."

Seeing Jackal's reaction, the Claymaster's smile deepened, revealing yellowed teeth.

"You know what the Rutters were before the war, don't you Jackal? They were bed slaves, mongrel stallions used to sate the twisted tastes of Hispartha's nobles. And not just the women. Polecat's a little young to remember that, but the Rutters' legacy has always attracted degenerates. He'll use her in ways an orc couldn't stomach and make whatever the Sludge Man did to her seem like a father's tender kisses. I wager he even lets the rest of us watch, share the entertainment."

Jackal was unrestrained, no chains or ropes bound him to the stump. He could easily pull an axe and split the chief's face. His palms burned with the desire. Hells, he could reach out and throttle him, snap his blistered neck before the others could even move. He didn't have enough friends in the room to survive the act. Not even Hobnail would back such a murder. It went against the code. And Jackal would destroy the Bastards if he slew the chief now. There was none strong enough to lead them out of the chaos that would follow, not with Oats lying up with a cracked skull. Jackal did not want his name to be remembered as the failed challenger who treacherously murdered his chief and brought about the fall of the Grey Bastards. More than that, he could not abandon Starling. He could die to spite the chief's plans or live, free to ride, with her safety in his hands.

There really was no choice.

"Give me the elf," Jackal said, "and I will go."

The Claymaster rolled his head backward slightly. "Tell them."

Jackal looked past the chief at the hoof and found his throat suddenly dry. The words needed to be said, but it was possible they would choke him for the betrayal. Swallowing hard, Jackal raised his voice.

"On the honored condition that I be allowed to leave with the Tine, Starling, I declare myself a free-rider and . . . renounce this hoof. I vow never again to set foot upon this Lot on penalty of death. From this moment, I am no longer a Grey Bastard."

The faces of his now former brethren turned truly to stone.

"Your hog and your kit are yours to take," the Claymaster proclaimed, "and the elf too. You have until dawn. If you remain on Bastard lands after that, you will be hunted down. Riders, retrieve your axes and mark this deserter."

One by one, the Grey Bastards approached the stump and wrenched their axes from the wood. They then took the blade and ran it across Jackal's skin, drawing ragged cuts across his tattoos. The pain of the sharp steel was nothing compared to the numb despair of a life erased. He had ridden with those who now cut him, ate with them, trained with them, fought with them, some were friends and some foes, but they were all family, loved and despised in unsteady measures over years of shared turmoil and celebrated victories. From his own mouth he had severed the kinship and now they came willingly to wound him, an oath of what they would do should he ever return. Gritting his teeth against the bite of the blades, Jackal waited for it to end.

When Fetching came, Jackal was already bleeding from cuts on both shoulders, both arms and his chest. Her eyes searched for a place to mark him and he saw hesitance shining through the flinty orbs. Jackal turned around and presented the tattoos upon his back, the proper place for her blade.

When it was all over, Jackal strode from the voting chamber for the last time, his body weeping crimson.

Outside, dusk had abdicated to darkness. The slopheads waiting in the yard stepped away from him when they saw the bleeding cuts reflecting wetly in the moonlight. They knew what the gashes signified. None of the hopefuls would help him now. He needed his wounds dressed, but did not want to distract Crafty away from Oats. There was only one place he could go.

Beryl's face melted and set, quick as candlewax, when she saw him. The Claymaster had not yet given the Winsome villagers permission to return home, so she and her orphans still lodged in the slophead barracks. Jackal tarried by the door as she approached.

"Nomad?" Beryl said, a hitch in her voice. She was relieved, but surprised. Her eyes wandered over his injuries and mourned. "The children shouldn't see you like this."

"Could you help me with the cuts?" Jackal ventured. "The Claymaster may take issue—"

"Fuck the Claymaster. I'll gather some things and meet you in your chamber."

Nodding gratefully, Jackal left.

The bunkhouse already felt foreign. As he stepped over the threshold, Jackal was seized by the same sense of trepidation he once felt as a slophead when it was his duty to clean the Bastards' quarters. He was an intruder once more. Moving quickly down the hall, Jackal entered the expiring solace of his room. There would be no time to sleep. The nearest border to the Bastards' lot was a ride of several hours. By the time his wounds were dressed, Hearth readied, and his gear collected, Jackal would be in a pressing need to leave. Plus, there was Starling to consider. With any luck she would go as docilely with him as she had done with Hoodwink. Resistance would only cause delay, and delay could get them both killed.

Beryl arrived, bearing a lit lamp and a laden sling bag. She came wordlessly into the room and sat next to him on the bed. He waited while she scrutinized his cuts by the light of the flame.

"None of them are too deep," she said softly. "Your brothers were kind to you. This one across your back won't even need a bandage."

Jackal laughed involuntarily, but bit it down when he heard the sob in his throat. Beryl began to clean his cuts, the wine-soaked rag more agonizing than the axe blades. Setting his jaw, Jackal sat slumped and staring.

"I'm sorry about Oats," he managed after a time.

"Slops say he is going to heal," Beryl replied. He could hear the chained anger in her voice and knew she held it back for his sake. How far had he fallen? What kind of pathetic thing had he become that he was spared the rancor he deserved from a woman who had never feared to scold him? It would have been better if Beryl had berated him, called him a fool, screamed all the truths of his folly. But he was beneath contempt now, just a shadow that would be gone with the sun. It was madness to scream at shadows.

"The Claymaster wants Oats to be chief," Jackal said, not entirely certain why.

"He will never take that seat, Jackal."

"He should. Tell him, from me, he should. And tell him not to seek revenge on Fetching, not when he wakes up and not once he sits at the head of the table."

Beryl's weary disapproval ran through her entire body. "Jackal, Jackal . . . you've always been blind when it comes to that one. How long are you going to protect her?"

"No," Jackal protested, "it isn't that. Oats should never trust her again, but he shouldn't go after her either. If he does, the Claymaster gets everything he's ever wanted. Me and Fetch gone, and Oats under his wing. She took a side. That was her right as a Grey Bastard. We, Oats and I, helped her get a place in this hoof, but her vote is her own. If Oats treats her with scorn once he's chief then he is no better than the Claymaster, and he has to be better, Beryl. He has to be better!"

There was silence for a long time while Beryl dressed his wounds and pretended not to see his tears.

"Where will you go?" she asked once the last bandage was tightened.

"I don't know," he admitted. "Never thought I would turn nomad. In my mind, this plan was always victory or death. Even if I had pondered life as a free-rider, I never would have imagined a pregnant woman I can't talk to sharing my saddle."

"You are going to be hard-pressed to keep you both alive out there, Jackal."

He could only nod shallowly.

Beryl leaned over and, grabbing his face, kissed him hard on the temple. She stood abruptly and went for the door, taking her lamp, but leaving the bag.

"Change your dressings daily," she instructed, her voice thickening. "Get the Tine to help you."

She was fleeing the pain of parting and Jackal did not hinder her.

"Tell your son I'm sorry."

Beryl made a pained noise of promise and was gone.

He sat there for a long time, knowing he should be preparing his departure, yet unable to move. Familiar sounds in the hall signaled the return of some of his hoofmates. Former hoofmates. Jackal knew who they were from the distinctive footfalls and the doors that closed along the hall. Hobnail. Polecat.

Fetching.

Jackal tensed when he heard her door, directly across from his, open and close. He sat in the dark, shivering with rage and no small amount of fear, a feeling so foreign, so unwelcome, that it only infuriated him further. For what seemed an eternity he wrestled against a thousand impulses, each defying sound judgment. Only when his body had ceased trembling did he stand and, decision made, take up his dagger.

Once in the corridor, he paused, seeing the door opposite was cracked. No light flickered, but Jackal knew Fetch, knew she would still be awake. Numbly, he pushed the door open.

She sat cross-legged on her bed. Boots, brigand, and riding leathers were thrown carelessly on the floor, leaving her clothed in nothing but a shirt and shadows. She looked up, but said nothing.

Jackal came fully into the room and closed the door without taking his eyes off her.

"I figured you'd bring a thrum," Fetching declared before he could say anything. "It's quicker. A dagger allows for a struggle . . . takes time."

Oddly, she had no weapons of her own close at hand, just a slack wineskin.

"I did not come here to kill you," Jackal told her.

To prove his words, he stabbed the dagger into the doorjamb and left it lodged there.

"Why, Fetch?"

She shook her head slowly, the motion causing her face to play in and out of the shadows. "That's a question I asked you often. Why. Why did you claim to kill Garcia? Why do you insist on protecting that Tine? Why did you trust that fucking wizard?"

Fetch's voice became softer with each question, but the anger grew, making quivering whispers of her last words.

"Why did I trust *you*?" Jackal growled.

Fetch's head twitched to look at him. "Did you? Because I recall you only worrying I would ruin your picky little plans. I couldn't squat to piss without you keeping one eye on me."

"I've been trying to keep you alive. To get the Claymaster out of his seat and stop him from handing you to Bermudo with a fucking apple in your mouth and a smile on his face. With Starling . . ."

Fetch scoffed. "All you've done with that point-ear is brought the Tines to our door. She didn't help us one damn cunt hair and you know it."

The desperation in her voice surprised Jackal and angered Fetching. She shot up, standing upon her bed for a moment before hopping down, every motion aggravated. Her hands came up to scrub her locks with frustrated rapidity. The motion caused her shirt to raise, the down of hair between her legs suddenly revealed in moonlight.

"You fucking know it!" she said again.

Jackal felt his blood go hot. "So which was it, Fetch? Who led me astray, Crafty or the girl?"

"Both!" She was in his face now, her breath edged with wine. "We got Tines sniffing around the Kiln because of you. We got a wizard in our ranks who makes puppets of dead orcs because of you. I thought you wanted to lead this hoof, Jackal, not bury it."

"Because of me?" Jackal repeated through clenched teeth. "Because of me you are a member of this hoof, Fetching. Because of me you are not warming one of our beds. You are a sworn rider of the Grey Bastards, sitting a hog, respected and feared. Because of me."

He could feel Fetching trembling with barely suppressed rage, the tiny twin fires of moonlight that were her eyes glimmering.

"And because of me," she countered, "you're not."

Snarling, Jackal seized Fetching by the throat. She jerked away, but he held fast and they stumbled across the small room. Fetching landed a blow across Jackal's face and pain bloomed in his teeth. He tangled her next strike with his free arm and kicked her feet out from under her. She grabbed a fistful of his hair as she fell, dragging him down with her. He would have gone anyway, not wanting to release his grip upon her neck. His clenching fingers burrowed deeper into the iron resistance of Fetching's muscles and felt the pulse of her quickening heartbeat. Jackal fixated on it, yearning to feel it slow beneath his touch, then cease completely.

They crashed to the floor.

Weathering blows from her fists, Jackal put both hands to the task of throttling her. The blows ceased and Fetching wrapped her legs about Jackal's waist, throwing him off with a powerful torsion. They rolled and she was now atop him, sending a punch down into his cheekbone. Through the dull flash of pain, Jackal felt her scramble off. He snatched for her while she was still on her hands and knees, catching her hair in his fingers. Wrapping his other arm about her waist he hauled back and pulled her back down. They both faced the ceiling now and Jackal removed his hand from her hair to seize her neck in the crook of his arm. Her head squirmed against his collarbone, but soon ceased as he increased the pressure.

A sound began to push through Fetching's short, choked breaths, a deeper constricted flutter.

She was laughing.

Jackal felt her hips revolving, grinding her buttocks down into him, drawing his attention to the object of her sudden mirth. Beneath his breeches, beneath the pressure of Fetching's body, Jackal was hard.

He must have relaxed his hold, for Fetch's laughter now escaped in a raw rush. Jackal removed his arm from her throat and clapped his hand over her mouth, wanting to end the sound. Amused blasts of breath besieged his hand and he became aware of his other hand upon the spasmodically flexing muscles of her stomach, the flesh smooth and near feverish. Fetching cocked one hip, rising slightly away from his crotch. Jackal tried to seize that escaping hip in a bid to pull it back down, but she knocked his hand away with her own before sliding it within the agonizing gap she had created between them, fumbling to loosen the ties of his breeches and failing.

Frustrated, she tore his hand away from her mouth and sat up. Straddling his stomach, she quickly set to unlacing him, but Jackal upset her attempts when the shadowed dimples above her ass forced him to scoot down and pull her down upon his face. He heard her breath catch as his tongue touched her. She tasted of sweet salt and saddle leather. Fetch must have given up on his breeches, for Jackal could feel his cock hardening further, half-free, the laces painfully tight against his flesh. He did not care, lost in the act of devouring her.

A voice called through the door, one Jackal could barely hear. Someone must have heard the scuffle and was now asking after Fetch.

"Fuck off!" she replied, an airy giggle escaping through her feigned anger.

Jackal reveled as her weight settled until he could barely breathe. Fetching allowed him to explore with abandon, then took control of her pleasure and rubbed against his tongue until her thighs quivered.

The warm, intoxicating weight left him. The bed was close and Fetching rose just long enough to fall back upon the blankets. Jackal got quickly to his feet, turning as he tore at his laces. Fetch was reclined on the bed, propped up on her elbows, one knee in the air. Jackal's breeches were around his thighs when she hooked her calf around his lower back and drug him toward her open legs. She reached and grabbed his fruits, tugging them down until his cod leveled, straining away from his body and toward hers. Falling forward, Jackal caught his weight on extended arms, his forehead pressing into Fetch's as she drug him inside. A groan escaped from low in his throat and Fetching hissed, her clenched teeth quickly separating into an openmouthed expression of feral delight. Their eyes met, and mated more than their bodies, the small span between suffused with a lifetime of shattered restraint. As Jackal thrust, Fetching met his gaze boldly, challenging him as she had always done, tempting him even now. He surged in that roiling, unconquerable gaze, trapped in the naked, unblinking pleasure reflected there. They seemed to sustain on a single, vicious breath, passing it between their open lips, a finger's breadth apart.

Entwining her fingers behind his neck, Fetching rolled Jackal onto his back. He slipped out of her and gnashed his teeth in aggravation, but Fetch quickly took him in hand, holding him upright as she lowered herself down. He bucked up into her, but she grasped his jaw firmly, shaking her head, until he lay still. Balancing on the balls of her feet, Fetching eased herself up and back down. Her hands were on his chest, but she soon moved them to her own knees, bracing herself as she rode him with greater fervor. Fetching bounced on him with increasing vigor, never allowing him to escape, her body in perfect control. Soon, Jackal was gritting his teeth, his eyes squinting shut against his will at the blissful pressure in his loins. No other part of her touched him but that furiously sliding heat. His ears roaring with blood, Jackal's entire body tensed as the end came. Fetching stood at the last moment, causing Jackal's jumping cock to thump heavily onto his body, his expulsions landing hotly on his chest, the lesser flows spattering his stomach. He groaned through teeth clenched with release and vexation.

After a moment he sat up, looking irritably down on the mess Fetch had forced him to make of himself. She stood on the floor, near the foot of the bed, grinning as she cocked her head.

"Serves you right for all the times you did that to a whore," she said huskily, removing her rumpled shirt and flinging it down on him. "Clean up. You have to get riding."

After wiping himself off, Jackal rose, feeling all the pains that wrath and lust had kept at bay. The cuts crisscrossing his body stung, some of them reopened and bleeding anew. The bones in his face ached from Fetch's pummeling and there was pain in his fruits as well, the dull kind that always settled after sex. Fetching's own injuries were suddenly apparent, as well. Even in the low light, Jackal could now see the bruise stains across her ribs, the gash above her eye, the swollen hump of her broken and reset nose. None of that was his work. They were all tokens from Oats.

"Just tell me why, Fetching."

They both heard the pleading in his voice. He expected her to mock him for it, but shockingly, she took a step toward him, and it looked as if she would reach up to touch his face, the barest intention of movement, so slight Jackal might have imagined it. Instead, she pulled his dagger from the doorjamb and offered it to him.

"You think I did this to you," she said firmly. "I didn't. I did this to save the hoof. If you think me a liar, then use this slicer and cut my damned heart out."

Jackal opened the door. His eyes flicked to the weapon in her outstretched hand.

"Keep it. Offer the same choice to Oats . . . if he wakes."

Turning his back, he left the room.

Chapter 20

There was only one figure waiting at the mouth of the tunnel gate to see Jackal and Starling off; a wide, turbaned silhouette standing at ease in the night.

"And so where we first met becomes where we part," Crafty said, his smile evident even in shadow.

Jackal pulled Hearth to a halt and sat for a moment in silence. "Whatever it is you came here for, Uhad, you must not have wanted it badly enough."

"Because you are not a successful usurper? Is this your meaning?"

Jackal snorted bitterly. Crafty's command of the Hisparthan tongue waxed and waned to suit his purpose. "You didn't help me get the chief's seat, so now I can't help you."

The wizard's pudgy, ring-laden fingers splayed out in a futile gesture.

"Had you come to me with your intentions, friend Jackal, I would have warned against untimely action."

"It doesn't take a wizard to see a shit future that is already yesterday."

"This is so," Crafty placated.

"What will you do now?"

"Truly, though it is far from ideal—"

"Enough," Jackal cut him off wearily. "It doesn't matter. It's not my place to care anymore."

He kicked his hog forward into the pure black of the tunnel, leaving Crafty to stand in the starlight.

In front of him, Starling went a bit taut as they rode blind. She did not know to trust the hog's instincts within the gullet of the wall.

"We're soon through," he told her, and tightened his hold about her waist.

Thankfully, she had not balked when he came to collect her from the supply hall. The slopheads tasked with guarding her would not meet his eye and offered him no aid. They went about their duties amongst the inventory, silently transferring care of the she-elf to Jackal as they would a bag of beans. That was what she had become, a commodity, to be stored amongst sacks of grain and barrels of olive oil, adopting their mute dullness. A mote of vitality appeared when she beheld the cuts on Jackal's arms and chest, but there was no trepidation on her face, only a grim curiosity. He took her from amongst the shelves with the rest of his allotted kit.

And now the Kiln was behind them both, forever.

Hearth wanted to run as soon as he cleared the tunnel. Jackal allowed him, checking the beast's stride just enough for Starling's ease. The whim of the hog was their only guide, for Jackal had no inclination of where they should head. Ul-wundulas was open to him, daring him to tread where he will. He was a free-rider, a nomad, with no oaths or pledges binding him, no sworn brothers to watch his flank. He and Starling would live or die on the choices he made, and that was if the Lots chose to be kind. If the sun rose to find them in Bastard lands, then die they would, bristling with thrumbolts if his former brethren could not stomach to get close for the killing.

The shortest distance out of the lot was north, toward the Umber Mountains, but that would bring them to the edge of Tine lands. Was that the best course? Simply turn Starling loose at familiar borders and be done? That was supposing he could get close enough without the elves feathering him quicker than the Grey Bastards. Even if he could, would they let Starling live? Would she allow herself to live once she learned the truth of her condition?

There were always the other hoofs.

The Skull Sowers' lot was the nearest, but the thought of living in the Furrow made Jackal's skin crawl. He had often found the Kiln too confining, to say nothing of that underground stronghold. The Orc Stains were just beyond Batayat Hill, but they accepted only thrice-bloods. The Fangs of Our Fathers were too obsessed with thick gods for Jackal's tastes, and there was already bad blood between him and the Shards. That only left three choices; the Cauldron Brotherhood, the Tusked Tide, and the Sons of Perdition. But none of them would consider taking him with Starling as baggage. If they did, they would want her as a whore. "The only thing rarer than seeing a she-elf is fucking one," the saying went. No, Jackal would have to forgo the other hoofs at least until he knew what to do with his companion.

That left only one place.

Strava.

It was the obvious choice, but Jackal was reluctant to return after agreeing to Zirko's mad bargain. He had not expected to go back until the Betrayer Moon, if then. Still, it made the most likely sanctuary for him and Starling. They had already been there together, received aid. Surely, they would be welcome again. Zirko believed Jackal was carrying one of the halflings' precious relics inside his arm, why would the little priest turn him away after asking he swear allegiance to the god Belico and some loon-brained crusade against the orcs? Plus, Zirko knew of the half-breed Starling carried, so there would be no need for lies, and it was unthinkable that the halflings or the Unyar would demand the she-elf as a plaything. It would be safe, as safe as anywhere in the Lots.

Jackal pulled the reins west.

It was at least a four-day journey, but they would be out of the Grey Bastards' lot once they crossed the Alhundra. There was enough time to make it before dawn, but only just.

Jackal pushed Hearth hard, though the hog needed little urging. A night ride across the badlands was nothing new for the barbarian and he took joy in the freedom, the chance to roam, to run, unburdened with the knowledge that home was forever closed. Jackal concentrated on the ride, watched the terrain for hazards and the darkness for foes. He tried to settle into familiar rhythms, but it was difficult with the smell of Starling's hair in his nostrils. His mind kept skulking back to Fetching, to the engulfing pain of her betrayal, the feel of her skin, the taste of her.

Briefly, he wondered if that was why she had lain with him, to eclipse the treachery, but he knew it was not the reason, had known even as he entered her. It was the last chance, for both of them. All kinship had been shattered by her actions, but so too had all impediments. No longer friends, no longer hoofmates, no longer living under Jackal's impending leadership, they were free to be lovers. Fetching had convinced the hoof that she lusted for women, and Jackal allowed himself to believe it over the years, despite the memories from their youth to the contrary. First kisses, first fondles, all awkward and shivering. But it had stopped when Fetch set her mind to the hoof. Jackal had not minded, he even understood. He wanted her to be one of them and knew that to do so she would need to *become* one of them. Besides, there had been plenty of other girls who were willing and generous, and that was all Jackal's youthful baseness required. After a few years and a handful of shared visits to Sancho's brothel, it was easy to support the falseness of Fetch's affections until they became truth.

In their worst moment, Fetch had set aside the impostor and taken what she wanted, what she knew they both wanted. The last chance. It was agonizing and infuriating, the pain and anger made all the more tempestuous by the fact that Jackal already wanted her again.

He called a quick halt to keep Starling from having to ride with a saddlehorn in front and behind. Reining Hearth up next to a rocky spur above a draw, Jackal dismounted quickly and turned to help Starling down, but she had already swung a leg over and ignored his reaching hands. Feigning stiffness in his legs, Jackal moved away to walk off the actual discomfort. Starling remained close to Hearth, the natural grace of her kind evident even in the small pacing steps she took. Beryl had scrounged clothes for her that fit properly; deerskin breeches, a linen shirt, a riding hood and mantle. Clean, garbed, and unguarded, she appeared less the cornered animal, yet still out of place. She reminded Jackal of rainfall during a day bright with sun, natural, yet rare and inharmonic. Her captivity in the Sludge Man's hut had been an atrocity, her confinement in the Kiln a crude necessity. Jackal could not imagine Strava would be much better. He wondered, was there a place in the world she would belong?

Hells, the same could be asked of him. Two people just got down from Hearth's saddle and both were strangers to Jackal.

He ambled up the shallow slope, giving Starling some space, and stood atop the spur. What he saw moving along their backtrail sent him rushing immediately back down.

"We must go," he told Starling, mounting up and reaching down for her. This time she did not ignore him, the urgency in his voice undeniable. He kicked Hearth into a gallop, guiding him along the draw as long as possible, sticking to the lower ground to avoid revealing a silhouette on the horizon to their pursuer.

A lone rider. On hogback. Not a mile behind.

Damn the Claymaster! He had already sent the boys out, which meant they weren't waiting for dawn. It was all a lie, the chief's mercy nothing but a ruse. The poxy cur never had any intention of letting Jackal and Starling live. There was no time now to try to lose them, cover his trail. Dawn was coming and life was now a race to the river.

"Reach forward," Jackal called behind Starling's ear. "Grab his bristles."

He took one of her hands and guided it into Hearth's mane, squeezing down on her knuckles until he felt her fingers clench. She understood and did the same with her other hand.

"Don't pull back, just hold steady and let your arms go with him."

Jackal did not know how much of that Starling would comprehend, but was relieved to see her follow his instruction. Hearth was surging now and Jackal counted half a dozen of the hog's deep exhales before letting go of Starling's waist. Gripping only with his legs, Jackal slung his stockbow around, pulled back on the string, and loaded a bolt. Jamming the butt of the weapon hard against his thigh and holding it one-handed, Jackal grabbed a fistful of Hearth's rough mane and bent to the task of a hard ride. There wasn't a barbarian in the Grey Bastards' stables that was faster than his, but none of his former brothers would be doubled up. As soon as they discovered he had given flight, they would kick their hogs to match. Once they were within thrumshot, it would be over.

Scrub and boulders, silvered with moonlight, rushed past as Hearth chewed up the dirt. Jackal ignored the ground immediately before them, trusting to his mount, and looked ahead, quickly assessing the oncoming terrain and making small adjustments to their course with the weight of his body. The hog responded without hesitation, anticipating the subtle commands. They stuck to the flats, thundering across sandy swaths lit with leeched starlight, bright white against the dark. The open ground would make them an easy mark, but it was the only way to gain a lead.

Jackal turned in the saddle and saw none giving chase. Not yet. They would need every heartbeat.

Starling was doing well holding her seat, her balance perfect. Hearth ran as if unaware of the extra weight. The Alhundra came into view ahead, the constellations sliding upon the skin of the water. Snatching a look behind, Jackal cursed. He did not know precisely how long the other rider had been in view, but he was certainly there now.

They would reach the river ahead of their pursuer, but perhaps not ahead of a bolt in the back. Jackal had a vague idea what stretch of the Alhundra lay before them, but there was only a single ford for miles in both directions. At night, after a desperate flight, the odds of striking the crossing were slim, and then there would be no choice but to turn and fight.

Hearth charged toward the flow, his sides heaving as he smelled water. The hog found reserves of speed and made directly for the bank, his hooves striking rocks as he jumped down into the gully bordering the wash. Jackal nearly pulled back on one of the hog's swine-yankers to prevent the beast from rushing headlong into the drink, but stayed his hand at the last moment. Water erupted beneath them as Hearth barged confidently across the ford.

Jackal smiled and nearly let loose a triumphal cry.

"Hearth, you beautiful, savvy son of a sow," he said, rubbing the pig vigorously.

They quickly reached the other side and Jackal tugged his mount around. It was time to see who chased them.

A moment later, the other rider came into view. The Alhundra was wide, but the pale, bald figure was unmistakable.

"Hoodwink."

Jackal cursed the name softly, his voice swallowed by the sound of the river, but Hood's gaze settled on him in that moment, as if he had heard. They stared at each other across the ephemeral barrier of the current, and suddenly it felt as if the water flowed down Jackal's spine. He saw Hoodwink's mind, the intention to cross written in the set of his shoulders.

Baring his teeth in a silent snarl, Jackal whirled his mount and made for the scrabble of boulders he had spied while crossing the ford. The other Bastards weren't in pursuit, he was sure of that now. The Claymaster had sent his pet murderer to ensure Jackal and Starling were found on hoof land come the morning, no matter where their feet stood when they died. Had it been anyone else, Jackal would have kept riding, knowing the tradition of safety would be upheld. But this was Hoodwink.

Riding swiftly up the rise, Jackal jumped from the saddle as soon as the rocks blocked him from view. Keeping low, thrum in hand, he left Starling astride Hearth and scrambled up the boulders. Nearing the uneven crest, he dropped and crawled on his belly until he gained vantage over the river. Just in time. Hood was already more than halfway across.

Jackal would rather have come to grips with the dead-eyed spook, vented his rage in the clash of blades, but he couldn't take the risk. He needed the Claymaster to know that coming after him was a mistake, to let the hoof know that any who hunted him would not return to the Kiln alive. Pulling the stock of his thrum tight into his shoulder, Jackal sighted down the shaft, leading Hoodwink with the barbed head of the bolt. The skulking wretch wasn't pushing his hog hard, his pace almost leisurely, mocking those who fled from him. Well, Jackal wasn't fleeing. He took a deep breath and held it in his lungs. Let Hood's cold confidence accompany him to every hell.

"Get your finger off that tickler, boy."

The voice was deep, gravel loosed by thunder, and uniquely resonant. You could never forget that voice.

Jackal cocked his head to the right to find an arrow trained on him, steady behind the straining string of a recurve bow. The archer stood amongst the boulders, his position perfectly chosen. Jackal would never be able to swing his thrum around and loose a bolt before receiving a shaft through the ribs. Complying with the command, he splayed his fingers away from the tickler and watched as a phantom from his past detached from the shadows.

Warbler.

The older half-orc had changed little in all the years. His thick, wavy mane of hair was now entirely silver, but it didn't appear one strand had been lost. The distantly familiar face was more wrinkled than Jackal remembered, housing the same flinty stare and prominent fangs that had often glowered at him as a child. Some softness had settled into his midsection, but his shoulders were still broad, and age had not bent his spine. Hells, he was still taller than Jackal. That was disappointing, yet not surprising. Warbler was a thrice-blood, after all.

"It's me, War-boar," Jackal said. "Look hard, it's Jaco."

"I ain't blind," came the low reply. "I know who you are, Jackal of the Grey Bastards. Though, judging from those cuts, perhaps not anymore."

Jackal was surprised to hear the use of his hoof name, a name he had not possessed when Warbler left the Kiln.

"You're making a mistake," Jackal told him.

The broadhead did not waver. "No, boy, I'm preventing one. Now, empty that runnel."

Gritting his teeth, Jackal reached with his left hand and pulled the bolt from his weapon.

"Thrum it," Warbler ordered.

Jackal hesitated. The string on the recurve bow groaned as Warbler pulled it tauter. With no choice, Jackal pulled the tickler on his unloaded stockbow, sending the string snapping forward on useless air.

"Leave it and stand up."

Abandoning his thrum, Jackal stood slowly. "I got a killer on my heels. He is going to be up these rocks soon. I know it's been a long span of years, Warbler, but you need to trust me."

"Killer?" Warbler seemed amused at the word, grinning for a long moment before unleashing a sharp, controlled whistle. "Hoodwink is a damn sight more than a killer."

Jackal heard footsteps on the lower rocks and Hood appeared, holding his tulwar loosely in one hand, Starling firm in the other.

"A damn sight more," Warbler said again as the pale devil climbed to stand beside him, "and right now, I trust him for all the hells more than I do you."

Chapter 21

Bound hand and foot, Jackal could only glare as Hoodwink and Warbler spoke in hushed tones. The familiarity in their furtive discourse was nearly impossible to reconcile. Warbler was clearly asking questions, and the answers were given readily, but with grim brevity. Though their words were lost to distance and whispers, this was the most Jackal had ever seen Hood speak. There were more than a few gestures and glances at Starling, who sat unbound less than a stone's throw from where Jackal knelt.

He wondered if she had even tried to run, though Hearth would not have responded favorably to commands from a strange rider. The hog was now tethered to a gorse bush beyond where Hood and Warbler stood, next to their own mounts, perfectly at ease. Likely Hoodwink had come up slowly, a familiar smell on a fellow pig, the cunning fuck. No doubt he simply reached out and took Hearth's swine-yanker without so much as a squeal of complaint. No, Starling had not tried to run. She was not as big a fool as Jackal.

He looked over and met her eyes.

"They won't harm you," he said, trying to sound resolved. She looked away almost immediately. Indeed not a fool, to ignore assurances from a captor now trussed up with leather straps.

"No, we won't harm you," Warbler announced gruffly as he strode toward them.

He went to Starling and squatted, waited calmly until she met his gaze. Then he spoke to her in the elf tongue. It did not sound beautiful, even with Warbler's distinctive voice, yet the old mongrel wielded the language with confidence. It seemed to Jackal that Starling gave a wordless affirmation. Warbler remained balanced on his haunches, deep in thought. He nodded shallowly to himself and drew a knife from his boot.

Jackal jumped up and managed to land on his yoked feet, but an unseen hand clamped around his neck and pushed him back to his knees.

"One day, Hood," Jackal snarled, "you'll fail to be so damn quiet."

With a deft motion, Warbler flipped the knife, caught it by the blade and slowly offered it, grip-first, to Starling. She took it readily, eagerly, her hand darting out with all the speed of a scorpion sting. Standing, she gazed at the blade for a moment, then her eyes flicked to Warbler. He remained where he was, giving nothing but a small permissive gesture with his hand. Jackal slumped beneath Hoodwink's hand. Warbler had just given Starling the choice he couldn't, and her decision was written in the haunted set of her face.

As she turned, her eyes settled on Jackal, brief as the landing of a butterfly, and then she was gone, hurrying into the night with the instrument of her salvation clutched in her hand.

Clenching his teeth in futile rage, Jackal hung his head. His hoof, his friends, his life, all now lost for the protection of a she-elf who wanted nothing but to die.

Warbler approached and resumed his squat.

"You challenged the Claymaster."

It wasn't a question.

Jackal looked up. "Same as you."

Warbler rubbed unconsciously at the web of raised scars on his arms. There had been more brothers during his day, more axes at the table.

"When I did it, the chief didn't have a wizard tickling his ear." Warbler snorted and shook his head. "You always had balls, Jaco. Waddled funnier than most toddlin' whelps because of them. I'd hoped some of that wrinkled flesh would find its way up inside your skull."

"My learning was cut a bit short . . . when my mentor exiled himself."

Warbler ignored this. "Hood says Isabet turned coat. Cost you the seat."

"It's Fetching," Jackal said through clenched teeth, "and Jackal. Not Isabet, not Jaco. Fetching and Jackal, our hoof names. We fucking earned them."

Warbler gave a solid nod of agreement. "You're right."

The old mongrel's gaze drifted up and his chin lifted. The bonds around Jackal's wrists parted. Another swift slice from Hoodwink freed his ankles. Jackal got to his feet and Warbler followed him up. Hood came around to stand between them, sheathing his knife.

"The Tyrkanian had a forked tongue from the beginning, Jackal," Warbler said. "He was just ferreting out the Claymaster's biggest rival. Tell him."

Hoodwink turned his unblinking stare on Jackal. "It was the wizard's idea. Send me out with the elf. Told the Claymaster it would provoke your challenge."

"And what were you supposed to do with her?" Jackal asked.

"Rape her and throw her off the top of Batayat," Hoodwink said woodenly. "Make it look the work of orcs."

Jackal bristled. "That what you did when you took her from Dog Fall? Make it look the work of orcs?"

"Wasn't me," Hood replied. "Wasn't the Claymaster. You had that wrong."

Jackal's mouth was dry, foul-tasting with bitter truths. Hells damn it all. Fetch was right. She hadn't done this to him. It was all his own fool-ass doing. The Claymaster's biggest rival? Jackal had never been close, not near as close to a rival as he'd been to his own ambitions. All the old man had to do was wait him out, watch as he ground himself to dust beneath the heels of his headlong flight to leadership. He'd thought it was his last chance, and been warned it was the wrong one to take. He could have done it differently at any one of a hundred moments. He could have done it all differently.

"And what if Crafty had it wrong?" Jackal demanded of Hoodwink. "What if I had let you leave with her?"

Warbler stepped in. "He would have brought her to me. As you saw, we did her no ill."

"No ill?" Jackal snapped. "She's still dead now, Warbler!"

"A clean death and an honorable one to her mind, boy. It's what you should have done when you found her."

Sliding the kerchief off his head, Jackal scrubbed at his hair, pacing away from the other two.

Strava. He was taking her to Strava! A place to be safe, a place to live. And now she was out there in the dark, preparing her own end, or already dead, limp and cooling in the moonlight. Come morning, only the carrion birds would know where she lay. In a month she would be nothing but another fetish of bleached bones adorning ancient, remorseless Ul-wundulas.

"And why would he bring her to you?" Jackal demanded, whirling and gesturing wildly between Warbler and Hoodwink. "What is this?"

"I've been a free-rider for nearly fifteen years," Warbler told him, "but Hood's been out here most of his life. I asked him to join the Bastards, get close to the Claymaster, be my eyes and ears. It took me a long time to find someone I trusted enough with the task."

Jackal shot a look at Hoodwink. "And why would you do this for him?"

There was no response.

"I never left, Jackal," Warbler went on, "not in my heart. They marred my Bastard tattoos, but the hoof lies deeper than flesh. The Claymaster has ruled too long. These last few months, Hood's been telling me it looked like you would take the seat. I just learned you failed. Claymaster must have thought you had a chance and took steps to bring you down."

Jackal chewed on this for a moment. "You think he knew Crafty all along, arranged to have him come to the Kiln?"

"I don't know," Warbler admitted.

"No," Jackal said, his mind working quickly. "That fat fuck has his own designs. He may have betrayed me, but he was no puppet of the Claymaster. It's the other way around."

"Yes," Hoodwink agreed.

Jackal took a deep breath, steeling himself for the answer to his next question.

"And Fetch? How long has she been heeling to the chief's commands?"

Hood's grave-mask did not slip.

"Never saw them speak. Not until after the vote. She volunteered to act as champion. Chief knew you were going to choose Oats. She claimed to be the only one who could beat him. Claymaster wasn't hearing it, then he talked to the wizard in private. After that, he said she could fight. No one foresaw her axe hitting that table."

It was true. Stunned as he was, Jackal still recalled the chief's face, equally slack-jawed.

"She made her choice," Warbler growled, "now it's time you made yours."

"And what is that?"

"Whether or not you want to continue trying to save the Grey Bastards."

A disgusted noise escaped from Jackal's lips. "From what? The Claymaster? We are both testaments to where that leads, Warbler. If you had just been patient, if *I* had just been patient, one of us might have succeeded him. He's going to be dead in a few years."

Warbler's thin smile bordered on mocking. "You believe so?"

"What do you know that I don't?" Jackal said.

"A hog's steaming heap," Warbler barked, "but there's much you can teach me too, especially concerning this swaddlehead sorcerer. Leaving the Claymaster with a wizard is woe on the wind, Jackal, no matter which is holding the reins. Help me break that oozing old shit's twisted back and take your revenge on the Tyrkanian."

It was Jackal's turn to display a mocking smile. "So you trust me now?"

"Not much," Warbler said, "but I don't know you anymore, boy. Seems to me you've made some fool-ass choices . . . so have I, though. Hood's vouched for you, says you've been dead set on booting the Claymaster. That gives us enough common ground to start, far as I can spit."

Jackal eyeballed Hoodwink and sneered. "Vouched for me. But didn't vote for me. Why is that, Hood? If you had sent your axe into the stump, the three of us wouldn't be standing here conspiring in the dust."

Hoodwink didn't seem likely to answer, so Warbler did.

"He had no choice. In the hoof's eyes, Hood has to be dog-loyal to the Claymaster until the very end."

"Had he thrown in with me, it would have been the end," Jackal replied bitterly.

Hood only turned away, unconcerned, and walked to the where the hogs were tethered.

"You don't trust him," Warbler said, "and that's good. You weren't supposed to. But give me eight days and I wager you'll begin to trust me. If you don't, well hells, you're a free-rider now and can go where you wish."

Hoodwink returned before Jackal could answer, bearing a thrum. Jackal's thrum.

"They'll never believe I didn't catch up to him," Hoodwink told Warbler as he handed him the weapon along with a single bolt.

Jackal tensed as the old mongrel loaded the stockbow.

"Could do the hog instead," Warbler offered. The look that Hoodwink gave him would have withered crops. Warbler chuckled darkly. Watching them, Jackal was suddenly reminded of the way he and Oats jested.

Until Warbler stepped back a pace and loosed the bolt into Hoodwink's thigh. He shot from the hip, yet the aim was unerring, piercing the meat while missing the bone. Hood's knee buckled slightly, but he remained upright, balancing on his uninjured leg. His breath came out in rapid, noisy pulses from his nostrils, but he did not so much as grunt against the pain.

Fucking hells. Jackal managed not to say it aloud.

"Well aimed, kid," Warbler proclaimed, tossing Jackal his empty stockbow. "Bring Hood his hog. Least you could do after feathering him like that."

Jackal did as ordered, slinging his stockbow across his back as he went. He gave Hearth a rub on the flank as he retrieved Hood's barbarian, a lean beast the color of old ash that had no name Jackal had ever heard. Hoodwink ignored all attempts by Warbler to help him mount and swung his skewered leg over the saddle.

"You know what to tell them?" Warbler asked.

Hoodwink nodded.

"Luck then, brother. Live in the saddle . . ."

Without responding, Hood clicked his tongue and rode off.

"Die on the hog," Jackal said, unable to let the creed remain unfinished. "He didn't say it."

"He never does," Warbler muttered, still watching the swiftly dwindling shadow. After a moment, he ambled over to the hogs and began tightening the cinch strap on his barbarian, clearly intending to ride. Jackal joined him and started adjusting Hearth's tack. He still hadn't decided what to do, but any choice made would involve his ass grinding leather. After a long silence, he looked over Hearth's back at Warbler's hog.

"When did you lose Border Lord?"

"First summer after leaving the Kiln," Warbler replied, still intent on his task. "Brush foot."

Jackal nodded sympathetically even though Warbler was not looking at him.

"And this one?" Jackal asked.

"I call him Mean Old Man," Warbler replied, giving the near pitch-black pig a final look-over.

"This is Hearth," Jackal said, then realized he had not been asked. Hells, his own voice sounded ten years younger, whining for approval. At that moment, he almost mounted up, put heel to hog and rode off. His old life was through. Why go wading deeper into the past with an old outcast who made him feel a child?

The answer was enthroned within his skull.

This old outcast made Jackal who he was. Made Fetch and Oats too. When they were younger, they all thought they would one day ride under his command, and spent long afternoons entertaining one another with certainties of that glorious, future life. Warbler would be their chief, and they his most trusted riders. They had not been able to fathom his sudden, grievous ousting. To this day there was still much Jackal did not know about Warbler's failed challenge. And he wanted to. He wanted to finally know this champion of his boyhood.

"What is Hood going to tell the Claymaster?" Jackal asked. "That I'm dead?"

Warbler chuffed. "That you're alive. That you escaped. The truth is the only choice. Sooner or later, you are going to meet other nomads and word will spread, free-rider to free-rider. Eventually it will get back to the Kiln. Hoodwink gets caught in that deep a lie, the Claymaster will sniff him out. Besides, knowing you're out here somewhere will make him sweat."

"Good enough," Jackal said. "Tell me, what will happen in eight days that you believe will make me want to help you?"

"A ride north," Warbler replied, climbing into the saddle.

"An eight-day northward ride," Jackal calculated, "would bring us to . . ."

He looked up sharply.

Warbler gave a quick, confirming nod. "Hispartha."

With that, the old thrice turned his hog, glanced at the stars for a bearing, and began riding.

Jackal lingered a moment to face a different direction, one guided only by a set of barely perceptible footprints in the dust. They disappeared into a still landscape rendered nearly featureless by night.

"Farewell, Starling."

CHAPTER 22

THE BONES OF KALBARCA SPRAWLED UPON THE BANKS OF THE river. Beneath the sunrise, the crumbling buildings composed a carcass, a decrepit pilgrim dead of thirst within reach of water. The long arches of the Old Imperial Bridge jutted from the ruins and spanned the muddy shallows of the Guadal-kabir, seeming to flee the decay of the once great city. The bridge was an ancient construction, yet stood sound while the surrounding buildings of Hisparthan architects slowly fell to rubble, shaming the genius of their Imperial forebears.

Three hard days in the saddle were needed to reach this place. At first, Jackal had been perplexed by the westward lean of their course, but now he understood.

Kalbarca resided above the heart of Ul-wundulas, backed to the north and west by the mountain range known as the Smelted Mounts, and though it had never recovered from its razing by orcs during the Incursion, the ruined city still remained an embarkation point for the Emperor's Road. Another invention of the now extinct Imperium, the cobbled marvel was not one road, but several that cut through the Lot Lands, maintaining courses once paramount to trade and the swift movement of legions. Jackal did not know what happened to the emperors, only that there was a first and a last, and much had changed since their days. The Hisparthan kings had risen after them, but they too lost their hold on Ul-wundulas. The sparsely populated badlands that Jackal called home had little use for roads and mile markers. The mongrel hoofs avoided them, preferring to ride cross-country amongst the scrub and the boulders. That is where any encroaching thicks would be, not marching down some neatly paved avenue.

However, the road was the swiftest route into Hispartha.

"We will rest the hogs here," Warbler declared, gazing down at

Kalbarca from their vantage upon a ridge. "Once the sun is high we will take the Emperor's, chew some distance before nightfall."

They proceeded down into the valley and reached the river while the morning was still young. The ruins rested in Crown lands, though Jackal saw no evidence of soldiery as they crossed the bridge and approached what was left of the walls. He knew from talks with Ignacio's men that patrols here were few. The Grey Bastards rarely had cause to intrude this far, and Jackal had only ridden within sight of Kalbarca once before.

Warbler clearly knew his way around. He guided them through the rubble-strewn alleys, past the shadowed sockets of doorways and windows long bereft of habitation. The orcs had occupied the city for years after breaking the defenses, and smears of their savage calligraphy stained the whitewash, boasts written in blood to their esurient gods. Thicks had no talent for building. Haphazard heaps of stone and timber were thrown into the breaches they made in the walls, all that was done to shore up their prize against a counterattack. Not that it mattered. Hispartha never attempted to retake the city. It was abandoned by the enemy only when the great plague swept through Ulwundulas, killing orcs and men in reaping strokes, ending the war.

"The frails never have come back," Jackal commented, craning his neck around to look at the puzzle of broken dwellings. "Must have been too ashamed."

Ahead of him, Warbler huffed. "They'll be back. Soon as some king orders the reclamation of the Lots, this warren will be crawling with more soldiers than rats."

Jackal was dubious, but he kept his mouth closed.

"For now," Warbler went on, "it's a good place for free-riders. Plenty of places to hole up, rest, hide if you need to. Just keep away from the old mausoleum and any tunnels leading beneath ground. The halflings have a permanent colony here, digging around for every shit Belico ever took. They think you've despoiled their work, you won't make it out of Kalbarca alive."

Jackal did not care for Warbler's instructional tone. This wasn't his first ride.

"I can handle halflings. Me and their high priest have an understanding."

Warbler twisted in the saddle and squinted at Jackal for a moment. He said nothing and soon turned back around.

They rode into what was left of a plaza and dismounted, quickly unsaddling their barbarians and stowing the tack within a nearby building.

"We'll walk the hogs down to a spot I know where they can drink, then come back and get some rest."

They slept the morning away in the cool shadows of the ruins. Jackal gave himself to slumber readily, but fell into fitful dreams of Starling. He awoke sore and sickened, with hours to spare before noon. Needing to feel the sun on his skin, he went out to the plaza and sat upon a cracked plinth. He busied himself with the care of his weapons, first cleaning his blades, before moving on to the longer task of his stockbow.

As he was refitting the bowstring to the prods, Warbler emerged.

"Best begin practice with a bow," the old thrice proclaimed. "That thrum won't last a year in this life."

"That why you use that piece of Unyar driftwood?" Jackal asked. "Couldn't maintain your stockbow?"

Warbler just laughed and shook his head, ducking back into the building to retrieve his saddle.

Jackal knew the old thrice wasn't wrong, but the constant advice was tickling at his temper. Every word out of Warbler's mouth, hells, his very presence, was a reminder that this life was permanent. Try as he might, Jackal could not shake the feeling that he was simply on another patrol, an extended ranging into unfamiliar territory, and when it was done he would ride back to the Kiln. But that fantasy only lived upon the surface of his mind. Pursuing it only dredged up pain as the truth of the past days poisoned the intimacy of years.

They left Kalbarca before noon, taking the ancient road. The straight, flat line of pale stones speared hypnotically toward the Smelteds, the foothills limned in shimmers of heat. Warbler set an even, tedious pace. Mean Old Man seemed well accustomed, but Hearth had difficulties. He wanted to run and, when held back, kept slowing to a plod. Jackal focused on getting control and was soon riding alongside his fellow nomad. They stopped rarely and spoke not at all.

The Emperor's Road led them northeast for most of the day, skirting the mountains. Finally, in the late afternoon, it split, the main body striking directly northward, while the smaller offshoot turned toward the descending sun. Warbler pulled his hog east, showing his ass to the Smelted Mounts. Dusk came, holding court over the sky with beautiful brevity before yielding gracefully to night. Still they rode on, and Jackal enjoyed the swiftly cooling air until Warbler called a halt. He led them off the road to a stand of stone pine and declared they would camp.

The rations in Jackal's kit would not last the ride unless stretched, so he took only pulls from his waterskin as he lay upon his bedroll, reclined against his saddle. He was drifting off to sleep when a rattling weight struck him in the chest. Plucking the flung sack from his chest, he unknotted the string.

"Almonds," he said, glancing up to look at the sack's thrower sitting beneath the opposite tree, but Warbler's scarred arms were crossed over his chest and his eyes were already closed.

They were in the saddle by dawn and rode hard before the heat was high. Warbler called a halt early, veering off the road to a grove of lemon trees. They stayed only long enough to pick some choice pieces and continued on, eating the fruit as they rode and saving the rinds for their hogs. The countryside grew noticeably lusher as they again turned north, though the dusty sun-bleached rocks still far outnumbered the greenery. Jackal was not certain exactly when it happened, but by midday he was unmistakably aware they were now in lands he had never before traveled. He wanted to ask why they were bound for Hispartha, but kept his questions locked behind his teeth.

The road was far from abandoned and they began to cross paths with other travelers, overtaking a lone halfling pilgrim on foot and, later, meeting a trio of mongrel free-riders coming south. Warbler stopped and spoke to them all. The discussions were brief, almost ritual.

Where have you come from?

Where are you bound?

What have you seen upon the road?

Answers to these questions were exchanged with no pleasantries, nor any guile. Warbler always responded truthfully and Jackal detected no dissembling from those they encountered. The information was sparse, yet valuable. Even no news was prized; an uneventful journey was often a safe one. With the halfling, names were not exchanged, but Warbler made a point of introducing Jackal to the half-orc nomads. Each of the three accepted his name with a terse nod, their dust-caked faces displaying a restrained mix of grief and scorn, as if they mourned and detested his choice to join their ranks.

Jackal found this same conflicted soup boiling in his own gut as he returned their stares. These were free-riders, outcasts, thrown out of their hoofs for all manner of unspoken reasons. Jackal was all too aware that the causes for exile were not always dishonorable, yet he could not help but think that he was now amongst a company of liars, cowards, and kin slayers. No doubt the same unproven condemnations were silently leveled at him.

Over the passing days they spoke with other free-riders, most riding alone, but some in pairs or small groups. All of them were filthy, careworn, and terse. Their hogs were lean and shabby, their weapons tarnished. Jackal noticed, with silent ill humor, there was not a single stockbow amongst them. He committed all of their names to memory, but wondered if he could ever tell one from another on a second meeting. Warbler was well known by all, yet commanded no unique respect. He was as they all were, just another masterless rider, drifting through the Lots.

Perhaps it was Jackal's well-fed hog or his supple saddle, perhaps his stockbow, but something about him seemed to sour the countenances of the other free-riders. At first he thought it was some customary derision given to all newcomers, but it was too unwavering and lacked any sense of the callous mirth directed at slopheads.

"It's as if they don't believe you," he finally said to Warbler at their sixth overnight camp. "As if they don't believe I've turned nomad."

"Difficult to believe a man has lost his hoof when he's bearing unmarked Bastard tattoos," Warbler replied, giving Jackal's arms a pointed look.

Glancing down, Jackal saw he was right. The cuts were gone. His flesh, and the ink beneath, was unmarred. He hadn't noticed, so used to them being a part of him.

Jackal ran a mystified hand from his shoulder to his wrist.

"I've been . . . I've been healing quickly," he offered in feeble explanation.

Warbler grunted. "You really make a deal with Zirko?"

The question forced Jackal away from the bemused exploration of his skin. He looked up to find the old thrice frowning at him, waiting upon an answer without demanding one.

"I went to him," Jackal admitted. "My arm was shattered and needed mending. It had gone too long. I knew it was going to have to be cut off, unless . . ."

"Unless you got some miracle."

"I'd heard the rumors about Strava. Hells, you used to tell us stories about it. Oats and Fe— . . . I was warned against it, but there wasn't a choice. Zirko said there would be a price. Two, in fact. I agreed to pay them. So yes, I made a deal. But the little fucker's half-crazy. Thinks his god is going to return and lead an army into Dhar'gest, destroy all the thicks."

Warbler gave a scoffing shake of his head. "It would take a god to do it. And even then . . ."

A distant, haunted pall melded with the shadows on the older half-orc's face.

"You've been there," Jackal realized aloud. "The Dark Lands. You've fucking been!"

Warbler shook his head again, but in distaste, not denial. "Once."

Jackal suddenly felt a child, begging for stories at War-boar's knee, but he could not help himself from asking the question.

"Why?"

"Same reason anyone goes into peril," Warbler responded slowly. "Because some things just have to be faced."

Unwilling to press further, lest he start to crave a tit full of milk, Jackal let the matter drop.

The seventh day of travel brought them to the edge of heavily forested highlands. The road continued on its course, rising to tackle the sloping terrain, but Warbler pulled Mean Old Man away from the cobbles, heading due east cross-country. Creeks and streams became prevalent, and Jackal marveled at the verdant plains splashed between the brown hills. He began to see trees he could not name, their leaves so thick and green they appeared nearly as black as the succoring shade they housed.

"Is this Tine land?" Jackal queried, turning south to see the distant, hazy peaks of the Umber Mountains.

"Far from it," Warbler told him. "This belongs to the Crown. Did you think the nobility would not keep the best lots for themselves?"

"Are there any castiles? Cavalry? Who keeps watch here?"

"No one. These are the borderlands, Jackal. There were few settlements here before the Incursion and none have been built since." Warbler pointed north across the rolling hills. "The Lots end less than half a day's ride from where we stand. Long before dark, we will be in Hispartha."

"And then?"

"Better seen than said."

Warbler did not speak again while they rode, not even to announce their departure from Ul-wundulas.

Yet Jackal felt it.

Lands weren't separated by names alone, they possessed their own natures, their own spirits. The country Hearth now trod was not the badlands of Jackal's birth. Yes, it was greener, the winds cooler, but the difference was imbued in more than beauty and fairer climes. This land was forgiven and forgiving, resting imperiously above its oft-raped sister. Ul-wundulas had no more tears, for itself or its people; it was used up, and bitter with the knowledge that its hideous, sun-scorched surface would not save it from another assault. Yet noble Hispartha was flush and unspoiled, content to ignore the ravages of time and invasion as long as the dusty thighs of Ul-wundulas lay spread between it and Dhar'gest.

When Jackal drank from his first Hisparthan stream, the water colder and cleaner than any that had touched his throat, he knew he never wanted to leave. Suddenly, shamefully, he understood why the thicks were so intent to reach this land.

"This what you wanted me to see?" he asked, standing away from the seductive brook. "The land we protect? The land denied us by the frails we keep safe?"

Warbler had not dismounted when they stopped. He squinted into the distance and shook his head.

"You're here to see that we don't keep anything safe."

They followed the stream as it ran through a sporadically wooded valley and eventually flowed into a sizable lake nestled amongst the hills. Across the calm surface of the water stood a blunt tooth of rock, its denuded hump sulking beneath the afternoon sky. Warbler led them toward it, riding along the western bank of the lake. The trees growing near were young, beginning to lead a charge up the slope to retake the lone peak. Jackal followed Warbler away from the shoreline, and they rode in the shadow of the tooth until the lake was lost from view. Ahead, the trees gave way to a blindingly white swath of dusty ground festooned with tall piles of loose stones.

The dust and detritus was the doorstep of a yawning cavity housed low in the base of the promontory. Evidence of wooden scaffolding lay bleaching in the harsh heat.

Warbler dismounted and left Mean Old Man standing in the shelter of the trees.

"What was this, a mine?" Jackal asked, following his lead.

Warbler loosed an affirmative grunt and retrieved a pair of prepared torches from his saddlebag. He doused the wrappings with a stream of oil from a skin and handed one of the staves over before heading off toward the entrance. As Jackal cleared the trees and entered the punishing sun, his nostrils flared.

The place smelled of home.

The mouth of the mine was larger than it appeared from a distance. As he walked closer, Jackal saw it was over twice his height and wide enough to admit a dozen men walking abreast. A palpable chill flowed out of the shaft, unpleasant despite the brutal heat of the sun. Drawing his knife and a piece of flint, Warbler struck sparks until both torches were alight. He looked up at the support lintel with a stubborn glare.

"The Imperium dug up so much silver, it is said they needed elephants to bring it out. Hispartha continued the work, but they used half-orcs . . . until the lodes gave out."

Jackal looked hard at the old thrice's profile. "You were a slave here?"

Warbler nodded. "I was born here. Well . . . I can't swear to that, but it's certainly the first cunt I remember crawling out of. Wish I was the worst that came from this womb."

"You mean the Claymaster."

Warbler's lips twitched into a sad smile. "No. He left here a hero. Come ahead."

Together they stepped into the cold tunnel, holding their torches aloft. The shaft was well shorn with timbers and cut deep into the rock. Jackal suppressed a shudder at the thought of an elephant emerging from the shadows at the edge of the torchlight, mad-eyed and trumpeting. He had seen only one of the immense creatures, when a troupe of entertainers came through the Lots. They had performed in Winsome and moved on, but were cut down by orc raiders before making it to the Skull Sowers' land. Oats had wept when they found the butchered elephant, though Jackal had pretended not to notice.

After what seemed an eternity of leading down, the shaft opened upon a shelf of rough-cut stone overlooking a vast sea of shadow that the torches could not hope to penetrate. Jackal sensed a vast openness as the queer subterranean breeze played through his hair. A massive ramp of earthworks rose to meet the shelf, and Warbler descended without pause. Jackal followed, sliding a bit on the loose stones carpeting the hard-packed dirt.

When they reached level ground, Warbler struck off into the abyss, his torch seeming to illuminate only him. Jackal trudged along behind, waving his own firebrand to coax shapes out of the darkness. The long runnels of deep shadow proved to be trenches, the briefly flaring crosses were revealed as the support beams of watchtowers. All the votives within this vast tomb of industry Warbler passed without a glance. He walked determinedly across the cavern until the darkness before him concentrated into an oculus of black on the far wall, the mouth of another tunnel. This too sloped downward, yet it was much smaller than the entrance shaft, forcing Jackal and Warbler to stoop as they went single file.

The air became warmer the deeper they went, and increasingly tinged with an acrid edge. By the time the tunnel debouched into a low chamber, Jackal was sweating and loath to take a deep breath, the air was so foul. The light from the torches exposed the source of the stench.

Heaps of tiny bones rose halfway up the cave walls, nested within the filth of long-moldered flesh and fur. Thousands of fist-sized rib cages stood out sharply from the refuse alongside uncountable pointed, fanged skulls.

"Rats?" Jackal guessed, his throat thick with stale decay.

Warbler did not respond. He swept the noxious chamber with his torch, taking in the pair of exit passages before deciding upon one.

"This way," he grunted, and led on.

They passed through more of the charnel caves, all filled with the remains of vermin hordes. Often they were piled against the walls, as if shoveled there, but some were deposited in deep pits cut into the center of the floor. After the first such room, Jackal ceased inspecting the pits and walked carefully around them without a glance. He followed after Warbler numbly, his mind drifting away to keep his body from fleeing back to the surface. Without a guide, such a flight would only fling him deeper into the twisting tunnels. He would be lost until the shadows claimed his torch and then his existence. Warbler moved with the hesitant surety born from memory. Any knowledge of these passages would take months of mapping, or years of imprisonment.

Jackal tried not to think on what it would have been like, existing entombed from your first memory. Thankfully, he had neither the imagination nor the madness to conjure a clear idea.

Until they reached the cages.

Lost in horrid reverie, Jackal was only dimly aware of entering the cavern. It was the smell that brought him around. Rust, tangy, and pungent. It was the stench of old metal, corroding not from water but from piss and sweat, the fearful humors that once leaked out of uncountable slaves, soaking the bars and chains that held them underground.

Warbler took in his surroundings for the first time since entering the mine. He held his torch high, but the light could not penetrate the upper reaches of the cages, stacked one atop the other until they vanished into the ink. Each was a wrought rectangle, big enough for a single occupant to stand within, as long as they weren't very tall. The meager light shone on mercifully little, but Jackal could still feel the hulking blocks of cages stretching beyond the darkness. Little avenues ran between the blocks. Warbler strode slowly down one until he reached a junction, where he stopped. The forest of iron bars dwarfed the old thrice.

"ANY ALIVE?!"

Jackal jumped, unprepared for Warbler's sonorous voice to challenge the cavern. The echo died quickly, as if ensnared by the flaking silhouettes of the bars.

"That's what they used to call out," Warbler said, lowering his voice. "After every trial, they would ask if any of us were still alive. Every time after the first, I thought about not answering. But we never saw what they did with the bodies . . . how they emptied the cages. I was more afraid of their arts than I was of the rats."

Jackal was having trouble hearing, but he could not bring his feet to venture forward. The prospect of walking down that aisle, between and beneath that legion of cages, held him paralyzed.

"Who?" he asked, sending his voice where his steps would not go.

"The wizards," Warbler answered. He bowed his head and let out a disgusted blow of air. "I hated the overseers when I was a boy, when this was still a mine. They had whips and loud voices, and used both. I hated them, but I never feared them. They were just men and could be killed . . . often were. Easy for a mongrel to kill a frail. Hells, they didn't even execute us for it. Just shattered a knee, made you keep working. Crippled like that, wouldn't be long before you would beg a fellow slave to cave in your skull. They had us digging down here long after the silver ran out. Once, I asked why, expecting a kicking. But the snapper just laughed and said, 'For a vein hope.' I didn't understand the jest until I was older.

"Sometime after, the war broke out, though none of us down here knew it. Even the overseers didn't think much of it, at first. They kept shouting and whipping, we kept digging. And then . . . the wizard arrived. The first one. He took control of the mine, brought in so many more slaves, I thought we would drown under each other."

Warbler pointed a finger upward and revolved it around. He loosed a curious little chuckle. "We cut this out and, fuck-all, we found silver. The wizard ordered it delved . . . and thrown in the slag pile with all the other rock. That's when we knew something had changed. That's when I started to fear. Another wizard arrived, then a third. I don't know how many there were, at the end, but we hated them more than we ever did the overseers. One of the new boys, one of the slaves brought in from the surface, he tried to kill one. None of us ever tried again."

Jackal didn't expect Warbler to elaborate, nor did he need him to. He had seen what Crafty was capable of, and yet, had never seen him do anything wrathful. It was always calm and calculated. The thought of a wizard driven to anger by an attempt on his life was not pleasant.

"The Great Orc Incursion," Warbler went on, "that's what the wizards called the war. Even down here, we started to get news of the battles. When they ordered us to drag these cages into the new excavation, we figured it was going to be a prison for the thicks. We found ourselves inside instead. I had spent my life as a slave underground. But that was the first time I felt trapped. The slave in the cage above me shat himself when they swung his door closed, dripped all over me. I swore to kill him next chance I got. Then they unleashed the rats, and my bowels ran down my legs too.

"They came like a flood. Chittering, chewing, biting. The screams from the cages as they crawled through the bars . . ."

Warbler paused, his deep voice faltering for a moment.

"I screamed too. But I stomped and grabbed and crushed and bit and chewed and choked. 'Any alive?' I awoke to that first call, chin-deep in dead rats. There was an answer, somewhere in another block, then another. Not sure how many before I cried out and they opened my cage. Not the one above. The rats had done for him what I swore to do. Perhaps a couple hundred of us had survived out of thousands. They took us away and chained us in another cavern. I slept. We all did. Still, no one had the strength to fight when they came to take us to the cages again. The dead were gone, rats and slaves both, but the cages were filled with more half-orcs from the surface. They didn't know what was coming.

"And the rats came again. I don't know how. Seemed they had unleashed every living one in the world the first time, but there it was again, that loathsome, deadly tide. Curse my luck, I survived again. And again. I don't know how many trials there were, only that fewer of us lived each time. Most that did got sick. Weeping sores, pustules all over, fingers black and swollen. They usually didn't survive the next trial, or died in the times between. I never got sick, don't know why, but there were a few dozen of us that never did. Fewer still were the ones who did, but wouldn't die. There were nine of them. And one tougher than the others."

Jackal swallowed hard and waited. Warbler cocked his head and looked back down the aisle, directly at him.

"He was already called the Claymaster, then. Had already thrown off the shackles of slavery and joined the war, leading his fellow potters on charges against the thicks on hogback. It was the frails that first called them the Grey Bastards, and the chief embraced the name as he won battles for his captors. Hispartha used him as a slave, then a soldier, now an experiment."

"The half-orc riders turned the tide," Jackal insisted, confused and growing agitated. "They were the reason the thicks were pushed back."

"Lies, son," Warbler told him. "Some of the slaves fought and were effective, for a time. Perhaps if Hispartha had allowed them to stay in the field, the history you believe would have been true. But the frails panicked and rounded up the mongrel troops, brought them down here as fodder for the wizards and their creation."

"What creation?"

"The plague. The damn thing wasn't natural. The wizards made it, down here, and used us to do it. I reckon they wanted to perfect it before unleashing it on the orcs, but they never had the chance."

"You escaped," Jackal said.

Warbler nodded. "We did. Led by the Claymaster. I don't recall him before the plague did its work. He was just another face in the herd. But I knew his voice. It was always the first to answer when they asked who was alive. No hesitation. 'Any alive?' And then there it was, his voice, strong and defiant. Every time I thought about staying silent, allowing them to dispose of me with the dead, I would hear that voice and it gave me the courage to live one more time. Hells, my suffering was nothing compared to his, all twisted up and ravaged like he was. But he just wouldn't die, so neither could I.

"One hundred and thirty-four of us made it out of this mine alive. We would never survive in Hispartha. So at the Claymaster's command we went south, into Ul-wundulas, where the war was still being waged. The conflict gave us room to move and we scavenged weapons and hogs, freed other half-orcs to swell our ranks. We fought everyone, man and orc, whoever we came across. We killed hundreds. The plague carried by the chief and the other eight did the rest. They were mongrels, human and orc, and the sorcerous sickness in their blood took hold in both armies. Within one summer, the war was done because there were none left to fight. In our hunger for vengeance, we brought peace. What orcs remained skulked back to Dhar'gest and the frails withdrew to glorious Hispartha."

"And we got the Lots," Jackal said.

"That was the price the Claymaster demanded. Otherwise, he threatened to ride north and bring the plague right to the king's throne room."

Jackal shook his head. "Why the lies? The Lots weren't given to you, they were taken. That should make us proud. Why hide it?"

"The Crown demanded the falsehood in order to keep its people calm. The mongrel hoofs had to appear beneath the king's rule, whether they were or not, to avoid hysteria throughout Hispartha. Those were the terms."

"But why keep them?"

"Because the kingdom was not without power. They still had their elf allies. And then there were the wizards. They escaped the mine when we revolted and scurried back to their masters. The Claymaster could have declared war on the kingdom and made good his threat, but without a way to counter sorcery, it was too great a risk. Better to take Ul-wundulas as prize and live in peace . . . or so I thought."

"He never stopped looking," Jackal proclaimed. "The Claymaster never stopped looking for a sorcerer of his own. And now he has one."

Warbler's chin dipped in grim agreement. "And now he has one."

CHAPTER 23

THE STARS HAD NEVER BEEN MORE BLISSFULLY DISTANT. Jackal drank the sight of them, allowing the millions of luminous saviors to lift the weight of the mine out of his bones. The edge of the lake lapped at the stones, inches from the toes of his boots. Behind him, Warbler had the campfire going strong. Soon, the smell of cooking fish drifted amongst the woodsmoke, and Jackal relinquished his succoring vigil of the heavens.

He turned to find Warbler already chewing, sitting with his share of the catch steaming upon the small spit in his hands. Jackal came and sat beside him, plucking the other spit away from the flames. He did not immediately eat, though he was ravenous. Food, fire, freedom. Somehow, it felt shameful to relish them in front of Warbler, knowing now what he had endured.

"If you like cold fish," the old thrice said with his mouth full, "then give me what's in your hand and go catch yourself another from the lake."

"You can have it," Jackal said without rancor and held his food out.

Warbler fixed him with a stern look. "Stop feeling sorry for me and eat your supper, Jaco."

Jackal let the name slide and took a bite.

Warbler huffed. "Time was, I didn't have to encourage you to eat."

"That's because Oats was around," Jackal recalled, grinning. "Had to swallow everything whole before he finished his helping, or you would find his hand in your mouth."

Warbler grunted fondly as he dug a bone out of his teeth. "Little fucker could eat. That's the only mongrel I ever knew who earned his hoof name while still pissing the bed."

"I remember!" Jackal declared, surprised at the recollection. "You said he should be called Porridge, but he could barely wait for it to cook."

"Barely?" Warbler said, his eyes going wide with exasperation. "He *couldn't* wait. I caught him with his hand in the pot while it was still cold so many times. Little shit was eating it raw! Raw fucking oats, like a damn donkey."

"So why not Donkey?"

Warbler shook his head ruefully. "His cock was too big."

Jackal sprayed flakes of fish into the fire, nearly choking as he laughed.

"That's where all the food was going," Warbler said, trying to hold back his own laughter. "Weighed his cod down like a feedbag. Hells overburdened! I'm surprised he can sit a hog."

"That's why he got so tall," Jackal put in, "to keep it from dragging in the dust."

"No, he didn't get tall enough. Those aren't muscles! Just his dick wrapped around his entire body."

It took them both some time to catch their breaths after that.

"I guess it's a good thing it was 'Oats' after all," Jackal said, still chuckling. "Beryl was pissed enough with that."

The broad smile on Warbler's face vanished. "He will always be her little Idris." Clearing his throat, he resumed eating and stared into the fire.

"You haven't asked me about her," Jackal said slowly.

Warbler's head snapped around. "No, I haven't. And don't go telling me anything either. Tell you the same as I told Hoodwink; no news of Beryl. Either she's with another or she's not. I don't know which would be more painful to hear and I don't want to find out."

Jackal nodded slowly, in what he hoped was an understanding way.

"You've seen us, though," he said.

Warbler's brow creased.

"You mentioned Oats's muscles," Jackal explained, "so you've seen us."

"Word gets around," Warbler replied. "But yes, I've seen you a few times over the years. Mostly from a distance. I was at Sancho's one time when you three rode in."

Jackal gave him a mocking grin. "Horny old goat."

"Just there for the baths, Jackal."

"Hells," Jackal curled his lip. "Small wonder I didn't see you. Why not just use the river?"

"Ask me again when your joints are as old as mine."

Jackal accepted that with a raise of his eyebrows and threw his fish bones into the fire. It was good to be talking to the old mongrel again.

"I understand why you brought me here," Jackal said after a long silence. "Without seeing the mine . . . those cages, the bones, I would have thought you mad."

Warbler hummed. "Too much time alone, brain baked by the sun? I know. I wish I was just some loony nomad. We would have a great deal less shit to handle."

"You said I was here to see that we didn't keep anything safe. What did you mean?"

Warbler took a deep breath. "I meant the hoofs don't. The Grey Bastards, the Orc Stains, the Fangs, the Sons, all of the rest. Before the Rutters were destroyed by the horse-cocks, there were nine half-orc hoofs. Nine. One for each of the mongrels who escaped that fucking mine carrying the plague. When the Incursion ended, the Claymaster demanded Ul-wundulas be ours. Fearing him, Hispartha agreed. But they countered by parceling it off between us, the Crown, and the elves, not to mention the parts already held by the 'taurs and the halflings. There wasn't anything the chief could do unless he wanted to go to war again. The elves were immune to the plague and we weren't certain of a victory against Hispartha even without their point-ear allies. So, we took what we could get and formed the Lots.

"The Claymaster divided our portion nine ways, and put one plague-bearer in each lot. The hoofs were formed to protect *them*, Jackal. As far as men and orcs were concerned, Ul-wundulas was filled with nine bear traps, any one of which could unleash the disease that nearly wiped them out during the war. The Claymaster was trying to ensure that neither the frails nor the thicks ever sought to retake the land that we had won."

Warbler stood briefly to throw some more wood on the fire. As he was sitting back down, he fixed Jackal with a pointed stare.

"The orcs don't stay out because a few gangs of half-breeds on hogs patrol the Lots, son. And Hispartha doesn't neglect to resettle cities like Kalbarca because of us either. They stay away because they fear the plague."

Jackal listened intently and chewed on Warbler's words. It all made a crushing sort of sense. Delia had said all the mongrel hoofs together could not stand against a single Hisparthan army. He had scoffed at that, full of empty pride. But she had been right. She was right about him too. He was a brave fool, living a lie within a land suitable only for the carrion eaters.

The vultures and the jackals.

"The thicks do come, though," he snarled, angry at his need for justification. "We have cut down scores of raiding parties!"

"And have for over thirty years," Warbler told him. "They're just scouting, Jackal. Looking for a bit of plunder and murder, most times. Other times, it's to see what has changed. To see how many of the nine remain."

"And how many do?" Jackal asked, knowing the answer already.

Warbler help up one finger. "Claymaster's been the last for a long time now."

"That's why he let those orcs go at Batayat Hill," Jackal realized aloud. "He wanted them to bring the news back to Dhar'gest that he was still alive."

"So long as he is, there won't be another Incursion."

Jackal's mind was reeling. "So why the fuck did you try and replace him?"

"Why did you?"

"Because I thought he was nothing but an aging cripple! I thought he was going soft and making piss-poor decisions. Because he was a hateful old fuck. Because I thought I would be a better chief! I didn't know he was preventing the Lots from being crushed between two enemies simply by breathing!"

At some point, Jackal had shot to his feet and Warbler looked up at him with a placid face etched in firelight.

"You're right," the old thrice said calmly.

"About what?"

"All of it. He is aging. And he was making poor decisions when I still sat at his right hand. Jackal, he is a hateful old fuck. It's all he is since he came out of the mine. For years, I tried not to judge him harshly. I went through it, too, survived the rats and the war, but I wasn't possessed by the wizards' foul creation. My body wasn't corrupted and bent. He is in constant pain, son, and it's a miracle he isn't mad. That's what happened to most of the others. They couldn't live with the plague using them as a vessel. It only nibbled at their bodies, but it devoured their minds. Within the first year of the Lots, two of them took their own lives. But not the Claymaster, not him! He lives, always. His need to see Hispartha suffer for what they did keeps him going. They locked him in a stalemate, and for nearly twenty years I stood by him while he searched for a way to break it. I hated, too, at the beginning, but time forced me to see what we had gained. A land. A home. Freedom. I had a brotherhood, and a woman . . . and you children.

"I urged the chief to focus on building up the Lots, to pursue better relations with Dog Fall and Strava. Hells, I even offered to take a ship east, to Traedria, Al-Unan, and Tyrkania, to forge alliances, but he wouldn't hear it. Couldn't see it! As the other plague-bearers died, one by one, Hispartha began creeping back. They stayed on their allotted lands, but they grew bolder. They had a wizard installed in the castile for months before we heard about it. I thought the chief was going to ride north right then and there, finally make good his threat to spread the pox throughout Hispartha. Fortunately, the other two remaining plague-bearers refused. Like me, they had grown to enjoy the new life and would not throw it away. It was the first time I had ever seen anyone not follow the Claymaster. He quickly lost his hold on the other hoofs after that. The years passed and he grew bitter behind the walls of the Kiln. By the time you were left at the Winsome orphanage, the Grey Bastards had ceased being the greatest power in the Lots. We were just another mongrel hoof, struggling to survive in the badlands."

His knees popping, Warbler stood again, ambled over to his saddlebags, and dug out a skin. Pulling the stopper, he took a long pull, then came back and handed the skin to Jackal.

"It's rude stuff," the old thrice admitted, "but I haven't talked this much in years. Figured we could use a little wetting."

Jackal took a drink and grimaced as the sour wine greased his tongue.

"You going to tell me why you finally challenged him?" he asked, belching unpleasantly.

Warbler took the skin back and drank. He wiped his mouth with the back of his hand and shook his head slowly.

"Wish I could say there was a story there. Truth is, I had wanted to do it for years, but never had the sack. Kept talking myself out of it."

Jackal watched as Warbler stared distantly into the fire. The old thrice's eyed welled, but whether it was from the smoke, the foul wine, or the memory, Jackal could not say.

"When we rebelled in the mine," Warbler said thickly, "I was injured. Took a spear thrust in the thigh. Once all the overseers were dead, the Claymaster put my arm over his shoulders, helped me walk out of that fucking hole. That . . . was the first time I saw the sun. This bright, hot, blinding beast that hurt far worse than the spear. But, Belico's Cock, I basked in that pain! So maybe you see why it took me years to throw my axe. Because it meant challenging the leader who carried me into the light."

Slapping the stopper back into the wineskin, Warbler tossed it down beside him and let out a long breath.

"Didn't matter anyway. As you know, I lost that vote."

"But the chief spared you," Jackal said. "He could have split your skull."

"Same as he could have you."

Jackal spit into the fire. "Hoodwink is proof that I was never meant to live. He just wanted to hurt me first. And he did. We may have both lost our challenges, War-boar, but did you have one of your most trusted allies knife you from behind?"

"No," Warbler said soberly. "In my vote, I was the betrayer."

Jackal leaned past the old thrice and retrieved the wineskin. Only the first few pulls had to be endured, after that, the draught became palatable.

"You know it was her that first called me that. Isa—" Warbler caught himself. "Fetching. She couldn't quite say my name. Kept coming out 'War-boar.' You talked early, never had a problem with it, but you switched when you knew she was having trouble. Oats did what you did, of course. In a day, the entire damn orphanage was calling me that, even the fuzz-lips a year away from joining the slopheads. Hells, I worried the brotherhood was going to start using it and change my hoof name."

"Sorry," Jackal told him, letting the word cover then and now. "I won't say it again."

"No need for that," Warbler groused, motioning for the wineskin. "It's not bad to hear after all this time."

Jackal allowed a small smile and watched the campfire as the old thrice drank. He must have got lost in the writhing of the flames, for Warbler bumped him with an elbow.

"What's bothering you, boy?"

"The Claymaster," Jackal admitted.

A half-drunk laugh bubbled out of Warbler. "Yeah, that's catching."

"But *he's* not. No one has gotten the plague that I can remember."

"Half-orcs are immune, Jackal, all except the original nine. I doubt that's what the wizards wanted, but we broke our chains before they could complete the fucker."

"I understand, but the chief has been around frails. Ignacio. Thistle. Countless others. Why isn't Winsome a graveyard?"

Warbler's eyes went dull. "Because he hasn't unleashed the pox in many years. Be grateful. I hope you never see it. I haven't since the war, and that was enough."

"He can control it?" Jackal asked, unnerved.

"More like he allows it to control him. I don't know. Can't claim to understand sorcery."

"But Crafty does."

Jackal had said it softly, almost to himself, but Warbler's somber expression was replaced with one of grim purpose.

"What is he capable of?"

Images filled Jackal's mind. The wizard standing unburned within the crucible of the Kiln walls. Sludges made inert by pipe smoke. The Sludge Man himself engulfed in a fiery, living breath. The orc assassin, dead yet screaming.

"Anything."

It was all the answer Jackal had.

Warbler ran a hand through his mane of silver hair, sighing. "In your time with him, this swaddlehead didn't say anything that might help us reckon out his plan?"

Starting slowly, Jackal went through it all. Crafty's sudden arrival, their time in the Old Maiden Marsh, his promise to help Jackal become chief in exchange for some unnamed favor, everything. When it was all said, Warbler sat for a long time frowning.

"He said 'only the Grey Bastards would do'? Those were his words?"

Jackal nodded. "Said he wanted to see Ul-wundulas . . . before it was gone."

"Shaft my ass," Warbler swore. "Singling out the Bastards points to needing the Claymaster for something. He's the only thing that makes us unique amongst the hoofs anymore."

"Us?" Jackal pointed out.

Warbler glared at him. "Tell me you don't still feel like one of them."

Jackal said nothing.

Seeing that his point had been made, Warbler thumped Jackal on the back. "So, what do we do, Bastard?"

"Try and do together what we couldn't do separately," Jackal replied. "Save our hoof."

"You sure?" Warbler asked with a grin and pointed off into the night. "You got all of Hispartha out there, and Anville beyond that. You could slip away, find work as a mercenary. Maybe turn to whoring. I'd wager there's plenty of noble ladies that would pay to have a pretty half-orc lick their quims."

Jackal smiled and shook his head. "The Lots are my home, Warboar. A pile of guts, gristle, and shit-smeared innards, according to another whore I know. Doesn't matter. Still home. And if Crafty thinks they're going to be gone soon, he knows something. The way I figure, the Lots could only disappear if they are retaken. So, which is it? Hispartha or the thicks? Crafty certainly thinks it's going to be one of them. Either way, we can't let it happen."

"No, we can't," Warbler agreed, rising. "So, he knows more than we do. Who knows more than him?"

"Another wizard," Jackal offered.

Warbler cocked his head north. "There's more than a few that way."

"And one that way," Jackal said, lifting his chin south, toward Ulwundulas. "One who knows the Lots. Besides, we go north I'm likely to get drunk on the smell of noble cunny and never return."

Warbler smirked. "So, it's the castile, then. You think they'll actually let us inside?"

"Certain of it."

"Why?"

Jackal shrugged. "There's a man there that really wants to hang me."

Chapter 24

Sancho shrieked when Jackal kicked through the door to his bedchamber. The shrill cry might have been caused solely from the shock, or it might have been that the girl with her mouth around the whoremaster's cock had accidentally bitten down in her own surprise. She crab-crawled quickly to a corner as Jackal barreled into the room. Sancho tried to stand, but panic and the breeches around his ankles conspired in tripping him. He fell backward over the chair he had just attempted to vacate and tumbled to the floor. Jackal flung the upset chair away and planted a heel upon the sweating pimp's small prick, barely protruding from between his lard-heavy thighs. The shriek came again and Sancho's eyes bulged as Jackal leaned forward.

"Where did the Tine girl come from?" he yelled. There was not much time and no need for silence.

Sancho tried to say his name, but all that came out was an airy, "Ja."

Jackal cast a quick look at the whore in the corner. It was the new girl, the one from Anville that he had enjoyed with Delia the night before Fetch killed Garcia.

"It's fine, darling," Jackal told her. "You're not the one who is going to get hurt here."

Removing his foot from Sancho's crotch, he reached down and hauled the tub of suet off the floor, spinning him around. Jackal wanted that broad back between himself and the door, just in case Bermudo's boys decided to come in swinging.

"Where, Sancho?" Jackal demanded, backhanding him across the mouth.

When the whoremaster's head snapped back, there was blood smeared across the black stubble on his jowls.

"Jackal," he whined, "you were cast out. I heard—"

"You heard true! I got no hoof now, fat man. Nothing to lose and nothing to hold me back. And you're half the reason why. Tell me! Before I start carving hocks off you."

Despite the threat, Jackal kept his knife sheathed. He hadn't even brought his thrum, leaving it with Warbler. All this was pointless if the soldiers killed him outright. Shaking Sancho roughly, Jackal got directly in his face.

"I want to know how you got an orc-raped Tine."

"But . . . I—I didn't—"

Jackal buried a knee in Sancho's sizable gut. "Lie to me again!"

The whoremaster was bent double, retching and wheezing. Jackal forced him upright once more.

"Spill your guts, you fat fucking frail or I'll kick them out through your damn throat."

Sancho shook his head weakly as a line of pink slaver fell from his quivering lips.

"The Sludge Man told me he traded for her," Jackal said. "He certainly had enough coin. Where else would he have gotten her but here?"

Defiance burned through the fear and pain in Sancho's eyes.

"I never had that fucking elf!" he exclaimed, quivering with feeble rage. "I told Ignacio she was a mistake. No elves from Dog Fall, he knew that! I said he had to take it up with the Sludge Man and be off."

Confusion boiled Jackal's blood.

"Ignacio? What are you going on about?" he demanded, nearly lifting the whoremaster off the floor by his stained tunic. But Sancho was barely listening.

"What was I . . . by all the hells' cunts, what was I supposed to do?" he rambled, his flash of anger had cooled as quick as it came, leaving him brittle. "What choices do I have, pinched between the Sludge Man and a captain of the castile?"

Damning all caution, Jackal snatched his knife from his belt and placed the flat of the blade against Sancho's cod. The whoremaster stilled, the feel of the cold metal refocusing his attention.

"Choices?" Jackal hissed. "I'll give you two. Talk sense and stay whole, or keep babbling and be gelded."

Jackal had never heard a man talk without breathing before, but somehow Sancho managed the feat.

"Ignacio's been bringing point-ears down from Hispartha. Slaves, singly, never more. Easier to hide amongst the other girls. They stay here until the Sludge Man comes. He pays in coin. That's it. I just hold them for a day or two and take my cut."

The sound of boots scraped in the hallway. Bermudo's cavaleros, four of them, the last four stationed at the brothel. They weren't hurrying. Jackal couldn't see them yet, but his ears told him they were coming carefully, likely trying to ascertain what was happening before committing themselves. Sancho wasn't a man to merit much haste.

"And the Tine?" Jackal growled, lowering his voice. "When was she here?"

"I told you," Sancho pleaded softly, "she wasn't. Not for more than a moment. I refused to take her. Sent Ignacio off. That pock-faced fuck must have got greedy, to risk taking a Tine."

"When was this?"

"The night before Fetching skewered that fop's skull."

"Hogshit!" Jackal yelled. "We were here! Oats and Fetch and me!"

"You were here," Sancho needled. "Drunk and fucking. Like always."

Jackal went numb. Some small voice in him had kept whispering the notion that the Claymaster had been involved, that he managed to hide his part from everyone. But now that whisper died. Starling was here and gone before Garcia died. She was never payment for his disposal, just one of hells knew how many taken and sold in an evil trade born from greed and the concert of three evil men. And the Sludge Man had fucking told him! He'd said Jackal was ignorant of his captain's dealings, but hadn't meant the captain of the Bastards, he meant the one under their control. Fucking Ignacio!

She'd been in here and gone, all while Jackal was blinded by willing flesh, deafened by flowing drink.

Over Sancho's shoulder, a helmeted head peered around the doorjamb.

Time for the gamble.

Quickly sheathing his blade, Jackal punched Sancho across the jaw. That sent the cavaleros rushing in, swords drawn.

Jackal left his tulwar in its scabbard and grabbed up the chair, shattering it on the breastplate of the first man through the door. He careened into the wall and fell on his ass, cursing. Swords were little use in the cramped space of the room. The ceiling was low and each man who came in made it harder on his fellows to properly maneuver. Deflecting an awkward sword stroke with the remains of the chair, Jackal stomped the attacker in the knee. As the stricken man crumpled with the pain, Jackal grabbed the plume on his helmet and jerked. Already off-balance, the soldier toppled. One of the remaining two had some sense and thrust with his sword, but his speed did not match his wits. Sidestepping the blade, Jackal caught the man's wrist and hammered his elbow. Crying out, the cavalero dropped his sword and Jackal used his arm to swing him into the last man. Their breastplates clattered as they jointly met the ground.

The first man had recovered and was gaining his feet. Jackal sprung and swatted the sword from his hand, but allowed him to rise. He needed to turn this into a brawl. He struck with fist and boot, trying to anger the cavaleros without inflicting serious injury. But he fought with more ferocity than intended, his temper lit by Sancho's revelations. Jackal had come here as a pretense, a means of being taken to the castile without arousing suspicion. There he hoped to find answers, but here he was met with more questions. Sick of riddles and mysteries and skullduggery, Jackal raged.

In the end, it was impossible to say who was more fortunate not to have been killed in the struggle, Jackal or the cavaleros. He barely felt their blows, most of which he let land, and two were missing teeth by the time he took a fall, permitting them to overpower him. Breathing heavily, Jackal was dragged to standing, his arms pinned.

The whoremaster had restored his breeches to a proper height, finding enough nerve to approach and pummel him once in the gut while the cavaleros held him still.

Jackal laughed. "You should keep to slapping whores around, you splinter-cocked tun."

Sancho smoothed his greasy hair and sniffed once. A wretched little smile appeared.

"I will," the whoremaster whispered, leaning close. "You know, Jackal, I've peddled quim since I was a boy. Started in the alleys of Magerit, collecting payment while my sisters spread their legs in the gutter. I learned a long time ago to spot a man who has feelings for a coin slot. So you should know, you fucking soot-skin, that when I do feel a need to slap one of my whores, from now on, I'll start with Delia."

Jackal returned the smile. "And you should know that when I leave the castile and begin killing, I'll start with you."

As the cavaleros manhandled Jackal out of the room, he fixed Sancho with a hard stare. The frail managed to keep to his smile, but his usually ruddy face had blanched considerably.

Out in the brothel yard, the cavaleros relieved Jackal of his blades and bound him with manacles before throwing him over the back of a mule. Blood rushing to his face, he waited while they secured him with ropes.

Once on their horses, one man rode point, one led the mule, and the other two brought up the rearguard. Jackal ate dust for miles. Somewhere, hidden amongst the scrub and the wavy phantoms caused by the heat, Warbler was following. He was supposed to make sure Jackal made it inside the castile, wait until morning, and present himself to the garrison to volunteer as a scout. The old thrice had a solid reputation in the Lots; the frails would be fools not to take him. At the very least, they would allow him through the gates to speak with one of the captains. They had counted on it being Ignacio, but Jackal hadn't expected to hear that Ignacio was involved in some black business with the Sludge Man. The captain was an unrepentant heap of shit, but smuggling elven slaves? And to the Sludge Man, no less, for whatever twisted purpose. That knowledge changed things.

Jackal considered goading the cavaleros with insults. If he forced them to beat on him, if it looked like they might kill him, then Warbler would surely intervene. That wasn't quite the plan, but if Sancho got word to Ignacio about what Jackal now knew, the march to the gallows would be quick.

However, the whoremaster had said nothing to the cavaleros that came to his rescue. They were noble-born, under Bermudo's command.

Sweat dripping from his face, Jackal grinned.

Bermudo knew. It must have been the reason he came to the brothel that morning. He was trying to catch Ignacio in the act. Slaves were a way of life in Hispartha, but elves were illegal, lest the alliance with the point-ears unravel.

The captains had always resented the other's presence in the Lots. Bermudo hated his low-born compatriot working so closely with the mongrel hoofs. Half-orcs were beneath the notice of a gentleman, after all. Ignacio viewed Bermudo with the inherited contempt all peasants hold for those that lord over them. That, and the man was all but useless in a place such as the Lots. Still, he'd managed to root out Ignacio's crime, somehow, and bit at the chance of being rid of him. Jackal wondered what the blue blood would think if he learned the Bastards had possessed living proof of Ignacio's traffic in flesh. If only the haughty captain had come to the brothel a little sooner, he'd have found Starling himself. If only Jackal had not been carousing . . .

Hells with it. Jackal would hold to the plan. Warbler would get in or not. Jackal would leave alive or not. No use yanking the hog to a stop now.

The castile appeared beneath the midday sky. From his inverted position, Jackal did not see the fortress so much as feel its presence. No fewer than six great towers lorded over the curtain wall, which crowned a steep, parched hill. The road switchbacked up the western slope toward the barbican. Jackal craned his neck to eyeball the battlements along the wall and above the gate. A pair of bartizans jutted imposingly from either side of the yawning arch, no doubt filled with archers.

This was the last fortification in Ul-wundulas still held by Hispartha. It must have once had a name, but none uttered it anymore. Home to a sizable standing garrison, as well as two companies of cavaleros, common and noble, the castile contained the largest armed force in the land. The towers commanded views for miles in every direction. And one of those towers was the residence of the castile's wizard. Like the stronghold, he had no spoken name, and like the stronghold, his simple presence was a reminder that the Crown still retained ample power in the Lots.

The castile was larger than the Kiln, its tallest tower double the height of the central chimney. The construction of the Bastards' home had borrowed the splayed-base walls found surrounding this citadel, but the Kiln did not come close to matching its imposing bulk. An army of orcs would be hard-pressed to breach these defenses. Countless waves would be broken on the hill, the entire ascent plagued by withering arrow flights. The bodies would be heaped beneath the talus before the battlements could be gained.

Since boyhood, the castile had been an arrogant, brutish fixture in Jackal's life, but never had he felt its slumbering oppression more keenly than he did now, trussed to a mule and entering the shadow of the gateway. Stableboys ran up and took the cavaleros' horses in hand as they dismounted. Orders were barked and Jackal was hauled roughly off the mule by a pair of guardsmen. He got a brief look at the sizable bailey beyond the barbican before being shoved through a low door set in the base of a square tower. Hells, he had been inside the walls for only a few heartbeats and had already seen at least two-score soldiers.

One of his guards lifted a grate in the floor, permitting access to a set of stairs spiraling down into darkness. As he began the descent, a voice in Jackal's head told him this may have been a fool-ass plan. The voice sounded too much like Fetching's. Clenching his jaw and squaring his shoulders, Jackal walked steadily downward. A long, dim corridor met them at the bottom of the stairs, lit by far-spaced torches. The guards must have been warned about him, or else had a healthy fear of half-orcs, for both leveled their halberds, one in front and one behind, before herding him down the passage, the lead man walking backward.

This tedious shuffle eventually brought them to a large, evil-smelling chamber with a heavy door in the opposite wall. The guards stopped well short of this, however, and Jackal heard the man behind him open one of ten iron grates in the floor.

"Down," the lead guard instructed with a punctuating jab of his halberd.

Turning, Jackal looked into the pit. It was a narrow shaft, and double his height in depth. Water stood at the bottom, dully reflecting the meager torchlight.

Spitting, Jackal squatted and sat on the edge of the pit. Turning to rest on his elbows, he let his legs dangle and gripped the edge with his manacled hands. He lowered himself down and hung with arms fully extended before letting go, landing with a heavy splash in the water. The unseen stone beneath the pool was slick with scum, but he kept his feet. He made a point not to look up, lest the guards decide to piss on him, a distinct possibility considering the smell of the ankle-deep liquid. Thankfully, he heard the grate slam shut above and the footsteps of the guards withdrawing, though not far. Jackal could hear their low voices muttering to one another in the chamber, but the sloshing cell swallowed the words. They conversed sporadically until they were relieved some time later by another pair. These two must not have liked each other much, for they said little.

The width of the cell might have permitted Jackal to sit, but the water made even that small comfort a miserable prospect. So, he stood, alternating between pacing the cramped, flooded square and leaning against the slimy walls.

Time rotted.

Jackal was just about to give in and sit when he heard the sound of the door open once more. The footsteps were not the ambling plod of bored soldiers, but the purposeful, resounding stride of one in command. A shadow fell across the square holes of the grate.

"I knew leaving men at Sancho's would prove fruitful," came a gloating voice. "Vengeance or lust. One of these was sure to bring you loping back to the brothel. Mongrels are ever driven by base needs."

"Glad to help you prove your capability, Bermudo," Jackal called up. "Someone needs to."

"The only proof you provide, half-orc, is the witlessness of your kind. Pride without brains, that's what disgusts me most about you ash-coloreds. Though, in this instance, I should be thankful for it, considering it was your need to avenge yourself on the brothel-keep's incompetence that delivered you in chains, where you belong."

Jackal bit back a laugh. Bermudo truly believed he had caught him through his own designs. Witlessness and pride were certainly present, just not where the captain claimed. This plan was perfect after all. At least, it would be without the manacles and the locked pit.

"It's that childish need for undeserved respect," Bermudo droned on, "which sours my stomach. That's what got the better of you, not me."

"Well, half of that is true," Jackal stated lightly.

The figure beyond the grate was silent for a moment.

"Eight years. That's how long I've been in Ul-wundulas. Eight years, every one of them a sweltering crawl. And then, delivered to my command, is a man that offers a chance of returning to civilian life. A chance you took from me."

Jackal snorted. "Garcia was likely spewing goose shit. You'd believe anyone with a whispered promise of going home. In earnest, Captain, you should be thanking me. Garcia was lording over you that morning. In your precious Hisparthan social standing hogshit, that harelip was every bit your superior. Another month, and he would have been commanding the blue bloods."

"You're right," Bermudo admitted, but Jackal could hear the smile. "I could not see it at the beginning, but that was a service, killing him. And doubly so now. I have just sent a messenger north with a letter to Garcia's mother. In the . . . pile of noble Hisparthan hogshit, she is a fat fly who buzzes close to the top."

"I heard," Jackal said.

"From Ignacio, I'm sure. The man's lack of honor is outpaced only by his stupidity."

"You were the one outpaced. Missed him at Sancho's."

"Because of you soot-skins."

Jackal shook his head, unsure if the man standing over him could even see the gesture. "You'll never believe this, but the Bastards weren't helping Ignacio. He was gone well before you arrived."

"True," Bermudo said, sounding far from pleased. "I don't believe it. I had hoped to catch him that unfortunate morning. He has bought off some of my own men, so I took only the fresh arrivals. Men that have since gone missing. Care to tell me what happened to them?"

"Let me out and I will. I'll also tell you where Ignacio takes those slaves."

"I'll get it all from you soon enough. Ignacio will hang beside you. The ruckus you half-breeds caused at the brothel saw my efforts against him stalled. But I am patient."

"Garcia was to blame for that ruckus and you know it."

"The man was a wretch," Bermudo agreed. "But even wretches have mothers that love them. When she hears I have the half-breed who murdered her son, she will insist that you be brought to her for justice.

I will, of course, respectfully refuse, informing Her Ladyship that you are simply too dangerous to transport. The chance of escape over so many leagues is quite high. I have never met the lady in question, but I soon will, for based upon her reputation I am confident she will make the journey into the Lot Lands, risking their myriad dangers, just so she can witness your eyes pop on the gallows. Such a visit will give me ample time to place myself beneath the grieving marquesa's good graces and provide the possibility of leaving this post behind. So yes, thank you for being a murderous cur, Jackal. Know that my gratitude will be even greater the day you swing from a rope."

Jackal hummed appreciatively. "Well, when you find yourself under the woman's good graces, you might see this pink little nub. Lick that. Believe me, it will help win her over."

"You really are an animal."

"Just trying to remain helpful, Captain. Since you've sucked cock your whole life, I figured you didn't know."

Bermudo expelled a clipped laugh. "I will be sure to come back and seek your advice often. There will be time. The marquesa won't arrive for a month or more, at the soonest. In the meantime, you can reside down there. Try not to waste away, Jackal. We don't want Garcia's slayer to appear too terribly weak and pitiful."

The shadow above turned on its heel.

"You know I wasn't even the one who killed him," Jackal said.

Bermudo paused. "Do you think it matters to me? I will claim it was you. Sancho will agree. The lady will believe justice done. The truth, Jackal, is that you are a nomad. I do not even need a reason to hang you. Without your hoof to protect you, you are nothing but a wild dog."

When Bermudo was gone, Jackal stewed in the reek of the cell.

The guards changed again, denoting the passage of innumerable hours. Jackal knew he had not been here a full day, not yet. His thirst and hunger would have been greater. Both were very likely to increase before long. It did not appear Bermudo had much interest in keeping him healthy. Knowing he would only get weaker, Jackal attempted to climb the shaft.

It was tricky with his bound hands, but the closeness of the walls made it possible for him to find solid leverage with his legs and he was soon at the top. The guards must have heard him, for no sooner had he pressed his face to the grate then the haft of a halberd was shoved through, striking him in the neck. He fell back down into the loathsome water, his heels sliding out from under him and planting his ass in the wet. Nothing else for it, Jackal remained slumped there.

Ignacio arrived later, his rough, perpetually tired voice giving the guards permission to wait without.

"Don't reckon you're here to free me?" Jackal asked as the captain's form darkened the grating.

The door of the pit swung open. Ignacio squatted at the edge and peered down, a lantern dangling from his hand. His ugly, pitted face was harried.

"You know I can't do that."

The captain's tone was almost regretful. Almost.

Jackal smiled up at him. "And here I thought you were a friend to the Bastards."

"You ain't a Bastard anymore, Jack."

"Well, this seems awfully severe a punishment for kicking a whoremonger around. Even for a nomad."

"This is about killing Garcia and you know it."

Jackal forced the snort of contempt down. "For Bermudo, it is. Surely, you don't give a shit about that."

"I don't," Ignacio admitted.

"So let me loose. A favor for old times."

"I won't be doing that. And neither will that old thrice."

"Who?"

Ignacio laughed at the attempt. "Hadn't seen Warbler in years. Actually made me smile when he turned up. Tempting, to take such a seasoned free-rider on. Almost did it. But I learned long ago to be wary of tempting things that make you smile in the Lots. So I had the boys turn him away. Imagine my . . . vindication when you arrive not long after. An old free-rider suddenly volunteering and a fresh nomad suddenly a captive, each a former Bastard. What are the chances? You almost pulled it off, Jackal, weren't for my gut. If I had known just how right I was, I would've let Warbler through the gates and tossed him into that pit beside you, 'stead of letting him ride off peaceful. So, what was the scheme? Why'd you two want in here?"

Jackal needed to keep Ignacio off the scent of his true quarry.

"To kill Bermudo," he lied, though it was quickly becoming part of the plan. "Figured he wasn't going to stop trying to put me in chains, so why not give him what he wants, then cut his throat for him? That could still happen. Can you say you wouldn't benefit with him gone? Let me out."

Ignacio didn't even consider. "No."

"Worried what I might say, Captain? What I might know?"

"What do you know, Jackal?"

It was a simple question, yet there was a cold menace in every word.

Ignacio's dispirited face tightened with annoyance when Jackal did not answer.

"I have to assume you know everything," he went on, "which means I don't have the time to squat here all damn night getting stiff in the knees while we bandy words back and forth."

"Afraid Bermudo might offer me a pardon once I tell him about you turning his men over to die?"

It was Ignacio's turn to laugh. "That noble son of a cunt would forgo the riches of Sardiz to see you hang! Nothing will sway him to spare you. He hates you, Jackal. Me, I don't have any feeling for you one way or another. But before you shit yourself on the gallows, I need to know where that Tine hussy got to."

"You mean your big mistake?" Jackal sneered. "How did you fumble that, Captain? Elf slaves are dangerous enough without provoking Dog Fall by nabbing one of their own."

"Her mistake, you mean," Ignacio said. "Fair little quim like that shouldn't wander too far alone. You have to take what comes in the Lots, Jack. Figured you knew that."

"What happened to being wary of tempting things?"

"Tempting things and profitable things are different. Besides, she never made me smile. Fought and screamed, all in a frenzy, every damn step."

Jackal was surprised when the image of Starling fighting back, crying out, came easily to his mind. The conjured picture brought pride to his heart before crushing it with regret.

"And what's the reward for you?" Jackal spat. "The Sludge Man gets his twisted perversions sated, but you? You get a few fistfuls of slimy gold. Think you can get enough to buy your way out of here before you get caught? You won't now. Sludge Man's dead."

Ignacio drug his fingernails beneath his chin for a moment. "I reckon you don't know everything, after all. Now . . . where's the elf?"

Jackal shrugged. "No reason to tell you. You're not going to let me loose, so you can't offer me anything. And threatening a condemned man is feeble. So the short of it, *Captain*, is—you're as useful as a limp cod."

Ignacio set the lantern down and stood, began unbuckling his belt. "Well . . . they have one use."

Jackal turned away. There was a brief silence and then came the stream of piss.

Once the warm liquid ceased spattering his skin, the door to the pit slammed shut.

It seemed Jackal would be lucky to make it to the gallows. The entire garrison was peasant stock, and no doubt any one of them would murder him in his cell if Ignacio ordered it, Bermudo be damned.

The sands of an hourglass were emptying all around him. His strength would not hold out in this wretched prison. And while he withered, Crafty and the Claymaster would continue to pursue whatever intentions they had for the Lots.

His survival had seemed far more certain while planning by a campfire.

Chapter 25

The sound of the door groaning open roused Jackal from a fitful doze. He heard the voices of the guards, and movement in the chamber above. Jerking upright, Jackal cursed as his numb legs and feet betrayed him, instantly forcing him back on his rump. The splashing drowned out all chance of catching what was being said. As the water settled and Jackal strained his ears, a burst of laughter resounded, followed quickly by the door shutting once more.

Silence followed. Jackal waited.

The quiet reigned for a long time, until he was convinced that the room above was vacant. Using the walls for support, Jackal stood again and rubbed some life back into his legs. He removed his boots and poured the water out of them before donning them once more, then climbed the shaft. No halberd shaft greeted him this time and he was able to push his cheekbone against the grate, revolving his eye around one of the holes to see what he could. The chamber appeared empty from his limited perspective, and his ears continued to testify to what his eyes could not completely confirm. He held himself there for as long as possible, but after a span his muscles began to cramp and quiver. Climbing down before he fell, Jackal stood in the cell and continued to listen, face turned upward.

At last, he heard the door open again, though the sound was softer. The play of shadows above implied furtive movement, before the holes in the grate darkened as a figure eclipsed them.

"Jack?" came a sharp whisper.

Jackal's guts jumped. "Delia?"

The sounds of a bolt sliding back rang stridently down the shaft. The grate slowly lifted and was laid aside soundlessly. The woman's familiar silhouette came into view once more.

"Can you climb up?"

Jackal did not waste time with an answer. Within moments he was hoisting himself over the lip of the pit. Still on his knees, he gawked at Delia. She too was crouched down and looked at him with a quick, nervous smile of relief, but her wide eyes kept flitting to the door.

"Help me put the grate back," she whispered.

Jackal did as she said and once they had carefully completed the task, Delia slid the bolt back into place, wincing at the noise. They both held their breath for a moment, but when no guards appeared, Delia took Jackal by the hand and led him toward the door. Opening it a crack, she checked the wide, vaulted passage beyond. All was still.

"The castile sleeps," she whispered, closing the door once more and turning to face Jackal. "But we must hurry. Rhecia is occupying your guards, but they will want to be back before their relief discovers them gone."

"Rhecia?" Jackal's brow creased, but then his mind began to settle. "The one from Anville . . . but how did you two get in here?"

"Let in through the southern sally port, same as always," Delia answered. "Whores never need to lay siege, Jackal. Let's get you out of those manacles."

"Did you steal the key?"

Delia shook her head and began gathering her skirts up behind her legs. "Too chancy."

Her mouth wrinkling with momentary discomfort, Delia's hand came back around, producing a thin, finger-long stick of wax. Letting her skirts fall, she moved quickly to one of the torches and held the sliver over the heat of the flames. The wax melted quickly, leaving behind a pair of lock picks.

Jackal expelled an amused breath. "Impressive. Though . . . couldn't you have just hidden those in the folds of your clothes?"

"Wasn't sure I would still be wearing clothes when I got in here," Delia replied with a purposefully exasperated sigh. "Besides, it's far from the most uncomfortable thing I've had up my arse."

"There I am a culprit," Jackal replied while she began on the first lock. "Though you may find some justice knowing I will now go everywhere similarly equipped."

"That might make riding a touch difficult," Delia replied, opening the first lock with a practiced hand.

"True," Jackal conceded.

Delia was having some difficulty with the second cuff. Jackal looked as the slight care-lines in her face deepened with growing concentration.

"Why did you risk this, Delia?"

She glanced up at him, briefly distracted by the gratitude in his voice.

"I saw you being hauled out," she replied, going back to her task. "Rhecia told me what happened. She needn't have bothered. Sancho was right behind her."

"That bloated fuck is dead," Jackal swore.

"Yes," Delia said as the second cuff opened. "He is."

The look on her face said it all.

"You killed him?"

Delia raised one freckled shoulder slightly. "Came at me with a scourge, so I opened his windpipe. All these years, he should have known I keep a knife close at hand."

"When was this?"

"Just after you were taken. Dust from the cavaleros' horses hadn't settled when Sancho choked on his own blood."

"Hells, woman," Jackal said, "they will hang you next to me."

"I'm not getting caught," she told him. "And neither are you, if you go now."

"I will," Jackal lied. It would do no good to confess why he had truly come here, especially now that she had burned her life down to aid him. He almost told her to go to Winsome, to have Beryl put her to work, but the notion perished in his head. Every soldier knew who she was, knew that he favored her. When word reached Bermudo of Sancho's death, she would not be safe.

"I'll find you," he said, "when this is all over."

Delia gave him a dubious squint. "If you could do that, I've failed at hiding. Come, I will lead you to the sally port."

"No," he said, taking the lock picks from her. "You go. If you're seen with me, they'll know."

Delia nodded reluctantly and went to the door. There, she paused.

"I need to tell you something," she said without turning.

Jackal waited.

When she faced him, he was taken aback to see fear in her eyes.

"It was me," she told him. "I was the one who let Garcia's horse loose."

Jackal only frowned, more confused than angry.

"I knew about the elf girls," Delia said, her breath fluttering. "They had been coming in, going with the Sludge Man . . . and never seen again. When I heard he was coming for the cavalero and the horse, I released it, hoping it would cause trouble for Sancho. I . . . I don't know, I thought if the castile started asking questions, all of it would end. I wasn't trying to hurt the Bastards, Jack, you have to believe that."

Jackal shushed her and took a step forward. "I do."

Delia searched his face frantically, as if doubting any absolution.

"But it worked, in the end? The one you rescued. She's safe?"

This lie came harder, as Jackal's throat constricted.

"Yes. She's safe."

"Good," Delia said, breathing out with relief. "Good."

Jackal put a gentle hand around the back of her neck. "You need to go."

She nodded and looked up at him. "Don't try to kiss me. I'm done with men that smell like piss."

Smiling, Jackal released her and she slipped out the door.

He stood for a moment, considering whether to wait and ambush the guards when they returned, weak-legged from fucking. It would provide a weapon and no small amount of satisfaction, but not time, and that was most important. His decision made, Jackal left the chamber, sodden and unarmed.

The wizard was said to lodge in a tower, which meant Jackal needed to go up. Up toward the bailey, up toward the walls, up toward where all the men who were not sleeping were standing watch.

"Fuck," Jackal sighed as he crept along the passage.

Eventually he came to the end of the vaulted corridor, finding an archway to the left and a small set of stairs leading up to an empty doorway. Sounds of Rhecia entertaining his erstwhile guards echoed from beyond the arch.

Jackal took the stairs.

Old rushes crunched under his boots as he entered the chamber at the top, finding himself in an undercroft made up of several adjoined square rooms. A bottlery to his left was secured by iron bars, but Jackal was free to move through the rest of the storage chambers, his eyes darting around for anything useful as he skulked between the barrels and sacks. He managed to find an old mason's mallet and a forgotten spar hook. Forgoing the heavy mallet, Jackal took up the spar hook. The single-edged curved blade was loose in the stubby handle, but it could still cut a throat, albeit with some sawing.

Emboldened by the blade in his hand, Jackal moved through the undercroft until he found stairs spiraling upward. They brought him to a room he surmised to be at the base of one of the towers, as it was nearly identical to the one he had entered before being ushered down to the dungeons.

Towers were what he wanted, but the castile contained at least half a dozen. Searching every one would be too treacherous. Dawn would likely come before he could sneak up them all, if he wasn't discovered first. He needed to know for certain where the wizard laired. But how? Not even Ignacio had ever betrayed that secret, despite all his dealings with the hoofs.

The tallest! It had to be the tallest tower. Obvious maybe, but Jackal could not imagine a powerful man dwelling in less. A humble wizard sounded as likely as a peaceful orc.

Jackal cracked the door and peered out into the yard. Silver light pooled in the bailey save where the shadows lay thickest beneath the walls. Fiery globs denoted torches along the battlements, some slowly moving, revealing the paths of sentries. The tallest tower was not immediately apparent. The central keep was largest, but the drum tower on the northeast corner of the fortress equaled it in height. The keep would be foolhardy. Bermudo was probably within, plowing the ass of some poor stableboy.

And then Jackal knew where to go.

He waited from the safety of the doorway, watching the pattern of the sentries for an opening. Before he felt comfortable venturing out, footsteps and a cough from the stairs above forced him to action. He slipped out into the yard, leaving the door slightly ajar lest the noise of it latching alert whomever was coming down the tower. He walked briskly across the yard, neither running nor creeping. Hopefully, from the wall he would look like a man crossing the bailey with genuine purpose, unless the watcher's eyes were particularly keen and noticed a shirtless, long-haired half-orc. He made it to the barracks without challenge and ducked into the shadows, trying not to think about the scores of men sleeping just beyond the wall he now used to conceal himself. Keeping low, he hurried beneath the windows, skirting the long side of the building until he reached the corner. The stables lay not fifty steps away, across an alarmingly bright stretch of yard.

Hells, was every damned star in the sky favoring that one cursed swath of dust?

He took his time watching the patrols on the battlements and, when he deemed it safe, made a run for it, hoping some sleepless soldier wasn't looking out from the barracks at that particular instant.

Skidding under the eaves of the stables, he stopped and listened. No cries were raised, no pounding of pursuing boots, just the occasional snort of a horse from the dozens of stalls beyond the chest-high stone enclosure. Columns supported the roof, allowing the wind to thread through the stables, relieving and carrying the strong odors of the steeds. Jackal remained outside, slinking along the wall until he found the wooden double gate. A wicket was set within it, allowing men to come and go without the need to swing the gates open. Fortunately, it was unbarred.

Jackal breathed easier once he was enveloped by the pungent darkness. Except it wasn't completely dark. A flicker of light outlined the closed door of the tack room to the right. The castile employed more than a dozen stableboys and Jackal could hear their soft snores in the hayloft above. One, however, was clearly working in the tack room, as none would have been foolish enough to leave a lit lamp unattended. As Jackal eased the door open, he hoped he was right about which individual was up so late.

The boy sat on the floor, barefoot, intent on repairing a bridle. He did not look up as Jackal entered the room, his head cocked far to the side as he squinted at his work. Like all the stableboys, his hair was shaved close to the scalp, to deter lice, but a white crescent of bald skin outlined a deep depression above his right ear. His mouth hung open slightly, his tongue making regular appearances, coinciding with the erratic tics of his face.

About seven years ago, Muro had been born to one of Sancho's whores. She died of some affliction passed to her by the cock of a Gubic merchant before the boy was weaned. Four years later, it was the mule of another merchant that kicked Muro while he was playing in the brothel yard. The lad had never been the same. Ignacio took him off Sancho's hands and brought him to live at the castile. Jackal had only seem him twice since, once when the hoof helped escort a caravan of goods to the castile and again when Delia brought him back to the brothel to nurse him through an illness that the garrison's horsemaster kept ignoring.

The boy looked up slowly as Jackal squatted down across from him. His eyes were slightly unaligned and blinked hard.

"I am to finish," Muro said, the words slow and dully pitched. He immediately turned his attention back to the bridle. He fussed dutifully at the leather, trying to braid the browband. It was a task that required nimble fingers, the work of an hour for someone of skill. This poor boy had neither, but had spent hells knew how long struggling until he was now half a finger's length from finished.

"Finish this?" Jackal asked, pointing to the bridle.

Muro gave a glacial nod. "Master tolds I am to finish before sleep."

Jackal breathed out hard through his nostrils and looked over his shoulder at the tack-room door. Perhaps he needed to go find where "Master" sleeps.

"Can I help you with it?" Jackal asked, turning back to the boy.

Muro held the bridle out. "Yes, thank you, please."

"Muro," Jackal said gently as he began threading the thongs, "do you remember me?"

"Noh."

"I'm Oats's friend."

Muro's slack jaw stretched up into a gleeful smile. "Bears and Moundtans."

Jackal sniggered. "That's right. Bears and Mountains."

Oats had spent more time at the brothel during the boy's convalescence than in the previous years put together. When Muro was finally strong enough to get out of bed, the two had played together for days and Oats had taught him every game he knew, then began inventing new ones. The big thrice was set on bringing the boy back to Winsome, but the Claymaster refused, saying the orphanage was only for mongrel children who might one day serve the hoof, not simpleton frails. If ever Oats might have thrown his axe, it was that day. He didn't, but his commitment to Jackal's bid for the chief seat became iron.

"Muro? Can you answer a question for me?"

The boy, still smiling with the memory of riding on Oats's shoulders, nodded.

"Where does the wizard live?"

It took a moment for the words to sink in, but when they did, the smile melted away.

"Noh."

"Is that a scary question?"

Muro nodded, shrinking back a little.

"I am sorry," Jackal told him gently. "I did not know. Do you think you can tell me anyway? It will be a secret between us."

"Noh."

The boy was shaking his head now, growing agitated. Worried he would begin to scream, Jackal held up his hands in a calming gesture.

"Muro, it's fine. You don't have to tell me. I'm sorry."

This eased the boy's distress and he settled. Jackal said nothing more, quickly finishing the bridle. Handing it back, he gave Muro a wink.

"Go on now. Get some sleep."

Muro stood and hung the bridle up with measured deliberateness. He passed Jackal without further acknowledgment and left the tack room. Tarrying only long enough to liberate a gelding knife from the racks, Jackal snuck from the room. This was folly. He would make for the sally port and escape, perhaps catch up with Delia and ensure she found a safe refuge. As he approached the stable gates, he noticed the wicket door was slightly open. Certain he had closed it earlier, Jackal proceeded cautiously, purloined knives in hand.

Glancing through the opening, he found Muro standing just outside. Tucking his blades away, Jackal hissed to get his attention. He needed to coax the boy back inside before he drew attention, but Muro only turned his head, regarded him for an instant, then looked back out across the yard. Slowly, his hand came up and he pointed. Stepping out to stand beside him, Jackal followed the direction of the stableboy's finger.

The eastern tower. The smallest tower.

Smiling, Jackal placed a grateful hand on Muro's head. "Brave boy. Get to bed now."

Muro returned to the stable and Jackal began working his way to the tower.

Chapter 26

THERE WERE NO GUARDS.

No one was posted near the doors of the small tower, nor were any of the sentries patrolling the nearby battlements. This made Jackal uneasy. He did not want to be seen, but the lack of protection around the tower bespoke of an inhabitant who needed none. Jackal was about to slip into the chambers of the most dangerous frail in Ul-wundulas. He wondered if he would be able to get a word out before serpents burst from his gut or his eyes turned into flesh-eating beetles.

"Move slow, talk fast," Jackal whispered to himself and went inside.

Stone steps snaked upward, unbroken by landings. Jackal took them up to the door of the garret. Breathing in, he did what he never dreamed might be his last living act.

He knocked.

There came the immediate sounds of movement from within. A clatter of unknown objects striking the floor was followed by a voice, the words indiscernible. The muttering beyond the door continued, but Jackal stood fast, expecting to die in agony as soon as the wizard finished what was likely an incantation. The words soon faded out. Jackal found he was still breathing. He could still hear movement, and then a low moan. Gripping the handle, Jackal slowly admitted himself into the room.

All attempts at silence were immediately snuffed as the smell assaulted his nostrils, forcing him to gag and cough. Old food, excrement, and unwashed feet bedded down in the air, an orgy of foul odors. Burying his nose in the crook of his elbow, Jackal surveyed the garret.

The furnishings were lost in warrens of damp parchment and swollen, moldy tomes. Several rats played about the piles, slinking from stacks of scrolls to plates of ancient food, their droppings ornamenting everything. A gaunt figure wandered aimlessly amidst the reeking detritus, shuffling in chaotic patterns between the largest heap and the vermin-laden nest of linens that must have served him as a bed. Beyond, the only window not obscured by refuse was barely able to admit the moonlight, its leaded glass made murky with thick films of filth.

The figure made an erratic turn, casting a crooked-neck look in Jackal's direction.

Removing his arm from his face, Jackal suffered the stench so he could speak.

"I must speak with you."

The figure made one last circuit before deciding to approach. It was an old man, clad in nothing but an open robe. Beneath, his body was wasted. Hard lines of rib roofed a ghastly potbelly. His old cods, more balls than shaft, swung pathetically between arrow-thin legs that quivered as he drew near.

"Another five hundred are required," the wretch proclaimed in a dusty voice.

Jackal could not help taking a step back as the wizard came closer. His eyes were rheumy and wild, the thin wisp of beard clinging to his quivering chin was crusted with dried food.

"I gave you a command," the old man complained.

A reedy arm crawled out from the crevasse of the filthy robe's voluminous sleeve and attempted to cuff Jackal. Reacting instinctually, he swatted the limb away. Still, the senile old fool kept coming, pawing and snatching with his skeletal hands until he managed to grasp Jackal's wrist. He stretched his vulture's neck up, his mouth agape and stinking of a corpse's asshole.

"You are no slave," he creaked.

"No," Jackal told him, "I am not."

The wizard's nostrils tightened, as if he were sniffing, and his eyes darted to and fro, crawling over Jackal's entire body.

"There is power in you," the man declared, and his mouth quavered into a nearly toothless smile of delight. "You are he! The Bastard!"

The wizard produced a look of triumphant realization, but his madness quickly snatched it away. His confused frown returned and he released Jackal, turning back into his miserable den. He ran a hand over his bald, flaking pate.

"Another five hundred, you ash-colored animal!" the wizard cried, whirling unsteadily to thrust a finger at Jackal. "Do it now, or you will be one of them!"

His patience fleeing along with his caution, Jackal took an aggressive step and seized the frail by his robe.

"I thought we agreed I was no slave," he growled.

The flicker of recognition returned as the wizard cowed. "It's you!"

"It's me," Jackal reminded him roughly. "The Bastard."

How this loon-brained skeleton knew him was a puzzle, but he supposed even demented wizards had ways. A wheezing laugh escaped from between the grey gums of the old man.

"Oh, but the queen will piss herself," the wizard gloated. "That the debaucheries of her uncle would manifest to haunt her as your magnificent person is delicious. A mongrel *and* a bastard, yet yours remains the better claim! Oh, it is sweet."

The wizard's right shoulder was revolving strangely. Jackal looked down to find the madman stroking his desiccated cock. With a disgusted shove, he sent the creep sprawling back on his vile mattress. While the coot continued to fondle his limp flesh, rasping laughter, Jackal mulled over his ramblings.

Bastard, he had said, but had not meant one of the hoof. No, he meant a natural child, some royal frail's half-blood by-blow. Hells, the man's brain was porridge.

"I need to know about a wizard," Jackal snarled down at the creature beneath him.

The old man ceased abusing himself, his laughter dying instantly. He rose, his quick yet labored movements reminding Jackal of an insect with broken legs that refuses to die.

"I am he," the wizard groveled. "Forgive me. I am Abzul, Communer of the Circle of Ul-zuwaqa, Strangler of the White She-Demon."

"I noticed," Jackal said, trying to avoid the fawning hands. "But you are not who I meant, coffin-dodger. I speak of a half-orc wizard, fresh to the Lots."

"Half-orcs," Abzul spat, "yes, many and more are required. If the high-born won't part with them for fair coin, take them! And kill one of the household. We will see what the noble families value more, their mongrel slaves or their wives and children. In this, we have the king's own blessing."

This forgotten old conjurer was useless. He was swimming in the past again, spewing nonsense at phantoms. Small wonder he was kept secret. He was just another lie, as capable of defending the castile as the hoofs were of protecting the Lots. Jackal gave him room as he fretted and paced.

Abzul suddenly shrieked at him. "Why do you stand there? Get to it! Use the survivors and the fresh arrivals. There is not time for separate crucibles. Five hundred more are required. Fill the cages!"

Jackal stiffened. Ignoring the raging old man, he looked around slowly, at the rats scavenging about the chamber.

Rats.

Cages.

"You," Jackal accused, taking a step toward Abzul. "You were one of them. You created the plague."

Pride bubbled past the wizard's befuddlement. "I did. An arduous working. Summoners. Communers. Vivamancers. Alchemists. Abjurers. All wisdoms were required. Oh, if we had but been allowed to complete . . ."

Abzul trailed off, his tongue running rapidly over his lower lip.

Overcome with loathing, Jackal snarled and seized the sorcerer by the throat.

"I think you've lived long enough, maggot."

Abzul's eyes popped and ceased their rolling to stare at Jackal's wrathful face. Whimpering, the wizard's knees buckled, but Jackal held him upright by the neck.

"I . . . am no threat to you," the wizard coughed out.

Jackal squeezed down further. "No, you are not."

"Truly," Abzul begged through his stifled airway, "there . . . is none who could challenge you, my lord . . . Ultani."

Jackal's spine went rigid. "What did you call me?"

He released Abzul, allowing him to drop. Cringing, the wizard held up a staying hand.

"Forgive me, I should not have used your name!"

"No, say it. The name. Say it!"

The old man's hands clenched together as he raised his arms imploringly. "I did not mean to offend—"

"Fucking say it!"

"Uhad Ul-badir Taruk Ultani!"

Slowly, Jackal's hands came up and rested in his dirty hair.

"Hells overburdened," he hissed.

He had come here to gather information about Crafty, not be mistaken for him by this addle-brained lecher.

"I will help you come into your kingdom, my lord!" Abzul declared. "I remain of use!"

The old wizard was starting to get loud, and though Jackal suspected mad ravings from this tower were common, he did not need some servant investigating the noise. Someone was still feeding this buzzard, though dropping a plate and hurrying away seemed to be the practice.

"Enough, Abzul," Jackal said, seeing his chance. "I will not harm you. You are of use. That is why I am here. I wish to know all that you do about me."

"Nothing, my lord," the old man baldly lied, shaking his head.

"You needn't fear," Jackal cajoled, "I know who my allies are, Abzul. It is my enemies I seek."

"Treasonous dogs! That is what they will be, my lord, when you sit your throne. Not I! I have waited here for you. I returned to Ul-wundulas when the others would not, to await your arrival. From your birth, I have waited."

"The throne of Hispartha," Jackal said lightly, carefully watching Abzul's reaction. "Do you think I can seize it?"

"It is yours to take, my lord. Your whore aunt and her pederast husband are pretenders to your grandfather's crown. I renounced their court in protest over your father's execution after he returned from exile, all the while making them believe I valorously returned to the Lots to help keep watch on the filthy soot-sk— . . . on the half-breeds, who are graced to count you as one of them!"

Jackal's jaw clenched. Abzul was a shit liar. He was trying to save his own skin from whatever danger he believed he faced. There wasn't enough courage left to hold allegiances, to Hispartha or any other. The prisons of his decrepit body and unhinged mind laid claim to all his loyalty. Still, fear had him locked in some semblance of clarity.

"Tell me of my father," Jackal urged. His corpulence aside, Crafty did not have the look of a frailing. If his father had been human, as

Abzul was suggesting, that could only mean his mother was a thick, and that was unheard-of. Female orcs were never seen outside of Dhar'gest. It would take a strong man to couple with one. A strong, utterly insane man.

"You should not heed gossip, my lord," Abzul said. "Can a prince of the blood truly be accused as a raper and a murderer, when it is of his own servants? I say not. And many, I amongst them, never believed he drowned the marquesa of Sparthis, nor hunted her sons with dogs. His exile was an unjust ploy. Yet he found friends in the east, yes? Friends who provided him entertainments worthy of his proclivities. Friends to all of Hispartha, indeed, for they ensured we had a worthy claimant to the throne. A half-breed! A sorcerer trained by the Black Womb! Who better to help us raze all of Dhar'gest and rid us of the orc threat?"

Abzul was now genuflecting with each lusty exclamation, ribbons of drool escaping from his toothless mouth.

"What of the Hisparthan wizards?" Jackal asked quickly, taking advantage of the old man's lucidity. "Are they a threat to me?"

"Not I, my lord," Abzul insisted passionately.

Jackal could not help but sneer. This man was a threat to nothing but the nose.

"And the others?"

"They would be fools to stand against you."

The way Abzul's yellowed eyes looked away when he made this claim revealed he was not only lying but wanted "Crafty" to attempt the contest and fail. So, there were magic wielders in Hispartha with the strength to challenge the Tyrkanian. But Crafty was no fool. He would not go unprepared into the lands of his enemies. No, he came first to Ul-wundulas, the long contested underbelly, and gathered powerful allies. The fucking Claymaster! Was Crafty truly about to help the chief take his revenge? If they unleashed the plague in Hispartha, what then?

Jackal found it difficult to care.

Hispartha was nothing to him. Its people were distant, faceless, seen in his mind's eye as fat and ignorant to all danger. Perhaps it was time that ignorance was shattered. It would inevitably happen. The Imperium had fallen and, one day, so would Hispartha, be it sacked by orcs or seized by a foreign half-breed with a claim to the crown. What did it matter to him? He was a free-rider now, with no loyalties save to the hog that bore him where he wished to tread. There was nothing holding him here. Delia could be his, she would ride with him if he asked, he was certain of that. They could go to Anville or Guabia, or points east. Hispartha was not the world, and Jackal had only ever known the Lots, the shit stuck to the boot heel of the kingdom. Fool-ass that he was, he loved the badlands, but like the northern frails in his imagination, he was ignorant of all else. He had wasted years trying to thwart the Claymaster. Was he truly willing to throw his life away trying to battle him and Crafty, all for a gaggle of lazy frails in the north?

As his brooding began to wane, Jackal found his eyes resting upon the nearest heap of hoarded parchment. There was a map near the top with only one corner buried. It was a map of the Lots. No, it was older than that, drawn up before the Incursion, when Ul-wundulas was held firm by Hispartha, save for Strava and the centaur woodlands. Both were definitively marked by the mapmaker. Jackal became intrigued by the map, and was mildly surprised to discover that without the lot borders, he found it difficult to orient. The whole seemed larger, no longer a quilt, but a seamless blanket. The Kiln had not existed, and Jackal had to find Batayat Hill and the Alhundra River before he was able to pinpoint the fortress's future site. The entire chart was dotted with castiles that now only existed as ink upon this map, each named and accompanied by a small illumination of the coats of arms of the noble families that held the stronghold before the orcs reduced them to ruins. One in particular drew Jackal's attention.

It was nestled within the grasp of the Old Maiden Marsh, where the concentration of settlements was sparse. There were only four castiles denoted in the entire region. One of them, deepest within the Maiden's interior, boasted a blazon Jackal had seen before; a yellow goat upon a black shield, surrounded by a purple belt. The colors had been less vibrant, but the overall image had been larger, so Jackal knew he was not mistaken. It was the same device he had seen upon the frayed and filthy banner within the Sludge Man's shed.

Reaching down for the cowering Abzul, Jackal lifted him up.

"What is this?" he demanded, jabbing a finger below the crest.

Abzul squinted hard at the map. "That . . . those are the arms of the House of Corigari. An ancient family with roots in the Imperium."

Jackal scowled at the map. "Any of them left?"

"Ha!" Abzul's bark of laughter told what he thought of that notion. "Everything in those marshlands was laid to waste by magic during the early Incursion. The elves met the thicks in battle there, both sides bolstered by sorcery. The hatred in the spells loosed that day will live for eternity."

"You mean the sludges."

Abzul leered down at the map. "Oh, yes."

"Was that your evil too, wizard?"

The old man shot him a withering look. "No. That was all point-ear shamanism and orc blood magic. Hispartha had no presence there, save the stubborn nobles who refused to abandon their holdings, and they all paid for their mulish pride with their lives." As Abzul spoke his face became suspicious and his nostrils drew thin again with that same queer sniffing he had done when Jackal first entered the garret.

"I would think you to have known this, my lord," the wizard declared.

Jackal nodded slowly, but not at the old man's words. The one Abzul mistook him for had known! Crafty had wanted to go to the Old Maiden, and he did have knowledge of the sludges, calling them children of conflicting spells. He had even shown some fear of them, yet he had been prepared, knowing how to stupefy them with whatever came from that queer pipe. He called the Sludge Man a demon and even awaited his arrival. Fuck, he had gone there to confront him! And why would he do that unless the Sludge Man was a threat? Crafty set out for the marsh in order to eliminate his greatest rival.

The sound of rustling parchment drew Jackal away from his revelation. All about him, the piles in the garret were shifting, sending small avalanches falling from the bigger heaps as they were upset from within. Abzul must have slunk off while Jackal was lost in thought, for the wizard was nowhere to be seen. His voice, however, carried over the increasing chittering coming from the refuse.

"Filthy mongrel! To dare deceive me! I will not be so abased by a soot-skin savage!"

Jackal tried to detect where the wizard was hiding, but his furious cries filled the room, coming from everywhere, yet nowhere. Drawing the spar hook, Jackal went for the door. He had not made it two strides before a pile of scrolls disgorged a mass of squealing rats. They spilled out in a stream of shiny fur and pallid tails. Jackal recoiled as the mass darted for him, but more sprang up from the debris, fleeing their hives to charge. The garret came alive as the moldering contents of the room heaved with vermin.

Surrounded by the oncoming tide, Jackal lashed out. He stomped upon those scurrying on the ground, and sent swaths flying off the furnishings with great sweeps of his arms.

And won nothing more than a heartbeat before the swarm was upon him.

Crawling up his legs, leaping upon his shoulders, the rats engulfed him in a wriggling cloud of biting teeth. Jackal cried out in horror and pain, whirling desperately, trying to sling the devouring mass off. He kept his eyes clenched shut against those on his face. He heard them hissing in his ears before their teeth sunk into the hard cartilage with a horrible popping. The spar hook fell from his grasp and he began yanking the rodents off his head, throwing them down after crushing their spines in his fist. Yet more always took their place.

Blind and stumbling, Jackal careened into a hard, flat surface. It must have been the door, for the garret's walls were moated by the nests. Slamming his body against the wood, again and again, rolling and grinding, Jackal crushed the rats, sending dozens falling limply away. It wasn't enough. He could feel himself getting weaker, his strength seeping red and hot from his body through hundreds of small punctures. Already he was shivering, his limbs beginning to convulse as an unnatural fever flared beneath his ravaged flesh. His joints throbbed as they swelled, filling with fluid, as were his lungs. He coughed, gagged and began to drown, horribly, from the inside.

Unable to breathe, Jackal fell to his knees. His entire body burned. He could no longer feel the agony of the rat bites, nor the terrifying constriction in his lungs. There was only the heat, seeming to rise from somewhere deep, searing his flesh from beneath. He screamed against the excruciation and in that scream, realized he could again breathe. The rats began falling away from him, twitching and dying in droves.

When his vision returned, he discovered he now knelt encircled in their still, loathsome forms. He continued to bleed from his teeth-torn flesh, but the ravages of the plague had fled. Rising out of the dead vermin, Jackal found Abzul standing across the garret.

"There *is* power in you, mongrel," the wizard declared, "but you are no magus of the Black Womb."

"No, old man, I am not. I am Jackal of the Grey Bastards. And I am about to start making a habit of slaying wizards."

He took a step forward, his strength returning with the promise of wrath.

Abzul began to laugh, his toothless mouth stretched into a rictus of crazed mirth.

"Oh, but there is sweet poetry to be found here!" he cried out with glee, his eyes flashing with more clarity and life than Jackal had yet seen. Holding up his hands, the wizard showed himself to be clutching a pair of ceramic jars. They were bulbous at the bottom, narrower at the neck and fluted at the top. They were nearly identical to the relics stored in the Claymaster's solar, except where those were empty, these were stoppered with wax.

Sapper pots.

Seeing them brought Jackal's advance to a halt.

Abzul was delighted by his sudden hesitance. "Ah! I see you recognize these. And well you should, they are your legacy after all, Grey Bastard. Fate has brought you here to die, it seems! That you should be slain by the implements made by the founders of your hoof in the days when half-breeds were properly chained is a delight I shall savor."

Jackal lunged as the wizard threw from both hands.

The casts were feebly aimed and Jackal ducked, hearing the pots break on the wall behind. There was a brief booming, quickly swallowed by a concussive pressure on the eardrums, before all sound was replaced by a piercing ring. Jackal saw the flash of flames and felt intense heat lick at his back as he was propelled furiously forward. He was catapulted directly at Abzul and wrapped his arms about the wizard's frail form as he smashed into him. Together they were hurled out the window, Jackal using Abzul as a ram to break the glass.

Wind and the wizard's buffeting robe slapped Jackal's face as they fell. Abzul's mouth was gaped in an unheard scream. Behind his skeletal head, the moonlit slope of the jagged hill rose quickly to meet them.

Chapter 27

Pain escorted Jackal back to consciousness. His ears were still ringing as he opened his eyes, finding the stars diluted by his swimming vision. Rocks dug into his back, cradling him ungently upon the slope. Sprawled with his boots higher than his head, he attempted to roll over, but his ribs screamed in complaint. Jackal heard the cry forced from his throat as a muffled grunt. Something bumped his leg. Lifting his throbbing skull, he saw Abzul a little farther uphill, writhing feebly. The wizard's robe must have come off after they landed, torn from his white body as they rolled. His limbs were bent at sickening angles, his jaw working in desperate gasps.

Gritting his teeth in preparation for the hurt, Jackal used his heels to drag his legs around until they faced downhill, and sat up. Dazed, he simply slumped there until his hearing began to return. Behind him came sounds of sliding stones and labored breathing as Abzul attempted to crawl away. Jackal did not bother to look. The worm would not get far.

An angry flicker on the rocks grew stronger as Jackal sat there, sending his shadow dancing down the slope. Craning his neck around, he saw the tower roof aflame, so distant it made him queasy. He thought he heard cries coming from along the battlements, but didn't trust his blasted ears enough to be sure. Either way, the alarms wouldn't be raised for him. The garrison would be too busy fighting the fire to look beyond the walls. Who could conceive that any would fall from that height and survive?

Turning back, Jackal saw movement amongst the scrub farther down the hill. He recognized the silhouettes. Two hogs, and one rider now dismounting to scramble up the boulders. Jackal tried to whistle, but found his mouth had no spit to wet his lips.

Warbler found him anyway.

"Fucking hells," the old thrice gasped, seeing him. The fire from the tower lit his craggy, worried face, which stared for a moment before rising to take in the blaze above the walls.

"I swore I heard a sapper pot," Warbler said.

Jackal cleared his raw throat. "At least two. Though he may have had more lost under all the rat shit."

"Who?"

Jackal didn't answer immediately, but held his hand up in a mute appeal for help standing. Grasping his forearm, Warbler pulled him to his feet. Moving gingerly, Jackal led him across the slope. Abzul had made it farther than he anticipated.

"Him," Jackal said, motioning down. Abzul must have heard, for he managed to roll his mangled body over. "He is—"

"I fucking know who he is," Warbler growled, his face turning grim. "Not even the age of thirty years could hide that face from me."

Abzul gawked at them, his pain-wracked visage convulsing.

"Amazing he's still alive," Jackal remarked with dark amusement.

"Wizards are damn hard to kill," Warbler said.

Abzul's mad eyes rolled about. "To . . . the cages. Both! You are for the cages." A crazed, choking laugh oozed past the wizard's tongue. "Any . . . any alive?"

Warbler took a step toward him. "Yes. I'm alive."

"Take your time," Jackal said, and moved away, finding a rock to sit upon.

What Warbler did was neither quick nor quiet. Even through the ringing, Jackal clearly heard Abzul's final shrieks.

"We should go," he said when Warbler returned. "The frails might have heard that. At the very least, they'll soon know I've escaped. The cavaleros will start beating the bushes for me."

"I couldn't get in," Warbler confessed. "They wouldn't even hear me out. Threatened to feather me from the gate if I didn't ride on."

Jackal gave a bitter snort. "Not your fault. It was a shit plan. Thankfully, the garrison likes to stick whores full of something other than arrows. Delia freed me."

"I know. I saw her. Almost snuck in the way she came out, but she said it was too chancy. Said you were coming soon. Reckon you got deterred. You learn anything?"

"Yes," Jackal said, standing. "Let's get to the hogs. Tell you once we are away."

They worked their way down the hill, going slower than Jackal liked, but his body rebelled against haste. When at last they reached the bottom, he stroked Hearth's face with both hands, briefly resting his forehead between the hog's eyes.

"Good to see you, you beautiful golden beast."

Hearth loosed a series of low, rhythmic grunts.

Once mounted, Warbler returned Jackal's thrum. "Where are we headed?"

"The Old Maiden," Jackal told him, slinging the weapon across his back.

The old thrice looked dubious. "For what?"

Jackal's response almost stuck in his throat. "To make an ally of the Sludge Man."

They rode for the remainder of the night, putting distance between themselves and the castile. Only once were they threatened with discovery, when a troop of cavaleros thundered up their back-trail, fast but noisy. Jackal and Warbler had plenty of time to get up into some rocks. They watched as the riders, unaware they had lost their quarry, sped by. Ignacio led them, his balding head and pockmarked face unmistakable. The commoner captain looked harried.

"That was blind luck," Warbler said when they were gone.

"For them," Jackal agreed. "They're just covering ground. Didn't even see our tracks. Only twenty riders."

Warbler huffed. "Spreading themselves thin. They must want to find you, Jackal-boy."

"Luck to them," Jackal said, grinning in the dark.

Dawn arrived with no more sign of soldiers. Hearth and Mean Old Man had pounded out some miles, their snouts pointed south and west. Confident that the cavaleros were well behind, Jackal and Warbler halted to rest beneath a rocky outcropping overlooking the River Lucia.

After draining his waterskin, Jackal slept.

When Warbler roused him, the sun was at its zenith.

"You smell like a sow's quim," the old thrice said. "Best go down and scrub, unless Lucia bends her current to avoid you."

Jackal took the suggestion readily. After a long dip in the blissfully cool river, he walked naked back up to the outcropping.

"Trade you," Warbler said, tossing him a pear and pointing to the filthy breeches in his hand. Jackal handed them over and bid a silent farewell as Warbler tossed them onto the fire he had kindled. Pear clutched in his teeth, Jackal dug fresh breeches from his saddlebags.

"Those already look better," Warbler said, squinting critically at the rat bites covering Jackal's body.

Jackal nodded, inspecting himself while eating. The wounds were fading. Those on his left forearm were almost invisible.

"You don't feel ill?" Warbler asked.

"I did," Jackal told him, hopping into his breeches. "Thought it was the end."

He laughed lightly when he said it, but Warbler didn't see the humor, and just continued to peer intently.

"What happened in there, Jackal?"

"What do you know about the king of Hispartha?"

Warbler's mouth wrinkled, annoyed to have his question answered with another. "Which one?"

"The one they got now."

The old thrice scratched through his white mane. "He's a king in name, but he married the true power. The queen holds the bloodline. Old king was her father. Why?"

"She have a brother?"

"More than one, I think."

"How about one that's older and blood-fuck crazy?"

Warbler raised his brows, deepening the wrinkles. "Oh, yes. They lopped his head for him, years back."

"Well, before they did that, he was exiled and survived shagging a she-orc. Probably arranged by some Tyrkanian caliph that was playing host, I don't know for certain."

Warbler was growing impatient. "What do you know, Jaco? What sunset are you riding for?"

"Crafty is his son," Jackal said. "The beheaded brother's half-breed son. Do you see? He is going to make a grab for the crown of Hispartha. That's why he's here."

Warbler accepted this with a long exhalation. "Does the Claymaster know?"

Jackal could only shrug.

"He must," Warbler decided. "It's what he's always wanted. A chance to destroy the frails. Hells, a half-orc king! His poxy cock is standing up at the thought and . . ."

The old-thrice broke off, his mouth slightly slack.

"You don't know that he's wrong," Jackal finished.

Warbler gave an aggravated shake of the head.

"I thought the same," Jackal told him, walking over to feed the remainder of the pear to Hearth.

Neither he nor Warbler said anything for a long time. The day was hot and the shade of the outcropping a relief, channeling the scant wind into a welcome flow across the skin. Gathering his tack, Jackal began to saddle his hog. By the time he was done, Warbler still hadn't moved a muscle.

"What's troubling you?" Jackal asked, though he suspected the answer.

The old thrice was a while in answering. When he did speak, he did not turn, but gazed out across the badlands.

"I just tasted vengeance, Jackal. Didn't know I still craved it. After this many years, hells take me, it was sweeter than it would have been if I had killed every wizard in that mine the day we escaped. Retribution does not sour, apparently. I . . . I'm not certain the Claymaster doesn't deserve to drink from that cup."

"He won't be sated with one wizard, Warbler."

"Why should he be? You weren't there, son. You cannot begin to know what it was like."

Jackal gestured angrily at his wounds. "I think I can."

"Could you suffer it again?" Warbler demanded, turning on him. "And again after that? What about again? And again and again and again, until you know nothing else! Until you can't recall a day without that gnashing, squeaking, wriggling torment! You think you understand? Even I don't understand! We are free from the plague, somehow, some way, we are free! He isn't! You say it took hold of you, said you thought it was the end. Now imagine living with that for thirty years, longer than you've fucking been alive! If anyone deserves to burn Hispartha to the ground it's him! The Claymaster has earned whatever he wants to do to those cunts up north!"

Jackal looked into Warbler's tortured face. "You still love him."

Tears appeared in the thrice's sun-squinted eyes, infuriating him further.

"He was my brother! My savior! My captain! And I betrayed him!"

Jackal shook his head. "If I had known it would take the fight out of you, I never would have allowed you to kill that wizard."

"Allowed?" Warbler demanded. "ALLOWED?"

The old thrice took two steps, reaping one arm across as he moved. His hard knuckles caught Jackal on the jaw, backhanding him to the ground.

"You are welcome to see what fight I got left, stripling!" Warbler threatened, looming.

Wiping the blood from his mouth, Jackal sprang back to his feet, causing Warbler to tense and clench his fists. But Jackal did not attack. He faced the old thrice, nearly nose to nose, and fixed him with an unblinking stare.

"The Claymaster doesn't want your pity, War-boar," Jackal said slowly. "He just wanted your blind loyalty. That's what he wanted from all of us. Nothing but to serve his grudge. You loved him, but you grew to love the hoof more, the brotherhood you helped create. What happens to the Grey Bastards in the pursuit of his vengeance? To Winsome and the orphanage and Beryl? You know the answer, have known since before I sat a hog. Why else have you continued the fight from the outside? To save our hoof. Tell me I'm wrong."

Warbler's ire visibly cooled. His face fell and he took a step away, unable to meet Jackal's eyes any longer.

"No, you're not wrong."

Shaking off the shame, the old thrice grabbed Jackal by the back of the neck and pulled him into a rough embrace.

"You always were too damn clever," Warbler said, his voice muddled by Jackal's shoulder. Releasing him, he stepped back and roughly pawed at his swollen jaw. "Sorry, son."

Jackal pardoned him with a dismissive wave. "I've had worse from Oats. You're getting old, War-boar."

"Must be. Because I am about to ask you what we are doing next."

Jackal thought a moment, tonguing his split lip.

"The Claymaster is being used," he announced at last. "If Crafty wanted to reign over a wasteland he would make himself king of Ul-wundulas. He will never allow the chief to spread the plague in His-partha, mark me. It's too . . . vulgar for him. Whatever he intends, it's farther reaching than the chief's vengeance."

Warbler loosed a weary sigh. "You must really want to stop him, if you think slogging through the Old Maiden in search of that naked scumsucker Sludge Man is the best way to do it."

"That's the trouble," Jackal laughed bitterly. "I don't want to stop him. In my time with the fat fuck, he proved to be wise, capable, a good ally. I liked him, Warbler. Still do. He would make a good Bas-tard and, being earnest, a good king, for the fuck-all I know about it."

"So why fight him?"

"*Because* I know fuck-all about it. About him. On first sight he's a half-orc. One of us. Below that, a wizard. Dig past that and you find the Black Womb, whatever that proves to be. There's so much buried within him, we'll be trapped if we attempt to reach the bottom. What-ever is at his core won't be good for us. The mongrel hoofs won't be sitting at King Uhad the Fat's side eating dates while virgins suck our cocks. The Claymaster may be the wizard's puppet, but Crafty's also dancing to the twitching fingers of others. Tyrkania, most likely, but we will always be guessing. Helping him to the throne will only de-stroy us."

"You don't sound sure."

"Because I'm not," Jackal said solemnly.

Warbler remained patiently silent.

Feeling the hurt begin to rise, Jackal cleared his throat. "But Fetch-ing was. She warned me against trusting him. From the start, she saw a scorpion in the blanket."

"And she didn't step on it," Warbler said. "She stepped on you."

"I know. And I'm not certain why. But I've been certain I had this all figured so many times . . . and every time I've been wrong."

Picking up a stone, Jackal rid himself of the creeping self-pity by flinging it far out toward the river.

"So," he proclaimed, "we are going with her gut now."

Warbler gave an amused grunt. "Which one of us still loves an enemy now?"

"Let's see," Jackal made a weighing motion with his hands. "A bent-backed, plague-ridden, pus-dripping vengeful old heap of hogshit, versus . . . Fetching. You have seen what she grew into? Between the two of us, War-boar, you are the tougher to understand."

"Straddle your razor, Jaco."

They rode hard until nightfall, made another rough camp, and were up with the sun. By midmorning on the fourth day, the dust began to slowly give way to the wetlands. Soon, they were bulling through thick reed beds and avoiding sinks of mire.

"All these years as a free-rider," Warbler groused, "and I managed to avoid this midge-infested armpit."

Jackal grinned over at him. "And yet you willingly soak in Sancho's baths. Don't see much of a difference."

He had led them to the northern edge of the marsh, purposefully skirting it for long miles west before finally turning south and intruding into its muddy clutches. Abzul's map was fixed in his mind.

"I think I can find the Sludge Man's huts again," Jackal told Warbler, "but there is something I want to try and see first."

"What?" the old thrice asked, swatting at the marsh flies gathering in front of his scowling face.

"A ruin," Jackal replied. "I think it was his family home before the Incursion. Hard to believe, but I figure he might have once been Hisparthan nobility."

Warbler grunted. "It always crawled at my spine the way he spoke like a blue blood, yet looked like his mother might also have been a sister. Of course, those two traits aren't entirely mismatched on further thought."

"And yet they call us half-breeds filthy."

"What do you hope to find in this ruin?"

"Not certain. An advantage, perhaps. If he still lives, and I suspect he does, the Sludge Man won't be pleased to see me again. Probably won't find anything but sunken stones, if that, but this course should bring us through the Corigari holdings. That was his name."

"Really think I need to know that?" Warbler asked grumpily, guiding Mean Old Man around a quagmire.

Jackal shrugged. "If he kills me outright, it might be a good idea for you to be . . . courteous."

"Since when are half-orcs courteous?"

"Didn't you hear? We are about to have our own king."

"What's got you all merry? Acting like your cock learned how to suck itself."

"Just trying to balance out your bile, old father."

Noon rose and began to recede. Jackal and Warbler had long been forced to dismount. They took turns leading, the acting scout proceeding with loaded thrum or bow in hand, while the other led Hearth and Mean Old Man a few paces behind. No matter his position, Jackal remained watchful for rokhs, and was relieved to have made it this far without encountering any of the giant birds. What he also had not seen, with an odd mixture of relief and doubt, were any sludges. Last time he and Crafty had come to the marsh, they hadn't intruded nearly this far before the off-putting creatures appeared. Granted, they had journeyed from the east, not the north, but surely that made little difference. The Sludge Man should have been tracking the presence of any visitors to what he believed was his exclusive domain. Could he truly be dead? Was this just another foolish endeavor?

"The sun's sinking fast, Jackal-boy," Warbler said during his third time on point.

Shielding his eyes against the diffused glare of dusk, Jackal surveyed the horizon in every direction.

"We need to find higher ground to camp," he said, "preferably with some trees. There, maybe."

He pointed off to the southeast, where he thought he spotted a distant rise.

"Give me the hogs, then," Warbler suggested. "My eyes aren't that good."

"Your eyes are fine," Jackal said, handing the leads over. "You just doubt me."

"That too."

Unslinging his stockbow and loading a bolt, Jackal began working his way to the hump, little more than a black smudge against the darkening sky. They picked carefully through the marsh, but as they went, the ground began to grow firmer. The bogs became shallower, the spongy ground bolstered by thick beds of marram grass. The land was already gradually rising. Halfway to their destination, Jackal could see he wasn't chasing a mirage. It was full night when they finally reached the mound, but the orc blood in their eyes showed them Jackal had been more than right.

"Luckier than a two-dicked hog," Warbler chuckled softly.

Jackal looked ahead with no small satisfaction.

It wasn't just a rise in the marsh, but the eroding remnants of a man-made bulwark, complete with the jagged teeth of a broken wall. Beyond, the shadows of an old keep stood brooding. Large sections of wall and the skeletons of fallen towers lay scattered around the mound, half-submerged in the mire. It was impossible to tell how tall the motte had been in its glory, but it was quickly succumbing to the sucking terrain and was now barely taller than Jackal, giving what was left of the stronghold a squat appearance, an old stone toad sulking in the marsh.

"This the one you were looking for?" Warbler asked.

"Likely," Jackal replied. "Regardless, it's a good camp. Come morning we—"

He broke off.

Something had moved in the ruins ahead, darting between the debris. Warbler saw it too, for he drew silently up beside Jackal, his bow now in hand with an arrow nocked.

Long before Jackal was a slophead, it was Warbler who had taught him the hand gestures used by the hoof when silence was needed. They used them to communicate now, quickly signaling that they each had seen one figure and verifying the location. Jackal suggested splitting up and Warbler agreed, immediately melting into the shadows. He would sneak along the skulker's rear, while Jackal moved to head it off. They left the hogs untethered, knowing they could better defend themselves if any were foolish enough to confront them.

Moving swiftly at a crouch, Jackal hurried to the closest piece of cover; a tumbled section of a once round tower, now a shattered egg in the muck. Pressing his back to the stones, he listened intently for a moment, then crept around and made his way furtively to the line of rubble lying thickly near the slope of the motte. The shadow he pursued should be making its way toward him on the other side.

He waited, ears straining. Soon, there came the faintest sound.

Cautious feet on sodden ground. Jackal waited for it to draw near and spun out from behind the masonry, stockbow aimed. He saw the dull reflection of moonlight on the dagger blade, raised to strike, but Jackal snatched his fingers away from his thrum's tickler, his eyes widening as they stared down the runnel at a fair, familiar face.

Starling recognized him with equal shock and arrested the plunge of her dagger. They stood for a long moment, both trembling, trying to reconcile each other's presence. Finally gaining his wits, Jackal lowered his thrum.

The she-elf was filthy, still wearing the garments Beryl had given her. Her short, knife-shorn hair clung to her grimy cheeks below the slightly slanted eyes, luminous with surprise. She spun around when Warbler emerged from the shadows behind, but relaxed when he quickly said some words in the Tine language.

"What is she doing here?" Jackal asked.

She turned back at his voice and her face settled with resolve. Motioning for them to follow, she went hurriedly up the slope of the motte, scrambling with her hands when the footing grew difficult. After sharing a look, Jackal and Warbler went after her. She waited for them at the top, then struck off along the curtain wall until she reached an opening large enough for them to all pass through.

Inside the murky yard, the keep lay before them. Starling paused, staring at the black walls of the structure. Standing behind her, Jackal was unable to see her face, yet still he felt the trepidation radiating from her slim shoulders. Quickly mastering her reluctance, the she-elf went forward again, leading them across the yard on nearly silent feet. The door to the keep had long since rotted away, but a thick curtain of bearded moss took its place in the archway. At the threshold, Starling again halted and her breath began to come in audible shudders. She stared at the entrance, fearful and furious, trembling. Placing a hand on her shoulder, Jackal stepped around in front of her and gave her a reassuring look, seeking permission to go in first.

Starling nodded.

Sweeping the moss aside, Jackal stepped into the keep.

The roof had collapsed, bringing the floors of the upper stories down with it. All that remained was a hollow shell. A shell alive with cruelty.

Jackal heard the others enter behind him, but he could not take his eyes off what he beheld, though, in truth, he had seen it before.

"Hells take me," Warbler marveled darkly.

The interior of the keep, from the rubble-strewn floor to the yawning hole at the top, was slick with gently moving sludge. Embedded within, held captive as Starling once was, were the naked, slack forms of female elves. Jackal counted maybe a dozen at a glance. Looking down at Starling, his mouth hanging open, he shook his head sorrowfully.

"She came back for the others."

CHAPTER 28

SIXTEEN WERE IMPRISONED WITHIN THE SLUDGE. THE EERIE black substance embraced them, holding them close as it moved sluggishly, almost imperceptibly, over their wrists and ankles, their thighs, necks, stomachs. Some were almost fully encased, others dangling from their extremities. Only their faces were left uniformly exposed, though none were conscious. Jackal was not certain they were all alive.

Next to him, Warbler came out of his disturbed torpor.

"We need to get them free of this shit," the old thrice declared, moving determinedly toward the nearest she-elf.

"Wait," Jackal warned, keeping his voice level but firm.

Warbler halted. "Will they attack?"

It was a direct question, posed by a seasoned warrior without fear.

Jackal looked at Starling, remembering when he had first seen her, the trepidation he had felt when reaching out to see if she were alive, wondering if the creature holding her would react aggressively to his meddling. It hadn't, but neither had he actually tried to remove her from the living muck. She stood now, surrounded by a horror she had escaped, a horror to which she had willingly returned for the sake of those still ensnared.

"I don't know," Jackal answered while continuing to look at Starling. "If they do, we are all dead."

"Did you know about this?" Warbler asked, his question tinged with accusation.

"No. Sancho confessed there were others before I was dragged away, but I figured them for dead. Delia did too. Starling was alone when Crafty and I found her. But she was within a shed near the Sludge Man's hut."

"Why separate her?"

"Perhaps because she was the only Tine. These others were all smuggled in from Hispartha by Ignacio."

Nearby, Starling was looking upon the plight of her fellow elves with a vague disgust, revolving slowly in place. She ignored Jackal and Warbler entirely as she surveyed the keep, giving the she-elves held in the highest reaches the longest consideration. Jackal watched as the despair on Starling's face ripened and soured. She had no notion what to do next, that much was plain. All her thought must have been bent on again reaching this prison, traveling on foot. Perhaps she did not expect to find any still alive. Whatever her hope, her innermost dread, she had arrived at last and the wet defeat in her eyes betrayed she did not know how to proceed.

That defeat hardened within a heartbeat.

Baring her own teeth in a silent snarl, she shook her head in denial of all fear, and moved swiftly toward one of the prisoners. Reaching with her free hand, she grabbed the captive by the arm and began to pull before Jackal could stop her. The sludge did not attack, but as the woman began to slide free, it resisted, growing taut to draw its charge back. Issuing an audible breath, Starling pulled harder and began using her knife to cut at the shiny black strands. Slinging his stock-bow, Jackal stepped to her aid. He plunged both hands deep into the sludge and seized the unconscious she-elf beneath the arms, hauling back. Out of the corner of his eye, he saw Warbler move to attempt a lone rescue of another. Jackal and Starling labored side by side and, measure by measure, they wrestled their captive free of the stubborn substance. She moaned weakly as she emerged, Jackal supporting her weight. Starling was already moving to the next girl.

A little down the wall, Warbler had also succeeded.

The she-elves close to the ground were soon freed. The next three required Warbler and Jackal to stack rubble until they could be reached. The footing was precarious and the rescues arduous, but they managed after what seemed an eternity.

"This one is gone," Warbler said softly, inspecting the last of the trio once they were safely on the ground.

Jackal looked down and nearly choked on the rage rising in his throat. Hells, they all looked half-dead. Their filthy, nude forms were frightfully wan. Half-dead, however, was a blessing when seen next to the corpse that Warbler knelt beside. She was just so still, devoid even of the shallow breaths of the others.

Jackal looked skyward, at the five remaining captives, and wondered how many of them were beyond saving.

"I don't know how we are going to reach them," he admitted aloud.

Starling's gaze was fixed on the same problem.

And so they both saw when the large sludge came crawling over the lip of the roofless keep. Briefly, it blotted out the rough square of visible sky, consuming the stars, before it began its descent of the wall.

Jackal alerted Warbler by simply saying his name, his tone enough to convey the danger that was approaching. Standing up, Warbler took his bow in hand and trained an arrow on the black mass. Knowing better, Jackal left his thrum slung. He watched and waited.

The sludge avoided the remaining captives, oozing past them. As it came closer to the ground, Jackal saw it had soaked up all the sludge in its path, leaving a wide trail of stones showing through on the walls. The absorbed muck from the keep added to the creature's size. When it reached the ground, it piled into a rough sphere, nearly the size of that damn elephant Oats had wept for.

Warbler took several paces backward, the instincts of an archer guiding his movement. Starling retreated but one step, then forced herself to hold firm. Jackal refused to give any ground.

The slick, rounded surface split, began peeling back and away, the opening petals of some great, putrid flower. The form enwombed within was familiar, yet dreadfully changed. Only a face and some of the torso were revealed, yet the injuries sustained from Crafty's magic were apparent. The skin was grey and withered, etched with deep, hard wrinkles, as if rancid meat had been smoked.

The Sludge Man was not burnt so much as exsiccated.

The black yolk surrounding him kept sliding over his exposed features and, for a moment, the petrified flesh would revive, only to visibly degrade once more. Only his eyes were constant. They bored into Jackal with the violence of flung spears.

"The villein returns to our demesne," the Sludge Man muttered. "You forfeit all with this, your final trespass."

Jackal set his jaw. "I have *risked* all to come here, Corigari. What is forfeit remains to be seen."

The name was said offhandedly, a way of unbalancing the Sludge Man. It worked, for his glare brightened.

"Our true name is too vaunted for mongrel tongues," he declared. "We will have only our appellation when you address us."

"I don't know what that means, Sludge Man," Jackal admitted lightly.

"Yet you are compliant in your ignorance." The Sludge Man's stare crawled over to Starling. "And you come bearing what you pilfered. Your chieftain is wise to deliver what was ours. Wiser still to have her deliverer be the Bastard that so affronted us."

Jackal nodded slowly, allowing the Sludge Man to believe they had been sent by the Claymaster.

"But he won't be delivering the one who truly caused you harm," he stated.

The Sludge Man glanced briefly at Warbler, as if just now realizing he wasn't fat and turbaned.

"The foreign wizard must know our displeasure!"

"The Tyrkanian is my chief's trusted adviser now," Jackal said, shaking his head. "The Claymaster will never allow him to be harmed. Nor will there be any more elf girls. That is why I have come, to tell you that the Claymaster has severed the bargain between you and Ignacio."

"That is foolish," the Sludge Man mused, "of him, and you. For your chieftain has sent you to die, and willingly did you march."

"Not if we make a new bargain," Jackal offered.

The Sludge Man's eyes narrowed. His inky cocoon roiled around his ruined visage.

Jackal pressed on. "I can give you the wizard. You can have revenge upon him. Him, and the Claymaster too."

"And you wish what for this, knave?"

"My life and the lives of those here. Release the elves, allow my companion to leave with them. Once they are safely outside the marsh, I will show you how to enter the Kiln. There, you can have your vengeance."

The sludge laved the bog trotter's face. When the blackness retreated, the Sludge Man's revivified cheeks were smiling.

"You would offer two lives for nearly a score. And for what? You believe that your holdfast would offer impediment to one such as we? Walls do not deter us."

"What about wizards?" Jackal asked. "I witnessed his defeat of you, Sludge Man. And you don't look hale enough to try him again, not without knowledge that I can give you. I rode with the Tyrkanian. I can ensure you are victorious."

It was a lie, of course, but Jackal sold it with the weight of his voice and the set of his stare.

"Why betray your hoof, mongrel?"

"In order to lead it," Jackal replied firmly.

The Sludge Man's smile vanished in another caress of muck.

"You seek to gain much for using us as your cat's-paw. Are we to be vassal to you? Is this the extent of your impudence?"

"If we both wish to prosper, this is the way," Jackal said. "You punish the Claymaster's pet wizard, I get what I deserve. All bargains resume. As chief, I can get elves coming back into the Old Maiden."

Another lie. They were piling up, as unstable as the surrounding piles of rubble.

"Yet you would rob us of what has already been purchased," the Sludge Man said, his head nodding down toward the prostrate forms of the she-elves.

"To appease the Tines," Jackal told him, indicating Starling with a tilt of his head. "Ignacio was never supposed to bring you any point-ears from the Lots. The Claymaster discovered his dealings and feared a war. He sent me and the wizard to bring the girl back to Dog Fall. We did, but she spoke to her kin of the others. The Tines have demanded their release."

The Sludge Man laughed and Jackal knew his tower of deceptions had crumbled.

"You knew naught of her when first you sullied our home. You spoke, slack-jawed, of whoremasters and horses. You prattle now to save yourself, caught again burgling."

"I'm not caught, Sludge Man," Jackal returned. "I came here to find you. To offer you a chance of retribution on the wizard. What I didn't expect to find was your fucking harem of dying elves! So why not come on out of that blob of shit and let me bash you in the cods again."

"What happened to courteous?" Warbler asked.

"Fuck it," Jackal answered without looking back.

"That's my boy."

The Sludge Man's unsightly face quivered with rage.

"Harem?" he repeated. "It is an altar! The Maiden demands sacrifice. Orc and elf defiled her, waging their blood feud. So it is with orc and elf blood that she will be made sacred again. We who rule her must first serve her, and lay her board with a bounty of her despoilers. The House of Corigari has done this faithfully, stooping to base dealings with grasping peasants to maintain the offerings!"

Sacrifice. That was what all this was, Jackal realized.

The Sludge Man would have been little more than a boy when the Incursion reached his family home. He must have witnessed the battles fought between the thicks and the elves, been caught in the devastation of their spells. That magic changed the marsh, sunk into the land, suffused the waters. The Sludge Man may very well have been the only survivor. Whatever happened, he clearly became mad and powerful. Perhaps he controlled the sludges, perhaps they controlled him, Jackal didn't know, but he understood enough.

Thicks often came through the Old Maiden after crossing the Gut to the south, using its treacherous and deserted expanse to enter the Lots. Even for them, the marsh had a sinister reputation, and for good reason. The Sludge Man culled the raiding parties or destroyed them entirely. But the Sludge Man wasn't killing orcs to help the Lots, he was giving the Old Maiden half of the blood he believed it desired.

Elves, however, were another matter. They were wise enough never to venture here. For them, the Sludge Man had been forced to barter. He just needed someone willing to smuggle point-ears in from Hispartha and other dens of slavery, someone with a heart black enough to agree to such evil.

"Captain Ignacio will soon be weighing down a noose," Jackal said. "His time as your faithful hound is over. Your days of murdering elves end now!"

The Sludge Man had grown quiet, yet the muck around him quivered with anger.

"They end, half-orc, because you have brought back all the Maiden demands, the she-elf with orc seed quickening in her belly."

Jackal forced himself not to look at Starling. His thoughts raced. So, that was why she was sequestered.

"She is no longer pregnant," Jackal proclaimed. "The Tines rid her of the get."

The Sludge Man's stare returned to Starling and she recoiled from the hungry menace lodged within. Jackal stepped between her and the demon.

"Your lies are feeble," the Sludge Man said. "It continues to grow. We can sense it. We sensed it the day we returned here to find the orcs had made merry with our larder. Fate led them here while we were away retrieving your dead man from the brothel. Their lust had overwhelmed their fear and they slaked their savagery, leaving only one alive. We gave the ravagers to the Maiden and would have done the same with the she-elf, but we heard the whispers of destiny wriggling in her belly. Orc-blood, elf-blood, made one. A rare and exquisite abomination. We took her to be close to us, to guard her until she birthed the Maiden's price. From the womb of the mother to the womb of the marsh will the babe go, and our lands will return to glory."

The cocoon began to slide forward. The sludge upon the walls of the keep was also moving, sliding down and carrying the remaining elves with the tide, depositing them upon the rubble before melding with the Sludge Man's dreadful palanquin. As the enlarging demon drew close, Jackal reached for his tulwar, only to remember the blade had been taken at the castile. An arrow sliced the air, speeding for the Sludge Man's eye. Warbler's aim was true, but a tendril of sludge darted from the mass and consumed the missile before it struck. Jackal began to step backward, unslinging his thrum and pulling back on the string. Before he had a bolt loaded, the Sludge Man stopped.

Starling stood before him, holding the knife to her own throat.

And she began to speak.

Her voice drifted back to Jackal, barely discernible. It was the elf tongue, complicated and mellifluous. She spoke softly, yet her jaw was set with firm certainty as she addressed the Sludge Man, the foreign words swimming elegantly in a school. The bog trotter's brow creased in concentration. He was listening.

Jackal moved quickly to Warbler's side. "What is she saying?"

"She just told the Sludge Man he is dying," the old thrice replied in a hush. "Says the wizard's magic is killing him. That he knows it too. She says her child is half a year from being born and that the Sludge Man won't last that long."

Jackal let out the breath he had been holding. She did know.

The Sludge Man spoke now, his low, mumbling voice rendering the elven tongue hideous. Starling tensed at his words, her knife arm flexing as she voiced a reply. Jackal could hear the threat.

"Sludge Man just claimed he would take her," Warbler related quickly. "Take his chances. Starling swore she would deny him. Kill herself."

Jackal leaned forward, readying himself to move.

"Stay put," Warbler hissed. Starling was still speaking and the old thrice was clearly struggling to keep up as her voice grew desperate. "She's offering a deal. Says she knows where to find another half-orc with elvish blood."

Jackal shot a confused look at Warbler and found his befuddlement reflected.

"What is she—"

Warbler growled him to silence, trying to hear.

"She is asking for our lives in exchange for the identity of the half-breed. An adult, she claims. One that will satisfy the Old Maiden. If he does not agree, she will open her own throat. She says he has no choice."

The Sludge Man withdrew slightly, the cocoon seeming to diminish as it bathed his wasted flesh. Within the embrace of pitch, the face nodded and spoke a word.

An agreement.

Starling began to speak again. Slower, now.

Warbler had no trouble catching her hesitant words, yet still he looked perplexed, the lines of his sun-creased face deepening.

"War-boar, what?" Jackal insisted.

"She says it's one of our own. Our hoof, the Bastards. I don't . . . hells."

The curse came out as barely a whisper, yet the Sludge Man raised his gaze to Warbler. Starling had ceased speaking and she turned now, her face issuing a plea for forgiveness.

"Warbler?" Jackal demanded. "What the fuck did she just say?"

The old thrice's face hardened once more and he peered hard at the Sludge Man.

"Fetching," he said. "She told him it is Fetching."

Jackal loosed a disbelieving breath, but as he looked at Warbler all words of challenge died in his throat.

"You don't deny this, old one?" the Sludge Man inquired.

Warbler shook his white-maned head. "No, I don't deny it. The she-elf tells you true. My woman cared for all the foundlings, so I know. Fetch is half-elven."

The Sludge Man smiled and his face began to sink back into the cocoon. The black mass sealed around him and moved back toward the wall.

"No!" Jackal shouted. "They are both lying to you, Sludge Man! This is insanity!"

He charged, but the sludge flowed swiftly up the wall. With a cry of frustration, Jackal loosed a bolt into its glistening form, uselessly. Ignoring the assault, the blob vanished over the lip of the keep. In a fury, Jackal whirled on Warbler.

"What the fuck was that?"

"That was her saving our skins," Warbler replied, pointing at Starling.

Jackal tried to glare at the she-elf, but found he could not even look at her.

"Is it even true?" he asked, striding toward Warbler. "About Fetch?"

The old thrice gave him a stern look. "What do you think? Her beauty. Her prowess. Have you ever seen a surer aim with a thrum?"

Jackal ran an aggravated hand through his hair. "And you knew?"

"Not for certain until now," Warbler told him. "But I suspected. Beryl was strangely guarded about that one. Had a laboring woman laid up that she wouldn't let anyone else see. I came back from a patrol and there was a new baby. Beryl said the mother had left, but there were blisters on her hands. I knew she had dug a grave, and she always had this same look when she lost one to the birthing bed. I never pressed it. Recognizing an elf-blood would only cause trouble between the Bastards and the Tines. Far as the hoof was concerned, Isabet was just another abandoned half-breed."

"And you just set that demon on her," Jackal said through gritted teeth.

"I set him on the Kiln. That was the plan, Jackal. You wanted him to take on the Tyrkanian, and the Claymaster, too, by the gambles you were making. Well, he is headed their way. If we're lucky, they'll kill each other and save us the trouble."

"And what if he just slithers in, takes Fetch, and slithers out? He'll bring her back here and drown her in some fucking bog."

"That's possible," Warbler said, moving toward the last five elves brought down from the wall. "But we won't be here when he does. We will be alive and far away. As will these poor girls."

Squatting by the she-elves, the old thrice checked them one at a time. Jackal could tell from his body language that only two still lived. Bile rose in his throat. The Sludge Man had said the orcs killed all of Starling's fellow captives. That meant these unfortunate women were all gathered and brought since her escape. Ignacio had been busy, the cur, likely bypassing Sancho's altogether and delivering these elves personally, as he'd been forced to do with Starling. She was now tending the seven survivors. Several were beginning to stir, coming out of the strange lethargy imposed by the sludge. Jackal could not allow this to happen to Fetching.

"I need to warn her," he said.

The older half-orc's shoulders slumped. "You won't make it in time."

"I have to try."

Warbler stood and faced him. "She betrayed you, Jaco."

"She cast her vote. It was her right as a Grey Bastard. She doesn't deserve to die for that."

"You're right, but she cast that vote for the Claymaster. Her chosen leader put her in danger with his scheming, not you."

"Hells, Warbler, the Sludge Man could kill the entire hoof!"

"That was a chance we took by involving him. You wanted him as an ally. What you got was an assassin. There's nothing you can do, but wait and see who dies."

Jackal fumed. "I can't do that."

"Then you ride," Warbler told him. "And hope to all hells your hog is faster than that tar. Even then, the Bastards will fuck you full of thrumbolts on sight."

Jackal both accepted and dismissed the warning with a tilt of his head. "What about you?"

"Me?" Warbler gave him a look that questioned his intelligence. "I'm going to guide these elves out of this sinkhole. Get them somewhere safe."

"Where?"

It was Starling who answered, making a short declaration. Warbler and Jackal both turned to see her giving them a determined look.

"Dog Fall," Warbler translated.

Jackal scoffed. "You do that, War-boar, and I won't be the only one in danger of sprouting feathered shafts."

"And you don't have time to worry on it."

He was right.

Jackal clapped the old thrice on the shoulder. "Live in the saddle."

"Die on the hog."

Warbler's reply sounded forebodingly like advice.

Slinging his thrum, Jackal sprinted for the archway and charged through the hanging moss. He found Hearth and was in the saddle before realizing he had not even given Starling a parting glance. She had done what she must, for the sake of more lives than her own. Now Jackal had to do the same.

Using the stars, he struck directly north. He rode when he could, dismounted and led Hearth when the ground was too boggy. Whether mounted or afoot, Jackal set a grueling pace, as quick as the Maiden would allow. Still, it took the meat of the night to traverse the sodden land.

Jackal could not allow a rest. Knowing the feel of firm ground would seduce Hearth to run, he slung himself into the saddle and rode hard. The sun soon rose directly before them, blinding in its denouncement of their success. The day would be long, hot, and impossible. The unforgiving glare was a mercy. Jackal could not see the arduous leagues before him, leagues that would only grow longer as the strength of half-orc and hog began to falter. The distance was tireless. To defeat this ride the land simply needed to exist.

Yet Jackal spurred Hearth onward.

The Sludge Man would be well ahead, the marsh having offered him no hindrance. If Jackal wished to make up the distance it would be now, with dust and rock beneath the cloven feet of a strong hog. Hearth was a prize amongst barbarians, but even his bestial endurance had limits. After two treks through the marsh, he was far from fresh, but neither was he spent.

Not yet.

Jackal pushed until they reached the banks of a stream, likely a tributary of the Alhundra. Here he stopped long enough for Hearth to drink. Eastward, the world was still bulwarked by the bright wall of morning. That was their course. Rather than continue on sun-blind, Jackal considered halting for a spell. A pause would allow the day to mature until the horizon was no longer afire, and provide a much-needed rest. A pause would allow the Sludge Man to get farther ahead.

Jackal pressed on.

Weary, squinting to keep the sun spears from his aching head, he rode. Hearth kept drifting north, trying to escape the punishing glare, forcing Jackal to constantly take the swine-yanker tusks in hand and wrestle to guide the hog. Knowing Hearth was tired, he listened closely to the animal's breathing, thankfully hearing no sounds of bloodlung.

Not yet.

The day hauled the sun higher, removing the blaze from their eyes, only to send it pounding down upon their flesh. Sweating, legs aching against the heaving barrel of an ornery hog, Jackal rode on, hoping to see the River Lucia join the Alhundra ahead. The Kiln was his destination, but it was a distant, dangerous hope. Jackal kept it from his mind, worried the very thought would claim the last of his vigor. So he concentrated on the river to his left and yearned to see the waters of its larger sister reflecting the burning heat.

Noon came, yet still the confluence did not appear. Twice now, Hearth had defied command and forded the river. Jackal had to take him firmly in hand, using all the power of muscle and voice to master the barbarian back to course. Temper flaring beneath his baking skull, Jackal kicked the hog into a gallop. He needed to run the willfulness out of Hearth. He needed to see the damned crossing of the rivers!

Sunspots punched into his eyes as the dust kicked up. He blinked hard at the white flashes dancing at the edges of vision, summoning dark, punctuating blobs. Those black blotches became sludge and Jackal urged Hearth to the chase, knowing he pursued the lies of his own scorched eyeballs. Blood throbbed against his eardrums, pounding away the sounds of Hearth's grunting breaths. A roar drowned out his furious heartbeat. The roar of water.

Ahead, the rivers joined and frolicked in a mating of white currents.

Hearth turned instinctively at the confluence, thundering eastward again until the ford. They crossed the merged waterway and surged, dripping, onto the flats beyond. Snorting in defiance of fatigue, the barbarian sped across the badlands, his hooves pummeling the earth. The heat was upon the hog. Some riders would fear they had pushed their mounts too far, driven them into a craze, but not Jackal. He knew Hearth, could feel the frenzy in his pumping limbs. He had more to give.

The miles began to fall, but the land fought back, throwing each dusty defeat down Jackal's parched throat. He coughed and choked and cursed and chewed on the grit. His legs screamed at him for ease as he bent low in the saddle, holding himself in perfect position for speed. Sweat and loose strands of hair stung his eyes, every muscle twisting into ever-tightening cramps. The sun began to sink and the hog ran on, transformed into a demon by his pursuit of one.

Jackal rode long after he should have stopped, long after he should have fallen from the saddle. Hearth should have collapsed, but he endured, hungry for the horizon. Hog and rider boiled in the cauldron of Ul-wundulas, but they did not succumb. The heat infused them, fed them, ushered them into a fever dream of indomitable will.

Dusk settled and there, impossibly, was an excruciating silhouette.

There, rising against the darkening skyline, was a finger of shadow thrusting upward from a brooding hump.

As Hearth stormed toward home, Jackal was overcome by a haunting disquiet. Above the dwindling flush of sunset, the coming night was a hideous bruise, the purple tinged with a sickly green. The moon emerged from a pall of cloud and, before his eyes, the old crescent waxed, brightening with a pallid light. Jackal's spine crawled and he looked ahead, unnerved.

The shadow of the Kiln no longer looked familiar. The chimney was too short, the walls too sloped. The surrounding lands were not covered with vineyards and olive groves, but a barren plain where a hive of low huts squatted.

Jackal then realized where he had truly ridden.

The hill and tower of Strava stood before him, meek beneath the menacing glow of the Betrayer Moon.

Chapter 29

Unyar horsemen teemed about the hill, so busy with preparation they did not give Jackal a second glance as he rode slowly through their village. Women were calmly herding children and sundries down into crude cellars dug beneath the huts. Strava had no walls, just the decaying mound and the broken tower, both nearly useless for defense. The halflings would hide within, but the humans had only the bows of their horsemen for protection. Holes in the ground would not deter the centaurs from slaughter if the riders failed to repel them.

Zirko stood at the crest of the hill, overseeing his industrious followers. Jackal expected to be challenged as he dismounted and began leading his hog up the slope, but the little priest was unguarded.

"The bad moon has risen," the halfling said with a nod of greeting. "I am glad to see you honor our bargain."

"I didn't have a choice," Jackal croaked through dry lips. "You brought me here through some sorcery."

Zirko shook his head sadly, causing the black twists of his bound hair to swing.

"I possess no sorcery. It was the will of Great Belico that brought you here. The Master Slave ensures his servants hold to their pledges . . . even when they swear oaths they do not intend to keep."

"Your god nearly ran my hog to death," Jackal said.

A small smile creased the halfling's face. "Surely, you have come to know, since receiving the bones of Attukhan, the winds of death find you difficult to stir."

Jackal set his jaw. He had known his freakish recovery from harm was tied to the healing of his shattered arm, but hearing the priest admit it was unsettling. He took a deep breath, swallowing his anger and his unease.

"I cannot be here, Zirko," he said bluntly.

"Ride where you will," the halfling shrugged, "but I think you will find that this night, all paths lead to holy Strava."

Gut-born rage boiled back up Jackal's throat. "Release me, priest!"

"And where will you go? The centaurs are leaving their shrines even now, to worship with murder and rapine. None are safe until the morning."

Jackal's thoughts turned to Warbler and the elves. Hopefully, the old thrice had not left the Old Maiden before the changing of the moon. Even that dread marsh was safer than being caught out during the horse-cocks' bloody ritual.

"Zirko, people will die if I delay."

"It is the Betrayer Moon. People always die."

"There are greater dangers than centaurs loose under this sky!"

"Not here."

Jackal fumed and his hand itched for the sword he did not bear. His aggression must have reeked, for Zirko's face became grave and his hand drifted to the grip of the stout Imperial blade at his side.

"You are blessed, Jackal," Belico's high priest said. "But it would be unwise to test the boundaries of your divine gifts, especially against me."

The halfling was barely half Jackal's height, yet his words were towers of iron.

Jackal refused to be cowed. "You were the one that said I found charging into danger comforting."

"True," Zirko replied, the whites of his eyes bright with the baleful moon. "And I still believe it. I believe many things. You took my beliefs for madness and swore an empty oath, yet where do you now stand? And now that you are here, willingly or not, what will you do? Stand with my people, as vowed, or break faith with Belico? Your choice will determine whether the soul of Attukhan resides in a worthy vessel. But I believe I chose rightly in you. I believe you will meet the danger that swiftly approaches and keep your word. Tell me, Jackal, does this belief further make me a madman?"

Jackal bore the intensity of the halfling's dark face as he awaited an answer.

"It's true," Jackal said after a moment. "I swore an empty oath.

I did not, I do not, believe your beloved warlord will return to life and destroy the orcs. Promising to serve a man who will never again draw breath cost me nothing. But the oath to defend Strava, that I did not knowingly break. I have been banished from my hoof and had no warning of the coming Betrayer."

"Then it is fortunate Belico kept his eye upon you and guided you hither."

The paltry amount of spit in Jackal's mouth was bitter. "Yes. Fortunate."

Zirko made no reply.

"I will need a sword," Jackal told him.

The high priest gave a call and motioned at one of the Unyar riders. The man obediently spurred his horse up the slope and made to dismount, but Zirko halted him with a word. He gave commands in the tongue of the Unyars, and the horseman bowed his head, then looked expectantly at Jackal.

"This man will see to your needs," Zirko said. "Yet again, Belico has answered my prayers and aided me in reading the portents. I was able to warn the half-orc hoofs of the coming rampage and they have sent aid, most of them, to Strava. No doubt, you shall wish to ride with them tonight."

Jackal nodded absently and looked up at the moon.

There was small hope the Betrayer would slow the Sludge Man, but it was possible. The centaurs were terrible beneath its light. Stronger, faster, their senses keener than any beast. Perhaps they would be crazed enough to attack the bog trotter, maybe even kill him. Either way, he was beyond Jackal's reach now. At least Fetching would be vigilant tonight, standing ready behind the walls of the Kiln with all the Bastards, save whomever the Claymaster had sent here to Strava.

Unless . . .

Jackal looked down at Zirko. "Is Fetch here?"

"No," the halfling replied soberly. "The Grey Bastards have sent no aid."

That was troubling. The Claymaster had unwaveringly honored the defense of Strava and never failed to send a rider. Why withhold support now? Zirko was the only one capable of predicting the waxing of the dread moon. If one of the mongrel hoofs refused to stand with the priest's followers, he withheld warning the next time. The Rutters were the last to deny him, and their losses during the following Betrayer led to the dissolution of the hoof. Why would the Claymaster risk the Bastards' safety after all this time?

Because he soon expected to be sitting beside the throne of Hispartha, at Crafty's right fucking hand, Jackal realized, far from the mercurial threat of centaurs.

He motioned impatiently for the Unyar to lead, and followed him down the hill without another word to Zirko. The horseman guided his steed expertly through the bustle of the village, but Jackal stayed afoot, wanting to rest Hearth as much as possible. The women and children had all disappeared beneath the huts, leaving only the warriors organizing themselves into fighting cavalcades. Scouts would already have ridden out into all directions of the night, ready to give warning of the centaurs' approach.

Along the way, Jackal's guide procured him a sword and handed it down. The Unyar blade was curved, but broader and heavier than a tulwar. The edge was well honed and the scabbard sturdy. Jackal hung the weapon from his belt, finding the weight welcome.

Coming around to the northeast of the hill, the tribesman brought Jackal to a patch of ground on the outskirts of the village. Rough laughter and the snorting of hogs emerged from the bulky silhouettes milling there. Ten half-orcs and their hogs were assembled, some mounted, others still securing weapons to their harnesses. Every head turned and looked at Jackal as he entered their midst, his guide depositing him and riding off.

"Pretty-boy Jackal," a vaguely familiar voice proclaimed with amusement.

One of the mongrels ambled away from his barbarian and approached.

Jackal clasped the proffered arm. "Cairn."

"For a moment, I thought the Bastards wouldn't attend," the Skull Sower remarked with a crooked smile.

"They still haven't," rumbled Stone Gut of the Orc Stains. "Word is he's one of them now."

The paunchy thrice-blood pointed to a trio of shabby riders standing apart from the others. Jackal recognized them as free-riders he had met with Warbler. Nomads were always welcome at Strava during the Betrayer, long as they fought. For some, it was the safest place they could be, having no other refuge to weather the evil night. However, as Jackal now knew all too well, knowledge of the moon's impending change did not often reach the nomads. Only those fortunate enough to have been told could ride to Strava in time.

Cairn scratched at a boil on his cheek, looking quizzically at Jackal's unmarred tattoos. "That true? You axed out?"

"Lost a challenge," Jackal confirmed.

"Shit," Cairn said. "We hadn't heard at the Furrow."

"Well, then he can ride with the other outcasts," said a young half-orc with fresh Shards tattoos.

"Fuck off, Pits," muttered old Red Nail of the Tusked Tide. "We stay together. I'm not getting a 'taur spear in the gut because some youngblood fresh out of the slops thinks he's too good to fight with nomads."

"And what if *I* say the scum keep to themselves?" Stone Gut threatened. "What do you say then, coot?"

"I say you know how this fucking works," Red Nail spat back. "Tonight, we're one hoof."

"That's right," agreed the rider from the Sons of Perdition.

Ignoring the growing argument, Jackal led Hearth through the middle of the group and joined the other free-riders.

"Gripper, right?" he asked the most familiar face.

The nomad nodded and motioned at his companions. "Slivers and Dumb Door, in case you don't recall."

"Welcome to the shit," Slivers said with gold shining in his smile. His small frame and paler flesh marked him as a frailing.

Dumb Door remained true to his name.

Gripper leaned and spat in the dirt. "Causing some dust there, Jackal."

Glancing back, Jackal saw the sworn brothers were still griping and posturing. All save one. He sat his hog at the edge of the argument, wearing nothing but a breechclout. A large tattoo of a gaping, toothed maw covered his muscle-etched belly, and bone fetishes hung from his stockbow. His barbarian stamped constantly, looking one generation removed from feral. The rider watched the others with thinly veiled contempt, running a hand over his shaved pate to rid it of sweat.

"I see the Fangs of Our Fathers have civilized some," Jackal said dryly.

Gripper snorted. "That one *may* cook his meat. Thick-loving fucks."

"I never met a free-rider thrown out of the Fangs," Slivers commented, idly tugging at his balls through his breeches. "Bastards. Sons. Hells, Dumb Door here was a Cauldron Brother. But never any Fangs."

"That's because they kill all their castoffs," Gripper said dourly.

Jackal had heard the same, but he kept his mouth shut. Walking over to a pitiful excuse for a persimmon tree, he picked what was left and shared the fruit with Hearth, continuing to watch the half-orcs snarl at one another. When it became clear there was no more food to be had, Hearth grunted with disappointment and settled down in the dust. Jackal joined him, stretching his legs out and leaning back on the hog.

Gripper turned.

"Sleeping during the Betrayer?" he asked, impressed. "You really don't want any friends."

Jackal just grinned and kept his eyes closed.

Some moons the 'taurs came late and sometimes not at all. Ulwundulas was vast. Many as there were, not even the centaurs could raid the entire land in a single night. Jackal still remembered the gloating Roundth had done upon returning from his turn at Strava and reporting the horse-cocks never showed. He had regaled them with lies about spending the entire night fucking pretty Unyar girls. Jackal dozed off to the fond memory of a dead friend, knowing that slumber would only summon trouble. Exhausted as he was, there was no choice.

It felt as if he only blinked before someone nudged him roughly on the shoulder, nearly knocking him sideways. His skin was wet from where they touched him. Cursing, Jackal righted himself and threw a sour look at his rouser. A flaring snout greeted him, the gateway to a warty, hideous face.

"Ugfuck?"

"Shouldn't sleep with your mouth open, brother," the big shadow next to the hog rumbled. "One of these heathens is likely to stick their cod in."

With a whoop, Jackal took the large hand extended down to him and allowed Oats to haul him up into a crushing embrace. They clung to each other in a vise of muscle, laughing. At last, Jackal broke free, stepping back to look at the big thrice, and took his bearded face between his hands.

"Hells, I'm glad to see you!"

Oats grabbed the back of his neck and thumped their foreheads together, then drew back smiling. Jackal found himself marveling, unable to let go.

"This is getting a touch backy," Oats said after a moment.

"Well then I will love on Ug!" Jackal proclaimed, hugging the smelly hog's head and humping his jowl until he squealed in complaint. The other half-orcs were watching and some laughed.

Nearby, Slivers snorted. "That is one ugly hog."

"Isn't he?" Oats beamed.

Sparing Ugfuck further affection, Jackal turned.

"Zirko thought the Bastards weren't going to show."

Oats shrugged his massive shoulders. "What does that waddler know?"

Jackal heard the forced levity and squinted at his friend. "Cut it close, though. You had at least, what, four days' warning?"

Oats tried, and failed, not to look over his shoulder at the other mongrels. Most had lost interest after Jackal stopped molesting Ug, but Stone Gut and the savage Fang brother still peered their way. The three free-riders stood closest and, with a motion of his head, Oats signaled Jackal to walk with him out of earshot.

"The Claymaster didn't send me," Oats admitted in a hush. "He's had the Kiln closed and fired since we got Zirko's bird about the Betrayer. Winsome was evacuated, as usual, but the chief hasn't let anyone out, even during the day. No patrols, no tending to crops, nothing. He said we weren't going to help Strava this time. I remembered the deal you made with Zirko and figured you'd be here, so I had to come."

"So how are you here?"

"I bullied the slops to lower the Hogback and left. Two nights ago."

Oats's face was a conflicted mask of defiance, doubt, shame, and anger.

"It's not the same, Jackal," the thrice went on, as if worried he was being judged. "Ever since your challenge nothing makes sense. When I woke up from the fight with . . . when I woke up, everything was all ass-end up. Glad as I was to hear you were alive, I couldn't figure why the Claymaster spared you. Seemed everyone was doing the last damn thing expected. So, that's what I did."

Oats would be branded a traitor. Abandoning your hoof during the Betrayer Moon was unforgivable. Jackal knew it, but said nothing, for nothing needed to be said. Oats knew what he had done, the weight of his choice was heavy upon his brow.

"I'm the reason you're out here, brother," Oats said, his voice thickening. "If I hadn't lost, then—"

"No," Jackal hissed, stepping forward. "Don't do that. Don't! This falls on a lot of heads, mine included, but not yours. Hear me?"

Oats dipped his chin sharply, embarrassed by his welling eyes.

Jackal put a hand on his shoulder. "Tell me about Crafty."

Oats sniffed hard and cleared his throat. "Crafty? Same. Smiles and jibes. Sometimes he and the chief stay shut away, like they did before, but no one knows what they talk about."

"Thrones and crowns, I'm sure," Jackal muttered.

Oats frown deepened. "Huh?"

"Crafty is making a play for Hispartha. His human blood is blue and he means to be king, with the Claymaster's help."

"Shit," Oats gasped. "Anything else I should know?"

Jackal ran a slow hand through his hair. "Warbler takes baths in the brothel, Hoodwink is spying on the hoof for him, the Claymaster can unleash the plague that ended the Incursion, and Fetch is a half-elf that the Sludge Man wants to sacrifice in the marsh."

"Hogshit!" Oats declared with raised eyebrows. "Warbler sits in those nasty tubs?"

"I mean to stop it, Oats."

"Well, sure, you wouldn't want the old man's cock falling off."

"Enough, fool-ass," Jackal held up a hand. "I get that you don't believe me."

Oats's face settled. "Of course I do. That's the most anything has made sense since I came to. Which do you want to tackle first?"

An Unyar horn sounded a warning in the distant darkness.

"Let's start by surviving the night," Jackal replied.

Chapter 30

"Mount up!" Red Nail yelled as the echo from the first horn was joined by a fresh blaring. "They're coming."

The half-orcs jumped to readiness, those not astride their hogs quickly swinging into the saddle. Oats removed a full quiver of thrumbolts from Ugfuck's heavily laden harness and tossed it to Jackal. Quickly affixing it to his own harness and checking his sheath of javelins, Jackal loaded his stockbow. Red Nail eyeballed the patchwork hoof as they assembled.

"If this is your first stand at Strava, listen well," the old-timer barked, giving Pits, the young Shard, a withering look. "Keep together. Keep moving. We got twelve riders here, more than I've seen most years, so no reason we shouldn't be breathing at dawn. The frails have horsemen around the hill to protect the waddlers. They're also riding the flats, thinning out any big herds, but the 'taurs don't fight with much order. Our job is to kill those that *will* break through into the village. You all harken?"

There were nods and grunts of agreement.

"And remember," Cairn said, grinning darkly. "We call them horse-cocks, but the females are the worst. If you see a pair of tits, you've already let the filly get too close."

This drew some laughs.

Jackal had carefully watched the others during Red Nail's instruction, reading their reactions. The loudmouth Shard and the rider from the Sons of Perdition were certainly virgins to a Betrayer at Strava. The Son looked a little spooked. That was good, honest, but Pits's eyes were too wide, his jaw too tight. His face was a brave, brittle mask. Jackal nudged Oats and lifted a chin at the youngblood.

"Yeah," Oats whispered.

Gripper caught Jackal's eye as well, confirming he saw the weak link.

"We'll ride six and six," Stone Gut proclaimed, looking at the free-riders with distaste.

"I just said we should stay together, thrice!" Red Nail complained.

The horns continued to sound and another dispute was beginning. Jackal urged Hearth forward a step.

"Red Nail," Jackal said respectfully. "Twelve will be too many in the press of the huts. Two groups, within sight, would be better. I will take Oats and the nomads and one other."

"*D'hez mulcudu suv'ghest s'ulyud wundu.*"

All eyes turned to the rider from the Fangs of Our Fathers. He looked fiercely pleased.

Pits curled his lip. "The fuck he say?"

"The Shards must not be teaching orcish to their slopheads anymore," Cairn muttered, shaking his head. "Ignorant little shit."

Pits bristled, but Stone Gut blustered before the youth could speak.

"Let the Fang ride with the nomads and the Bastard, then!" he declared, looking at Oats. "I'd invite you to ride with us, brother-thrice, but I know you won't be parted from your outcast lover."

"When morning comes, Orc Stain," Oats promised, "you and me are going have us a disagreement."

"Enough," Red Nail growled. "Two groups it is. Let's get on with this damned night."

The riders divided.

The Fang approached on his ornery hog and joined Jackal's group.

"You got a name?" Gripper asked.

"Kul'huun," the savage mongrel replied. All the Fangs of Our Fathers took orc names, and never spoke Hisparthan, believing the frail tongue weakened them.

Slivers screwed up his face. "What was that you were spouting? My orcish was never all that good."

"He said, 'We fight with the hands of the orcs,'" Jackal replied. "Groups of six. Like an *ulyud*."

Kul'huun inclined his head and gestured at Jackal. "*T'huruuk*."

Slivers snapped his fingers. "That one I know! 'The arm.' Right?"

Oats raised his eyebrows at Jackal. "Looks like the Fang wants you as leader, brother."

Jackal turned to Gripper. "Unless you would rather."

"Not me." The nomad snorted and deftly strung his bow. None of the nomads carried thrums.

"Hells, I'd say give the job to Dumb Door," Slivers sniggered, "but our war cry might be a little lacking."

Dumb Door glanced down at his frailing companion. And said nothing.

"All right." Jackal sighed, shouldering the task. "We will go broadhead. Kul'huun and I are the point. Dumb Door, Slivers, you're up behind us on the shoulders."

"That leaves me and Gripper on the flanks," Oats said.

"Everyone good?" Jackal asked to nods of agreement. "Let's kill some 'taurs."

They all fell into position as Jackal rode off, Kul'huun on his left, with Dumb Door trailing Hearth's right haunch. Oats was behind the mute. It felt good to have a trusted friend watching the rear. It felt good being part of a hoof again.

Going at a trot, they moved back into the Unyar village and circulated through the huts. The tower of Strava stood blackly against the stars before them. Off to the left, within thrumshot, Red Nail's group kept pace.

"Keep an eye on the others, boys," Jackal called to his companions. "They've got two untested riders. If they come to grips with the horsecocks, we go to aid."

This was Jackal's third stand with the Unyars, same as Oats. He suspected the riders with him had equal experience, possibly more. Half-orcs were a small, yet crucial, force in Strava's defense. The halflings were no match for the centaurs, and their human protectors relied solely on their incomparable skills as mounted archers. An Unyar bowman could shoot quickly and accurately at a gallop, but if pressed into close combat, the odds of survival were grim. Centaurs were far stronger than frails, even when not frenzied beneath the Betrayer Moon. Half-orcs carried by the might of a barbarian mount, however, were capable of matching the ferocity of the 'taurs. That was why Zirko needed them here, to crush the enemy that survived the flights of arrows from his faithful Unyars. Still, it was an unwise warrior who became too eager for close quarters. Thrumbolt and javelin remained the best weapons against the 'taurs, though it was a rare Betrayer that passed without empty quivers, and hand-to-hand was often inescapable.

An ululating cry split the night, a sound that eschewed the ears and went directly for the spine.

Off to the left, Jackal saw Red Nail respond and turn his riders toward the sound. It had come from the western borders of the Unyar village. The centaurs never attacked from a single direction, but Jackal could not leave Red Nail unsupported. He pulled Hearth to pursue and his column followed.

The huts and animal pens of the tribesmen prevented a direct route. Through the gaps in the low structures, Jackal saw the other hoof winding through the village, searching for the enemy. Keeping them in view, he guided his own riders, drifting a bit to cover more ground. The chilling war cry came again, much closer, and nearly drowned out Oats's warning.

"To the right!"

A pack of centaurs thundered from behind a cluster of huts, leaping the fences of a goat pen as they screamed lustily. Filthy, dark hair streamed from their shrieking heads. Jackal counted four at a glance, charging fast and leveling their great spears.

"Snail left!" he yelled.

Kul'huun took hold of his hog's swine-yanker and pulled. An instant later, Jackal did the same. The hoof followed them in a tight wheel, spiraling around to meet the oncoming enemy. The maneuver was perfectly done, but they narrowly avoided being flanked. Jackal hardly had time to pull the tickler as he faced the ravening beast-men.

His bolt slapped into the corded chest of the lead centaur, turning its gallop into a careen of flailing limbs. Thrum and bow strings snapped as the hoof let fly, felling two more of the 'taurs, but the last made it through the volley. Screeching fiercely, it charged the small gap between the point riders. Jackal now saw it was a female, sinewy and enraged. Hearth and Kul'huun's hog squealed as the 'taur collided. The moon-crazed cunt just threw herself upon their tusks, stabbing with her spear. For one terrible instant she was dragged along before the force of the barbarians snapped her forelegs, gored her belly, and sent her bowling over to be trampled by the rest of the hoof.

When they were well clear of the corpses, Jackal signaled a halt. Turning in the saddle, he was rewarded to see all five of his riders.

"We whole?"

"You're the only one seeping, chief," Slivers said, pointing.

Jackal looked down and found he was bleeding from a gash along his left shoulder. The last centaur must have just missed her thrust.

"It's nothing," Jackal said. Looking about, he saw no sign of the other hoof. Red Nail had either been unaware that they were attacked or chose not to lend aid. The latter was unlikely, seeing as the old Tusker had wanted to stay together from the onset. It was more likely he had been forced to respond to a different threat.

"Let's find the others," Jackal ordered.

They found more horse-cocks first.

Nine of the savages had caught a company of Unyar horsemen and were finishing the butchery when Jackal's hoof came upon them. Stamping and hewing, the cocks of the males erect with bloodlust, the centaurs failed to notice the arrival of the half-orcs. Reining up, Jackal silently assigned targets. Six bowstrings hummed and six 'taurs died. The remaining three turned, raised their dripping weapons, and charged, kicking up blood. The gore-splattered muscles of their horse limbs rippled as they surged forward, emitting hollers from frothing lips. Jackal and his companions calmly reloaded and sent the beasts to whatever hell they held dear.

"Loony fucks," Slivers said disgustedly as they searched the carnage of the Unyars for survivors. There were none. The centaurs had spared neither horse nor man. Thankfully, none of the nearby huts were despoiled, the hidden occupants spared by the sacrifice of their menfolk.

Others were less fortunate.

Farther on, they found the ruins of several huts, probably razed by the same band they had just slain. The Unyar innocents had been dragged from their hiding holes. Skewered by spear, crushed by hoof, pulled apart by lasso, the slain were strewn amongst the wreckage.

Kul'huun dismounted, squatting briefly to inspect the churned earth before pointing deeper into the heart of the village.

"*Hesuun m'het Strava rhul.*"

"How many?" Jackal asked.

Kul'huun held up a splayed hand.

Jackal regarded his hoof. "Five split off. We are going to track them. And fast."

They pushed deeper into the village, going as quickly as the buildings allowed. The night was pregnant with foreboding sounds. A chorus of horse screams, agonized man cries, and ecstatic bellows sailed upon the moonlight, each an elusive chance to lend aid, spill blood, come too late, or be killed. They held to the centaur tracks, a north star of vengeance twinkling upon a sea of death. Kul'huun led them now, the bones that hung from his weapons clattering. They caught up to the centaurs near a large training corral, and found the five they hunted had joined with another group.

Jackal counted eleven, all kill-drunk and wild.

He signaled the charge.

This time, the centaurs saw them coming and surged to welcome them. Jackal shot his bolt, wounding his target but failing to drop him. He allowed his stockbow to fall to the end of its tether and snatched a javelin from the harness, hurling it into the gut of another 'taur. There was just enough time to draw his sword before the crush.

A spear came for his chest, but Jackal knocked it away with his blade, using the return swing to slash another centaur as he passed. Hearth whipped his head to either side, scattering the onrushing foes as they dodged away from his tusks. To the left, Kul'huun smote with his orcish scimitar, the heavy, cruel blade cleaving the arm from a screeching female. Four of the man-beasts reared before them, a wall of kicking hooves and striking spears. Jackal was forced to rein up and the charge stalled. Pressed and outnumbered, Jackal and Kul'huun waded in, standing in the saddle to fend off spear thrusts with their curved blades.

The centaurs split up to deal with the half-orcs, and Jackal found himself fighting two, while Kul'huun engaged the other pair. They fought, trusting to their brothers behind to deal with the rest.

The height and reach of the centaurs was greater, making it difficult to find an opening. Jackal managed to slice the head off one stabbing spear, but its wielder quickly whipped it around and struck him across the ribs with the splintered haft. Reeling in the saddle, Jackal slashed wildly to keep from being overwhelmed. Crazed though they were, the centaurs recoiled from the whirling steel. Angry and snarling, Jackal used the moment to fling his sword overhand, sending it cartwheeling into the skull of one of the horse-cocks, where it lodged with a woody thud. Hollering with rage, the remaining centaur lunged. Twisting in the saddle, Jackal grabbed the spear in both hands and pulled. The centaur clung to his weapon and was hauled forward, close enough for Hearth to viciously sweep the legs from under him. Jackal finished him off with a downward stab of the stolen spear.

Nearby, Kul'huun, bloody from several small wounds, struck the head off his remaining foe.

Behind them, a hog squealed in agony. Looking quickly, Jackal saw Dumb Door unseated, his barbarian writhing upon the ground with two spear shafts protruding from its body. A pair of 'taurs circled the fallen rider, preparing to lance him in the back. Jackal threw his stolen spear, sending it sinking into the haunch of one of the horse-cocks. It bucked in agony before an arrow put it down, shot by Slivers. The other 'taur was distracted long enough for Dumb Door to roll to his feet, slashing upward with his tulwar. Horse guts spilled to the ground as the man half wailed.

Three 'taurs remained.

Gripper battled one, while the other two had managed to get lassos around Oats, one about his wrist, the other his neck. Still astride Ugfuck, the hulking thrice strained against the ropes that pulled him in opposing directions.

"*T'huruuk!*"

Jackal turned at Kul'huun's shout and the savage mongrel tossed him the orc scimitar. Catching the weapon, Jackal kicked Hearth toward his stricken friend. He sliced the rope binding Oats's wrist, the sudden release in tension causing both the centaur and the half-orc to spill to the ground. Jackal split the skull of the fallen 'taur, but the other began to gallop away, dragging Oats by the neck.

"Fuck," Jackal hissed, and slung his stockbow around.

Before he could get it loaded, Oats managed to get his feet under him, skidding for a moment before finding purchase. Grabbing the rope in both hands he pulled with a grunt, slowing the centaur until it was forced to stop.

Jackal's bolt hit the 'taur at the same moment as Ugfuck. Barreled off its feet, the horse-cock quickly lost hold of the rope and life.

Slivers came to Gripper's aid and together they dispatched the last 'taur. Jackal breathed a sigh of relief to see every one of his hoof alive. Dumb Door's hog now lay silent and still, their only loss. The mute mongrel knelt briefly beside the animal and placed a farewell hand upon its snout.

Jackal rode over to Oats, who was having a chore pulling his hog away from the mangled centaur. Dismounting, Jackal grabbed hold of Ugfuck's other swine-yanker and helped haul the barbarian away from his victim.

Oats rubbed at his throat.

"You all right?" Jackal asked.

"Good," Oats grunted. "Be glad when this cursed night's over."

"We all will."

The rest of the hoof was quickly salvaging what javelins they could. Kul'huun approached, Jackal's sword in hand. He held the weapon out and Jackal took it, breathing a laugh as he returned the Fang's scimitar.

"There is no orcish word for gratitude," Jackal mused.

Kul'huun grinned. "No. There is not."

"Ohhh!" Oats teased Kul'huun. "Buy me a whore or I'll tell the other Fangs on you."

"*S'hak ruut ulu.*"

Oats snorted. "He just told me to go fuck myself."

"I heard," Jackal said, grinning.

The others had gathered, Dumb Door now riding double with Slivers.

"What now?" Gripper asked, looking tired.

Before Jackal could answer, the sound of hoofbeats snatched their attention. Gripper, Slivers, and Dumb Door trained their bows toward the sound while the rest mounted. Once astride Hearth, Jackal quickly loaded his thrum and pressed it tight to his shoulder. The hoofbeats were slow, heavy, approaching from the huts behind the corral.

"Sounds like ours," Oats said, a heartbeat after Jackal had come to the same conclusion.

Red Nail and his group rode out from behind the huts. Most of them.

Four mongrels on three hogs.

Jackal kicked Hearth forward to meet them, his hoof following.

"Looks like you found trouble," Red Nail said, taking in the eleven slain centaurs.

"You too," Jackal replied.

The old Tusker nodded. Stone Gut and the young Son were with him. Cairn rode behind Stone Gut, barely able to stay in the saddle. His face was waxy, his eyes open but blank. Stone Gut's saddle and the haunches of his hog were soaked with blood. The fletching of a thrumbolt stuck out from low in Cairn's side.

"Pits panicked," Red Nail explained. "Fucking useless Shard! Horse-cocks hit us and he misreads my signal, loosed a damn bolt right into Cairn. Then he turned tail. The 'taurs cracked us like an egg, killed that Cauldron brother."

"Rinds," Slivers said.

Red Nail nodded, a little ashamed he had not known the name.

"We managed to win free," Stone Gut said and pointed at the Son. "Duster kept his head."

They all gave the younger mongrel an approving nod, which he accepted with tremulous pride.

"All my stands, we took downed riders to the hill," Jackal said, looking to the others for confirmation.

"Way it's always been done," Gripper agreed.

Red Nail nodded once.

"So that's what we do," Jackal decided. "The halflings might be able to help Cairn, and Dumb Door can aid in the defense there. The rest of us will ride back out together. Any who object can stay at the hill or fucking ride alone."

Jackal directed this last statement at Stone Gut, but the Orc Stain merely scowled for a moment before dipping his chin in acceptance.

"That will put us at eight," Gripper said, breathing out heavily. "It's certainly been worse."

"The 'taurs came late this time," Jackal said, looking at the Betrayer Moon. "Dawn is not far off."

Even as he checked the sky, an Unyar horn blasted through the night. Four long peals, a pause, then the same four long peals.

Oats's brow furrowed. "Never heard that one."

"I have," Red Nail said grimly. "Only once in seventeen stands at Strava. It means the hill and the tower are in danger of being overrun."

"Sounds like our signal to put heel to hog and get the fuck gone," Slivers declared.

"Nomad scum!" Stone Gut spat.

"That's right," the frailing snapped back. "I come here to survive the Betrayer. What are the waddlers going to do to me if I run? I got no hoof that needs warning next time. If the 'taurs don't massacre all those little black shits, they will welcome me back whenever I choose to come."

Silently, Dumb Door climbed down from behind Slivers and stared with disappointment at the smaller half-orc.

"Slivers," Gripper said. "You run and you'll be alone."

The little mongrel shrugged. "Safer than riding directly to where the horse-cocks are heaviest."

Without further comment, Slivers turned his hog and, after a brief consideration of the shadowed huts, chose a direction. Stone Gut snarled low in his throat and raised his stockbow, taking aim at the retreating rider.

Jackal jerked his own weapon up and pointed the bolt at the thrice.

"He's a free-rider," Jackal warned. "Which word do you not understand? Now take your finger off that tickler, Stain, or I'll change your name to Worm Food."

His expression curdling, Stone Gut did as instructed.

"You done with that shit?" Red Nail demanded. "You don't prove your worth by killing deserters. You do it by doing what needs to be fucking done! Now, let's get to the hill."

"Ride," Jackal told his hoof, and set off.

They thundered through the deserted village, the silhouette of the tower beckoning them onward. Long before they cleared the huts, the sounds of centaur war cries filled the air. Slowing, they came around the corner of a large stable and got a look at the temple.

"Oh shit," Duster gasped.

The base of the hill writhed with centaurs. Whooping and screaming, they assaulted the slope in droves. The tribesmen had clustered at the top of the hill, surrounding the tower and pouring volleys of arrows downward. Many were afoot, the bodies of their mounts littering the slope, and piled at the base. One company of mounted men, no more than thirty, valiantly strove to harass the horse-cocks with the hit-and-run tactics they had perfected, but were greatly outnumbered. Their horses were flagging, their quivers nearly spent. So far, they were preventing the centaurs from reaching the top, but the defenders would soon be overwhelmed.

"That has to be a hundred centaurs," Stone Gut said.

"With as many more attacking the opposite slope, like as not," Gripper added.

"What do we do?" Duster asked, his eyes wide.

Jackal looked at Oats, then Red Nail, Kul'huun, and Gripper. All four nodded.

"Dumb Door," Jackal said. "Take Cairn into one of the huts. Keep him safe."

The mute half-orc nodded and got off Gripper's hog. He went and lifted Cairn gently as able from Duster's saddle. The Skull Sower cried out weakly and seemed to pass out. Jackal hoped he had not just died. Hells, they were likely to join him very soon.

"We're going up that hill," Jackal said, directing his words at the group while looking at Duster.

Kul'huun drew his scimitar. Oats's tulwar was already in his hand.

"We are going up that hill," Jackal repeated, freeing his borrowed blade. "Ride hard, hit harder, and don't stop until we reach the summit."

"And if we reach the summit?" Stone Gut challenged. "Then what?"

"We go right down the other side," Jackal told him.

"Where just as many horse-cocks will be waiting to greet us," Stone Gut realized with grudging respect, cracking a smile. The thrice clapped Duster heartily on the back. "Fill your hand, Son of Perdition. We are going to follow this pretty outcast up the ass of one centaur and down the throat of another!"

Duster gave a resigned nod and drew his tulwar.

Jackal took point and the others fanned out in a tight wedge behind him. Oats was at his right, Kul'huun his left. The rumps of over a hundred jostling centaurs lay a little more than a thrumshot away. As he kicked Hearth forward, Jackal wondered which one would bring him down.

The hog pounded beneath him, quickening his heart, kindling his guts until he wanted to scream, but Jackal kept his teeth clenched, not wanting to alert the enemy. If they were fortunate, the shock of the attack might carry them through. The base of Strava Hill was wide, forcing the 'taurs to spread thin. Jackal just needed to punch through their ranks to gain the slope. After that it was only a matter of reaching the top before they were overtaken or struck down by errant Unyar arrows.

Gripping Hearth's mane tighter, Jackal leaned forward and silently willed him to greater speed.

So intent on their prey upon the hill, the centaurs never saw them coming.

Swinging his blade viciously, Jackal took the hind legs out from the first one to come within reach, and kept swinging as Hearth burrowed bloodily through. Oats and Kul'huun hit with the force of a gale, widening the gap. Centaurs were crying out in pain and alarm as the hogs shattered their ranks. Another cry went up from the crest of the hill, this one thrown from the throats of the tribesmen, and the arrows began to fall with renewed vengeance. The aim of the Unyars was uncanny and Jackal rode safely through a maelstrom of shafts that felled only centaurs.

The slope lay ahead, but the horse-cocks had begun to turn. Spears and roars of challenge rose ahead of the hoof's charge. Jackal did scream now, a wordless, savage cry of defiance. Behind, his brothers added their voices to his, and seven became a horde. Jackal smashed into the bulwark of centaurs, his sword arm whirling. A woman's face shrieked at him, teeth bared, and he split it with his blade. The coarse weight of a rope struck him in the eyes, the loop of the flung lasso failing to snare him. Spears struck with the fearsomeness of serpents, but he batted them aside and slew their wielders. He felt a great impact beneath his left arm that nearly spilled him from the saddle, but with a growl, he righted himself and continued to kill. Slicing one last centaur across the throat, Jackal won through and Hearth's hooves struck the slope. Arrows fell in a whistling rain as they surged up the hillside, riding over the corpses of man, horse, and the awful pairing of the two.

Above, the tower.

Behind, the vindictive wails of the enemy.

Oats drew even on Jackal's right, his sword blade broken. To the left came Duster. The youth was smiling and looked over to catch Jackal's eye, proud and triumphant. He was still smiling when the lasso fell over his head and jerked him savagely out of sight.

An overwhelming rage took hold of Jackal. He would not lose a brother to these animals!

Commanding Hearth to keep running, Jackal flung his legs up and flipped out of the saddle, his spine rolling along the hog's rump. His boots struck the uneven ground and he spun, seeing Duster being dragged toward the oncoming horde of frothing centaurs. Jackal gave chase, bounding down the slope. He dove and slashed, parting the cord. Duster's limp form came to a rough stop as Jackal rolled to his feet between the youngblood and the howling wave of 'taurs. Even charging uphill, their speed was ferocious. Spears and hooves and whirling lassos surged closer. Many in the forefront suddenly reared, arrows appearing to sprout from their bodies. The shafts fell in a storm, but the centaurs merely rode over their fallen and kept coming. But they had been stalled enough. Jackal hoisted Duster across his shoulders and fled up the hill. His legs burning beneath the weight, he slogged up the grade, hoping the arrows of the Unyars could keep the 'taurs at bay long enough for him to reach the top. From the sound of the nearing screams at his back, it was a vain hope. But then his hoof was there, charging past him, back down the hill, the barbarians kicking up grit. Jackal kept running, hearing the sounds of his brethren meeting the centaurs.

He gained the top and the Unyar archers parted to let him through. Zirko was there, his stout sword in hand, commanding the tribesmen with calm resolve. No other halflings were present.

"Your arrival is once again timely, half-orc," the little priest proclaimed.

Ignoring him, Jackal lowered Duster to the ground and whistled for Hearth. He needed to join his hoof, if any still survived.

Before he was in the saddle, Oats rode through the gap, followed by Kul'huun. The Fang had a gaping wound across his brow and a dripping puncture beneath his ribs, but his eyes had lost none of their untamed luster. There was a long delay and then Stone Gut rode up. His namesake was slick with blood, but none of it appeared to be his. Gripper was on the thrice's heels, Red Nail behind him. The old Tusker looked dazed and slid from the saddle shaking his head.

"You're as crazy as a 'taur!" he accused Jackal, though there was a respectful awe in his voice. "Who goes back for a youngblood yanked off his hog?"

Jackal swept the hoof with a look. "Didn't expect you all to be as foolish as me. How were you not slaughtered?"

"We had help," Gripper replied as a dozen Unyar horsemen came through the line of archers, all that was left of the thirty harriers they had seen defending the base of the hill.

Their wide, slant-eyed faces were smiling and all looked directly at Jackal. One of them said something, his words foreign and breathless.

Ignoring the men, Jackal turned to find Oats.

"Get ready. We need to go down the other side."

His friend's concerned eyes drifted down. Following his gaze, Jackal saw a centaur spear sticking out from under his left arm. With a frustrated snarl, he pulled it free and cast it down upon the ground.

"Gripper, Kul'huun! Form up, we're going again. Stone Gut!"

"Jackal," Oats said slowly.

"We have to go now!" Jackal told him. "Before they recover."

Zirko stepped up beside his hog.

"There is no need," the halfling said calmly, and cocked his eye at the horizon.

Jackal looked and saw the sky was blushing with the beginnings of dawn. Ensconced in the besieged band of night, the Betrayer Moon waned, returning to a pale crescent. Below, the centaurs were riding off in living currents, back to their ancient, shadowy groves and vine-strangled temples. Troops of returning Unyar outriders sped the horse-cocks' departure with volleys of vengeful arrows.

"It is over," Zirko proclaimed.

The surrounding tribesmen continued to marvel at Jackal and each began repeating the words of the first. The archers on the hill turned and began to gather. One of them plucked the spear that Jackal had removed from his body and held it reverently before punching it aloft.

"*Va gara Attukhan!*" he cried, and his kindred let loose a victorious cheer.

The call was taken up and the tower reverberated with the chant of the Unyars.

Jackal looked down at Zirko.

"What are they saying?"

"They hail you," the priest replied. "They recognize you for what you are."

"And what is he?" Oats asked, his face mirroring Jackal's own confusion.

"The Arm of Attukhan," Zirko answered solemnly with a small, pleased smile.

Jackal looked wearily about him. Everywhere were the gleeful faces of the Unyars, men he had never known to smile. Every voice was lifted, every arm was thrust into the air. Whatever exhaustion they felt after so bloody a night, whatever despair was in their hearts at the losses they had suffered, none of it showed as they chanted, saluting Jackal with words and beliefs he did not understand.

"*Va! Gara! ATTUKHAN!*"

"*Va! GARA! ATTUKHAN!*"

"*VA! GARA! ATTUKHAN!*"

Chapter 31

The morning was infused with a rare rain. It fell thinly, not even audible upon the roof of the corral shed. The near-invisible drops brought a chill to the early air, summoned it seemed, by the funerary song of the Unyars.

Jackal sat listening to their voices, carried on the damp breeze for some time now. Somewhere, out of sight, the tribesmen buried their dead, entombing the warriors within Strava Hill, the women and children entrusted to familial mounds. The half-orcs had not been invited to attend, all offers of aid denied. They were given food and a place to rest, but Jackal had been unable to sleep, unlike the rest, who slumbered around him. At his side, Oats snored softly, despite the singing, his head pillowed by a bedroll. Even Kul'huun slept, sitting upright in a corner of the shed. Red Nail had stirred long enough to walk stiff-legged out into the rain for a piss, then immediately returned to his blanket. Stone Gut was the first to fully rouse and sauntered out into the corral while finishing off the contents of a milk jar.

Jackal was anxious to ride, but Hearth was in need of a decent rest. He lay out in the corral, huddled beneath the low roof of a foaling pen with the other barbarians. Stone Gut barked a curse when he discovered his hog had been bullied out from beneath the shelter by Ugfuck. The paunchy thrice saddled his drenched mount in a frustrated hurry and rode away without so much as a parting glance. Eyes still closed, Oats smiled widely, and went back to sleep.

Jackal bid the surly Orc Stain a silent riddance with a grin. This was the way of the hoofs at Strava. You stood, you fought and, if you survived, you left, duty done. Depending on the number of riders sworn to the Stains, Stone Gut would not have to spend another Betrayer here for years to come. Jackal envied him that comfort.

The singing wore on. The swath of sunlight behind the seamless grey of watery clouds spread across the sky. By noon, the dirge had ceased, but the rain fell on, aging the day. At the back of the shed, Gripper and Dumb Door were stirring. Looking down, Jackal saw that Oats was awake. He lay on his back, but his head was turned, his eyes fixed upon Jackal's ribs.

"See that's already closed," the big thrice said quietly.

Raising his arm, Jackal inspected the spot where the centaur spear had pierced him. It had been a deep wound, though he had felt no pain. Now, it was nothing but a slightly ragged puckering of the skin.

Oats sat up, grunting out a long breath and shaking his head, communicating a litany of opinions without a word.

"We need to saddle up," Jackal told him, handing over the last heel of bread.

"To the Kiln?" Oats asked, his mouth full.

Jackal nodded. "I set out to warn Fetch about the Sludge Man and that's what I am going to do."

It was probably far too late, but he left that unsaid.

Oats gave voice to the fear anyway. "Sludge Man could have already been there and left, brother."

The look on the thrice's face reflected what they both knew but would not utter. The Sludge Man was capable of killing everyone within the Kiln, and all of Winsome would have been lodged in the fortress due to the Betrayer Moon. Beryl. Thistle. Cissy. The orphans. None of them would be safe from the bog trotter.

The only person Jackal knew with the power to stand against the Sludge Man was Crafty, but trust in the wizard was a knife that cut both ways.

"I need to see for myself," Jackal said. "And so do you."

The set of Oats's bearded jaw was all the agreement needed. They stood at the same time and began gathering their gear.

"*D'hubest mar kuul.*"

Jackal shot a look over at Kul'huun and saw he was awake too. His eyes were cocked and staring out across the corral. Jackal followed his gaze and found Zirko approaching through the spitting rain. The high priest was alone, his short steps tired. Arriving under the eaves of the shed, the halfling wiped the wet from his face and looked up.

"I trust you have managed some rest?" he asked the gathering half-orcs.

"We have, thankfully," Gripper answered, stepping forward. "How are Cairn and Duster?"

"I tended them," Zirko replied, "but Cairn could not be saved. I am sorry. The younger one was more fortunate. He remains unconscious, though I believe he will wake. Some of my most skilled priests are with him, and I have sent a bird to the Sons of Perdition, telling them of their brother's injury. Another I sent to the Skull Sowers to inform them of their loss."

"And what about Pits?" Red Nail snarled, a knee popping as he rose from the ground. "Did you find any sign of that craven shit?"

"Or Slivers?" Gripper added.

Zirko inclined his head gravely. "My riders found the Shard slain. The centaurs had torn him asunder, so there is little left for his hoof to retrieve. His mount was found alive and will be brought here to use as you please. Of the free-rider, there is no sign."

Red Nail gave a grunt of grim satisfaction.

"Well," Gripper waved a thumb between himself and Dumb Door, "if none of you object, my mute friend will claim the Shard's barbarian and we'll be on our way. Any who want to ride with us are welcome."

Jackal knew the offer was directed at him, but merely clapped his fellow nomad on the shoulder in a respectful farewell.

As the free-riders maneuvered out of the shed, Red Nail looked to Zirko.

"I trust the Tusked Tide will receive warning of the next Betrayer."

"Of course," the priest promised solemnly. "Ride with the blessings of Great Belico."

Stepping past the halfling, Red Nail followed the nomads into the rain. Kul'huun continued to sit in his corner, watching Jackal, Oats, and Zirko with naked interest.

"I hope your losses weren't great," Jackal told the little priest.

Zirko bowed slightly, folding his hands before him. "Greater than some Moons, yet fewer than most. Belico will receive many faithful this morn, borne to his side on the voices of we who live to await the Master Slave's return."

"The way those frails were carrying on at dawn," Oats grumbled, "I'm surprised half of them aren't here trying to give Jackal their daughters."

Jackal gave his friend a horrified look, but Zirko was smiling.

"The Unyars have witnessed many of the god's gifts throughout the generations and celebrate their arrival, yet will always remain an insular folk. Even we halflings live apart from them."

Oats scratched at his bald head. "So . . . if Duster lives, he going to be some unkillable loon-brain like Jackal?"

Abandoning the scathing looks, Jackal slapped the thrice across the shoulder.

"The fuck is wrong with you?"

Oats shrugged. "You weren't going to ask."

Kul'huun was chuckling silently in his corner.

Zirko's face, however, lost its smile.

"Attukhan was a great warrior in life," the halfling said, "but death claimed him, as it did all of Belico's loyal sworn men." The priest's cunning black face settled on Jackal and grasped his attention. "Do not mistake gifts for miracles, half-orc. You carry a soul within you favored by a god, but your own is still there, and can be torn from life. It is difficult to blow out a candle that resides behind a roaring waterfall. Difficult, but not impossible."

"He's saying you're not invulnerable," Oats said out the side of his mouth.

"I fucking heard him," Jackal groused.

"Just making sure."

Jackal looked boldly down at the high priest. "If you and your god are done with me, Hero Father, I have matters to settle."

He had tried to bury the bitterness in his voice, but it scuttled to the surface nonetheless.

"Of course," Zirko said. "Until the next Betrayer Moon."

The sword Jackal had borrowed was propped against the wall. He pointed it out to Zirko with a lift of his chin.

"Could you see that gets back to its owner? All the Unyars look the same to me."

"Keep it," the halfling told him. "The look in your eye tells me you will soon have need of it."

"My thanks."

Shouldering his saddle and taking up the blade, Jackal left the shed, Oats following. Kul'huun unfolded from his corner and came with them.

Outside the foaling pen, Gripper and Dumb Door were already mounted, the mute having adopted Pits's mount. Red Nail was giving his hog's girth strap a final tug.

"Where are you bound?" the grizzled Tusker asked.

"The Kiln," Jackal told him simply.

"That wise?" Gripper asked. "You know your life is forfeit if you set foot on your former hoof's lot."

Jackal slung his saddle over Hearth's back. "We don't have a choice. Gripper, if you see Warbler, tell him I was here at Strava and where I went after. Spread the message to any nomads you meet."

"I will."

Red Nail winced as he climbed atop his hog. "Luck to you boys. Hopefully I'll be dead before my turn here comes up again, old as I am. But if you find yourselves on Tide lands, you will be welcome at the Wallow. I will vouch for you."

"Our thanks," Gripper said, smiling as he hooked a thumb at Dumb Door. "Though this one is likely to have trouble saying who—"

The nomad ceased speaking, his attention suddenly drawn by something that caused him to frown.

Looking over his shoulder, Jackal saw a group of Unyar horsemen swiftly approaching. There were ten of them, surrounding a lone half-orc on a barbarian.

"Is that . . . ?" Oats began.

"Slivers," Gripper confirmed.

The frailing was escorted into the corral and the horsemen reined up, their leader breaking away and trotting toward Zirko. The little priest listened to a quick report, then pointed at Jackal and the others. At a bellowed command, the horsemen allowed Slivers to ride up to the foaling pen. His face was tight and worried.

"They catch you stealing a goat?" Red Nail accused.

Slivers shook his head and tried to speak, but his throat only croaked wordlessly. Gripper tossed him a waterskin. As he drank, Zirko and the Unyar leader came up.

"My men tell me you have spotted orcs nearby," the halfling said, looking intently at Slivers.

Oats grunted out a laugh. "You run to save your hide from centaurs, then come running right back at the sight of an *ulyud*. Hells, mongrel, you got any balls left?"

Slivers tore the skin away from his panting, dripping mouth. "Not . . . not an *ulyud*."

Everyone stilled, all eyes locking upon the spooked frailing.

"How many?" Red Nail asked.

Slivers gave a searching shrug, mouth agape. "More thicks than I've ever seen."

"How far?" Zirko demanded.

"Not ten leagues east."

The halfling was implacable. "Are they coming this way?"

Slivers shook his head. "North. They're moving north."

Zirko gave a string of commands to the Unyar rider in the tribesman's own tongue, sending him riding away immediately.

"You will lead my men to have a look," the little priest said in a voice that allowed no chance for denial.

"And us," Gripper said as Dumb Door gave a solid nod.

"I would see them, too," Red Nail declared.

Jackal and Oats shared a look, a look that agreed the Kiln would have to wait.

Two hundred horsemen were assembled at the base of the hill. A swift war chariot drawn by a pair of horses waited at the head of the column. The Unyar driver bowed as Zirko mounted the conveyance, stepping up onto a platform that allowed the halfling to stand equal to the man. The little priest motioned the men to ride. Slivers was placed in the lead, while Jackal and the other half-orcs formed up around him. Strava dwindled behind them in a storm of thundering hooves.

For all the jabs at his bravery, Slivers was an experienced rider and led the troop hard to the northeast. Not knowing the numbers of the orcs made this a scouting run. Catching up without overtaking was the goal. The Unyar horses were a hardy breed, but some care had to be taken when leading them. Barbarians were slower, but the hogs could traverse ground that could prove treacherous for a horse. Slivers kept this in mind as he guided the column through scrubby flats and dry gulches, avoiding the rocks and hardscrabble. The pitiful rain was transformed into swift sheets of tickling mites by the speed of the ride.

It was not long before they came upon the orcs' tracks. The damp dust was churned into weak mud, carelessly sculpted by heavy footprints. Zirko called a halt and ordered four outriders to proceed ahead. Kul'huun jumped down and studied the tracks, his face etched with concentration.

"How many?" Jackal asked, but the Fang only frowned and remounted without answering.

"Well, that's unsettling," Oats complained.

The Unyar outriders were not long in returning. Jackal and the others watched intently as they reported to Zirko in low, foreign voices. The halfling's face was grim. The tribesmen's report ended quickly and, after a moment's consideration, Zirko stepped down from the chariot and allowed the driver to help him up onto one of the outriders' saddles. The high priest's bearing was undented, even sitting a horse in front of its rider like a child. The scouts approached the half-orcs and Zirko gave them all a look.

"Come."

Without waiting for a response, Zirko commanded his four riders onward, leaving the barbarians to fall in behind. Four horses and seven hogs made their way slowly over the orc tracks until the Unyars diverted after half a league. The ground folded uphill, rocky shelves jutting from the creases. The way grew difficult as the boulders began to hold dominion over the scrub. To the left, the rain-darkened flats lay down a rugged slope. Picking their way through the rocks, the riders skirted the lower ground, the black line of orc passage still visible. Soon, they caught up to the marching mass leaving that dark trail.

"Damn all the hells," Red Nail growled as they reined up on a stony overlook.

Looking down, they watched the long, dense column of dark-limbed shapes pass. They were only a little beyond thrumshot, close enough to see the scimitars in their hands, see them turn their gazes uphill to watch their watchers. Close enough to begin a count.

"What is that, two hundred?" Gripper guessed.

Dumb Door held up three correcting fingers.

"Shaft my ass," Oats said. "The hells are they playing at? There is nothing around here but the Rutters' old lot. It's abandoned for miles. There's nothing to take, no one to kill."

Jackal's spine went cold. "And no one to report their movements."

"Well, *we* see them," Slivers said.

"We weren't supposed to," Jackal told him. "They came close to Strava, but did not attack, they're making directly for Rutter land, land they know to be empty. Look, they see us and are doing nothing."

It was true. No raiders were detaching from the main body, no attempts were made to rush the slope. The thicks just continued their mile-eating pace, hungrily intent on the northern horizon.

"They are going to Hispartha," Jackal realized aloud.

He felt the stares settle. The others frowned at him, all but Zirko and Kul'huun, who both continued to watch the orcs.

Slivers was the first to scoff. "Let them! Hispartha can handle three hundred orcs."

"Be good for them to fight for once," Gripper agreed.

Oats was studying Jackal's face. "What are you thinking, brother?"

Jackal only shook his head, a head filled with a whirling mass of disturbed thoughts.

"It's another Incursion."

It was not Jackal who had answered, though the words reflected those in his mind. All looked at Zirko. The halfling continued to gaze at the swiftly passing tail of the orc column.

"No offense, priest," Red Nail said, "but that is far from an Incursion. I saw it the first time, and there were a heap more thicks than those down there."

"I was there, too," Zirko replied. "This is simply the beginning."

"That's hogshit," Slivers declared airily.

"No, the halfling is right," Kul'huun said, surprising all but Jackal and Oats with his use of Hisparthan. "That down there is an *ul'usuun*. A tongue. It has come to taste the enemy's blood, test the courage of those they mean to devour."

"So we cut off the tongue," Oats said. "Surely we got enough Unyars back there to get it done if we hit hard and run harder, again and again until the orcs got more feathers than a buzzard. Thicks won't find blood so delicious when it's their own."

"That will be a decision for the Hero Father," Kul'huun replied.

"But killing these only ends one *ul'usuun*. The orcs never taste just one dish. They will be lapping at Hispartha with a pronged tongue. Three, at the least."

Oats ran an aggravated hand through his beard. "You saying we got close to a thousand orcs moving through the Lots?"

Kul'huun looked squarely at the thrice. "Again, at the least. All probing, all preparing for what comes behind."

"And what's that?"

"The teeth," Jackal answered.

"*Duulv M'har*," Kul'huun agreed with a nod. "Forty thousand orcs."

The three hundred below were dwindling while every mind on the ridge tried to imagine them swelled to such a force. There was a long silence.

The tide pool in Jackal's head began to settle, and nightmarish bits rose to float upon the surface. The details were loathsome, but now that they lay still, he found them easier to sift. Jackal studied the bloated remnants of long-rotting questions and found the drifting answers incapable of escape.

"He sent them."

Jackal had barely whispered, had not meant to even speak aloud.

"Jack?" Oats pressed.

Shaking out of his dark musings, Jackal met his friend's concerned frown.

"Crafty," he said, knowing the others would not understand, and refusing to care. "He wants to rule Hispartha. To do that he has to conquer it. He would need an army." Jackal extended an arm at the backs of the orc war band. "There it is! He doesn't need to do a damn thing to bring the kingdom to its knees, except allow the orcs to pass. Another Incursion will likely end Hispartha, especially if the Lots do nothing to stall the advance."

"I don't follow all your raving, boy," Red Nail grumbled, "but, these days, all the hoofs riding together would be hard-pressed to stop just one of those *ul'usuun*, to say naught of forty fucking thousand. A second Incursion was never within our power to stop, even at our height."

"You're wrong," Jackal told the aging Tusker. "In the early years, any of the nine hoofs could have done it, and done it alone. Tell me, Red Nail, tell me you didn't have a rider in the Tusked Tide years ago, one twisted from the plague. Some tough mongrel who endured weeping sores and swollen joints long after he should have been dead."

Red Nail wore a perplexed expression. "Yeah, called him Quicklime."

Jackal looked to Kul'huun. "What about in the Fangs of Our Fathers?"

The savage mongrel thought briefly, then gave a quick nod.

"Before I was cast out of the Shards," Slivers recalled slowly, "the old-timers used to talk about some poxy brother they used to ride with. Said he hung himself one day."

"Every hoof had one," Jackal said. "A plague-bearer from the days of the Incursion. They were what kept the thicks from returning, from trying again. Not the hoofs, just nine tortured mongrels. Now, there is only one left."

"The fucking Claymaster," Oats rumbled.

"And Crafty's got him hiding behind the walls of the Kiln," Jackal said. "That's why he was so intent on the Grey Bastards. Our chief was the last thing the thicks feared, the best weapon against them. And now, at a wizard's insistence, the Claymaster is going to stay away. The orcs will march unchallenged across Ul-wundulas. Maybe Hispartha can repel them, maybe not, but it doesn't matter. They will be weakened and Crafty will set his fat ass on the throne."

Oats made an apologetic face. "Might not be a bad thing, Jack, having one of us as king."

"This wizard's a half-orc?" Slivers gawked. "Hells, why aren't we helping him?"

Jackal opened his mouth to respond, but faltered. He had feared that reaction and been unprepared with a counter. It was Zirko who provided one.

"History is littered with the tyranny of sorcerer-kings," the priest intoned. "I have beheld this wizard and, though I believe he masked some of his potency, I can tell you he serves greater masters."

Jackal recalled the vile Abzul's words in the castile tower. "The Black Womb."

The looks he received showed none were familiar. That ignorance quickly turned to disquiet.

"I tell you," Zirko went on, "this is not one you wish to see wear a crown. That he has made allies with Dhar'gest is enough for me to oppose him. I believe Jackal has the right of it. More, I think this wizard used the Betrayer Moon as a signal, one the orcs would be certain to see."

Further realization dawned at the halfling's words.

"The Lots are practically empty," Jackal said to Zirko. "All the hoofs holed up. Free-riders hiding. Your own horsemen drawn close to Strava. All the orcs need do is use the most remote stretches in a land already made sparse by the centaurs."

"Like the Rutters' lot," Gripper offered.

"The Old Maiden too, I wager," Red Nail added.

Jackal felt as if a nauseating fist drove his fruits into his gut. Hells, the thicks had always favored the marsh for entry into the Lots. The only thing there to oppose them was the occasional rokh and the cursed Sludge Man. A man Crafty had made a point to eliminate. A man who, even now, had vacated his precious home in order to assault the very walls the wizard now dwelt behind. Jackal had thought Crafty wanted to rid himself of a potential rival, but it was possible he was simply trying to open another road for the orcs to tread without restraint. By seeking the Sludge Man's help, Jackal had unknowingly aided Crafty's plan, putting Fetch, Warbler, Starling, and the other captives in danger with the same folly.

"This has to end," Jackal said, his private rage honing his voice.

"A thousand orcs?" Slivers reminded him. "Coming in from . . . we're fucking guessing where! With forty times that number right on their heels? How we supposed to end that?"

Jackal looked at Zirko. "You going to let this *ul'usuun* live?"

The high priest of Belico shook his head. "None will return to Dhar'gest."

"That's one tongue," Gripper said with an approving smile.

"Red Nail is right," Jackal decided. "Another will be coming through the Old Maiden. But they will be the slowest. Gripper, if you can warn the castile, they might have a chance to muster enough cavaleros. At the very least, they can get word to Hispartha. I think Crafty planned to have the castile's wizard on his side, probably have the mad fuck murder the garrison, but seeing as he is now dead, we may have a chance of getting the frails in this fight. Captain Bermudo won't want to speak to you, and he won't believe you. Force him to do both! And don't talk to Captain Ignacio. He's too entwined with the Claymaster to be trusted."

"That leaves one *ul'usuun*," Red Nail muttered. "If we're lucky."

"And we are not going to be," Jackal said. "I would wager the thicks are sending in more than we want to think about. There could be ten tongues out there. If there are, we need to know. Red Nail, Kul'huun, you need to get back to your hoofs, warn them of what's coming. We need riders ranging the Lots, so we know where the tongues are, and when and where the damn teeth are coming from. Slivers, go to the Skull Sowers. Dumb Door, to the Sons of Perdition. Can you make them understand you?"

The big mute gave a nod that promised mountains.

"Good. We can only hope that Stone Gut sees some of this and tells the Orc Stains."

"Jackal," Oats put in, "that leaves the Shards and the Cauldron Brotherhood in the dark."

"Pick one," Jackal told him. "That's where you are going."

"And you're taking the other?" Oats asked, doubtful.

"I'm going to the Kiln."

"Then fuck if I'm not going with you."

"What good is warning the Bastards anyway?" Slivers put in. "If you're right about this, they know all about it."

"I'm not going to warn them," Jackal replied. "I am going so I can drag the Claymaster out of his hole and ram his swollen carcass down the throat of the orcs. The plague is our only chance to stop this. If the thicks discover it's being used again, this Incursion might end before it begins."

"Our only chance," Oats repeated gruffly. "Doesn't sound like something we should trust to just one rider, even if that rider is you. I'm going."

"And me," Gripper said. "The thrice is right. You will need help. Slivers can ride to the castile."

"Fuck that," the smaller half-orc said. "I'm going with you boys."

Jackal grit his teeth, distracted by Zirko whispering briefly to the Unyars before two of the scouts rode off. He took a deep breath.

"We don't have the numbers. The castile and the other hoofs must be warned."

"And they will be," Zirko told him. "Those riders go with all haste back to Strava. They will have my priests send birds across the Lots. Messages will reach every stronghold before any of you. Messages that will be believed, as they will bear my name."

Oats grinned triumphantly. "See there. Little waddler's right fucking useful. I'm going."

"Yeah," Red Nail said.

"What about your hoof?" Jackal asked.

The older half-orc frowned. "Seems the best way I can help them is to help you."

Jackal turned to look at Kul'huun. "You coming too?"

The Fang's eyes gleamed. "*Sul m'huk tulghest, t'huruuk.*"

"That's what I thought," Jackal said with a small laugh. He gave Kul'huun an appraising look. "The orcs have no word for saddle. That means the Fangs of Our Fathers must have a different creed than the rest of us."

"*Thrul s'ul suvash. G'zul ufkuul,*" Kul'huun recited, lifting his chest.

Jackal looked gravely at the six mongrels choosing to ride with him.

"You heard him, brothers. 'Live in the battle. Die in a fury.' "

Chapter 32

THE GLOW FROM THE TOP OF THE KILN'S CHIMNEY WAS EVIL. Visible from over a league, a green, eldritch light flickered and winked, a disturbing eye mounted upon a stalk of stone. Smoke drenched the sky above, flooding the night with a dense, living blackness. The stars were drowned, the pale corpse of the moon bobbing just beneath the surface.

Jackal and his riders gazed at the fortress. Someone breathed a curse.

"Never seen it lit," Slivers said. "Does it always look like that?"

Jackal shared a dark look with Oats.

"No," the thrice answered.

"No doubt the ovens have burned continuously since before the Betrayer," Jackal said. "They've exhausted their timber."

"Then what, they're using that alchemist shit that Mead's been mucking with?"

"Al-Unan fire?" Red Nail asked, his face troubled.

Jackal could only nod.

"I thought it burned too hot," Oats grumbled. "Mead couldn't manage it."

"It's Crafty," Jackal said. "If anyone knows the secret to that eastern substance, it's him. And it *is* him."

Together, the makeshift hoof gazed at the hunkered shadow of the fortress as the eerie light belched a steady torrent of smoke.

They had ridden through the day and into the night, halting scarcely and briefly, ever-watchful for orcs. Fortunately, they saw no more *ul'usuuns*, nor any sign of their passage. It was cold comfort. They were out there, somewhere, but not knowing their roads of invasion was the least of Jackal's worries. There had been plenty of time to think during the long ride, hours in the saddle yielding a simple plan, one that was easily communicated to the others during their fleeting rests. Yet that plan was nearly crushed by doubt when the Kiln came into view.

Jackal had expected the stronghold to be closed to him, but the sight of that green, unnatural glow made his former home something sorcerous and unreachable. Getting inside was always going to be difficult, but now it seemed impossible. Gritting his teeth against a rising outcry, Jackal inwardly cursed Crafty's keen mind. The wizard had sealed himself up in the most imposing fortification in the Lots, and bolstered its defenses with his arts. Immured with him was the only living being the orcs feared. By keeping the Claymaster close, Crafty gave the thicks free rein to march across Ul-wundulas, while also ensuring they did not attempt to murder him on their way to do his bloody work. All he need do was sit on his broad rump and wait until Hispartha was in ruins.

"*T'huruuk?*"

Kul'huun's voice pulled Jackal out of his brooding. He found the others staring at him expectantly.

"You know what to do," Jackal told them.

Red Nail and Kul'huun nodded, and spurred their hogs toward the Kiln without another question. Jackal led the rest to Winsome.

The small village was deserted. A sleepy, stray goat and a few errant geese were all that remained. The buildings were dark and shuttered, the homes vacant and quietly foreboding. Jackal had seen Winsome sleep many times over the years, but this was the first time he had seen it dead. The sight was unsettling, though far from unexpected. It was now nearly two days since the Betrayer. The villagers should have already returned, but Crafty and the Claymaster knew the orcs were coming. They were keeping everyone safe in the Kiln until the thicks moved through. That's why the chief wouldn't allow a rider to go to Strava. No way for them to get back.

Going to the mule skinner's empty stables, Jackal dismounted and allowed Hearth to root around in the old straw for a moment. Oats did the same, but Gripper, Slivers, and Dumb Door remained on their hogs.

"Tie Ug up," Jackal told Oats, quickly securing Hearth as he spoke. "This close to home, they are likely to follow."

Oats did as instructed before removing one quiver from his harness and hanging it off his belt.

Securing his own weapons, Jackal swung up behind Gripper. Oats rode double with Dumb Door. They left Winsome as quickly as they had come, keeping to the track leading to the Kiln for mere heartbeats before Jackal wordlessly guided Gripper into the scrub. They approached the fortress from the northeast, close to the top curve of the oval. Jackal signaled a halt several furlongs from the wall. The Hogback was still half raised, the ramp sticking up vertically above the parapet.

Jackal pointed and whispered a reminder in Gripper's ear. "When you see that come down."

The nomad gave a confirming grunt and Jackal dismounted. Oats was already on the ground, crouched and ready.

"Lead the way, brother," he rumbled quietly.

Bent nearly double, they scurried toward the walls, creeping between the shadows of boulder and scrub. Their swords were sheathed, their stockbows slung. They made for the Kiln, as furtive as cutthroats. Just out of thrumshot, Jackal paused. He could see the heavy shape of the orc assassin he had killed still affixed to the raised Hogback. Other silhouettes moved behind the parapet, fewer than Jackal had expected. Usually, the Hogback was the most heavily defended section of the walls, but there seemed to be only a handful of guards. Still, this was not the place for an ascent. Jackal had simply wanted to be sure the enchanted corpse of the orc was not going to scream a warning at their approach. When all remained silent, they continued on. They went no closer to the walls, but snuck along, following the curve around to the west.

Hunkering down in the scrub, Jackal and Oats waited, listening.

Unseen, on the opposite side of the Kiln, Kul'huun and Red Nail would have reached the gatehouse by now. Their task was to hail the sentries and simply tell the truth. Orcs were invading the Lots and word needed to be spread. As members of the Tusked Tide and the Fangs of Our Fathers, the pair would be viewed for what they were, sworn brothers of allied hoofs riding to the stronghold of the Grey Bastards with dire news. The reaction to that news would be telling.

Oats had known nothing of the coming Incursion when he left the Kiln, and it was likely all within remained ignorant, save Crafty and the chief. Jackal could not imagine his former brothers would consent to such a plan. In truth, he was relying on it.

Regardless, word would be brought to the Claymaster about the riders at the gate. They would request shelter for the night and, Jackal suspected, be turned away. This would spark an outrage, one that would necessitate Red Nail and Kul'huun shouting abuses at the walls. That would be Oats and Jackal's signal to move.

Of course, it was possible that the Claymaster would allow the messengers entry, in which case the Hogback would need to be lowered, signaling Gripper, Slivers, and Dumb Door to ride. If a pair of hoof riders were granted entry, then surely a trio of nomads would not be turned away, as long as there were no former Bastards amongst them. That would put five swords loyal to Jackal within the walls, five conspirators that could aid his and Oats's skulking entry with nothing more than a little time, keen wits, and a few distractions.

So, they kept their eyes on the Hogback and their ears open.

A long span passed, and then abrasive voices echoed through the night. Sounded like someone cursing vehemently in orcish.

"Inhospitable Bastards tonight, ain't we?" Oats whispered.

So, the chief was not risking outsiders. That was cautious, which meant he was not wholly confident.

"Let's go," Jackal said in a hush and sped for the walls, hoping all eyes were turned to the commotion at the far end of the fortress. If not, he may never know it, especially if the slophead on guard was a good shot.

Halfway to the wall Jackal was struck. Not by a thrumbolt or a javelin, but by the heat. He was nearly repelled by a stifling, invisible barrier, forcing his eyes closed. He steeled himself, plowing through the air-robbing waves. Somewhere behind him, Oats grunted in surprise and discomfort. The walls of the Kiln were designed to be hot when the ovens were lit, the conducting tunnel within being a death trap for any who entered, but this was unlike anything Jackal had known during his years living within the stronghold. Flinching and sweating, he stumbled against the bricks and immediately recoiled to save his flesh. He was amazed the stonework had not begun to crack. Oats appeared beside him, his beard dripping. Mouth agape, the thrice shook his head, denying the possibility of a climb.

Setting his jaw against the futility, Jackal snatched the kerchief from his head and tore it into rough halves. Oats watched as he wrapped his hands, and followed his example. The thrice also shrugged out of his brigand, leaving him bare-chested like Jackal. Almost as one, they sprang up, and grabbed the top of the angled, triangular buttresses that supported the slope of the wall. Oats growled in his throat, the exclamation no doubt caused by the burning of his exposed fingertips, a pain that Jackal shared. Nevertheless, they each managed to scramble up and anchor themselves within the first row of recessed arches. Oats was now hidden from view, but Jackal could hear his hissing breaths. The arches were too short to allow them to stand upright, but were just deep enough for a balanced crouch. Though his skin was saved contact from the stone, Jackal still suffered the hellish heat. He could feel it cooking through his boots.

Licking the tips of his fingers quickly, he grabbed the right edge of the arch and swung out, pushing off the shelf with one foot. At the end of his spring, he managed to catch a fissure in the bricks with his left hand and tried to ignore the sizzling sound. The slope of the wall was less pronounced now, but it aided him enough to reach a second, near-vertical buttress. Seizing either side of the stone support, Jackal crawled apelike up its length, grinding the balls of his feet into the bricks for purchase. He ground his teeth as his fingers seared. At the end of the buttress the wall rose straight up for nearly two lengths of Jackal's body. Beyond, the latticework of the palisade beckoned, promising an end to the scorching stone. Accepting the pain, he climbed, his burning hands speeding his ascent. There was no time for care, to search for the next handhold, there was only the need to escape the agonizing touch of the rock. To halt was to burn.

The latticework was within reach. Jackal snatched for it, knifing his fingers through the crumbling render to seize the dry wattle beneath. The wood snapped and broke under his weight, but he threw his other hand up, grabbing hold to prevent a plummet. His throbbing fingers entwined blissfully in the rough lattice, Jackal planted his boots into the stone below and held for a moment, looking to his right. Oats too clung to the bottom of the palisade, a little more than arm's length away. The sweating thrice gave him an exasperated look of triumph, a look that quickly fled as his eyes darted up above Jackal and widened. Oats opened his mouth to voice a warning, but forced himself to silence.

Looking up, Jackal saw the silhouette of a sentry directly above him, leaning over the parapet. An arm rose, holding a javelin. There was nothing Jackal could do. The shaft of the weapon eased down. Jackal found himself staring at the butt end.

"Grab it," an eager voice hissed.

Taking hold of the shaft in one hand, Jackal finished the climb, aided by the upward pull of the javelin. Scrambling over the edge of the parapet, he came face-to-face with a panting slophead. Jackal knew the youth's face, hells he knew all their faces, but names were another matter. Hopefuls weren't worth remembering until they had proven themselves. Without a word, the slop went over to help Oats. Glancing about quickly, Jackal saw no sign of any other sentries close by, though the shadowy forms of those clustered by the Hogback were distinguishable across the curve. Jackal sat for a moment, putting his back against the parapet and breathing deeply. The heat was easier to take up here away from the radiating stones, but it was still uncomfortable. Small wonder there were fewer guards along the wall. The heat must have forced them to shorter shifts. Oats sank down next to him, gingerly flexing his fingers.

"You all right?" Jackal whispered.

"Good," Oats grunted.

The slophead came and squatted down in front of them. If he'd had a tail sprouting from his ass crack, it would have been wagging. Jackal studied his face. Finally, it came to him.

"You're the slop who came down to Beryl's that day. Berno."

"Biro," the youth corrected, though it sounded more like an apology. "I also saddled Hearth for you when you left with that swaddlehe— . . . with the wizard."

Jackal nodded, remembering. "You can call him a swaddlehead, Biro, no harm."

"Hells, you can call him a fat, backy, Tyrkanian fuck-mule for all we care," Oats declared.

Biro laughed, but the sound of his own mirth seemed to spook him and he cast quick looks down the parapet.

"Why are you helping us, slop?" Jackal asked, snatching his attention back.

The question confused the youth. He searched for an answer, trying to read one from Jackal's face, but was too timid to look for long.

"An exile and a deserter climb the wall at your post and you help them," Jackal said, his voice hard with suspicion. Biro's uncertainty was palpable.

Jackal and Oats lunged at the same time, the thrice wrenching the javelin from the slop's hand. Jackal caught Biro by the throat, twisting quickly until they had switched places, planting the boy on his rump.

"This reeks of Crafty," Jackal accused, getting nearly nose to nose with the wide-eyed slophead. "What does he want you to do?"

Biro attempted to shake his head and speak, but Jackal's grip around his neck prevented both.

"Quietly," Jackal warned, easing his hold.

"The . . . wizard's been hidden away in the keep," Biro whispered. "I've never even spoken to him."

Jackal smelled the trepidation, but he couldn't detect a lie.

"You know hoof code," he said. "Outcasts are to be killed if they return to the lot. Tell me why you would help us? The truth!"

Beneath his grip, Biro slumped. Shame settled into his body, his downcast gaze.

"I know what I was supposed to do," the young mongrel said meekly, "but you're . . ." He exhaled with agitation, then looked up and managed to keep his gaze steady. "You're *Jackal*."

Frowning, Jackal looked over at Oats.

The big thrice shook his head ruefully and snorted. "You got the luck of demons, brother. Thirty-odd slopheads and we crawl up under the one who smells the dust after you take a piss."

"I don't do that," Biro protested, then flinched when Oats glowered at him.

Jackal released the youth. "Stand up. We don't need some sharp-eyed slop noticing us three lounging about. Oats, give him back his javelin."

Both did as he bid. Jackal and Oats remained sitting in the shadow of the parapet while Biro made a display of standing his watch.

"It's not just me," he told them. "A lot of the slops might have helped you. The younger ones might not have had the courage, but . . . Petro still talks about the time you showed him how to reload a thrum on the run, and Egila says that yours is the best-trained hog in the hoof. Well, said."

"Said?" Jackal pressed.

Biro glanced at the raised shadow of the Hogback. "He was killed in the stables the night that thick snuck in."

Jackal recalled the three slops he found slaughtered in the straw. The orc had killed two other hopefuls that night, but Jackal had never learned any of their names. That was just the way of the hoof. And yet, here this young half-orc stood, defying tradition.

"Is it true, what those riders said?" Biro asked, unable to weather the silence. "Are the orcs invading the Lots?"

"Yes," Jackal replied. "The Claymaster and the Tyrkanian have incited another Incursion."

Biro's eyes mirrored the moon as they widened.

"But we can stop them," Jackal told him, "if we can get to the Claymaster."

"He won't—" Biro began heatedly, then snapped his mouth closed.

"What?" Oats growled.

Biro shook his head. "Nothing. I'm not supposed to speak against the chief."

"We ain't gonna tell on you," Oats chuckled. "You're looking at the last two mongrels who would give a fuck over shit-talk about the Claymaster."

"What is it, Biro?" Jackal asked.

"Things just aren't right," the youth declared. "We been holed up since before the Betrayer, still can't leave. The wizard's done something to the fires to where it's almost too hot to stand a post. Claymaster's been in a fury ever since you left, Oats. Sent Hoodwink to bring you back and brought the cavaleros in—"

Jackal held up a hand. "Hold. What?"

"Captain Ignacio's men," Biro said, turning to point at something down in the yard.

Standing momentarily and looking over the roof of the supply hall, Jackal saw a temporary corral had been staked out. Within, the moonlight shone smoothly off the backs of dozens of horses.

"They weren't here when I left," Oats protested.

"They rode in the day before the Betrayer," Biro said. "The chief had us lower the Hogback to let them in."

"How many?" Jackal demanded.

"Sixty."

"Hells," Jackal swore, sitting back down. Ignacio and his men were a problem he had not foreseen. The Claymaster must have expected them, marshaling his every ally. A thought smote Jackal. "Biro? Any sign of the Sludge Man?"

The very name took the youth aback. "I never even seen him before."

Jackal exhaled deeply, relieved. It was one fewer foe to worry over, at least for the present.

"Shit, Jack," Oats said, "even if we get Gripper and the other boys inside, the seven of us won't be enough."

"Not with Ignacio's men here," Jackal agreed. "He'll have told the Claymaster I escaped from the castile." Hoodwink's absence was also a blow. It meant one less solid ally. The fact that he had not caught up with Oats was also troubling. Had he run afoul of centaurs? Hood was a dangerous cur, but the Betrayer could claim even the most formidable. "Oats, you ever see Hood on your backtrail?"

The thrice's brow creased. "No. Chief must have really wanted my hide, sending that pale shit to kill me."

"Not to kill," Biro put in tremulously. "I heard the Claymaster say he wanted you back alive. The whole Kiln heard it, he was yelling so loud."

"Generous of him," Oats grunted.

Jackal didn't like it. The Claymaster's expressions of mercy usually hid a knife. A knife named Hoodwink. The chief had promised Jackal and Starling their lives, then immediately sent Hood out to murder them, ignorant of his true loyalties. Likely all his insistence of retrieving Oats alive was posturing for the hoof, soften the blow of losing yet another member.

"What do you want to do, Jack?" Oats asked. "Ignacio's boys make this slightly more fucked."

"The cavaleros are nothing," Biro declared boldly. "Frails on foals! I know a dozen of us slops that would fight them. Maybe more."

"No," Jackal answered sternly. "Too risky."

"One mongrel is worth three men," the youth insisted.

"I said no," Jackal hissed, rising swiftly and staring the youth down. "I'm not risking the lives of the hopefuls if it can be helped. That includes you. Besides, we are not here to fight. If it comes to that, we've already failed."

Biro tried to remain resolute. "Then . . . what?"

"Do you know where the Claymaster is?"

"In the keep with the wizard when my watch started. Where he's been, mostly, since the Betrayer. They ousted everyone else, including the slops that normally help with the ovens."

"And the Bastards?"

"Hobnail is at the Hogback. I don't know about the others."

"I haven't seen anyone riding patrol in the yard," Jackal said.

"The wall is too hot down there," Biro told him. "The hogs can't stay near it for long."

Jackal looked at Oats. "That only makes it easier to get where we need to go."

The thrice rose. "Let's move, then."

Jackal clapped a hand on Biro's shoulder. "You want to help?"

The youth nodded.

"Oats and I are going to make our way down to the yard. Once we are gone, I need you to find all the Bastards. Just you. Don't send anyone else looking for them. Tell them to gather at the table immediately."

"I can do that," Biro said, but a ripple of doubt moved across his face. "What if they ask me what for?"

Jackal smiled reassuringly. "Just tell them their chief wants a word."

Chapter 33

Lying on their bellies atop the roof of the claymaster's domicile, Jackal and Oats watched as the Grey Bastards entered the meeting hall. Mostly, they came one at a time, only Hobnail and Polecat arrived together. Grocer was yawning, clearly roused from his bed. Mead kept trying not to look up at the Kiln's chimney, his shoulders slumped.

Fetching came last.

As she rode up, Jackal felt his guts twist. He stayed perfectly still, less than a javelin's throw away, worried she would feel his eyes and turn, spot them in the upper shadows. Yet that foolish fear was not enough to deter his gaze. She swung agilely off the saddle, her every fluid motion sending currents of uncertainty directly into his bloodstream. Four heartbeats and she passed from sight, swallowed by the door of the hall. Four heartbeats that nearly caused Jackal to sneak away from the Kiln, from Ul-wundulas, and never return.

"They all took their thrums inside, Jack," Oats whispered beside him.

"I saw."

"You still want to do this?"

Jackal grinned. "You tell me. Do you believe the chief really wants you back alive?"

"No," Oats decided bluntly. "Let's just hope someone in that meeting hall does."

"I'll be right behind you."

"Great. You'll have time to scamper when their bolts skewer me."

Quietly, they lowered themselves off the roof and dropped down to the yard. Hurrying to the door of the meeting hall, they paused, listening. Oats eased the door open and peered inside, nodding when he found the common room clear. They slipped inside.

Familiar voices drifted from the closed voting chamber. Voices, but no laughter. Oats made his way across the common room, causing enough noise to be heard. The voices began to grow quiet, thinking the Claymaster was about to enter. Jackal held his breath, remaining out of sight, as Oats slowly pulled the double doors open. There was a storm of exclamations, but Hobnail's rough voice usurped the rest.

"Fuck all the hells!"

A silence followed, a silence where Oats merely stood there, his broad, corded shoulders filling the doorway.

"You got guts coming back here, deserter," Jackal heard Grocer growl.

"Put a cock in it, you coot," Polecat said. "Hood was told to bring him back breathing. Why do you think we're sitting here? We got to vote his punishment. Soon as the chief gets here."

"Chief ain't coming," Oats tolled. "Neither is Hoodwink. I never saw him. Came back on my own."

"Why did you leave?"

Mead. Sounding like any answer would shatter him.

"To stand at Strava," Oats replied. "As the Bastards always have."

Another pause.

"That the only reason?"

Fetch's voice. Sympathy buried deep, inaudible to most. Jackal heard it, along with the faintest echo of a plea to look at her. From the set of his neck, Oats did not oblige.

"I'm sure you all heard about the riders at the gate," the thrice said, ignoring her question. "Members of the Tusked Tide and the Fangs. I fought with them during the Betrayer. Good mongrels. They brought news of thicks in the Lots."

"We heard," Grocer said, sharp and hostile.

"And what did you think?" Oats demanded, returning the ire. "That they were fucking lying? That why you turned them away?"

"We turned them away because that is what the Claymaster ordered." Grocer, again. "Same reason you should have stayed put when he said none were riding to Strava."

"There are orcs in the Lots," Oats repeated, refusing to be baited. "I've seen them. And they are coming in numbers most of us can't count. There's more. More you need to hear. But not from me. Remember, if you keep calm, keep your hands away from your weapons, this don't need to get bloody. But I fucking swear, if it does, it's getting bloody on both sides."

"What in the hells are you saying, Oats?" Hob asked, laughing uncomfortably.

Jackal was already moving. He had hoped to do this with Kul'huun, Red Nail, and the nomads at his back, force his former hoof to think twice about fighting, but there was nothing for it now. He had Oats and whatever affection still existed at that table. He also had the truth.

Oats moved aside at his approach, his shoulders swinging away, leaving Jackal facing the Grey Bastards.

In a frozen moment, five faces stared at him in disbelief at the far end of the long, coffin-shaped table. Hob, Polecat, and Grocer sat on the left, Mead and Fetching on the right. She was closer to the door, and closer to Jackal. In a glance, he took in the stockbows propped against the walls behind every occupied chair and the voting axes on the table before them. The stunned inertia was over in a blink, broken as Polecat lurched to his feet, upsetting his chair.

"You can't be here," the hatchet-faced mongrel said.

The instant Jackal focused on Polecat, Grocer's arm moved, quick as a snake, drawing and hurling his knife. The wiry old coin clipper was fast, but Oats had kept an eye on him, and a hand on an empty chair. He snatched it up and knocked the blade away, using the return swing to throw the chair at Grocer. Unprepared, the aging frailing was sent sprawling. Hobnail was on his feet now, but his hands were empty, his bearded face awash with agitated indecision. Mead went for his stockbow. His hands were shaking, his eyes spooked, unable to make sense of what was happening. In his hurry, he fumbled the load, dropping the bolt.

"This isn't what I want!" Jackal declared, but the ears in the room were deaf to all but the rising tidewaters of violence.

Polecat had drawn his tulwar. He jumped up on the table and began charging down its length. Snarling, Oats tore his own sword free. Polecat made it only a few pounding steps before Fetching's hand darted out, seizing his ankle and yanking him off his feet. He fell hard in front of her, chin striking the dark wood of the table. Rising, Fetch snatched the thrum from Mead's hands, threw a back kick that knocked him into the wall, and loaded the weapon swiftly from her own quiver. Stretching one leg up onto the table she placed a knee over the back of Polecat's neck, pinning him with her weight while pressing the stockbow firmly into her shoulder and aiming at the half-recovered Grocer.

"Hob?" she asked, without taking her eyes off the quartermaster. "Do I need to do anything to you?"

Across the table, Hobnail raised his hands casually and retook his seat. "No."

Jackal reached over and lowered Oats's sword arm, inwardly thanking all the hells his instincts had not lied to him. Had he been wrong, if Fetch had intervened differently . . . fuck, right up until the moment she moved he had not been certain. For one moment, everything felt normal. He and Oats and Fetching were on their feet, triumphant against the world. But the moment fled quickly, leaving behind nothing but the cold touch of recent events that had twisted the faces of family into threatening strangers.

"I don't know how many times you need to hear it," Jackal said to the room, "but the thicks are in the Lots. It's the beginning of another Incursion. Hells, it may already be too late, but if it's not, we don't have much time. I need to talk fast and you need to listen. If turning other hoofs away from your gate sits right with you, if the evil-looking shit coming out of the chimney doesn't unnerve you, if you are content to ride the trail of ruination that the chief has led this hoof down, then keep trying to stick daggers in me. But if you want some answers, then get up, sit down, and open your ears."

Polecat's strained and muffled voice echoed off the table. "Fetch. Let me up."

"Let go of the slicer, Cat," Fetch told him.

Splaying his fingers, Polecat allowed his sword to rest on the table. Fetch removed her knee. Rising up to sit on his heels, the former Rutter rubbed at his chin and set his beady eyes on Fetching.

"If I had known that's what it took for us to grapple," he leered, "I would have tried to kill Jackal and Oats years ago."

"Get off the table, limp-cock," Fetching instructed him lightly. "And Grocer, you keep giving me that shit-filled stare, I'll put a bolt in your throat just to change your expression."

The thin old frailing redirected his sour grimace at Jackal and got to his feet, his long, ropy hair dragging the floor as he pushed up. Righting the chair that had felled him, Grocer sat down.

"Mead," Jackal said, inviting the youngblood to take a place with an inclination of his chin. With a look of downcast contrition, Mead picked himself up and obliged. "Fetch, I'd feel better if there were no loaded thrums."

The last time Jackal had seen Fetching, she was bruised and swollen from her fight with Oats. Those hurts had mostly healed and her alluring face regarded him boldly for a moment. He saw the expectation of ill will in her eyes. She was waiting for him to look away in distaste or peer at her in judgment. He did neither. He gave her a small, oft-used smile, perfected during their youth, and motioned at her thrum. Giving him a mocking sneer, Fetch removed the bolt, put the thrum on the table, and straddled a chair. Resting her arms on the chair back with her chin atop, she blinked up at him in a mockery of rapt attention. But just at the end, he saw her notice his Bastard tattoos, whole and free of axe cuts. Her brow furrowed, ever so slightly, and her concentration became real.

Sweeping the countenances of the others, Jackal took a deep breath.

"The Claymaster and Crafty have conspired with the orcs. They are using the thicks to bring Hispartha down, so the wizard can take the throne."

"Oh, this is hogshit," Grocer groaned.

"The chief can stop it," Jackal went on, undeterred. "He still carries the plague, and can release it at will. There used to be eight others like him. They were the true protection against the thicks, not the hoofs. We were formed to protect *them*."

"I helped found this hoof, you arrogant cunt!" Grocer snapped, nearly standing, but a warning look from Oats put him back in his seat. "I was there when you were still a rape waiting to happen, so you can stop your lies."

"You were there for the start of the Bastards," Jackal agreed evenly, "but you didn't fight with the chief during the Incursion. He freed you from a quarry after the fighting. Didn't he?"

Scowling, Grocer did not respond.

"I've seen the place where the plague was created," Jackal said.

"Seen the cages used to hold the slaves. I spoke to one of the wizards who concocted the damn thing."

The others were barely listening. Grocer was too busy contriving ways to kill him, Mead was lost in despondency. Polecat kept staring at Fetch, fantasizing, while Hobnail wore a gormless grin, as if waiting for the end of a long jest. Only Fetching truly heard him, yet his every word darkened her face, the revelations forming storm clouds in her stare.

"I must sound mad," Jackal said, shaking his head.

Oats came to his aid.

"Tell them how you know all this, brother."

Jackal gave his friend a grateful look and turned back to the table. "Warbler."

A change came over the hoof. They all tensed and their eyes settled on him. Hobnail's grin began to fade. He had been a fresh slop when the old mongrel left, but the name still carried weight. Mead's eyes drifted to the stump behind the chief's empty seat, where Warbler's axe had long resided, the only evidence of him the young half-orc had ever known.

"He told me about the plague," Jackal said, seizing the opportunity. "Brought me to the mine where he and the chief were slaves, prisoners. Where they were tortured. He has long believed the Claymaster was leading this hoof to destruction and has never stopped trying to find a way to wrest the Grey Bastards from his control."

Jackal almost told them about Hoodwink's years-long deception, but held his tongue. Some secrets were not his to reveal.

"I know how this sounds," Jackal conceded. "But think about what you've seen. The Claymaster let those orcs go at Batayat Hill because he wanted them to bring word back to Dhar'gest that he still lived. That's why the thick assassin came. He was sent for the chief. With him dead, the orcs have nothing left to fear."

Polecat shifted in his chair, agitated. "You just said he was allied with them."

"He's allied with Crafty, and I think the wizard made a bargain, one the thicks didn't readily accept. It's not their way. The assassin was a test or a message. Either way, Crafty made sure the orcs knew what he was capable of. He answered the message by hanging their cutthroat's corpse from our fortress and giving it a voice. The thicks must have listened. They have been promised the Claymaster will not oppose them, keeping them safe from the plague while they march north. And now they are coming."

"That's a tale with a long cod, Jack," Hobnail declared.

"Makes a heap of sense, though," Mead said quietly.

A disgusted noise rattled out of Grocer's throat. "Good on you, Jackal. You got Oats and Mead convinced. Tough job, there! But you've always been too clever by half. It's a fool that would take the word of a free-rider, especially one ousted for failing to replace the chief."

"And how did I fail?" Jackal asked, seeing the dreaded moment had finally come. He struggled not to look at Fetching, a struggle made all the more difficult by the feel of her eyes on him. "It's the one answer I haven't been able to grasp. I made my challenge knowing I had the chair. That day, even the chief was shocked when I lost. But there was one person close to me who didn't want me at the head of this table. One person who had promised loyalty and delivered betrayal. One whose motives I was too blind to see."

He turned to Fetching now, to her hard, set jaw, her fierce, lovely face.

"And that person was *not* you. Was it, Fetch?"

Her nostrils flared, almost imperceptibly, as she let out a silent, relieved breath. She shook her head, just for him, then turned to the hoof.

"Crafty," she told them, her voice steady. "He threatened to destroy the hoof, kill us all, if I didn't vote for the Claymaster."

Next to him, Jackal heard Oats's breath catch painfully in his chest. All around the room, the mongrels were listening, not liking what they heard. Mead started to look awake. Polecat's mouth slowly fell open. Even Grocer was changed, the malice smoothed from his pinched face by the slack of unwelcome understanding.

"It was also the wizard's idea that I volunteer as champion," Fetch went on. She paused. The muscles in her throat constricting. She looked directly, and only, at Oats. "He said there was no one that could beat you . . . only one you would refuse to beat."

Oats had difficulty returning her gaze. His jaw bulged and he tried to clear his throat. Only when his eyes had welled beyond his control was he able to look at Fetch.

"But I didn't hold back, Fetching," Oats admitted, his voice wet and quivering. "Not at the last."

"I know," she told him. "And neither could I. I had to win. That fat tub said he would burn us all if Jackal got the chief's seat."

Towering over the table, tears making their way down into his beard, Oats nodded slowly. Casting a stern glance at his brothers, daring them to mock him at their peril, he opened his massive arms and beckoned Fetch.

"You going to get in here, or do I have to come haul your ass out of that chair?"

Springing up, Fetch went to the thrice's crushing embrace. Jackal could not keep the smile from his face and found it reflected by all but Grocer, who sat in an unblinking brood. Twice Fetch tried to break free and twice Oats refused to let her go, until her laughter emerged in muffled bursts from beneath mounds of muscle. Finally released, she looked at Jackal and quickly grew ashamed of her smile.

"I couldn't tell you," she said. "Even after it was over. I knew you would confront him if you found out. After what he did in the Old Maiden and to that thick's corpse, I feared he would kill you."

"I understand," Jackal told her. "You were right. About him. About what you had to do. You were right."

Fetch's mouth twisted and she gave a careless shrug. "I know."

Yet a gleam appeared in her eyes, one that promised to make up for all hurts in a very specific fashion. Without a word, Jackal returned that promise before addressing the others.

"You heard it. The chief is not in control of this hoof. It is Crafty giving the orders now. I suspect he has been since the day he arrived. So, what's it going to be, boys? You going to wait until the Kiln is an island in a sea of orcs before you do something?"

Before any could answer, Grocer's hand slapped down on the axe in front of him. His knuckles went pale as he gripped the haft. Jackal tensed and his hand went to his sword.

"Our votes are sacred," the old frailing said through clenched teeth.

Twisting quickly as he stood, Grocer flung his axe into the stump.

There was a moment of stillness. Grocer looked as if he were about to be sick, glowering at his choice. Nodding with approval, Hobnail stood and another woody thud resounded in the chamber. Mead and Polecat followed, casting their votes in quick succession, both into the stump.

Striding to the table, Jackal reached and retrieved two more axes. He handed them to Oats and Fetch.

"Bury him."

They threw as one, their flung blades sinking deep into the wood.

Jackal basked in the sight of eight axes blooming from the grey, ringed face of the stump. Hoodwink's axe was still on the table. By hoof code, the vote wasn't solemn until all sworn members had cast, but it did not matter. The Bastards had made their displeasure known. In their minds, the Claymaster was no longer chief.

"Let's go deliver the news," Hobnail said with relish.

"Remember," Jackal reminded the group, "we still need him. If the orc tongues see that he stands against them, they will turn back and inform the teeth that the plague still protects the Lots. We have to get the Claymaster out from Crafty's clutches."

Mead raised a finger. "How are we going to do that? He threatened to kill us all, and Fetch thinks he can, which is proof enough for me. So . . . what is going to prevent him from doing that?"

Before Jackal could speak, Oats hooked a thumb at him.

"He is. Crafty may be a wizard, but our pretty-boy here is the Cock of Armakhan."

Hobnail's lip curled beneath his red-dyed beard. "What the fuck is that?"

"And how can I be it?" Polecat asked peevishly.

"It's Arm of Attukhan," Jackal corrected Oats wearily. "And I don't know exactly. Something Zirko gave me. It helped me handle one wizard. No reason it shouldn't give me an edge against the Tyrkanian. You all just get the Claymaster out and away. And avoid Ignacio. He may try to stand in your way. Get the Hogback lowered. There are five riders outside the walls ready to help."

"That will still put us far from matching the cavaleros' numbers, Jack," Mead pointed out.

Jackal gave him a reassuring clap on the shoulder. "Let's get the first task done before we start sweating the next."

Gathering their weapons, the mongrels left the meeting hall. As a group they crossed the yard. Jackal strode purposefully in their midst, free from any more skulking in the shadows. There was no more need to hide. Fetch was right about him. Had he known of Crafty's treachery sooner, he would have faced the wizard immediately. But he would have done it ignorant and alone. Now, he was whetted with knowledge and bolstered by six mongrels with a grudge. The Claymaster had shaped them all, but chosen to abandon them for the machinations of a devious outsider. The hoof was a thrumbolt the chief had removed from his quiver, and now the barbed head of that bolt was speeding toward his heart.

The question remained, would they be able to punch through Crafty if the wizard chose to stand in their way? Jackal may very well have just set the Bastards on the path of their destruction, but braving that path was the only way this would all end.

He had wanted to be the instrument of the Claymaster's fall since before he was a slophead. He daydreamed of power and went to sleep with flattering images of leadership stewing in his head. In youth, it was a selfish scheme, an unfocused lust for importance. Once he was a sworn brother, his reasons matured somewhat, becoming dimly driven by a need for change, lest the hoof continue to decline. Now, it had nothing to do with vain rivalry, or worthiness for leadership, or even what was best for the hoof. The Claymaster was a weapon. Hells, to Crafty he was a toy, one the wizard needed to be deprived of for the sake of the Lots.

The central keep loomed ahead.

Mead pulled the heavy door open and the Grey Bastards filed inside, loaded stockbows held low. Jackal took the lead.

CHAPTER 34

ODDLY, THE AIR WITHIN WAS CHILL. EXPECTING AN OPPRESSIVE furnace, the hoof cast quizzical glances at one another. They moved smoothly down the curving passage, passing the kitchen, forges, and storage rooms until they emerged into the great, central chamber. The base of the massive chimney awaited them. Honeycombed within its bloated form, the edges of the closed iron doors of the ovens were etched with that horrible green light.

The Claymaster stood beneath the imposing works he had designed. He turned at the sound of their steps, his bent back slowly revolving beneath the uneven hunch of his shoulders. Swaddled in bandages and covered in layers of boiled leather, the misshapen mongrel was a bulky, intimidating presence. He watched as the remnants of the hoof he had led for nearly thirty years approached.

"What the fuck is this?" the Claymaster demanded, seeing Jackal at the head of the group.

"You know," Jackal told him.

A sudden glare appeared above as an oven door set higher in the chimney was opened. Revealed by roaring jade flames, Crafty stood upon the gantry and, removing a handful of something from the bag at his hip, tossed it into the inferno. Jackal had failed to notice him, but now his stockbow, along with those of his companions, jerked upward to train upon the scaffolding. Crafty calmly pushed the oven door shut with a bare hand, and turned. Looking down, he made a show of noticing the hoof, his broad smile visible from the ground.

"Ah, friend Jackal!" he said, leaning his sizable frame upon the railing. "You have returned. It pleases me to see you."

Sighting down the runnel of his stockbow, Jackal got the distinct, disturbing impression that the wizard's pleasure was genuine.

"We are taking the Claymaster, Uhad," Jackal called up.

"I think that unwise," the wizard replied.

The calm in his voice, the good humor, was infuriating.

"Hob, Polecat. Lead him out."

Out of his periphery, Jackal saw the pair move to do as he instructed. He heard the Claymaster snarl as he ripped his tulwar free, slashing out on the draw, forcing Hobnail and Polecat to recoil. For all his infirmities, the old mongrel was dangerously fast.

"Don't try it again," the Claymaster warned. "You blind sucklings don't know what the fuck you're doing!"

"We know," Grocer said bitterly. "And we know what you are doing."

"Fucking hiding!" Hobnail spat.

From beneath the putrid wrappings, the Claymaster's eyes burned. "Hiding? Hiding? You mewling, miserable cunts!"

In a growing rage, the Claymaster advanced on the hoof, brandishing his tulwar. Everyone pulled back a pace, stockbows leveled.

"Watch those ticklers!" Jackal yelled. "We need him alive!"

"If I may, perhaps, interrupt," Crafty's voice drifted down. "Truly, I think this rash action is a mistake. Claymaster, please. Anger will not do."

The Claymaster halted, though his venomous gaze, undaunted by the pointed thrums, promised murder.

"Friend Jackal," Crafty continued, satisfied with the stillness. "What is it you think to accomplish?"

"An end to your lies and your schemes. To repel the orcs you invited into our lands."

"I see," Crafty said, standing up straight. "And I believe you could accomplish this. Once. Yet, I must ask, what will you do the next time?"

Jackal hesitated and the wizard gave him a fond smile.

"I fear you may have misread my . . . schemes, friend Jackal."

"Have I?" Jackal challenged. "You hold claim to the Hisparthan throne through your human father. You intend to win that throne using the fury of the orcs and the complacence of the Claymaster. You are both going to allow Ul-wundulas to be trampled beneath the conquering heels of a thick war host. You told me that you wanted to see the Lots before they were gone. You sounded so fucking certain! Now I know why. Your tongue is silvered and forked, Uhad. Tell me I have misread, and all I hear is how close to the mark I truly am!"

"I have given you cause to distrust me," Crafty admitted, "but suspicion shall not be outweighing your cleverness, I think. In this moment, you are correct. But what about the days to come? What is the future of these lands once you have thwarted me?"

"We didn't come here to listen to you, jowly!" Fetch said. "Counsel. Lies. Threats! Whatever comes out of your mouth, we are not hearing it."

"Then hear it from me!" the Claymaster said. He pointed at the hoof with his sword, moving it slowly across as he addressed them. "You all came in here with a mind to, what? Drag me out, force me to face the orcs? Jackal talks of silver tongues. What do you think is in his mouth, when it ain't licking quim?" The blade came to a stop, pointing at Jackal. "Did you tell them I was the last? Convince them I was the only way to turn the tide of an Incursion? Well, boy, you are right. Probably makes you hard, hearing that. You are right." The Claymaster's bandaged head swung to look at all who had him at thrum-point. "Did you hear? My tongue ain't silver. It's black. Decayed. There are no pretty words in me. So just maybe you will believe me when I tell you, Jackal is right. I am all that stands between us and the hordes of Dhar'gest. AND I SHOULDN'T BE!!!"

Without warning, the Claymaster flung his sword upon the ground, the blade ringing stridently upon the stones. He stepped fiercely into the ring of stockbows, leaning his face toward the points of the bolts. Mead and Polecat took another step back, spooked. Jackal tensed, hoping not to hear the snap of a bowstring.

"LOOK AT ME!" the Claymaster roared, his mouth opening so wide it stretched and loosened the wrappings beneath his jaw. "Look at me! I'm old! I'm rotten! Haven't been able to sit a hog in years. How many wars do you think I have left in me? How many battles? And you!" The quivering mass of rage swung on Jackal. "You arrogant, pretty little fuck. You come in here with my hoof turned against me and demand I go out and fight. To save you. To save the Lots. And fucking Hispartha! Well, you are not the only one who is right, Jackal-boy. The wizard's right too. I may be able to do it. *Once*. One last time. Maybe! And what then? WHAT?!"

The Claymaster's voice was raw, his voice hitched with small coughs. His shoulders slumped as his rage diminished, replaced with a resigned weariness. Stepping away from Jackal, he looked again at the group.

"The Lots are an hourglass, boys. The orcs were always coming back, one year or another. Hispartha gave us these lands knowing that. They feared us plague-bearers, but they also used us. We bought them time to rebuild, to prepare. All for a hot, dusty swath of badlands." The stained, loose wrappings swung as the Claymaster shook his head. "I could get on my chariot, ride out, let this hideous shit loose that the frails put into me. Orcs would die. The plague might scare them away again for another few years. Another few years for Hispartha to train armies, build towers, indulge wizards. None of which they are going to use to protect the Lots once I'm dead and you are facing this again. The sand is about to run out. I have spent years looking for a way to stop it. The Tyrkanian is that way."

"What is he going to do?"

It was Mead that asked, his voice filled with curiosity and reluctant hope.

"Turn the hourglass over," Crafty answered from above.

Realization struck Jackal.

"You're going to give the plague to another," he said.

Crafty produced a respectful little bow. "As I said, your cleverness abounds."

"Not me," Jackal surmised, "or else you never would have arranged to have me ousted."

"Again, you are correct."

"Then why work so hard befriending me? Making promises to help me become chief?"

Crafty's smile widened, as if relieved Jackal did not have it worked out.

"Because the friend of my friend is mine too," the wizard replied. "You command great loyalty, Jackal. The influence you have over the one required could not be discounted."

Reflexively, Jackal's head turned to look at Fetching.

Her eyes narrowed as she steadied her aim at the wizard. "You're not putting anything in me, suet-ass. Especially not anything coming out of the Claymaster."

Crafty's bright teeth showed as he rejoiced in her vitriol. "Dear Fetching, you have many strengths, but a thrice-blood you are not."

Jackal's spine went cold.

Oats's heavy brows knit together. "Me? He saying he wants me? I knew it, you backy swaddlehead!"

Crafty's amusement grew. "Yes, I must admit it. Though, strong Oats, my need for you is less base than you imagine. I simply do not wish to rule over a kingdom of corpses."

"The fuck are you on about?" Hobnail demanded.

Mead lowered his stockbow slightly, pondering.

"A thrice is more orc than man," the youngblood said. "Oats carrying the plague would make it more deadly to thicks and less to frails."

"Be careful, friend Jackal," Crafty said, clicking his tongue, "you may not be the most clever amongst your brotherhood."

"You've tricked the orcs," Jackal said. "Lured them with the promise of Hispartha. But you do mean to fight them."

The wizard's broad cheeks inflated as he blew out a breath. "Oh, I am giving them Hispartha. For a time. Enough time for the kingdom to bleed, to despair. Their defenses are not as potent as they believe. Those I serve have seen to that."

"The Black Womb," Jackal said sourly. "Abzul was not alone. You have others at your command."

"Quite so," Crafty said. "Messages will be lost. Garrisons will abandon their castiles. Wells will be poisoned. A number of little catastrophes to allow the orcs to penetrate into the heart of Hispartha, near enough for the queen and her court to smell them coming. That is when we will strike."

Grocer wrinkled his face. "We?"

"Half-orcs," Crafty clarified amiably. "The hoofs of Ul-wundulas. We will rally all mongrel riders under the new plague-bearer and come to Hispartha's rescue, routing the horde and sending those that survive the pox back to Dhar'gest." Placing a thick-fingered hand on his chest, the wizard smiled. "But not before what is left of Hispartha's nobility recognizes the half-breed grandson of their late, beloved king. A king whose legitimate daughter so recently failed to protect the kingdom and its people. With no other honorable course, she will graciously abdicate the throne."

"To you," Jackal said, unable to suppress a small laugh of admiration.

Crafty's turbaned head nodded humbly. "Just so."

Jackal was filled with a bitter curiosity. "Tell me, Uhad. Are you truly some prince's mongrel son?"

The question was not met with the smugness Jackal had anticipated. From his vantage on the scaffold, Crafty grew pensive, even mournful. He was silent for a long moment, his eyes blank. When he responded, his voice was solemn.

"One thousand and one half-orc youths were taken by the Black Womb and tested in the crucibles of sorcery. To say that only I lived would be a falsehood. To say that only I survived would not. One thousand souls broken in the contractions of rebirth. I ask you, which is more possible? That the Hisparthan prince's bastard was the one to overcome all the trials? Or that the one to overcome all the trials was the Hisparthan prince's bastard? A blood tie to nobility needs only be claimed, but the mastery of wizardry must be real. Tyrkania desires to make a satrapy of Hispartha, this I know, and to this purpose I am tasked by potent masters. Yet for me to succeed they were forced to give me power equal to their own. My paternity may be a lie, but my arts are truth. Hispartha will allow itself to be deceived. They will crown their savior, half-orc and wizard though I am, comforting themselves with the knowledge that I am connected by blood to their precious, though perverted, lineage."

"You have it all solved, don't you?" Jackal mocked.

"Much of this was set into motion before you and I were born, my friend. The east has long yearned to make a puppet of Hispartha, at last turning to arcane counsel for the means. For my part, adjustments had to be made. Some of them regrettable."

"Like squeezing Fetch's vote?" Grocer growled. "Find it hard to fathom you weeping over that."

"Weep? No," Crafty confessed. "But causing one I had grown to admire to become outcast gave me no pleasure." The wizard looked at Jackal directly, his face steady and earnest. "It did not take long to see you would oppose me, my friend. You hold such love for this land, and you are ever bold in your vain struggles against rule. I had hoped to make you an ally. I still wish it, for you would be a strong one, but it is a false hope. Seek potent allies and you shall find the most grievous of your future foes. We need simply look around to see I was correct. Here you stand, with the Grey Bastards at your command, willing to defy their master of moments ago. Willing, also, to defy me, though there is no hope in the doing."

"Wizards can be killed," Jackal said. "I've done it with a lot less help."

"You should not be mistaking me for a toothless, twice-mad communer residing with his pet vermin in a reeking tower," Crafty said. The words were a warning, but the tone was strangely affectionate.

Jackal snorted. "Why? Because you can do what Hispartha's wizards could not? Make the plague only sicken orcs and not humans?"

"Humans will still sicken," Crafty told him flatly. "Fewer in number, thankfully, but some will die."

"And the survivors will hate you for spreading it," Fetch exclaimed.

"The survivors will fear him," the Claymaster muttered. "And they will kiss his feet, so that he doesn't unleash it further."

Oats glared at him and Crafty. "You two think I'm going to be the cause of all that, you got runny hogshit in your skulls."

"You have to, son," the Claymaster said. There was reason in his voice, and guilt, Jackal noticed. Fetch must have heard it too, and shifted uneasily.

"Why does he have to?" she demanded.

The Claymaster didn't answer.

Jackal snapped a look up at the gantry. "Crafty?"

The wizard made a small, apologetic gesture with his hands. "It is rare that we half-breeds know a mother's love. For many of us, not being killed at birth is all the evidence of her affection we have. But a lifetime of that love, reflected in an actual face? That is a rare blessing. Truly, Oats, you are fortunate."

Oats did not immediately understand what he was hearing, his face perplexed.

"Damn you, Crafty," Jackal growled.

The venom in his voice burned through Oats's confusion.

"Beryl?" he said, his voice weak, then boiling over with rage. "My mother? My fucking mother! What have you done?!"

"She is safe," Crafty insisted. "Watched by the trusted Captain Ignacio, who awaits to hear word that you have accepted your chief's mantle."

Jackal began to shiver with fury. Of course. No one else would agree to hurt her, not even at the Claymaster's order. Every sworn brother, slophead, and bedwarmer loved Beryl. Hells, she had raised most of them.

Dropping his stockbow, Oats surged at the Claymaster. "WHY WOULD YOU DO THIS?"

Up on the gantry, Crafty leaned forward eagerly. Too late, Jackal saw the trap.

"Oats, don't!"

Deaf to all, the thrice seized the Claymaster, his huge hands curling around the old mongrel's neck. As soon as they touched, both stiffened, screams erupting from their gaping jaws. The Bastards cursed in alarm and stepped back as a palpable miasma poured from beneath the Claymaster's bandages. The visible fetor was a churning, living cloud of pale brown, limned with sickly yellow light and veined with tendrils of putrescent green. Reaching forth from its host, the plague cloud ensnared Oats, the tendrils caressing and encircling his limbs, his neck, while the vapor crawled into his mouth and nostrils. Choking noises bubbled from the thrice's retching throat as he convulsed violently, his hands still throttling the Claymaster.

Jackal snatched a look at Crafty and found the wizard standing transfixed, his eyes rolled to white above a mouth moving wordlessly.

"Take him!" Jackal yelled, raising his stockbow.

The Bastards responded swiftly and six bowstrings thrummed. The bolts sped for the wizard, each a killing shot, but none touched their mark, turning to shafts of smoke just before they pierced flesh, passing through harmlessly and becoming solid once again to splinter against the chimney behind.

"Fuck!" Polecat exclaimed, his curse wild with anger and fear.

"We have to do something, Jack!" Fetching screamed, her head darting between him and Oats. The thrice was almost completely hidden within the noxious cloud, his beleaguered cries of anguish ringing through the chamber. The Claymaster appeared in equal agony, yet he was mostly free from the roiling murk.

Grocer had reloaded his stockbow and, with a scowl of pure loathing, stepped up close to his former chief, heedless of the cloud.

"Time to put this cur down," the old frailing said, taking aim at the Claymaster's temple.

A wrathful cry came from Crafty and, before Grocer could pull the tickler, the plague snapped away from Oats. The sorcerous tendrils wrapped around the quartermaster's throat and lifted him off his feet. Pustules formed and erupted on Grocer's strangling face, his protruding tongue awash in a torrent of bile. His flesh blackened and sloughed away, melting from his shaking body. As quick as it had entangled him, the cloud released Grocer, letting his corpse fall in a wet heap upon the ground.

"Hells overburdened!" Hobnail said, his forearm pressed firmly against his mouth. Next to him, Mead fell to his knees, heaving.

Fetching gave a cry of helpless fury as the plague renewed its claim upon Oats's stricken form. Eyes lifting, she fixed Crafty with a vengeful stare.

"Fetch, wait," Jackal urged, but she did not listen.

Slinging her stockbow, she ran for the chimney, sprung up on the nearest ladder, and began to swiftly ascend the scaffolding, intent on the wizard. As she climbed, the mingled screams of Oats and the Claymaster intensified.

Jackal gnashed his teeth and, dropping his thrum, charged the ensorcelled pair. His mind was filled with images of rats and Abzul's leering visage. The plague had not been able to touch him in the tower. He could wrest Oats free. There was still time.

But Hobnail and Polecat intercepted him, grabbing his arms and waist.

"Are you mad?" Hob yelled.

"Let go!"

Polecat held firm. "Do you want to fucking die?"

"I won't!" Jackal struggled against them. "Let me go!"

"Jackal!"

It was Mead's voice, hoarse from vomiting. The younger half-orc was still crouched on the ground, but his gaze and extended arm were pointed upward. Still held fast, Jackal looked. At first, he thought Mead was indicating Fetch, now one platform below Crafty and making her way swiftly for the next ladder, but then his eyes alighted on movement above the wizard. A darkness crawled on the surface of the chimney, glistening and clinging to the bricks as it progressed downward.

The Sludge Man.

"Go!" Jackal ordered, slinging Hobnail and Polecat off of him. "He's here for Fetch! Help her!"

Without waiting to see if they listened, Jackal bolted forward and dove into the cloud.

CHAPTER 35

THE PLAGUE BEGAN RIPPING HIM APART FROM THE INSIDE. HE felt it fill his lungs, the vapor turning into liquid. Drowning in acid, Jackal tried to scream and choked on the geyser of his guts. He was blind within the tempest, but could still feel his flesh bubbling, lit from beneath with the boiling humors of his body. All was pain.

Groping, his hands met resistance. He pulled against the entwined forms of Oats and the Claymaster, but his swollen, fluid-flooded knuckles had no strength. The thrice's iron thews were locked with seizures of agony. There was no breaking his hold. Yet Jackal sensed that his own assault had drawn the plague away from Oats. He just needed to endure, to keep the wrathful magic focused on trying to kill him until his friend was forgotten.

Adrift in a feverish sea, buffeted by tidal waves of nausea, Jackal drank the pain. He welcomed the plague, cursed it, laughed at it, and devoured it with the lethal appetite of the starved. But this was not the sickness of Abzul's rats, it was the beast which fed on them. Savaging his insides, lapping at his flesh with a corrosive tongue, the monster toyed with its food, waiting for the prey to grow weak and frightful before swallowing it whole. Jackal knew he was going to die, but he continued to bite back, a poisoned weasel still trying to kill the snake.

Spitting and hissing at the face of oblivion, he felt the end coming. The maw of the plague opened, its patience spent, and descended. But the final strike never fell. The serpent suddenly retreated. Jackal felt most of the pain flee as well, the absence of it a relief that sent him reeling to the ground. His stinging eyesight began to clear, focusing on the Claymaster and Oats sprawled unconscious nearby. There was no sign of the cloud, nor had it left any mark upon Oats. He lay pale and limp, half-supported by Mead. The younger half-orc stared with wide, horror-filled eyes.

Sitting up, Jackal looked down at his chest and stomach, finding them riddled with weeping sores and straining pustules. His right hand was black, swollen to the point of bursting. Yet his left was whole. Even as he watched, the healthy flush of skin began to creep over his forearm, the sores closing, the plague-blisters receding. The healing spread from his left arm into his torso, and Jackal took an exquisite, clear breath as his throat was rid of acrid bile. He got to his feet, and by the time he stood straight, the evil disease had completely fled, chased away by the might of Attukhan.

"Fuck. Me," Mead whispered.

Looking up, Jackal found the source of his salvation.

Fetch had reached Crafty. Her tulwar flashed as she set upon him, forcing the wizard to break his trance and defend himself. For all his bulk, Crafty danced nimbly away, backing down the gantry. His hand darted into his satchel and came out again in an arc, scattering an azure powder that hung in the air. Fetch kept coming, heedless to all but her quarry. Jackal tensed, dreading the effects of whatever foul magic she had just ignored. Crafty paused in anticipation, but whatever he expected to befall Fetch did not manifest. The powder swirled harmlessly as she rushed through and slashed at the stunned wizard. Crafty dove backward and barely avoided having his sizable gut opened. He reached the edge of the gantry. There was no more room to run.

Less than three javelin lengths separated Fetching from her vengeance. Balanced perfectly, ready to pounce, she savored the wizard's plight. Flummoxed with her immunity to his arts, Crafty merely stood. So intent were they upon the other, both failed to notice the large, black mass detach from the chimney above and plummet.

The sludge slammed down upon the gantry, directly between the half-orcs. The planks splintered as the entire scaffolding shook. Crafty lost his balance and spilled onto his back, his weight causing his end of the gantry to creak and bend, threatening to snap. A sinuous black tentacle shot forth from the sludge and wrapped around the wizard's legs. With monstrous speed, Crafty was whipped into the air and dashed headfirst against the chimney. The first blow would have been enough to kill, but the sludge swung its captive again and again, battering his skull until the bricks loosened and fell in, leaving a ragged, green-glowing hole. Dangling Crafty's limp, prodigious body, the featureless sludge dropped it disdainfully to the gantry.

Holding to a railing, Fetching had kept her feet, transfixed by the rapid, brutal attack, and now stared as the thing re-formed and began to rise up before her. Jackal too had been rooted in place, but his wits began to return. Scanning the scaffold, he saw Polecat and Hobnail were still two levels below, moving with all the speed the ladders allowed. Jackal hurried to follow them, yelling as he broke into a sprint.

"Fetch! Run!"

He ran beneath the scaffold and all was hidden from view. Clambering up the first ladder, he heard forceful impacts resound above, shaking the timber. Reaching the second level, he pounded down to the far side of the gantry, where the next ladder waited to slow him. Cries and curses from familiar voices reached his ears. The third landing. The fight was now directly above. Steps away from the final ladder, a shape crashed through the opening, snapping rungs as it tumbled. Jackal skidded to a halt and found Polecat lying at his feet. Kneeling quickly, he found the mongrel unconscious but alive. The ladder was in ruins. Vaulting to plant a boot on the side rail, Jackal jumped for the opening, caught the edge, and pulled himself up.

The sludge dominated the center of the quaking gantry. Half a dozen of the whiplike tentacles launched from its mass, swatting at Hobnail, who stood before the onslaught, desperately trying to reach Fetch. She was down on her back, one hand grasping a support beam while the other wielded her tulwar, slashing at the inky limb hauling on her leg. Keeping his own blade sheathed, Jackal dashed forward.

Fresh tentacles sprouted violently from the mass as soon as he started moving, spearing and swatting. One caught him brutally across the shoulder, sending him careening hard into the side rail, which split. He felt the grip of a long fall almost claim him, but then Hob was there, snatching his arm at the last moment and pulling him back onto the gantry. There was no time for gratitude. The sludge sought relentlessly to crush them, every blow they ducked rocking the gantry.

Fetch had managed to sever the tentacle holding her, but no sooner was she free than another spat forth to wrap around her legs. Jackal could see her grip was slipping. He dove, belly-down, and seized Fetch's hand just as it slid, fingernails gouging, from the beam. Hobnail scrambled up, reaching for Jackal's other hand, but was blindsided by a punching tentacle and knocked backward. Thrusting his fingers between the boards of the gantry, Jackal tried to hold firm, but the sludge pulled inexhaustibly. Groaning, the board began to peel up. The nails gave a final, surrendering squeak and pulled free.

Fetching was yanked toward the belly of the beast. Jackal went with her, unwilling to let go. She continued to hack at the creature as she sank up to her waist in the living tar, but the cuts of her blade immediately closed. Her grip on Jackal's hand began to slacken and he saw her strength fading as the soporific effects of the sludge's touch took hold. In a moment she would be lost in torpor, like all the she-elves, and taken by the Sludge Man. Issuing a desperate groan through clenched teeth, Jackal tried to find purchase and pulled with everything left within him. It wasn't enough. Fetch sank to her neck and her eyes closed. A hand emerged from the sludge, a man's hand, and slowly, tenderly, awfully, began to stroke Fetch's cheek. Jackal could only cry out in repulsed rage and watch as she vanished.

A gout of green fire tore through the middle of the sludge. Jackal felt the heat upon his face as it streaked past. The monster convulsed violently, its slick surface rippling as it tried to seal the puckered wound. Another font of flame erupted through its body with a wet, tearing sound. Jackal felt the resistance upon Fetch weaken. Redoubling his efforts, he pulled. Immediately, she began to emerge as Jackal yanked and the sludge retreated. Bolts of flame continued to pierce through as the gelatinous mass leapt for the side of the chimney and fled, slithering swiftly away into the upper shadows.

Jackal pulled Fetch close and she came around swiftly, shaking off the unnatural lethargy with a deep, curse-infused breath. Across from them, standing stoutly on the far end of the sagging gantry was Crafty. The turban had come undone from his head and he smiled through swollen lips leaking blood, but was otherwise disconcertingly unharmed. Casting sidelong looks at the reaches of the chimney, the wizard approached. Jackal and Fetching disentangled from each other and jumped to their feet. Hobnail hurried to stand beside them, a loaded stockbow aimed.

"You should be fucking dead," Fetch announced angrily.

Jackal drew his Unyar sword. "Wizards are damn tough to kill."

"I'm all for a challenge," Fetch said. "Hob?"

"With you," Hobnail growled.

"I am not your present worry," Crafty chided, looking only at Jackal. "That demon will not stop coming for her. A half-elf, friend Jackal? I am most impressed you managed to hide that from me."

"I'm disappointed you didn't already know," Jackal returned. "And he won't stop coming for you either, Uhad. Sludge Man wants you dead nearly as much as he wants Fetch alive."

Fetch looked put out. "The fuck does he want me for?"

"To sacrifice you in the Old Maiden, far as I can figure," Jackal told her. "Half your blood is elven. He thinks that will restore the marsh."

Fetch accepted this with a rueful shrug. "All right . . ."

Hobnail squinted at her critically. "You just found out you're half point-ear and that's what you say?"

"A crazy, inbred, sludge-covered, bog man wants to cut my throat in a marsh. Who gives a heap of hogshit who my mother was?"

Hob conceded the point with a raise of his eyebrows.

Crafty gave Jackal an earnest look. "You will never defeat him without me."

"Fuck that," Hobnail declared, pointing at the wizard with his thrum. "And fuck you."

He was within a heartbeat of pulling the tickler. Reaching out, Fetch touched him on the shoulder.

"We got brothers down," she said. "Sludge Man is loose in the Kiln. Now is not the time."

Jackal had to agree. He wasn't so quick to believe Crafty's insistence on his necessity, but he couldn't outright deny it either. Besides, fighting the wizard was an unwelcome prospect even without the Sludge Man to contend with. Crafty would have to wait. But he would wait on Jackal's terms.

Thrusting his left hand out, he seized the Tyrkanian's thick neck with his left hand. Squeezing down, he pulled the wizard toward him.

"Feel that?" Jackal asked. "It's power. One I don't understand. And I don't think you do either. I have a sneaking suspicion, Uhad, the reason you got rid of me was because of whatever Zirko did to me at Strava. I think you fear it."

"You may be wrong," Crafty croaked out, his eyes dancing with amusement.

"Try anything," Jackal promised, "and we will find out."

He pushed the wizard away and released his grasp. Crafty did not so much as shoot him a nasty look, but simply folded his hands below his sizable waist and waited expectantly.

Keeping a lookout for the Sludge Man, Jackal led them down off the scaffolding, picking up Polecat on the way. Thankfully, he was already coming to and descended the ladders mostly under his own power. Mead was still tending Oats, but there was no change in the thrice. Nearby, the Claymaster also lay motionless.

"They're breathing," Mead told Jackal as soon as he approached, "but it's shallow."

Jackal whirled on Crafty. "Will Oats recover?"

The wizard regarded the prone thrice for a moment before shifting his gaze to the Claymaster. "Perhaps. The plague remains in its familiar host, but allowing it to remain there is foolish. If the—"

"That's enough!" Jackal snapped.

"We need to get him out of here," Fetch said, staring grimly at Oats.

Jackal nodded. He retrieved a coal cart, and loaded Oats into it with Hob and Fetch's help. Polecat stood bleary-eyed, supported by Mead.

"You all get out of here," Jackal told the hoof. "Crafty and I will deal with the Sludge Man."

"Have you lost your mind?" Fetching gawked at him. "I'm not going anywhere."

"Crafty and I will deal with the Sludge Man, Fetch," Jackal repeated insistently.

"He wants *me*, fool-ass," Fetch replied. "Unless you want to chase him all over the Kiln, I suggest I stay here. Fuck suggest, I *am* staying here! I don't care if you do have a magic bone inside you!"

Hobnail snorted.

Knowing there was no argument, Jackal turned on him.

"Get gone. The three of us will cover your back."

"What about the Claymaster?" Mead asked.

"Leave him," Jackal said. "We can't risk Ignacio seeing him. Far as he can know, everything went as planned. Soon as you're out, get Oats and Cat to the meeting hall, then go find out where Beryl is. Free her if you can. And lower the Hogback. We need those other five mongrels in here. Anyone asks, it's the Claymaster's orders."

"Right," Hob said, and began pushing the cart out. Mead and Polecat followed.

When they were gone, Jackal turned to look at his remaining companions.

"Ready to hunt?" he asked.

Fetch met his eyes and calmly loaded her stockbow.

Crafty ambled over to the large furnace doors and pulled them open. The Al-Unan fire danced within, fueled by nothing but itself. Without hesitance, Crafty stuck his fists into the blaze, drawing them out encased in green flame. Turning, he smiled, and walked back, his hands trailing smoke.

The three of them waited in the cavernous chamber, listening to the hollow roar from the ovens. Standing slightly apart, they each faced a different direction, keeping vigilance on the dark, towering recesses. They did not speak, they did not plan. There was no need. The Sludge Man would come to them. He had to. All he desired was within this keep, all those he wished dead, imminently or in time. Jackal could feel his lust for a reckoning filling the great chamber, as potent as the musk of an animal.

Fetch was the first to spot the sludge, drawing Jackal and Crafty's attention to it with a small hiss. The pitch-dark mass oozed from around the lengthy curve of the chimney, nearly at ground level, barely visible in the enshrouding shadows beneath the scaffolds. It stopped moving as their eyes rested upon it, the barest reflection on its slick surface the only evidence it was there at all. Motionless, it waited, holding their gazes. Holding their . . .

"It's a distraction!" Jackal exclaimed, spinning around.

But the monster sludge was already upon them, nearly silent even as it barreled across the ground. A tentacle scythed out, knocking Jackal's feet from under him. He had hardly struck the ground when his foot was seized and his vision blurred as he was flung upward. His shoulders and neck were smote upon the ground, his spine wrenching as he was again hauled skyward. A green flash intruded upon the duller lights already dancing in his skull and he felt himself tumbling through the air. Again, the ground struck, but only with the force of his fall. His addled sight cleared and he saw an arm's length of smoldering tentacle detach from his leg to crawl away, wormlike, making quickly back toward the larger mass, which was embattled with Crafty. The wizard stood firm amidst the writhing multitude of tendrils, bringing his burning hands up to his mouth and blowing great gusts of flame that sheared through the appendages. Fetching must have danced away from the initial charge, for she knelt out of the sludge's reach, her stockbow aimed, clearly waiting for a shot at the man hidden within the loathsome vessel. Jackal knew firsthand the folly of trying to slay the Sludge Man with a thrumbolt, but what choice did they have? Likely, they would never get the chance, for Crafty could not seem to burn through the muck to reveal the bog trotter, his efforts focused entirely on the flailing coils.

Jackal made to rise, but a clinging, cold weight bore down on his back, forcing him to his knees. Craning his neck, he saw the smaller sludge had hold of him, crept from beneath the scaffold. He reached over his shoulder, grabbed the writhing muck, and tried to fling it away, but the sludge sucked at his hand, holding it fast. The ichor was quickly flooding around to his chest, crawling up his neck, flowing over his head. An undeniable drowsiness began to claim him, his eyelids drooping even as the sludge began to descend over his face.

Pain awakened him. Burning pain.

His eyes snapped open and he felt the sludge dribbling down his back, forming a scorched pool around his knees. He found Fetch behind him, holding a coal shovel, the metal spade alight with Al-Unan fire and quickly being consumed. A tentacle lanced at her and she severed it with the shovel, then tossed it down lest the flames reach her hand. Crafty stood directly in front of them, fending off the living bulwark of thrashing sludge that threatened to encompass them all. Fetch must have rushed to Jackal's aid, drawing the creature, its fury forcing Crafty to give ground. The flames wreathing the wizard's hands were guttering with each warding breath.

"Prepare to run!" the wizard called. "I can give but a moment!"

Aided by Fetch, Jackal struggled to his feet. His sword was gone, lost when he was thrown. Fetching hacked at the ever-encroaching tentacles with her tulwar, but every length she severed crawled back to be reabsorbed by the mass.

Crafty suddenly flung his arms wide, swinging them back together with tremendous speed. His flaming hands clapped with a thunderous resonance, producing a dense wave of green fire and hellish wind that collided with the sludge. The creature was thrown backward, the black membrane blistering as it was carried on the sorcerous tide. The smoking mass was borne into the air for a moment before striking the ground to tumble over itself, coming to a rest across the chamber, near the mouth of the passage out.

"Go!" Crafty yelled, turning to make for the scaffolding. With nowhere else to retreat, Jackal and Fetch followed. As soon as the wizard passed beneath the timber, he halted, sinking down to rest with his back against a support beam.

"Get off your fat sacks," Fetch told him. "Go stick your hands back in the damn furnace!"

"Not so simple, I am fearing," Crafty replied breathlessly. "The spirits within the flame will only suffer servitude for so long."

Jackal saw the sludge already stirring.

"We don't have long," he warned.

"I have had it with this bog sucker!" Fetch raged, following his gaze. "What can we do?"

Crafty gave a tired, helpless gesture.

Fetch got in his face. "Think! You were just crowing about how we needed you!"

"Have to kill the man within," Crafty offered, "but I cannot reach him."

"Then I'll fucking go in and get him!" Fetch declared.

"That's madness," Jackal said.

Ignoring him, she pressed Crafty. "Got anything in that bag to keep me from going to sleep?"

The wizard shook his head. "No. Were there such, it would be little use. Elf-blood quickly dispels most all—"

Crafty's eyes went wide with inspiration.

"Friend Jackal, give me your knife!"

Snatching the dagger from his boot, Jackal handed it over. Crafty grabbed Fetch and sliced her across the inner forearm. She winced and hissed, instinctively tried to pull away, but the wizard held her firmly, opening her flesh again across the shoulder.

"The hells are you doing?" Jackal demanded.

"Her own blood may protect her. Help me!"

Seeing Jackal's hesitance, Fetch grit her teeth, drew her own dagger and quickly drew three cuts across her thigh, slicing through her breeches.

The sludge had been roiling since it landed and was now gathering its shape once more.

Fetching jerked away from Crafty after he cut her a fourth time. "Enough! Leave some where it belongs."

"You won't have long," the wizard cautioned.

Peering out through the support beams, Jackal saw the sludge begin to move forward. It was no longer crawling, but rolling, sloughing over itself and quickly gaining speed.

"It's coming!"

"Be ready," Fetching said, winding her way out from under the scaffolding.

There was a fleeting moment, as she passed, when Jackal could have reached out and tried to stop her. He did not take it.

"Right behind you."

Fetch broke into a run as soon as she reached open ground and rushed to meet the creature. The sludge increased its pace as she emerged, barreling ravenously to reach the object of its desire. Screaming with a fury, Fetch leapt, her formidable legs launching her headfirst into the black mass. Her entire body disappeared within its inky embrace.

The sludge's rush was immediately arrested, the ripples from Fetch's entry replaced by a violent quivering across the viscid skin. Jackal moved quickly toward the creature, his heart hammering. A tentacle birthed to strike at him, but was pulled back before it came close. The entire creature writhed with inner turmoil, swelling and constricting haphazardly. Jackal circled it, uncertain where Fetch would emerge, if she would emerge. As he watched, an irregular protuberance began to form. The flesh of the sludge stretched outward, thinning, as the bulge grew. Jackal began to see the outline of shoulder blades, the back of a head. The tension upon the greying membrane snapped and Fetching burst forth, back-first, her arms encircled about the waist of the Sludge Man.

Using their combined weights to speed her escape, Fetch fell out of the sludge and rolled, planting her feet in the Sludge Man's gut and kicking him over her head. The heavy-limbed, naked form landed hard. And Jackal was there to greet him.

The Sludge Man's eyes lolled in his calcified face. His grey flesh creased and cracked even as Jackal hooked a hand beneath his chin and drug him along the ground. The sludge was in pursuit, flowing over and around Fetch as she coughed on her hands and knees. The doors to the great furnace still hung open and Jackal pounded toward them, bent low. The Sludge Man began to struggle and kick, wriggling pitifully as the threshold to the oven loomed. Hauling him up by the throat, Jackal flung the decaying demon at the roaring flames. The Sludge Man's long arms splayed wide and grabbed the jamb. He glared hatefully at Jackal from the brink of the inferno.

"Filthy half-breed! You dare lay besmirched hands upon us!"

"Enjoy all the hells, Corigari," Jackal growled, and booted the Sludge Man into the emerald flames.

The onrushing tide of sludge was at his back. Jackal dove to the side as the river of tar went after its master, pouring into the furnace. As soon as the last flowed through, Jackal jumped to his feet and slammed the doors shut, burning his hands on the hot iron. Through the thick metal the final shrieks of the Sludge Man could still be heard.

A great booming sounded within the furnace and the doors buckled. Jackal jumped back as the works began to rumble. The roar from the ovens was increasing as concussions blossomed within the belly of the chimney, sending bricks shrieking through the air on jets of steam. The scaffolding shivered and timbers began to snap. The entire keep began to shake.

Fetch ran up. "What is happening?!"

Jackal could hardly hear her over the din. He shook his head. A strident metal scream cut through the thundering as the door to the furnace, glowing white-hot, warped violently.

Jackal put his mouth near Fetch's ear. "Crafty will know!"

"Jack! He's fucking gone!"

A massive explosion rocked the chimney midway up its length, vomiting green flame and large chunks of stone.

"Go!" Jackal yelled, pointing at the passage.

Staying together, they ran, reeling and flinching as the keep cracked and belched.

Outside, they found the Kiln in chaos. The eruptions could be felt in the yard, and flares of flame were already fountaining out of the wall, beacons of jade against the foredawn sky. Slopheads were scurrying down off the shaking palisade.

"The Al-Unan fire," Jackal gasped, "it's burning out of control."

"We have to get everyone out," Fetch said, her eyes taking in the fortress and seeing the destruction to come.

Jackal bit down on a scream as her words reminded him.

"The Claymaster," he said, turning back to the door of the keep. "He is still inside."

"Let him burn," Fetching declared, grabbing his arm.

Jackal looked back at her. "We need him."

"Go," Fetch told him, setting her jaw. "I'll get everyone out."

Giving her hand a grateful squeeze, Jackal flung the door open and ran back into the dying keep.

Chapter 36

The Claymaster stood in the middle of a green hell. Heedless of the falling stones, the collapsing timber, the fonts of flame shooting from the walls and the floor, he simply stared up at the crumbling chimney. Jackal remained in the fragile shelter of the sweltering passage and called out to him. Slowly, the Claymaster turned.

"Come to revel in what you've done, Jackal?"

The rancor in the old mongrel's voice could be heard over the tumbling brick and sibilant fire.

"This wasn't my doing, chief!"

"No?" the Claymaster said, flinging an arm back at the chimney. "I built it. You destroyed it!"

Jackal took a single stride out of the passage. "The hoof isn't destroyed. Even now. The Grey Bastards are more than the Kiln!"

"And we could have been more than a hoof! But for you."

"We would have been bowing before a foreign sorcerer! Servants to a king!"

"A half-orc king!" the Claymaster shot back.

Another of the oven doors gave way under the building pressure, cannoning off its hinges to slam against the wall.

"Doesn't matter," Jackal said. "He will always be the Tyrkanian cat's-paw who allowed the orcs to destroy the Lots."

"The Lots!" the Claymaster spat. "Ul-wundulas is a blight, Jackal. If you had ever seen Hisparth—"

"I've seen it! It's beautiful. And it's not home."

Phantom waves of heat distorted the Claymaster. "You only know what a home is because of me, boy! You are not living in chains because of me!"

Jackal took another step. "That's true. You gave us this land. So why are you not defending it? Why have you abandoned your prize to help Crafty win his?"

"No one can fight forever, Jackal. You'll discover that when you're old and done."

"You're wrong. You fight forever if you fight to the end."

The Claymaster laughed and spread his arms. "Wiseass whelp! This is my end!"

"It doesn't have to be! Come with me. Ride against the orcs. Remind them why they fear you. Remind the Bastards why we followed you."

Behind the hunched form of the Claymaster, half the chimney fell in on itself. The heat within the keep was nearly unbearable. The chief regarded the jagged throat of bricks for a moment before making his way toward Jackal, stepping over steaming fissures and around burning debris.

"Remind them?" the old mongrel asked as he drew close. "Remind them with what? The truth is . . ."

The Claymaster's hand came up. The bandages about his head were loose, heavy with sweat. Clawing at them with fingers no longer swollen, the chief pulled the wrappings down to hang about his neck. Jackal looked upon the old mongrel's face. Wrinkles and the creases of long cares dwelled there, but no pustules, no sores. The ravages of plague were gone.

". . . I no longer have it in me."

Jackal felt his guts roll over. "Oats."

The Claymaster smiled, amused at his astonishment. His hands darted out and seized Jackal by the shoulders, dragging him nearly nose to nose.

"Jackal," the old mongrel said, invoking the name as a curse. "I am half-tempted to keep you here. Force you to watch the fall of everything I created. Allow our mistakes to burn us both."

"Half-tempted?" Jackal asked, grinning at the unmasked, unfamiliar face. "I am wholly hoping you will try."

The Claymaster's mirth faded, replaced with a resigned regret. Dropping his eyes and his hands, the chief turned and strode back into the burning ruin of his works.

Jackal was halfway down the passage, running for all he was worth, when he felt the furnace chamber implode. Overtaken by a fist of roaring wind and smoldering dust, he was punched forward, slammed to the ground, where he slid until striking the curved wall. Picking himself up, he ran on, choking on grit. He could feel the weight of the entire shuddering structure above him, ready to expire. The door appeared ahead and Jackal kicked it open, fleeing the calamity. He ran for the bunkhouse, darting around the corner to the far side of the building just as the heart of the stronghold succumbed. Hunkering, he put his arms over his head. Stones fell in a rain, many of them awash in Al-Unan fire. They besieged Jackal's shelter with a terrifying clamor. He heard the roof of the bunkhouse collapse and the wall at his back felt made of wind-blown cloth. For what seemed an eternity, he existed in a world of cacophony and tremors. He could do nothing but shield himself with his own flesh and weather what could not be stopped.

When the stones finally ceased falling, Jackal opened his eyes to dust and smoke. All was illuminated by the alchemist's fire. The broken tooth of the bunkhouse stuck up from a sea of rubble. Looking around the corner Jackal saw the keep, reduced to nothing but a hill of burning stones. Stumbling away from the wreckage, he hurried across the quaking yard, making for the Hogback. Vaulting strewn stones and lurching away from blasts of flame and steam, he moved through the destruction, watchful for signs of any others. Thankfully, he saw no stragglers. None would be foolish enough to remain.

The Kiln was tearing itself apart.

Even as he ran, a stretch of the palisade ignited on the wall ahead. The white render vanished as the flames dined upon the latticework beneath. The fire spread swiftly in both directions. Soon, the entire wall would wear a dancing jade crown. Jackal raced the flames.

The great ramp came into view. Upon its crest, at the top of the wall, a lone figure sat astride a hog, watching the yard. The smoke was thick in the air, but Jackal knew it was Fetching. She had ensured everyone fled, and now waited on the last occupant. The fire was coming, chewing its way toward the wooden Hogback from both directions.

Jackal halted. He would never make it.

Fetching had not yet spied him. She would come for him when she did. And then neither of them would make it out. Even her hog could not outrun the alchemist's fire. His choice made, Jackal ducked behind what was left of the Claymaster's domicile. Peering around the shattered wall, he watched the one who watched for him, and waited. He willed Fetch to leave, fearing she would gallop down into the doomed fortress to search for him. It was a near thing. She almost waited too long. The flames were licking at the hooves of her barbarian when she turned and vanished over the edge of the wall.

Weary to the bone, Jackal sat down, leaning against the wall of the domicile. He had never had the Kiln all to himself before. The thought made him laugh aloud, the sound dry and humorless.

An explosion erupted in the wall nearby, making him flinch and killing his laughter. A gaping hole stared at him, an eye with green lashes, weeping smoke. Jackal stared at it dully for a moment, wondering how long it would be before the walls completely fell. He wouldn't live to see it. The conducting channels underground were already beginning to burst. Soon the entire yard would be a lake of fire. Jackal stared at the hole in the wall, the tunnel inside exposed.

Slowly, he rose.

The tunnel.

He could feel the heat from where he stood. Hells, he would never survive. But it was a chance. The hole was just south of the upper curve of the wall. He would have a little more than half the circuit to traverse. It was madness. The gate at the other end would be closed. Even if he made it before he cooked, he would be trapped. Unless other holes had been blown in the wall. He only needed one on the outer-facing side to escape.

"Going to burn anyway."

Jackal walked to the mouth of the hole. The heat pouring out of it was bearable, but it would be worse once he was inside. Stepping back to get a running start, Jackal took several deep breaths and rushed in, jumping through the ring of flames. Landing, he turned left and sprinted up the tunnel.

He had light from the opening until he turned the upper curve, then all was darkness. Sticking his right hand out, Jackal placed it on the wall, dragging it along the scorching stones to guide him as he ran. And still he fell. Unseen debris, shaken loose from the failing masonry, tripped him up. Each time he hit the ground, it was harder to rise. The air was leaden. He was blind not just from the lightless tunnel, but the necessity to keep his eyes closed against the blowing heat lest they be boiled in their sockets. His first steps had drenched him with sweat. By his second fall, he was encased in dry, tightening flesh. Nothing flowed through his nostrils, nor his open, parched mouth. Yet he got to his feet, again and again, continuing to run.

The curve of the wall was never-ending. He despaired of ever making it to the downward side of the oval, much less to the gate at the bottom end. His skin split. And mended. He could feel the blessing of Attukhan striving to save him, but it could not conjure air into his lungs. Zirko had said even a candle behind a rushing waterfall could be snuffed. Jackal could not have blown out a candle directly in front of his lips. Wheezing, suffocating, he fell again, and this time nothing had impaired his feet.

He did not rise. The tunnel floor seared his cheek, his chest and stomach, but there was no strength within him to do anything but burn. The pain was excruciating. Jackal eagerly awaited his breathless body to drag him into darkness so he could escape. The tunnel pounded up ahead. Stones falling. Good. He would be crushed, buried. Whatever would bring an end. Through the rumble, the pounding continued, louder now, closer.

Rhythmic.

Jackal could feel it now in the floor beneath his chest, melding with the beats of his heart. Beats. Hoofbeats. A squeal echoed through the tunnel. Jackal raised his head, knowing that sound.

It was Hearth.

The hog stopped right in front him, unseen, yet heard, smelled. A dry snout, pulsing with labored breaths, nudged his arm. *No!* Jackal tried to call out, tried to tell him to go back, but his tongue was useless in his barren mouth. *Turn around! Run!* The hog squealed again, agitated, his own voice raspy and weak. *Hells, Hearth, you are dying! Go!* But the hog remained, buffeting him with the sides of his tusk, trying to hook his arm, force him to stand. Raising an arm, Jackal gripped the barbarian's mane, the bristles dry and brittle. With an effort, he mounted.

Hearth turned immediately and sped away.

Lying upon his hog's neck, Jackal felt the heat rushing around him, a torturous breath from every hell. Galloping down the tunnel he had traversed countless times, Hearth ran. The bellows of his belly heaved, less with every breath. Beneath his thighs, Jackal could feel his mount giving out. He reached weakly for one of the swine-yanker tusks, instinct telling him to slow the beast, but Hearth jerked his head and snorted, denying him. His every breath was audible, painfully punctuated by flagging squeals. The rider within him told Jackal he was astride an animal already dead. He screamed into his beloved hog's smoldering mane as a mote of light appeared before them, growing larger as the beast thundered on. Leaping the shattered and twisted gate, Hearth bore Jackal out of the tunnel, his legs buckling as he landed. Without the strength to hold on, Jackal was thrown, landing beneath the arch of the gatehouse. Hearth was less than a stone's throw away, spilled on his side. Jackal crawled, watching the barbarian's last breaths rise and fall, wanting only to reach him before the end, place a hand upon him in parting.

He did not make it in time.

Dragging himself the last infuriatingly small span, Jackal rested his head upon Hearth's face and wept in a futile rage.

Above him, the gatehouse groaned. Small cascades of dust and powdered mortar drifted down as the stones loosened in the arch. Jackal got to his knees, then his feet, remaining in a squat as he took hold of Hearth's tusks and dragged him out from beneath the gatehouse, not stopping until they were well clear. Kneeling beside his dead mount, he watched as the walls of the Kiln tumbled to rubble.

The sun appeared over the horizon and still Jackal remained, bitterly feeling his unnatural strength return. He was still sitting there when a shadow fell over him and a strong hand clasped down on his shoulder.

"I'm sorry, brother."

Jackal put his own hand over the thick, powerful fingers, relieved, but reluctant to look up for fear of what he might find. After a moment, he did.

Oats stood above, soot-stained and a little haggard, but otherwise unchanged. Jackal let out a long breath.

"Claymaster made me think you now carried the plague," he said.

Oats's face fell. "Not me."

The mournful tone roused Jackal. "Then who?"

Oats bade him follow with a small motion of his head. Getting to his feet, Jackal complied and the thrice led him a little farther away from the Kiln, where they found Fetching and the Grey Bastards, mounted and waiting. Red Nail, Kul'huun, Gripper, Dumb Door, and Slivers were with them. Beyond, the Winsome villagers milled about in the scrub, watched over by the slops. All appeared dirty and unnerved, some gazing fixedly at the conflagration of the Kiln, while others avoided looking in its direction. Jackal's own stare settled on a familiar figure, standing amongst the hoof, holding a bundle wrapped in a blanket.

Beryl watched as he approached, moving the folds of the blanket aside when he drew close so he could see. It was Wily, the toddling thrice-blood from the orphanage. He lay asleep in Beryl's arms, his little brow creasing as he whimpered slightly. His round face was flush and pustules had already formed on his neck.

Jackal's heart sank and he looked at Beryl aghast. "I . . . I don't understand. How?"

For the first time in his life, he saw cracks form in the matron's resilience, threatening to break her. Her voice came from quivering lips, barely a whisper.

"This . . . fog. It came into the room. It was so fast, and . . . I thought he was going to die right then. But he didn't. Jackal . . . he hasn't woken up."

"Captain Ignacio was with her, Jack," Fetch said softly from the back of her hog, clearly having heard the story. "He told Beryl the Claymaster wanted her and the boy protected."

"Crafty wanted a thrice to bear the plague," Jackal said through clenched teeth, running a thumb gently across Wily's forehead.

"There was only one other in the Kiln after I left for Strava," Oats said, his voice breaking. "This is my fault."

Beryl snapped a hard look at her son. "I already told you to stop that. This is on the chief's head. His, and that wizard's."

"The Claymaster's dead," Jackal said to no one in particular. He couldn't take his eyes off the afflicted boy. Had he known this was where the plague would flee, he never would have chased it away.

The guilt would kill Oats, no matter what Beryl said. "What about Ignacio?"

"He fled when the plague entered the room," Fetch replied, saving Beryl the account. "Forced the slops to lower the Hogback, took his cavaleros and rode away."

"That got us in," Gripper uttered.

"Your new boys were damn helpful getting everyone out, Jack," Hobnail said, trying to sound hopeful.

"Our thanks," Jackal told them.

"It was our honor," Red Nail said, though his face held great pity. "All of your folk may shelter at the Wallow, if you wish."

Jackal nodded gratefully.

"Any sign of Crafty?" he asked Fetch, but she only tightened her lips and shook her head.

"I will hunt him down," Jackal vowed to Beryl. "Make him undo this."

She wanted to believe him, he could see, but despair had taken root, refreshed every time she looked down at the child in her arms.

A noise resounded in the early morning air. It was faint, but protracted, drawing the attention of all.

"It's . . . a voice," Mead said, squinting in concentration.

Jackal thought so too, and it was coming from the ruin of the Kiln.

"Hob, Mead," Fetch said. "Let's go have a look."

Uninvited, Kul'huun rode with them. They weren't gone long. When they returned, all four wore grim faces.

"It's the orc's corpse, isn't it?" Jackal said, knowing the answer. He had suspected as soon as he heard the sound.

"Half-burnt and buried," Fetch replied. "But the fucker's still howling."

Slivers screwed up his face. "What the hells does that mean?"

"Crafty said it would only do that for one thing," Oats tolled, staring at nothing.

"Thicks," Jackal said.

Polecat, recovered enough from his fall to sit a hog, swore under his breath. After that, all were silent. They stood displaced beneath a morning sky stained with the black fumes of their stronghold, listening to a corpse's voice trumpet the coming of his kin. Looking at the people of Winsome and the slops, Jackal saw more than two hundred lives, nearly a quarter of them children. Most of the folk who came to live under the protection of the hoof were mongrels, orphans once, and now orphans again. Exposed in the badlands, the orcs would find them, sniff them out even with all the smoke. And slaughter would follow.

Jackal set his tongue against his teeth to whistle for Hearth before remembering. Biting back the grief, he called to the slops.

"Get me Grocer's barbarian!"

Soon, Biro rode up on Winnow. Dismounting, he turned the animal over, along with a tulwar, stockbow, and full quiver. Jackal gave the youth an approving look and climbed into the saddle to face the assembled riders.

"Red Nail. The people of Winsome will accept the offer of shelter from the Tusked Tide. Will you lead them and our slopheads to your lot?"

"I will," the older half-orc replied. "What do you mean to do?"

"Give you as much time as we can," Jackal replied.

Slivers barked a laugh. "We?"

Slowly, Jackal looked at five faces. Polecat. Mead. Hobnail. Oats. And Fetching. He saw steel in the eyes of each.

"Grey Bastards. We got orcs in our lot. Do I have to say how we deal with that?"

"No, you don't," Oats rumbled, hauling himself atop Ugfuck.

Mead began to nod, slowly at first, then building into an emphatic, feral motion. Hob smiled behind his red beard. Fetch's stockbow was already loaded.

Polecat grinned and shifted in the saddle. "All the hells, I'm hard."

"Six of you?" Slivers said, his voice high and incredulous. "That's at least three hundred thicks out there. Could be the, the . . . what did you call the big fucking horde?"

"*Duulv M'har*," Kul'huun said lustily.

Slivers hooked a thumb at the Fang. "That! Forty thousand strong? Are you mad?"

"We don't count them, frailing," Fetch told him, winking at her brothers. "We kill them."

The Bastards chuckled.

"Would you count another to ride with you?" Gripper asked.

Dumb Door thumped himself hard in the chest.

"Make that two more," Gripper amended.

Jackal gave the nomads a pardoning look. "No need for you to die for our lot."

"How about this?" Gripper returned. "We survive, we become sworn brothers."

Jackal looked at his hoofmates. "What do you say?"

There was a collective shout of approval.

"Eight it is."

"*G'haan*," Kul'huun said.

"Nine, then," Jackal announced with a smirk. "Though *you* have to go back to the Fangs of Our Fathers when this is over." He turned to Biro. "Get our nomad brothers some stockbows."

"Well, don't look to me to be the tenth fool," Slivers whined.

"You can ride with me," Red Nail growled. "Help escort the innocents."

Slivers gave a sullen nod. "I can do that."

"My thanks," Jackal told him earnestly. He was about to give the order to ride when he saw Beryl step up beside Ugfuck. Oats looked down at his mother from the saddle and a silent commiseration passed between them. She, who had lived with the ways of the hoof before he ever drew breath, was torn between respecting the rider and fearing for the son. Oats placed a broad hand over Wily's head for a moment, then leaned down and kissed Beryl, his fierce beard lingering against her raised cheek. Everyone looked away.

Only when Oats reined up beside him did Jackal give the command.

"Let's ride!"

They went roughly south, passing the broken pyre of the Kiln, the bellow of the enchanted orc still ringing out from the wreckage. It did not take them long to find the thicks. They were less than a mile below the Kiln, a column of tall, swarthy figures moving within a cloud of dust. It was another *ul'usuun*, three hundred marauders armed with spear and scimitar. The hoof reined up directly in their path.

"That it?" Polecat complained. "I thought they were bringing an army."

Laughing, they all checked their weapons. The orcs marched

steadily closer and a guttural cry arose from their ranks when they spotted the riders. The tongue began to increase its pace, eager to run off the enemy or, better, come to grips and slay them.

Jackal's hoof waited, raising their stockbows.

The orcs charged.

As soon as the thicks stepped within range, they loosed. If any fell to their bolts, Jackal did not see, focused solely on reloading. To his right, Fetch's thrum was already snapping again. After the fourth volley, Jackal called the withdrawal. Turning, they spurred their hogs away. The orcs gave chase, growling and snarling, their long, powerful legs eating up the ground. But the riders had the lead and soon turned, unleashing another swarm of thrumbolts before breaking away once more. Again and again they baited the orcs, until their quivers were spent. They rode farther away after the final volley, but Jackal signaled a turn before the enemy was lost from view. Baying for vengeance, the thicks pursued. If the *ul'usuun* was thinned, it was difficult to see.

"How many did we get?" Mead asked, his face flushed.

"A score, maybe," Hobnail guessed. "No more."

Jackal freed himself from the strap of his stockbow and let the weapon fall. All around him, the others did the same, filling their hands with swords. Looking over, he found Fetch beside him, flush with the thrill of battle, savage and beautiful.

She smiled at him. "Tusker, Jack?"

"Down their throats," he replied.

Oats was a bulwark at his right, his brutish face fixed on the oncoming foe, whiskered jaw pulsing.

The rest of the hoof formed up in a wedge behind, the Bastards trailing Fetch, while Kul'huun and the free-riders fanned out on the other side. Unspoken, they had all arrived at the same decision. There was no need to scout for good ground or search out ambush sites. When nine stood against hundreds, such tactics were simply tiring. They wanted to be seen, to be counted. For years they had lived a lie, believing they protected the Lots. And for years the thicks had been deterred by only one mongrel. Now, the Claymaster was dead, his legacy unjustly foisted upon a child. It was time for the half-orcs of the Lot Lands to mold their false purpose into something real. And they would do it with blood.

Pointing his tulwar at the surging wall of orcs, Jackal kicked his mount forward.

"Live in the saddle!"

"DIE ON THE HOG!"

Hooves thundered behind, orcs swarmed ahead, swelling as the distance closed. It was a howling sea of bulging muscles, fanged jaws, curved swords, and heavy-bladed spears. The riders plunged into those bloodthirsty waters with no hope of returning.

The wedge slammed into the massed orcs and pierced deep. At its head, Jackal slashed with his tulwar, severing spear shafts and ringing scimitars. Beneath him, his barbarian cleaved a path with its tusks. The charge scattered the orcs, trampling those directly in its path, but their numbers made it impossible to win through. Closing the wound, the thicks bulled back in, pressing the sides of the wedge, squeezing it until it was forced to halt.

Jackal heard a hog squeal in agony behind him, but he could not spare a look. Life shrank to the multitude of snarling faces before him and the swinging of his sword. Spears lunged at him, orcs screamed at him, and he lashed out at all. His tulwar lopped down upon necks and shoulders, but the thicks' primordial frames feasted upon the edge of the blade, turning death strokes into flesh wounds. Fetch and Oats were by his side, preventing the thicks from reaching his flanks. Trained to battle, the barbarians bucked in tight arcs, sweeping and rending with their tusks. Jackal knew, even without seeing, that the wedge had become a ring. The hoof was surrounded, resisting the inevitable.

A spear made it past Jackal's warding blade, scraping across his hip to lodge in his saddle. He opened the offender's throat with a reaping stroke, but there was no end to those wanting his blood. A scimitar swept in, wielded by a swart brute. Jackal turned the stroke, the force of it knocking him off balance. The orc seized the opening, and lunged, dropping his weapon to seize Winnow by the tusks. The hog tried to rear, but the brute held her fast, fell muscles bulging. Horribly, impossibly, the orc dominated the swine as four spears punched into her chest and neck. Screaming, unable to escape the pain, Winnow began to spin wildly, her fear allowing her to break free. Jackal fought to keep his seat, but the hog was frenzied, spooked beyond control. With no other choice, Jackal jumped from the saddle. Winnow attempted to flee. Powerful in her pain-fueled rage, she barreled forward, trampling and goring, cutting a swath through the orcs, but her strength was flagging and they drug her down to be butchered.

Fetch and Oats closed ranks, shielding Jackal. He rose in the center of the ring and saw the end was near. Kul'huun's hog was dead. The Fang fought on foot, covered in blood, a scimitar in each hand. He raged with a savagery to match his enemies, screaming abuses at the orcs in their own tongue. The rest were still mounted, but as Jackal watched, Hobnail took a spear through the chest, the blow so fierce it came through his back and knocked him from his hog. Bounding forward, Jackal vaulted onto the barbarian's back, taking it in hand and slaying Hob's killer. But the thicks struck with renewed furor. Next to Jackal, Mead let out a horrendous cry as his hand was hacked off by a scimitar. Gripper was dragged from his saddle and vanished amidst the ravaging press. Fetch's hog was killed beneath her. She rolled free and, using her dead mount as a barricade, fought on.

The ring began to collapse.

Letting loose shouts and curses, Jackal kicked Hob's hog forward. Ignoring his own defense, he allowed the orcs to surround him, hoping to draw them away from his brethren, even for a moment. He felt the edges of scimitars and the points of spears kiss his flesh. Damning the wounds, he continued forward, hells-bent on testing the limits of Attukhan's relic to his final breath. He did not know when he was dismounted, only that somewhere in the red world he found himself again fighting on foot. His tulwar was broken, shattered on the skull of an orc. Taking up a spear, he slew until it too was sundered. Taller than he, stronger than he, the orcs threw themselves at him. They cut him, stabbed him, knocked him down and pummeled him with iron knuckles, yet he rose, cutting, stabbing, pummeling in return.

Dozens lay beneath his feet. Yet scores stood before him. Gathering themselves, slavering with the coming kill, they stared at him with dark, animal eyes. He braced himself to receive them.

A great cry went up amongst the orc ranks, a single word bellowed in their savage tongue that Jackal did not catch. Every thick turned directly away from him and raised their weapons, howling as they charged. Bewildered, Jackal cast about and saw groups of riders coming in from all sides. Their mounts were great stags, the antlers imbued with a pale, ghostly light. On their backs were warriors with wild, plaited hair, shaven to the scalp down the sides of the skull. They loosed arrows from bows on the run, or impaled the orcs with wood-hafted war lances. The riders let loose an ululating cry as they killed, but the stags, though they ran mightily, were eerily quiet.

Behind, Jackal heard a familiar voice lifted in elation. Turning, he found his hoof a javelin's throw away, relieved of all foes, clustered together amidst the orcs they had killed. It was Polecat who cried out, laughing and pointing out the newcomers to Mead, whom he held close.

"The Tines! Hells overburdened, it's the Tines!"

The elven hoof set upon the thicks without mercy. Riding in troops of ten, they seemed to hit from everywhere at once, never slowing. They were so swift, Jackal could not say how many they numbered. Eighty, at least. But the mongrels who rode with them were unmistakable.

Warbler and Hoodwink were at the head of one troop, their stout hogs leading the harrow stags. They crashed into the nearest cohesive group of orcs and had at them. Other troops converged, herding and surrounding the soon-to-be outnumbered thicks.

Jackal ran back to his hoof.

Oats was still mounted, riding a protective circle around the others on Ugfuck, the only hog to have survived. Fetch was on her feet. The relief in Jackal's face at seeing her alive must have shown, for she grinned wearily. Polecat had managed to get Mead's stump bound, but the youngblood was ghastly pale and on the verge of passing out. Dumb Door had pulled Gripper's body out from amongst the dead thicks and stood beside it, staring blankly. Stumbling into their midst, Jackal's eyes settled on Hobnail's still, impaled form. Kneeling down, he put a hand on his fallen brother's shoulder. Fetch joined him, placing her hand atop his.

"Kul'huun?" Jackal asked, his voice raw.

Fetch lifted her chin toward the direction of the fighting. "Went chasing after the orcs when they attacked the elves. That is one loony fuck."

Jackal tried to laugh, but it died in his throat.

"Looked like Hood with them," Fetch said. "But that other? Is that War-boar?"

"It is."

"Never thought to see him again."

It wasn't long before she did. The Tines finished off the orcs and the old thrice rode up with a pair of elves. Dismounting, Warbler picked his way through the carnage, giving nods to the hoof, his eyes lingering longer on Oats and Fetch. She stood. Jackal did not bother to rise. Squatting down, Warbler regarded the body between them, but remained silent.

"How?" Jackal asked at last. "How did you get the Tines to help?"

Warbler shook his white head. "You know it wasn't me, Jaco."

". . . Starling."

"We had to hole up for the Betrayer. After, we were moving slow. Hood found us. Told me about being sent after Oats and all the strangeness at the Kiln. Figured the Claymaster was making his move. Word had already spread amongst the nomads about the orc tongues in the Lots. Still, I had to get those she-elves someplace safe, and that Starling was insistent on Dog Fall. Tines were on us long before we even made it into their territory. They were already looking for her. Hoodwink and I were a sow's whisker from being lanced, but Starling vouched for us. Told her kin she had a debt owed. To you. Next I know, the she-elves are being taken away and I got a pack of whooping point-ear warriors asking where we're going. Made for the Kiln . . . you weren't hard to find after that. Still a heap I don't understand, Jackal, but I figure that can wait."

"It can. What about Starling? The Tines accept her back?"

Warbler's face answered the question before his words. "No, son. Maybe they would have. But . . . she went off alone."

Jackal managed a nod of acceptance and fought not to cast dark looks at the two elves now tending Mead's injury.

A terrible howl went up over the battlefield, coming from the site of the Tines' last skirmish with the orcs.

"That's probably the work of your Fang friend," Warbler said as the questioning glances fell upon him. "He insisted on letting one orc live. He's pulling all its teeth. Hoodwink and some of the point-ears were happy to help him. Says it will bring a message back to the rest."

The scream rang out again.

"Brutal. Simple," Fetch said. "Might just work."

Jackal was too tired to agree, but he did hope.

No teeth.

Chapter 37

JACKAL THANKED THE UNYAR MESSENGER AND WALKED BACK to the orphanage. Entering the cool shade, he blinked the sunspots from his eyes. The Bastards waited expectantly.

"Well?" Polecat asked, sitting atop one of the long, low dining tables used by the children.

"Strava has seen no sign of any orcs," Jackal told the room.

Polecat spread his hands. "That's it. That's all the Lots."

Dumb Door nodded slowly in agreement. Leaning against the wall next to the door, Hoodwink continued to clean his fingernails with a knife, saying nothing.

"You want to do another patrol, Jack?" Fetch asked from her usual stool.

Jackal didn't immediately answer. Near the fireplace, Oats shrugged, giving him the decision.

"It's been nearly a fortnight," Warbler said. "They ain't coming."

"They will always be coming," Jackal replied, staring at the floor.

Polecat slumped a little. "Our people can't stay with the Tusked Tide forever."

"Some of them will," Mead said quietly, hand cradling his bandaged stump.

There was silence for a long time.

The Incursion had not come.

Jackal knew he needed to accept that the orcs had chosen to heed the warning, but his mind was plagued with visions of the *Duulv M'har* marching across Ul-wundulas. Five *ul'usuuns* had been sent. None of them made it back to Dhar'gest. Zirko and the Unyars dealt with one, Bermudo and his cavaleros another, though it was rumored the captain was grievously wounded and not likely to live. Two of the tongues came through the Old Maiden and made it into Hispartha, but the kingdom had been warned. The thicks were ambushed and every last one ridden down. Still, Jackal could not bring himself to say, to believe, that they were not coming.

"Let's put it to a vote," Fetch said, at last. "Bring Winsome and the slops home?"

"Can we have a separate vote for the slops?" Polecat suggested playfully.

Fetch ignored him and raised her hand in favor. Cat's went up readily, a grin on his hatchet face. Mead held up his good hand. Dumb Door, still unsure of his new place within the hoof, waited to see what Jackal would do. Warbler, too, was reluctant to vote.

"What do you say, War-boar?" Oats goaded, his own hand going up.

The old-timer shook his head and gave a little laugh of self-mockery. "Keep forgetting I get a say."

"You're a Bastard again," Jackal told him.

A mote of panic appeared in the old thrice's eyes as he considered. After a moment, he shook his head rapidly. "I say no. Too soon."

A knife seemed to sprout from the table next to Warbler's hand. All eyes snapped to the mongrel that had thrown the blade.

"Hand up," Hoodwink told Warbler evenly. "See her again."

"Oh, right," Polecat said, swinging a finger toward Oats. "He used to fuck your mother."

Oats came away from the fireplace just as Warbler stood up, both wearing the same threatening look. Polecat, sitting between two glaring thrice-bloods, bared his teeth sheepishly and mouthed an apology.

"Just vote for the old man, Hood, and let's get this done," Fetch said, trying and failing to hide a smile.

Hoodwink raised a finger languidly.

"Five to three," Jackal said. "Who wants to escort them home?"

Polecat bounded to his feet. "Me!"

"By the hells, you want some quim!" Fetching criticized.

Polecat nodded excitedly and thumped his knuckles on Mead's shoulder. "We'll both go!"

Jackal saw the younger half-orc hide his stump under the table, not looking at anyone.

"Ride with me," Polecat urged, sitting down next to him and leaning in. "The hogs the Fangs gave us are spirited. We would be at the Wallow in a few days. *And*. I wager, Cissy would go for being spitted between us."

"I would just slow you down," Mead protested.

With visible effort, Polecat managed not to make a jest. "Hogshit."

"You need to get back in the saddle," Fetch said.

"Plenty of one-handed riders, son," Warbler put in.

Jackal found Mead's eyes on him. "What are you looking at me for? Go if you want. Or don't. Your choice."

"I just thought . . ."

"We haven't voted a new chief yet, Mead," Jackal reminded him.

"Needs doing, though," Oats said pointedly.

Jackal shared a look with Warbler.

"Let's not rush a vote," the old thrice said. "It can wait until your . . . our folk get back."

Most of the hoof let it go at that, but Jackal could feel Fetching and Oats eyeing him, while Hoodwink gave Warbler a passive, yet fixed look.

Polecat rode out with Mead as soon as their gear was gathered. Mead was unsteady in the saddle at first, but had begun to adjust before he was even out of sight.

Winsome had been left untended since before the Betrayer Moon. Houses needed to be swept out and vermin chased away before the villagers returned, but that could wait a day. For now, the hoof was ready and eager to relax. Hoodwink went hunting, while Dumb Door, unaccustomed to sleeping in a bed, snored loudly on the floor of the orphanage.

"That's the most noise I've heard him make," Fetch said in a hush as she, Oats, and Jackal crept out to scrounge some wine. The cooper's shop next door provided and they sat on the roof, passing the bottle for a while in silence.

"You going to tell us why you're dragging your heels on the chief vote?" Oats finally asked, handing the wine to his left so Fetch could take a pull.

"Not dragging," Jackal said, waiting for the bottle to come his way.

"Hogshit," Fetch said, smiling as she turned it over. Jackal felt her fingers slide off his and was all too aware of their thighs touching.

"After all that's happened? With the Claymaster? You two think a chief is what this hoof needs?"

"Yes," Oats replied without thought.

But Fetch considered the question. "The people of Winsome will need one, Jack. The Kiln's gone. They're not going to feel safe. Having a leader is going to be necessary for those that do return or they won't remain. Besides, what are the other hoofs going to think if the Grey Bastards don't have a chief?"

"I don't know," Jackal said, drinking.

Fetch robbed him of the bottle before he could take another pull and then refused to hand it over to Oats. A tugging match ensued, with Fetch defending her prize while being assailed from either side. Try as they might, Jackal and Oats could not pry the bottle from her agile and laughing form. At last, she allowed Oats to win. He finished the bottle in one long guzzle while Jackal and Fetch groaned at him. Flushed with wine, Jackal watched Fetch bite down on her lower lip, trying not to speak, but the words were building on her tongue and would not be imprisoned.

They came out in a drunken giggle. "Warbler and Beryl are going to fuck so hard when she gets back."

Oats spewed off the roof.

Jackal erupted with laughter. "Oh, hells! It's true! Remember the noise they used to make?"

Crying and shaking, Fetch nodded adamantly.

"Shit on you both," Oats complained, his beard full of red droplets. "I'm going to push you off."

Fetch was struggling to breathe. "Remember Warbler? When he would finish?"

Jackal launched into an imitation, sounding something akin to a dying bear. Fetch pointed and reeled back into Oats, who was fighting a growing smile.

"Damn," the thrice said. "I'm gonna take Ugfuck on a really long patrol when they get back."

Soon, the three of them were laughing so hard, Dumb Door

emerged from the orphanage, roused from slumber, to glare up at them.

"Come join us!" Jackal said, inviting the mute mongrel with a wave of his arm.

"We're out of wine," Fetch pointed out.

"I'll find more," Jackal volunteered, and made his way down.

He was rummaging through one of the vintners' cellars when Warbler found him. Turning around at the sound of the old thrice coming down the ladder, Jackal held up a bottle and wobbled it questioningly. Warbler declined with a wave of his hand, propping himself against one of the lower rungs. They looked at each other for a moment, neither speaking. At last, Warbler took a deep breath.

"The hoof is starting to think there is going to be a contest between us for the chief's seat," he said.

"There won't," Jackal replied simply.

"I know," Warbler said. "You still sure about this?"

"I could ask you the same."

"And I would say no, being truthsome. Besides none of this is certain."

"It's the best decision for the hoof, War-boar."

"They might not see it that way."

"They will. You'll see. Now, if you will kindly remove your rump from the ladder, these bottles are sorely needed."

Warbler moved out of the way with a grin.

Jackal put a foot on the lower rung. "You are welcome to join us. Of course, you might not want to carouse too much. Save your strength."

"For what?" Warbler asked frowning.

Smiling, Jackal began climbing the ladder and did his impression of the dying bear.

That night, head pleasantly humming, he bedded down on the cot he had pulled out onto the portico of the orphanage. The air was hot and pregnant with the constant song of cicadas. He slept fitfully, the wine unable to drown the dreams of orcs on the march. He was awoken by a more pleasant dream, yet one he feared would come true. And feared it would not.

Fetching crawled atop him, clothed only in silence. The warmth of her smooth skin was cool compared with the night's heat. The simple weight of her hardened him and he slid in before he was fully aware. Her mouth found his, her tongue languid and searching. It was over embarrassingly, blissfully, quick. She bit at his neck and grinned as he continued to pulsate. They lay together, and Jackal reveled in the slight breeze cooling the sweat that had formed in the crease between their bodies.

"I grew tired of waiting for you," she whispered.

"Wasn't sure. Last time was . . ."

"I know," she said, absolving him. "I didn't know either. Most nights, we've been on patrol. And when we were here, it didn't seem right with Mead hurt. Be like cutting his cods off along with his hand if he found out."

"And Oats?" Jackal added. "No telling what he would do."

"Nothing," Fetch laughed. "Who do you think dared me to come out here?"

Jackal shifted to look at her, seeing little more than the line of her exquisite jaw and the slivers of moonlight in her eyes. "You're jesting."

"I'm not. He said I was a lily if I didn't try."

"That still works? He said the same thing when we were children to get you to try and ride Border Lord."

"Oh, I remember. I remember the broken collarbone too."

Jackal smiled in the night, the fond thoughts of the past pushing his mind to the unknown future. He ran his fingers gently down Fetching's spine. The motion, the affection, came more naturally than he wanted to ponder. He tried only to think about the moment, to live in the presence of the breeze and the cicadas and the feel of Fetch's stomach against his. He tried not to think about how all this must end, and soon.

"You are not allowed to brood," Fetch chided, lifting herself up.

"What am I allowed then?"

She shrugged. "Sleep. But you're a lily if you do." She revolved her hips in a wonderfully torturous way.

Jackal sat up and kissed her fiercely, their arms entwining. Rolling her beneath him, he bent to the task of not sleeping.

It was another twelve days before Polecat and Mead returned with Winsome's inhabitants. Jackal and Fetch spent much of that time together, sneaking off and fooling no one. When Polecat rode in ahead of the main group, their time was over and they both knew it. Fetching pulled Jackal into an empty house and they sacrificed all that had become so recently familiar in a final, desperate coupling. They emerged just ahead of the tired folk. Hogs carried some of the slopheads and donkeys some of the villagers, but most were walking. They flowed sore-footed into their village and the hoof turned out to meet them.

Fewer villagers returned than Jackal had hoped, but they lost fewer slops than he anticipated. Only four of the hopefuls chose to test their worthiness with the Tusked Tide. Biro was one of them. Jackal could not judge the youth harshly. The Grey Bastards were not the hoof they once were. Cissy returned, much to Polecat's satisfaction, as did Thistle, both helping herd the flock of orphans who ran back to their home with gleeful enthusiasm. Beryl walked at the rear of that shrieking gaggle, leading a lone, wide-gaited child by the hand.

"Thank all the gods I can't name," Oats declared at seeing Wily alive.

Jackal sighed in agreement. As they walked down the dusty avenue to meet Beryl, they saw that the little thrice was already wearing bandages to conceal his affliction.

"Most of the other children won't play with him anymore," Beryl confessed softly as she embraced them both.

Jackal gave Oats a knowing look. "Well, who needs them when you've got—"

"Bears and Mountains!" Oats bellowed, stooping to hoist Wily into the air and planting him astride his massive shoulders. The thrice-bloods went away together, the little one giggling from the furthest reaches of his round belly as the big one bounded and hollered.

Beryl watched them play, a small, tremulous smile on her face. "He's in pain, Jackal. You wouldn't know it to look at that joyful face, but he is."

"You need some rest," Jackal told her. "But I should warn you, there is someone here that wants to see you."

"Mead told me," Beryl said, her face tight with a bevy of controlled emotions. "Where is he?"

"Waiting by the farrier's well. If you would rather wait, I can tell him later would be best."

Beryl shook her head. "No. Waiting isn't much of a virtue."

Jackal had never laid eyes upon a queen, wouldn't know it if he had, but if they carried themselves with any less strength than the half-breed matron walking away from him, they weren't worthy of any regal title.

There was no more putting it off. Jackal spread the word that the hoof would meet after sundown in the cooper's shop, one of many that would remain empty because its proprietor had chosen not to return.

Perched atop barrels and lounging on half-finished coffins, the mongrels waited for everyone to arrive. Polecat was the straggler, still out of breath and lacing his breeches. There was some good-natured ridicule and shaking of heads, but then everyone settled, every face reflecting the importance of the meet. There was no table, no voting axes, no stump, no chief's seat. Just eight sworn brethren sitting in a rough cluster. Jackal had placed himself on a workbench, no more prominent than the others, yet he found all eyes looking at him.

"We are here to select a new chief," he said, accepting that he had to speak first. "Likely, most of you know who you want leading this hoof. I know my mind is made up. But before we vote, there are some things you need to hear."

Jackal looked at Warbler and the attention in the room shifted.

The old thrice took a deep breath, remaining seated as he spoke.

"I helped found this hoof. Hells, in some ways I helped found them all. I remember the day we laid the first stone of the Kiln. I followed our chief loyally for years, until I began to see what he was becoming. After a time, I wanted to lead the Grey Bastards, felt it was my duty. I still do." Warbler paused for a moment, seemed to lose his thoughts. He ran a hand through his thick, white hair. "None of you truly know me, saving Hoodwink, but I have been struggling to save this hoof for longer than some of you have been alive. It was a damn fool thing to try. One mongrel can't do it. A hoof has to survive as a hoof. The Grey Bastards are far from saved, though we have been freed from the Claymaster's madness. I'm proud to be back where I belong, where my heart always was. I could lead this hoof. I could, and do it well. But there is another duty for me. Far more important. One mongrel can't save a hoof, but one mongrel can save one child."

The room was still.

"I am taking Wily to live at Dog Fall," Warbler continued with a small, hopeful smile. "The Tines have agreed to try and help him, rid him of that damn plague. I don't know a heap of hogshit about wizardry, but the elves do. They think that, in time, they can cure him. If not, they have assured me they can do what that swaddlehead did, and force the plague to move."

"Into you?" Mead said.

Warbler nodded. "They suspect it can go from one thrice into another. Something about how the Tyrkanian . . . crafted it."

"Then I should be the one to go," Oats insisted. "That backy tub wanted to put it in me. Stop laughing, Polecat!"

"You can't go, Oats," Jackal said. "Warbler knows the Tine tongue. You don't."

"Still doesn't account for him being allowed to enter Dog Fall," Mead said. "The Tines are known for rarely allowing other elves within their land, much less two half-orcs."

"We understand less about their ways than we think," Warbler said. "They took in those elves I brought out of the marsh, and not one of them was a Tine. They trust me, as far as they can, I think. Even if they don't, I suspect they know how important the plague still is to protecting the Lots. Perhaps they're simply using me. Either way, they have agreed to allow the three of us to come live in their gorge."

Polecat's brow creased. "Three?"

Warbler looked at Oats. "It's the other reason you can't go, Idris. Your mother would never allow you to take on that sickness."

"Beryl's going with you?" Fetching asked, wearing a bemused smile.

"Do you think she would be separated from the boy?" Warbler returned.

Mead looked at Jackal. "How? How did you get them to agree to this?"

"They didn't take much convincing," Jackal admitted. "Warbler's right. The Tines know the importance of the plague. It's dangerous. And useful. We're lucky the orcs did not proceed with the Incursion. If they had, we wouldn't have been able to stop them. Until Ul-wundulas is stronger, more united, the plague is necessary. We also gave the Tines something they wanted. Revenge on those who were delivering elf slaves to the Sludge Man. Sancho and the bog trotter himself are dead. But there was one more still alive. Captain Ignacio. Warbler told the Tines about him. They were eager to pursue. Likely he is seeing Dog Fall at this very moment, but he will never leave alive."

Warbler blew out his cheeks. "So there it is, lads . . . and Fetch. I can't lead the Grey Bastards, much as I want to, but I would be grateful to remain sworn to the hoof."

"Vote it," Oats barked. "Hands up to let the old man call himself a Bastard while languishing in the Umber Mountains!"

Every hand went high.

"Hells, War-boar," Fetching teased, "you only had Hood's vote anyway."

"No," Polecat said lightly. "I was going to throw for him. Sorry, Jack. Now, if *you* had been fucking Oats's mother . . ."

An empty bucket went down over Cat's head and Oats drummed hard on the sides.

As the raucous laughter reached its pitch, Oats yelled gleefully over the ruckus.

"Jackal as chief! Hands up!"

There was a shout of approval and the vote went up, every arm raised save for Warbler's, who looked at Jackal solidly. Fetch caught that look before the rest.

"I'm leaving," Jackal said, meeting her eyes.

The hoof, hearing his words, grew silent.

Oats's smile vanished. "What?"

"I'm leaving," Jackal repeated, louder. "I can't be chief."

"The fuck you can't," Oats declared.

Fetch was horribly silent.

Jackal swept the Grey Bastards. "This hoof has a long ride ahead. If I am with you, leading you, we won't survive. Hispartha wants my head. Bermudo had already sent word to powerful nobles about me, and that was before I escaped from the castile and killed their wizard. As a nomad, they have little hope in finding me."

"So you're running to save your hide?"

It was Fetch, her teeth clenched.

"To help this hoof," Jackal replied. "You are going to need Hispartha's aid to build a stronghold. With me in your ranks, they will never trade with you. And it's not just the blue bloods up north who demand payment from me. Brethren, I don't know what Zirko truly did to me, but I can tell you his hold is real. I made a bargain, willingly, and it saved my life, more than once. I cannot escape my pledge to stand at Strava. The Betrayer Moon will find me there until I am dead, that much has been proven. But it goes deeper than that. Zirko may demand more of me, and if he does, I will not have a choice. You don't need a chief that is pulled away by the whims of a priest.

"But most important. I cannot remain because I have to find Crafty. So long as he's alive, we are not safe. The Lots are not safe. I won't have us rebuild all we have lost only to have him return and pull it all down. He came to us and the Claymaster welcomed him, brought him into our midst, but we allowed it . . . I allowed it. I rode with him, fought with him, even grew to think of him as a friend. But one of us saw the wizard for what he was from the very start and cautioned me against him. One of us put the lives of the hoof before all other loyalties. That is the one you need leading you. That is the one I now raise my hand for."

Jackal stood and put his hand up.

"Fetching."

She looked sharply up at him, thinking, for a heartbeat, she was being mocked, but then she saw the stolid resolve he directed at her and grew very still.

"You are the best shot in the hoof," he told her, not looking at the reactions of the others nor caring. "You are the fiercest fighter we have. Fearless. Bold. Frightening. The Tines know you carry their blood. Our alliance with them will strengthen once they see your existence does not sully them, but honors them. And they *will* see it, because you will show them, as chief. You are not charmed by wizards nor cowed by Hispartha. You would spit into the eye of every noble they have with a thrumbolt if they dared challenge you, as you did the day you killed that cavalero. Let Hispartha chase me for that crime, while the true threat grows stronger, bringing this hoof back from the brink with her leadership.

"Grey Bastards, I call a vote! Fetching for our chief!"

Looking beyond him, Fetch produced a wry smile. "Their hands were already in the air, Jack."

Turning, Jackal found she was right.

"Mine was up right after yours, brother," Oats said.

Fetch stood and looked at her hoof. "You fool-asses going to do what I say?"

"Oh, yes," Polecat said, his eyes glazing. "Anything. You tell me to lick your quim and I will serve without question."

"If I need that done, I'll ask Cissy," Fetch returned. "She tells me you're hopeless at it."

Laughter boomed through the cooper's shop, needling Polecat.

"So," Jackal addressed Fetch when all was calm, "do I have your leave to ride alone, yet still call myself a Grey Bastard?"

Fetching's eyes narrowed. "No."

The silence stiffened and Jackal lowered his eyes.

"None of you do," Fetch declared. "The Grey Bastards were the Claymaster's hoof. We need to leave that behind." She looked at Jackal and Warbler. "In honor of the two mongrels that challenged our founder and, even in defeat, stayed loyal, I say we become what they always remained. True Bastards."

Jackal glanced at Warbler.

"It's a good name," the old thrice said, clearing his throat against rising emotion.

Fetch put a hand on their shoulders. "And these two, no matter where they go, will forever be members of our hoof. Brothers, if you're opposed, stick a knife in that table."

No one moved.

Fetch winked at Jackal. "There's your answer."

"Thank you."

"When will you leave?" she asked, keeping her voice steady.

"Dawn."

The True Bastards spent the night in celebration with the people of Winsome. At last, the last jug was drained, the last echoes of song and laughter faded. Jackal went to his usual spot and lay there, sleepless, until the sky began to brighten. It was an uninviting sight.

She had not come to him, nor he to her, though he fought the urge with every long moment. Unwilling to listlessly watch the impending pain of the day draw closer, Jackal rose and gathered his gear. The village slept as he made his furtive preparations. Walking to the stables, he saw a wain moving toward him, pulled by the massive, grunting form of Big Pox, the Claymaster's hog. Warbler and Beryl sat upon the seat, and the old thrice pulled the hog to a stop as Jackal approached. Peeking over the side, he found Wily asleep on a pallet amongst the supplies.

"Getting out before the others are awake," he said quietly.

"You too," Beryl said with a hint of reprimand.

Jackal smiled at her and looked at Warbler. "Not taking Mean Old Man?"

"Left him for you," the old thrice said. "A hog like that is wasted cooped up in a gorge. Besides, the point-ears are likely to force me to ride a harrow stag before long. That pig was born for the nomad life. He'll serve you well, wherever you go."

"I'll take good care of him," Jackal said. "And thank you."

Beryl leaned down and kissed him once, giving his face a fond pat as she withdrew. "We didn't make it out wholly unseen. You'll find two in the stables waiting to ambush you."

Jackal smiled and felt his heart flutter.

The wain continued on down the avenue.

Oats was already astride Ugfuck when Jackal entered the stables. It took him a moment to understand these were the two Beryl meant. He tried to mask his disappointment, but Oats caught it all the same.

"She isn't one for farewells, brother."

"That is true," Jackal agreed, pulling Mean Old Man's harness from a peg.

"Besides, she said watching us part was going to get all backy and she didn't want to see it."

Jackal hummed a laugh. Oats waited in silence for him to get his hog saddled. At last, he was mounted and ready, but he did not turn his hog toward the stable doors. Instead, he looked at Oats.

"You should stay here," he said.

Oats frowned. "Just keeping you company until the edge of the lot."

"You go too far and you won't come back."

"I know," Oats admitted. "Cornered me good, you cunning shit."

"She is going to need you at her side, Oats."

The thrice nodded once, sharply. "Then that's where I will be. Until you get back."

Urging his hog up alongside Ugfuck, Jackal leaned in the saddle and embraced his friend. Pulling away, they looked at each other for a moment.

"Hells," Oats groaned, "she was right."

Jackal laughed and clapped the thrice on the shoulder. "See you at the Betrayer."

"Fuck that! I'm letting someone else take a turn watching you get worshiped by waddlers, Arm of Cock-in-Hand."

Shaking his head as he turned away, Jackal spurred his hog out of the stables. As he rode down the avenue at a healthy trot, he saw Fetching standing on the roof of the cooper's shop. He did not pause, knowing it would be impossible to leave if he did. Her voice called down to him as he passed.

"Bring me a wizard's head back from Tyrkania!"

He waved. "Yes, chief!"

Leaving Winsome behind, he went east. Mean Old Man's gait was smooth and strong. He did not have Hearth's raw speed, but his girth felt solid, a deep well of endurance. The sun climbed higher and the heat of Ul-wundulas rose with the dust beneath the barbarian's hooves. Jackal's home grew more distant with each pounding step.

The unridden surface of the world lay ahead.

Acknowledgments

This book is even more of a mutt than its main characters are. It was inspired by *Sons of Anarchy*, Middle-earth, spaghetti westerns, and the history of Reconquista-era Spain. That makes Kurt Sutter, J. R. R. Tolkien, Sergio Leone, and El Cid the Bastards' beloved godfathers. I hope that enthusiasts of any/all these men will enjoy the homages and tips of the hat within this chimera of a fantasy, and that anyone who's enjoyed riding with the Bastards will be moved to spend more time with their illustrious ancestors. Only time and readers will determine whether these inspirations formed an endearing mongrel love-child or a monstrous abomination. I certainly hope it's the former.

The Bastards' ride into the world has been a complex one. A few will recall its days as a self-published book. To those few, I would like to express immense gratitude, especially to Thomas J. C. for becoming a fan and inviting me to the Grimdark Readers & Writers Facebook group. It was there that I discovered the SPFBO hosted by Mark Lawrence. Had my mongrels not entered that contest, their story would still exist, but their reach would not be what it is today.

To Mr. Lawrence, there is no amount of profound thanks I can offer that won't sound feeble or, worse, hyperbolic. But I must try. The SPFBO is a game-changer, for some it will be a life-changer. I firmly believe the contest's positive impact exists only because it is an extension of the open mind and generous heart that invented it. You're a damn fine man, Mark, and if we ever meet in person it's likely to get a touch backy.

Another in danger of an imminent, crushing man-hug is Julian Pavia, an editor who sent an email I thought was fake; a belief only truly dispelled when the female robot voice of my caller ID announced between rings, "Call from. Penguin, Random." I will likely remain ignorant of all his efforts on behalf of this book, but I can imagine they were immense. His feedback was beyond brilliant and the book is better for it. I am beyond thankful for his involvement, especially for putting me in contact with . . .

Cameron McClure, an agent who puts Burgess Meredith to shame as a cornerman. I used to cringe reading author acknowledgments that extolled the endless virtues of their agents, but I have drunk the Kool-Aid and am now converted. I can no longer imagine how I ever did this without her.

If there is a real-world hoof in my life, it is made up of my test readers. Once again, they rose to the challenge of scrutinizing this story. They earned hoof names this go-round. Thank you, "Shenanigans" Matt, "Grim" Rob, "Left Coast" James, "Doppelwulf" Chael, and Mom (no quotations needed).

Likely I have forgotten many fine folks, but True Bastard status is due:

To Angeline Rodriguez at Crown for putting fresh eyes on the story and for likely much else I know nothing about.

To Anna Jackson at Orbit UK for bringing the book across the pond and fulfilling my mother's dream that I one day be published in our former home.

To any and every reader that ever reached out with something positive to say (like Tony D. & Mike E.), your encouragement kept me writing when I wanted to quit.

To Lizbeth, for being on the team during the indie days.

To Chris & Angela (and by extension all of CONjuration), for predicting this book would "go places."

To Rick, thanks for being an open ear, a great friend, and a stellar uncle to my little boy.

To my fellow SPFBO entrants, especially Dyrk Ashton, Phil Tucker, and Josiah Bancroft, thanks for the continued camaraderie and commiseration.

To the SPFBO judges, with a scraping bow to Ria and a brisk high-five to Laura, much appreciation for taking the time to read and, shockingly, enjoy the grimy tale of these half-orc hog riders.

And miles ahead of the rest, much love and gratitude to my wife,

Liza, for convincing me the Bastards deserved a book. Without her, this story may have remained simply a creative exercise. Hopefully, darlin', there weren't too many days when you regretted encouraging me . . .

Finally, to Wyatt, my beautiful son. It will be many, many, *many* years before this particular book is appropriate for you, but you have my deepest gratitude for being a ceaseless source of joy during its creation.

Until next time,
Live in the saddle!

Look out for

THE TRUE BASTARDS

Book Two of the Lot Lands

by

Jonathan French

Back in the saddle!

Fetching was once the only female rider in the Lot Lands. Now she is the leader of her own hoof, a band of loyal half-orcs sworn to her command. But over a year has passed since the Claymaster's demise and the pitiless appetite of the Lots remains eager to consume everything she's struggled to protect. Her people are starving. Is the famine a harsh reality of life in the badlands or Crafty's vengeful sorcery at work? Either way, time is running out for the True Bastards.

With Hispartha reasserting its claims on the Lots and her fellow hoofmasters pressuring the Bastards to disband, Fetch is tested to the breaking point by the burdens of leadership. Fortunately, she's no stranger to battling the world, greeting these new threats with the same boundless spite and ferocity that made her a mongrel chieftain. Yet sharp steel and a strong hog are useless when an old enemy finds a way to strike from beyond the grave . . .

extras

www.orbitbooks.net

about the author

Jonathan French resides in Atlanta with his wife, son and cat. He is a devoted reader of comic books, an expert thrower of oddly-shaped dice and a serial con attendee.

Find out more about Jonathan French and other Orbit authors by registering for the free monthly newsletter at www.orbitbooks.net.

interview

When did you first start writing?

Creative writing assignments were the only ones I ever bothered with in school and I usually turned in much more than the teachers required. During my acting years, my college improv instructor flunked me because I was "A hopeless playwright" – meaning I wasn't using my feelings and being spontaneous so much as I was quickly scripting everything in my head and going from there. And then of course there were the roleplaying campaigns I wrote for my gaming group. As far as pursuing writing with a mind to a career, it didn't happen until 2008. In a bid to pursue professional theatre, I moved from Atlanta to Chicago… in February. I had little money, few friends, and HOLY SHIT IT WAS COLD! I started writing as a cheap and therapeutic way to fight boredom and loneliness. By that Christmas, the loneliness was alleviated by the woman that would become my wife, but the writing bug had bitten hard, so I kept at it until I finished my first novel.

Who are some of your most significant authorial influences?
As a reader, I'm a fan of many: Tad Williams, Tolkien, Terry Pratchett, but I can't honestly call them influences because I don't think I'm capable of their particular brands of artistry. The author that made me start writing seriously was Robert E. Howard. I had read Conan stories as a teen, but when Del Rey released his complete works scrubbed of all the garble pastiche writers had added to his stories over the years, I was bitten by how brilliant he truly was. It just ignited something in my head and I hit the keyboard with this sudden confidence. I'm also greatly influenced by Lloyd Alexander and Guy Gavriel Kay.

***How did you come up with the idea for* The Grey Bastards?**
It was a weird stew of ideas and I'm not confident I have the chronology straight, but I can hit the highlights. I was playing way too much D&D (fifth edition had just come out) and I was obsessed with painting any miniatures sculpted by Tre Manor, especially his orcs and half-orcs. At some point I was wearing a *Sons of Anarchy* T-shirt with the simple SAMCRO logo (fans of the show will know what this is). I looked down and, rather stupidly, noticed CRO spelled backwards was ORC and immediately conceptualised this T-shirt parody for gaming nerds that said HAFORC in the same font (sidebar: I firmly believe someone should still produce said shirt). So, I told my wife, "My next D&D game is going to be *Sons of Anarchy* with half-orcs." And she replied, "You mean on hogs

instead of…*hogs*?" And I said, "Yes," like it had been my plan all along (it wasn't). And she said, "Why do it as a game? Write the fucking book." So the more I thought about it, the more I thought it could work and I started pulling in ideas from Spaghetti Western films, many of which were filmed in Andalusia, Spain so that led me to the historical era of the Reconquista…then I just threw in a bunch of ripped half-orcs, foul language, violence, sexual humour, whisked liberally and…

Were there particular themes you wanted to explore in creating the world of the Lot Lands?

I wanted to present something that had the same dramatic, semi-historical grit I was seeing on shows like *Black Sails* and *Spartacus*, but with the fantasy elements I loved so much added to the mix. Bigotry, racism, and sexism were certainly a part of this world, so I was forced to face them down. I think the idea of a tightknit band of rough-around-the-edges outcasts trying to survive in a harsh environment will always resonate with me. On more meta level, I think I was on a personal crusade to get men reading again. At least in my home country of the USA, I felt there was an alarming trend of males (especially teens and twenty-somethings) having no interest in books. Video games, television, and film seemed to hold most of the male attention, so I set out to write a novel that resonated with the trends found in those mediums. Time will tell whether I was successful. And hells, I got no problems if the ladies love the book, as well!

If you had to pick one character from this novel, who is your favourite? Who was the most difficult to write?
Oats is easily my favourite. Mostly because he never gave me any problems. I always knew what he was going to say and how he was going to react. Plus, he's both over-estimated and underestimated at the same time; he's pretty vulnerable despite his size and strength, and also far from stupid despite initial appearances. PS My inspiration for him was a mix of Jayne Cobb (from my favourite TV show *Firefly*) and the late, great MMA fighter Kimbo Slice.

The most difficult to write was definitely Starling. I knew having a female character that was seemingly help-less through most of the book would cause trouble for some readers. But I was (and still am) playing a rather long game with her, so I kept the course despite second-guessing it on many, MANY occasions.

Go on, tell us – what would your half-Orc nickname be?
Man, tough one. The thing about nicknames is they're only good if given to you by someone that really knows you. I think that goes double for hoofnames since they have to be earned. I'd likely never make it out of the slopheads, being honest. But to play along, my wife asserts my hoof-name would be Malcontent, 'cause apparently I'm never happy about anything.

What can readers expect from the next story, The True Bastards?

Three words: Fetching in charge. More broadly, the next Bastards is a book about the immense burdens of leadership. Pulling the hoof out of the ruin left behind by Crafty and the Claymaster is not going to be an easy task. And what about this elven blood in Fetch's veins? Blessing? Curse? Also, more twists, more revelations, and lots more foul-mouthed mongrels killing shit!

if you enjoyed
THE GREY BASTARDS

look out for

YOU DIE WHEN YOU DIE

West of West: Book One

by

Angus Watson

YOU DIE WHEN YOU DIE . . .

You can't change your fate – so throw yourself into battle, because you'll either end the day a hero or drinking mead in the halls of the gods. That's what Finn's people believe. But Finn wants to live. When his settlement is massacred by a hostile nation, Finn plus several friends and rivals must make their escape across a brutal, unfamiliar landscape, and to survive, Finn will fight harder than he's ever fought before.

Chapter 1

Finnbogi Is in Love

Two weeks before everyone died and the world changed for ever, Finnbogi the Boggy was fantasising about Thyri Treelegs.

He was picking his way between water-stripped logs with a tree stump on one shoulder, heading home along the shore of Olaf's Fresh Sea. No doubt, he reasoned, Thyri would fall in love with him the moment he presented her with the wonderful artwork he was going to carve from the tree stump. But what would he make? Maybe a racoon. But how would you go about . . .

His planning was interrupted by a wasp the size of a chipmunk launching from the shingle and making a beeline for his face.

The young Hardworker yelped, ducked, dropped the stump and spun to face his foe. Man and insect circled each other crabwise. The hefty wasp bobbed impossibly in the air. Finnbogi fumbled his sax from its sheath. He flailed with the short sword, but the wasp danced clear of every inept swipe, floating closer and louder. Finnbogi threw his blade aside and squatted, flapping his hands above his head. Through his terror he realised that this manoeuvre was exactly the same as his rabbit-in-a-tornado impression that could make his young adoptive siblings giggle so much they fell over. Then he noticed he could no longer hear the wasp.

He stood. The great lake of Olaf's Fresh Sea glimmered

calmly and expansively to the east. To the west a stand of trees whispered like gossips who'd witnessed his cowardice in the face of an insect. Behind them, great clouds floated indifferently above lands he'd never seen. The beast itself – surely "wasp" was insufficient a word for such a creature – was flying southwards like a hurled wooden toy that had forgotten to land, along the beach towards Hardwork.

He watched until he could see it no longer, then followed.

Finnbogi had overheard Thyri Treelegs say she'd be training in the woods to the north of Hardwork that morning, so he'd donned his best blue tunic and stripy trousers and headed there in order to accidentally bump into her. All he'd found was the tree stump that he would carve into something wonderful for her, and, of course, the sort of wasp that Tor would have battled in a saga. He'd never seen its like before, and guessed it had been blown north by the warm winds from the south which were the latest and most pleasant phenomenon in the recent extraordinary weather.

If any of the others – Wulf the Fat, Garth Anvilchin or, worst of all, Thyri herself – had seen him throw away his sax and cower like Loakie before Oaden's wrath, they'd have mocked him mercilessly.

Maybe, he thought, he could tell Thyri that he'd killed the wasp? But she'd never believe how big it had been. What he needed to do was kill an animal known for its size and violence . . . That was it! That's how he'd win her love! He would break the Scraylings' confinement, venture west and track down one of the ferocious dagger-tooth cats that the Scraylings banged on about. It would be like Tor and Loakie's quest into the land of the giants, except that Finnbogi would be brawny Tor and brainy Loakie all rolled into one unstoppable hero.

The Scraylings were basically their captors, not that any Hardworker apart from Finnbogi would ever admit that.

Olaf the Worldfinder and the Hardworkers' other ancestors had arrived from the old world five generations before at the beginning of winter. Within a week the lake had frozen and the unrelenting snow was drifted higher than a longboat's mast. The Hardworkers had been unable to find food, walk anywhere or sail on the frozen lake, so they'd dug into the snow drifts and waited to die.

The local tribe of Scraylings, the Goachica, had come to their rescue, but only on two big conditions. One, that the Hardworkers learn to speak the universal Scrayling tongue and forsake their own language, and, two, that no Hardworker, nor their descendants, would ever stray further than ten miles in any direction from their landing spot.

It had been meant as a temporary fix, but some Scrayling god had decreed that Goachica continue to venerate and feed the Hardworkers, and the Hardworkers were happy to avoid foraging and farming and devote their days to sport, fighting practice, fishing, dancing, art or whatever else took their fancy.

Five generations later, still the Goachica gave them everything they needed, and still no Hardworker strayed more than ten miles from Olaf's landing spot. Why would they? Ten miles up and down the coast and inland from Olaf's Fresh Sea gave them more than enough space to do whatever they wanted to do. Few ever went more than a mile from the town.

But Finnbogi was a hero and an adventurer, and he was going to travel. If he were to break the confinement and track down a dagger-tooth cat . . . He'd be the first Hardworker to see one, let alone kill one, so if he dragged the monster home and made Thyri a necklace from its oversized fangs surely she'd see that he was the man for her? Actually, she'd prefer a knife to a necklace. And it would be easier to make.

A few minutes later Finnbogi started to feel as though he was being followed. He slowed and turned. There was nothing on the beach, but there was a dark cloud far to the north. For an alarming moment he thought there was another great storm on the way – there'd been a few groundshakers recently that had washed away the fishing nets and had people talking about Ragnarok ending the world – but then realised the cloud was a flock of crowd pigeons. One of the insanely huge flocks had flown over Hardwork before, millions upon millions of birds that had taken days to pass and left everything coated with pigeon shit. Finnbogi quickened his pace – he did not want to return to Hardwork covered in bird crap – and resumed his musings on Thyri.

He climbed over a bark-stripped log obstructing a narrow, sandy headland and heard voices and laughter ahead. Finnbogi knew who it was before he trudged up the rise in the beach and saw them. It was the gang of friends a few years older than he was.

Wulf the Fat ran into the sea, naked, waving his arms and yelling, and dived with a mighty splash. Sassa Lipchewer smiled at her husband's antics and Bodil Gooseface screeched. Bjarni Chickenhead laughed. Garth Anvilchin splashed Bodil and she screeched all the more.

Keef the Berserker stood further out in Olaf's Fresh Sea, his wet, waist-length blond hair and beard covering his torso like a sleeveless shirt. He swung his long axe, Arse Splitter, from side to side above the waves, blocking imaginary blows and felling imaginary foes.

Finnbogi twisted his face into a friendly smile in case they caught him looking. Up ahead their clothes and weapons were laid out on the shingle. Bodil and Sassa's neatly embroidered dresses were hanging on poles. Both garments would have been Sassa Lipchewer creations; she spent painstaking hours sewing, knitting and weaving the most stylish clothes in Hardwork. She'd made the blue tunic and stripy trousers that Finnbogi was wearing, for example, and very nice they were too.

The four men's clothes, tossed with manly abandon on the shingle, were leathers, plus Garth Anvilchin's oiled chain-mail. Garth's metal shirt weighed as much as a fat child, yet Garth wore it all day, every day. He said that it would rust if the rings didn't move against each other regularly so he had to wear it, and also he wanted to be totally comfortable when he was in battle.

In battle! Ha! The Hird's only battles were play fights with each other. The likelihood of them seeing real action was about the same as Finnbogi travelling west and taking on a dagger-tooth cat. He knew the real reason Garth wore the mail shirt all the time. It was because he was a prick.

Despite the pointlessness of it, many of the hundred or so Hardworkers spent much time learning to fight with the weapons brought over from the old world. All four of the bathing men were in the Hird, the elite fighting group comprising Hardwork's ten best fighters.

Finnbogi *had* expected to be asked to join the Hird last summer when someone had become too old and left, but Jarl Brodir had chosen Thyri Treelegs. That had smarted somewhat, given that she was a girl and only sixteen at the time – two years younger than him. It was true that she had been making weapons, practising moves and generally training to be a warrior every waking hour since she was about two, so she probably wouldn't be a terrible Hird member. And he supposed it was good to see a woman included.

All Hardwork's children learnt the reasons that Olaf the Worldfinder and Hardwork's other founders had left the east, sailed a salty sea more vast than anyone of Finnbogi's generation could supposedly imagine, then travelled up rivers and across great lakes to establish the settlement of Hardwork. Unfair treatment of women was one of those reasons. So it was good that they were finally putting a woman in the Hird, but it was a shame that it had robbed Finnbogi of what he felt was his rightful place. Not that he wanted to be in the stupid Hird anyway, leaping about and waving weapons around all day. He had better things to do.

Out to sea, Wulf the Fat dived under – he could stay down for an age – and Garth Anvilchin caught sight of Finnbogi on the beach. "Hey, Boggy!" he shouted, "Don't even think about touching our weapons or I'll get one of the girls to beat you up!"

Finnbogi felt himself flush and he looked down at the weapons – Garth's over-elaborately inlaid hand axes the Biter Twins, Bjarni's beautiful sword Lion Slayer, Wulf's thuggish hammer Thunderbolt and Sassa's bow which wasn't an old world weapon so it didn't have a name.

"And nice outfit!" yelled Garth. "How lovely that you dress up when you go wanking in the woods. You have to treat your hand well when it's your only sexual partner, don't you, you curly-haired cocksucker?"

Finnbogi tried to think of a clever comeback based on the idea that if he sucked cocks then he clearly had more sexual partners than just his hand, but he didn't want to accept and develop the him-sucking-cocks theme.

"Fuck off then, Boggy, you're spoiling the view," Garth added before any pithy reply came to Finnbogi, curse him to Hel. Garth might be stupid but he had all the smart lines.

"Leave him alone," said Sassa Lipchewer. Finnbogi reddened further. Sassa was lovely.

"Yes, Garth," Bodil piped up. "Come for a wash, Finnbogi!"

"Yes, Boggy boy! Clean yourself off after all that wanking!" Garth laughed.

Wulf surfaced and smiled warmly at Finnbogi, the sun glinting off his huge round shoulders. "Come on in, Finn!" he called. Finally, somebody was calling him by the name he liked.

"Come in, Finn!" Bodil called. "Come in, Finn! Come in, Finn!" she chanted.

Sassa beckoned and smiled, which made Finnbogi gibber a little.

Behind them, Keef, who hadn't acknowledged Finnbogi's presence, continued to split the arses of imaginary enemies with his axe Arse Splitter.

"I can't swim now, I've got to . . . um . . ." Finnbogi nodded at the stump on his shoulder.

"Sure thing, man, do what you've got to do, see you later!" Wulf leapt like a salmon and disappeared underwater.

"Bye, Finn!" shouted Bodil. Sassa and Bjarni waved. Garth, towering out of the water, muscular chest shining, smiled and looked Finnbogi up and down as if he knew all about the wasp, why he was wearing his best clothes and what he had planned for the stump.

"I don't know why you give that guy any time . . ." he heard Garth say as he walked away.

He didn't know why the others gave any time to Garth Anvilchin. He was *such* a dick. They were okay, the rest of them. Wulf the Fat had never said a mean word to anyone. Bjarni Chickenhead was friendly and happy, Sassa Lipchewer was lovely. And Bodil Gooseface . . . Bodil was Bodil, called Gooseface not because she looked like a goose, but because Finnbogi had once announced that she had the same facial expressions as a clever goose, which she did, and the name had stuck. Finnbogi felt a bit bad about that, but it wasn't his fault that he was so incisively observant.

He walked on, composing cutting replies to Garth's cocksucking comments. The best two were "Why don't you swim out to sea and keep on swimming?" and "Spoiling the view am I? You're the only person here with a good view because you're not in it!"

He wished he'd thought of them at the time.

Chapter 2

A Scrayling City

Three hundred and fifty miles to the south of Hardwork, Chamberlain Hatho marched through the main western gateway of Calnia, capital of the Calnian empire and greatest city in the world. After almost a year away, the teeming industry of his home town was such a joyful shock that he stopped and shook his head. Had he been one of Calnia's uncouth Low, he would have gawped and possibly cursed.

He inhaled slowly through his nose to calm himself, swelling his chest with sweet Calnian air. By Innowak the Sun God and the Swan Empress herself, Calnia was an impressive sight.

As the Swan Empress Ayanna's ambassador to the other empires, Chamberlain Hatho had travelled thousands of miles. Some of the cities he'd seen did in fact rival Calnia in size and splendour, but for the last few weeks he'd been travelling by dog-drawn travois and boat through less sophisticated lands. The greatest settlements he'd seen for a good while had been casual collections of crooked cabins, tents and other meagre dwellings. Staying in those village's finest lodgings had made Chamberlain Hatho itch all over. How did the Low live like such animals?

"Chippaminka, does Calnia not rise above every other town and city like an elk towering over a herd of deermice?"

His young alchemical bundle carrier and bed mate Chippaminka gripped his arm and pressed her oiled torso against his flank.

"It is truly amazing," she replied, her bright eyes satisfyingly widened.

He held the girl at arm's length. She was wearing a breechcloth embroidered with an exquisite porcupine-quill swan, the gold swan necklace that he'd given her to reflect light and her new allegiance to Innowak the Sun God, and nothing else. She held his gaze with a coquettish smile then licked her top lip.

He had to look away.

He was pleased with his new alchemical bundle carrier. Very pleased. The woman who'd fulfilled the role previously had disappeared early on his embassy, in the great port town at the mouth of the Water Mother. Walking along, he'd turned to ask her something and she hadn't been there. He'd never seen her again.

That evening a serving girl had seen he was morose and claimed her dancing would cheer him up. He'd told her to clear off and protested as she'd started to dance anyway, but his angry words had turned to dry squeaks as her sinuous slinkiness, smouldering smile and sparkling eyes had stunned him like a snake spellbinding a squirrel.

At the end of her dance he'd asked Chippaminka to be his new alchemical bundle carrier. She'd been at his side ever since. She was the perfect companion. She knew when he needed to eat, when he wanted time on his own, when to let him sleep, when to talk, when to stay silent and, most joyfully of all, when to make love and how to leave him smiling for hours.

Chamberlain Hatho was forty-five years old. He'd always thought that love was at best a delusion, at worst an affectation. But now he knew what love was. Chippaminka had shown him. At least once every waking hour and often in his dreams, he thanked Innowak that he'd met her.

She gripped his hand. "It is a wonderful city. But what are all these people *doing*?"

He pointed out the various stations of industry that lined the road running into the city from the western gate. "Those are knappers knapping flint, then there are metalworkers heating and hammering copper, lead and iron nuggets dug from soil to the north. Next are tanners curing skins with brains, marrow and liver, then there are artisans working with shells, clay, marble, feathers, chert, porcupine quills, turquoise and all manner of other materials to create tools, pipes, baskets, carvings, beads, pottery and more. That next group are tailors who sew, knit, twine, plait and weave cotton, bark fibres and wool from every furry animal in the Swan Empress's domain."

"They seem so *diligent*. They must be very intelligent."

"On the contrary," smiled Chamberlain Hatho. "These are the Low, the simple people who perform mundane but skilled roles so that people like me – and you, dear Chippaminka – might soar higher than our fellow men and women."

The girl nodded. "What are those Low doing?" She pointed at a team of women spraying white clay paint from their mouths in ritualistic unison onto leather shields.

"They are using paint and saliva as alchemy to create magic shields."

"Magic! Whatever next?"

Chamberlain Hatho surveyed the wondrous, teeming array of sophisticated industry and nodded proudly. "Yes, you must find it simply amazing; like something from one of your tribe's legends, I should imagine. And this is just the artisan quarter. As you'll see when we explore, there are thousands of others beavering away throughout Calnia, all dedicated to the tasks essential for keeping a city of twenty-five thousand people clothed, fed and ruling over the empire."

"So many?"

"The empire stretches north and south from Calnia for hundreds of miles along the eastern side of the Water Mother, so, yes, that many are needed."

"And what are those mountains, Chamberlain Hatho?"

Chippaminka nodded at the dozens of flat-topped pyramids rising from the Low's pole and thatch dwellings like lush islands in a muddy sea. The flanks of the largest were coated with a solid-hued black clay and topped with gold-roofed buildings blazing bright in the sun.

"They are pyramids, constructions of great magic that house Calnia's finest. The highest is the Mountain of the Sun, where we are headed now to see the Swan Empress Ayanna herself. You see that pyramid behind it?"

"The little one on the right? The much less impressive one?"

"Yes . . . That is my pyramid. It is not as high as the Mountain of the Sun, but broad enough that its summit holds my own house, slave dormitory and sweat lodge. It is where we will live."

"*We?*"

"If you will consent to live with me?" He felt the surge of fear, that terrible fear that had grown with his love, as if Innowak could not allow love without fear. The terror that Chippaminka might leave him dizzied him and loosened his bowels.

"I would *love* to live with you," she said and he resisted the urge to jump and clap. That would not look good in front of the Low. He'd never known such a swing of emotions was possible. He'd been terrified. Now, because of a few words from a girl, he had never been happier. Had humans always been so complicated, he wondered, or had the Calnians reached a pinnacle of cultural sophistication which was necessarily accompanied by such conflicting and high emotion?

"Come, let us report to the empress, then you will see your new home."

He headed off along the road with Chippaminka half walking, half dancing to keep up. Her dancing walk was one of the thousand things he loved about her.

He wrinkled his nose at the acrid whiff from the tanners and turned to Chippaminka. She'd already delved into the alchemical bundle and was holding out a wad of tobacco to render the stench bearable. He opened his mouth and she popped it in, fingers lingering on his lips for an exquisite moment. He squashed the tobacco ball between his molars, then pressed it into his cheek with his tongue. Its sharp taste banished the foul smell immediately.

Industry banged, chimed and scraped around them like a serenading orchestra and the joy in his heart soared to harmonise with its euphoric tune.

Ahead on the broad road children who'd been playing with bean shooters, pipestone animals, wooden boats and other toys cleared the way and watched open-mouthed as he passed. As well they might. It was not every day that the Chamberlain, the second equal most important person in Calnia, walked among them. Moreover, his demeanour, outfit and coiffure were enough to strike awe into any that saw him.

Chippaminka had plucked the hair from his face and the back of his head with fish-bone tweezers that morning. Tweezers gave a much fresher look than the barbaric shell-scraping method of the Low. Long hair fanned out like a downward pointing turkey tail from the nape of his neck, stiffened with bear fat and red dye. The hair on the top of his head was set into a spiked crown with elk fat and black dye, enhanced by the clever positioning of the black feathers plucked from living magnificent split tail birds. He could have used ravens' feathers, but those were for the Low. Magnificent split tail birds were long-winged creatures that soared on the tropical airs in the sea to the south. Young men and women would prove their skill and bravery by collecting feathers from the adult birds without harming them. It was nigh on impossible, so the feathers were fearfully valuable;

the six in Chamberlain Hatho's hair were worth more than the collected baubles of every Low in Calnia.

His breechcloth was the supplest fawn leather, his shoes the toughest buffalo. The crowning garment was as wonderful as any of Empress Ayanna's robes, commissioned in a fit of joy the day after he'd met Chippaminka. Six artisans had worked on it for months while he'd travelled south. It was a cape in the shape of swans' wings, inlaid with twenty-five thousand tiny conch beads. The whole was to honour the Swan Empress, with each bead representing one citizen in her capital city. He hoped it would impress her.

Despite his splendid cape, his most subtle adornment was his favourite. It was his strangulation cord. He hoped that he would die before Empress Ayanna. However, if she were to die before him, he would be strangled with the cord of buffalo leather that he'd tanned himself, cut and worn around his neck ever since. He might love Chippaminka with all his heart, but that did not dim his devotion to Ayanna, Swan Empress and worldly embodiment of the Sun God Innowak who flew across the sky every day, bathing the world in warmth and light.

"Will we be safe from the weather now that we are here, Chamberlain Hatho?" Chippaminka asked. Their journey had been plagued by mighty storms. They'd seen two tornados larger than any he'd heard of and passed through a coastal town which had been destroyed by a great wave two days before. The root of the astonishing weather was the chief finding of Chamberlain Hatho's mission. He hoped that Empress Ayanna already knew about it and, more importantly, had laid plans to deal with it.

"Yes," he said. "You will always be safe with me."

They passed from the industrial zone into the musicians' quarter, where the air vibrated and shook with the music of reed trumpets, deer-hoof and tortoise-shell rattles, clappers, flutes and a variety of drums. A choir started up. The singers held a high note then stepped progressively lower, in a sophisticated, well-practised harmony so beautiful that every hair that Chippaminka hadn't plucked from Chamberlain Hatho's body stood on end.

Two other voices rang out, sounding almost exactly like screams of terror. Hatho looked about for the source, intending to admonish them and to have them executed if they did not apologise to a satisfactorily fawning degree.

Instead, his mouth dropped open.

Several of the choir had stone axes in their hands and were attacking other singers. It was no musicians' squabble over a muddled melody; these were full-strength, killer blows to the head. Blood was spraying. Time slowed as a chunk of brain the size and colour of a heartberry arced through the air and splatted onto Chamberlain Hath's eye-wateringly valuable cape.

Further along the road, more men and women were producing weapons and setting about unarmed musicians and other Low. By their look, the attackers were Goachica.

Chamberlain Hatho guessed what was happening. This was the Goachica strike that he'd warned about for years. The northern province of Goachica had been part of the Calnian empire for two hundred years. Many Goachica lived and worked in Calnia. One of Hatho's direct underlings – which made her one of the highest ranking people in Calnia – was Goachica.

Five years before, a few Goachica had stopped paying tribute. This happened every now and then in the empire and it was simple to deal with. You either flattered the rebels into restarting their payments with a visit from a high official such as himself, or you found the ringleader or ringleaders and tortured him, her or them to death in front of the rest.

However, the previous emperor, Zaltan, had overreacted with the Goachica. He'd sent an army with the orders to kill all who'd withheld taxes. Dozens of Goachica had failed to give tribute only because Goachica's leaders had told their tax collectors not to collect it. To any objective eye these people were as near to innocent as makes no difference; many even had the bags of wild rice that was Goachica's main contribution stacked and ready to go to Calnia.

The Calnian army had killed the lot of them.

Many relatives and friends of the slain Goachica lived in Calnia and many more had moved there since. Chamberlain Hatho had warned that these people would make trouble and advocated either apologising and giving reparations, or slaughtering them. Other issues, however, had taken precedence, not least Ayanna slaying Zaltan and becoming empress herself.

Because the massacre was entirely Zaltan's doing, and because actions like that one had been the chief reason for his assassination, people had thought the Goachica would have forgiven Calnia. Chamberlain Hatho's had warned that this was unlikely. He was less happy than usual to be proven correct.

To his right, several of the choir were fighting back with their instruments as weapons and the attackers were held.

Up ahead, he saw to his relief, three of the Owsla – Malilla Leaper, Sitsi Kestrel and the Owsla's captain, Sofi Tornado – had appeared. They were making short work of the attackers.

Malilla Leaper leapt over a man, braining him with her heavy kill staff as she flew. Sitsi Kestrel was standing on a roof, legs planted wide, her huge eyes picking targets, her bow alive in her hands as she loosed arrow after arrow. Sofi Tornado was dancing like a leaf in a gale, dodging attacks and felling Goachica with forehand and backhand blows from her hand axe. They said that Sofi could see a second into the future, which made her impossible to kill. Certainly none of the attacking Goachica came close to landing a blow on her.

Chamberlain Hatho felt a thrill to see the Owsla again. He had been ashamed when Emperor Zaltan created an elite squad based on his perverted desire for seeing attractive young women hurting and killing people in varied, often grim ways. However, the Owsla had proven to be a fearsomely effective squad of killers. More than that, the unbeatable ten had come to symbolise the success, power and beauty of Calnia.

Just as their chief god Innowak had tricked Wangobok and stolen the sun, so Calnia's rise to power had begun with alchemy-charged warriors rising up and freeing the ancient Calnians from imperial tyrants. Now Calnia ruled its own, much larger empire and the Owsla were its cultural and martial pinnacle; the beautiful, skilful, magical deterrent that kept peace across the empire. No chief dared antagonise Ayanna, knowing that a visit from the Calnian Owsla could follow.

There was a roar as a crowd of Goachica warriors rushed from a side street and charged the three Owsla.

Chamberlain Hatho gulped. Surely even Sofi Tornado, Malilla Leaper and Sitsi Kestrel would be overwhelmed by such a number? This was a much larger attack than he'd imagined the Goachica capable of.

He turned to Chippaminka, determined to save her. Their escape lay back the way they had come, surely, into the industrial sector where the Low craftspeople would be better armed and more inclined to fight than the musicians.

Chippaminka smiled at him sweetly, the same look she gave him before they made love. Had she not seen what was happening?

Her arm flashed upwards and he felt something strike his neck. A gout of blood splashed onto Chippaminka's bare chest.

What was this?

A second pump of hot blood soaked his smiling love. He

saw that she was holding a bloodied blade. No, not a blade. It was her gold Innowak swan necklace.

She'd slit his throat! His love had slit his throat! With the necklace he'd given her!

She winked then nodded, as if to say *yes, that's right*.

The world swirled. He collapsed to his knees. He reached up to Chippaminka. This was wrong, it must be a dream, she wouldn't have, she couldn't have . . .

He felt her small hand grip his wonderfully coiffed hair – coiffed by her with such love and attention. She pulled his head back, then wrenched it downwards as she brought up her hard little knee to meet it. He felt his nose pop. Blood blinded him.

Then he felt her arms around him.

"No!" she cried. "They've killed Chamberlain Hatho!"

But I'm still alive, he thought. But oh he was tired. So tired. But he was warm in her arms. As good a place as any to sleep, he thought, drifting away.